— 6/96 —

Jennifer,
I just thought this
might interest you.
keep it on your shelf.

All my love

Writers of Italy

Zanzotto

Writers of Italy

edited by
LINO PERTILE
and
PETER BRAND

Zanzotto

VIVIENNE HAND

EDINBURGH UNIVERSITY PRESS

© Vivienne Hand, 1994

Edinburgh University Press Ltd
22 George Square, Edinburgh

Typeset in Bembo
by Æsthetex Ltd, Edinburgh, and
printed and bound in Great Britain by
Redwood Books, Trowbridge

A CIP record for this book is
available from the British Library.

ISBN 0 7486 0411 1

Contents

Acknowledgements

I should like to express my deep gratitude to Mr Peter Hainsworth, Dr Diego Zancani, Professor John Woodhouse and Professor Giulio Lepschy for their valuable comments on the original typescript of this book. My thanks also extend to a number of other people: first and foremost to Andrea Zanzotto for his interest, for his very warm and copious correspondence, and for permission to reproduce material from 'Microfilm' and *Galateo*; Professors Lino Pertile and Peter Brand for their constant care and encouragement; the Italian Department at Royal Holloway College; Tom Glynn for his original sketch of Zanzotto; Isobel McLean for her careful indexing; Nicholas Buxton and Luigi Suvini who provided me with the musical distractions I so very much needed; Michael, Séan, and my parents, as always; and finally, the late Professor John Dinwiddy, to whose memory I dedicate this work.

Most of Chapter 4 and a section of Chapter 5 in the present study have already appeared in *Italian Studies* and *Romance Studies* respectively. I wish to thank the editors of these journals for their kind permission to allow me to reprint these parts.

V. H.
London, 1993

Abbreviations

ACV	*A che valse?* (*What was the Point?*)
DIP	*Dietro il paesaggio* (*Behind the Landscape*) DIP 1, DIP 2 and DIP 3 indicate the three sections into which the book is divided.
EAV	*Elegia e altri versi* (*Elegy and Other Verses*)
IXE	*IX Ecloghe* (*IX Eclogues*)
LB	*La Beltà* (*Beauty*)
'Possibili prefazi'	'Possibili prefazi o riprese o conclusioni' ('Possible prefaces or refrains or conclusions')
'Profezie'	'Profezie o memorie o giornali murali' ('Prophecies or memories or placards')
PSQ	*Pasque* (*Easters*)
SA	*Sull'altopiano* (*On the Plateau*)
VCT	*Vocativo* (*Vocative*)

With the exception of *Filò* and *Idioma*, the emphases in the quotations from poetry and prose are all mine, as are all the English translations. I have tried to keep the translation of Zanzotto's works and their punctuation as close as possible to the Italian. These translations are literal, and in no way attempt to reproduce the literary qualities of the originals.

Andrea Zanzotto by Tom Glynn, 1993.

Introduction

Andrea Zanzotto was born in 1921 in Pieve di Soligo, a small town near Treviso in the Venetian provinces. He gained a degree in literature at the University of Padua in 1942, participated in the Resistance, and thereafter lived in France and Switzerland before returning to work for over forty years as a secondary-school teacher in Pieve di Soligo, where he currently resides.

Zanzotto has written thirteen books of poetry, for which he has won major literary prizes, including the Saint-Vincent prize in 1950, the Viareggio prize in 1978, and the Eugenio Montale-Librex prize in 1983. He has also written two prose works, critical articles, and has translated several French literary works. The present study examines each of Zanzotto's major collections of poetry from *A che valse?* (composed between 1938 and 1942) up until *Idioma* – his last work to date, published in 1986.

The three major areas of emphasis are language, self, and reality. Zanzotto's interest in language and the self – themes treated in a personal manner in his first five collections – *A che valse?*, *Dietro il paesaggio* (1940–8), *Elegia e altri versi* (1949–54), *Vocativo* (1949–56), and *IX Ecloghe* (1957–60) – leads him to exploit poetically the theories of language and being, which were circulating in France in the 1960s, in *La Beltà* (1961–7) and *Pasque* (1968–73) which follow. Correspondingly the analyses here assess the importance of semiotic and psychoanalytical features of Zanzotto's work. The discussion of language also takes into consideration Zanzotto's view of the role of dialect *vis-à-vis* standard Italian, since dialect is a medium that becomes increasingly important for Zanzotto after *Pasque*.

The realities that Zanzotto examines, always in relationship to either language, the self or both, fluctuate, for circumstantial or biographical reasons, from one collection to another. The chronological sequence is broadly as follows: nature and Zanzotto's local landscape; political history; science; extra-linguistic realities in general; pedagogy and religion. But there is little clear distinction to be made on this basis between the various books.

Both Agosti and Contini have described Zanzotto as the most interesting and important poet since Montale. The interest which Zanzotto generates lies largely in the fact that his writings have always remained divorced from literary trends. Zanzotto's first four books were written during and immediately after the Second World War. When the majority of poets were jumping on the bandwagon of committed writing and the Neo-Realist tradition, Zanzotto was remodelling traditions recently expired – Hermeticism and Surrealism – into a mode of his own. His reasons for doing so were carefully thought out and interwoven into the fabric of the poems themselves.

On the publication of *La Beltà* in 1968 critics quickly pointed out that here was a work that could not be associated with the contemporary Neo-Avant-garde, even though it bore superficial resemblances to it. The very fact that in *La Beltà* Zanzotto continued to develop those issues that were present in his earlier collections, showed that he was moving in his own, personal direction, rather than collaborating with the anti-institutional aims of the *Novissimi*.

It is for *La Beltà* and his subsequent works – which, apart from the dialectal compositions, are more experimental in technique than the earlier ones – that Zanzotto has received greatest critical acclaim. The importance of these works lies in their presenting an Italian point of view on language and the functioning of language: an important intellectual concern of our age, and a dominant topic in most Italian poetry being written today.

The late 1960s was a period when, along with the revival of interest in Ferdinand de Saussure's *Cours de linguistique générale*, there emerged the deconstructionist philosophy of Jacques Derrida and the psychoanalytical writings of Jacques Lacan, both of which centred on linguistic principles. This study examines how *La Beltà* and *Pasque* are informed by the writings of Saussure, Derrida and Lacan, and how the theme of language is present from the beginning of Zanzotto's poetry and is pursued and developed from one collection to another – language as a general phenomenon, but also as a specifically Italian one. Zanzotto's lexical registers in the texts examined comprise the lofty tones of the *lingua aulica* (especially of Leopardi, Petrarch and Dante); a scientific and technological language derived from Latin; the language of the mass media (Italian pop songs, publicity slogans and advertisement jingles); archaisms; neologisms and dialect. The depth and consistency with which this theme of language is examined is one of the features which distinguishes Zanzotto from his other contemporaries who take language as the subject of poetry: Cagnone, Lumelli and Spatola being significant names in this field. Furthermore, Zanzotto's treatment of language is more comprehensive than that of his contemporaries. Whereas Cagnone, Lumelli and Spatola write about language *per se*, Zanzotto places language in relation to several major disciplines, such as politics, psychoanalysis, philosophy, pedagogy, religion and history. Also, whereas in the poems of Zanzotto's contemporaries there tends to be an obfuscation of meaning, in Zanzotto's there is a plurality of meaning that is skilfully structured.

The approach taken here to Zanzotto's poetry is literary and critical, not historical, for the main problem is one of interpretation. Indeed, most critics writing on Zanzotto concede that his work is difficult. In spite of this, criticism on Zanzotto is vast. Together with an abundance of articles, predominantly Italian, it includes five book-length studies: three in Italian and two in English. Giuliana Nuvoli's work, in the Castoro series, presents clear but necessarily cursory examinations of all of Zanzotto's works written from 1938 to 1978. Piero Falchetta and Lucia Conti-Bertini both concentrate on collections of poetry written from 1957 onwards, and highlight the philosophical and psycho-analytical aspects of Zanzotto's thought. Like Beverly Allen, they tend to use Zanzotto to advance the cause of modern theories of language and being. The approach here is more traditional: because of Zanzotto's proverbial difficulty, an attempt has been made to define through detailed textual analyses the range of meanings in his poems, and, in so far as it is possible, to establish particular meanings in each case. The readings are neither Structuralist (Saussurian) nor Post-Structuralist (Lacanian and Derridean), and the expositions of the thought of these writers which are given in this volume are intended to show how originally and creatively Zanzotto has exploited their ideas.

While the themes of language, self and their relationship to reality are ones constantly present in the work of Zanzotto, they do not always develop in a strictly linear fashion, nor are they given equal weight in each collection. As successive chapters in this volume demonstrate, in the earliest works – *A che valse?*, *Dietro il paesaggio*, and *Elegia e altri versi* – composed between 1938 and 1954, Zanzotto insists upon the importance of poetry as a response to what he perceives as a dying culture in wartime Italy. He does this in two ways: by poeticizing his local landscape – that is, by presenting it in a deliberately inventive, as opposed to prosaic, manner – and by imitating, in the process, the languages and styles of major Italian and European poets of the past. The language of these works is therefore intentionally literary. The self is involved in the poeticization of the landscape: landscape phenomena have a psychic symbolism. Reality is to be understood as the local landscape, presented as an antithesis to man and historical reality.

The next collection, *Vocativo*, reveals some radical new developments. Whereas in the earlier works Zanzotto was presenting a case for poetry, now he feels that a division exists between literature and reality which leads him to question the authenticity of poetry. The division is investigated from three different angles: he debates what relevance his earlier, idyllic poetry has had to the real (and sometimes historical) world about him. He considers the relationship between a pragmatic and a romantic (in the literary sense) attitude towards life; and he doubts the ability of the written word to present subjectivity and reality with any degree of precision. Language is therefore metapoetic, that is to say, Zanzotto's poems are self-referential in that they discuss the problems of writing poetry and of presenting the self linguistically. The poet begins to consider the historical reality that he had deliberately ignored in his earlier works.

IX Ecloghe, which follows, contains a fuller inquiry into the theme of history, examined, as in *Vocativo*, in relationship to poetry. What characterizes *IX Ecloghe* is, however, Zanzotto's treatment of the new issue of science, for certain scientific explorations of the late 1950s lead him to consider both science *per se* – technological, anatomical, medical and chemical – and the relationship between scientific and literary language. Language, therefore, continues to be self-referential; the reality considered is now scientific as well as historical; while the theme of the self temporarily disappears.

In the following collection, *La Beltà*, Zanzotto develops an idea from *Vocativo*: that there may be a dichotomy between language and reality. His views about language achieve a greater precision, and now have a decidedly Saussurian slant: Zanzotto acknowledges that there is no necessary relationship between signifiers (sound-images) and signifieds (concepts). He begins to view the linguistic system as a false convention. By thwarting the reader's attempts to give meaning to his poems, he is attempting to undermine the logocentric tradition that considers language to be 'centred' by meaning (a 'logos'). In this, he is prefiguring Derrida. Language in *La Beltà* is therefore 'decentred'. The theme of the self reappears in the form of a creative interpretation of Lacanian theories. Reality is purely extralinguistic.

The question of logocentrism is continued in *Pasque*. Zanzotto condemns pedagogy and religion: two institutions which, in his opinion, encourage one to read and think in the logocentric tradition. The poet is now familiar with Derrida's work, which began to be published in 1967, and he undermines or 'deconstructs' both pedagogy and religion, partly by using in the writing of his poems the Derridean, deconstructionist theory of language, coupled with the Lacanian theory of being. Hence, whereas Zanzotto's treatment of language and the self does not differ radically from the preceding collection, the realities that he considers – pedagogy and religion – are now much more specific than in *La Beltà*.

The poetry published since *Pasque* comprises *Filò* (1976), a book of poetry written entirely in dialect, and three collections which together form what the poet has referred to as a 'pseudo-trilogy' – *Il Galateo in bosco*, *Fosfeni* and *Idioma* (1975–84). *Filò* came to be written on the request of Fellini, who wanted some verses in Venetian to accompany two scenes involving female figures for his film, *Casanova*. The 'Venetian Recitative' and the 'London Lullaby' which Zanzotto offered are contained in section 1 of *Filò*, whereas section 2 is composed of one long poem, written in the dialect of the Soligo valley, and which, among other things, discusses the nature of dialect. It is this section of *Filò*, therefore, which is coherent with Zanzotto's previous work in its investigations into another aspect of language.

The two nouns in the title of the first book of the 'trilogy' represent for Zanzotto an impossible symbiosis. 'Galateo' refers to the original *Il Galateo* – a sixteenth-century book of manners by Giovanni della Casa, which was written near the Montello wood, and in which Della Casa offered an exhaustive codification of the speech and behaviour appropriate to a courtly (and civilized) society. In opposition to this, Zanzotto foregrounds with the term 'bosco' the uncodifiability of contemporary language (which in the collection oscillates between vulgarisms in dialect and a Petrarchan *lingua aulica*), the self, and a society which has been irreversibly shattered by the events of historical reality, such as the battles between Austria and Hungary fought in the Montello region in 1918. The inability to apply clear-cut rules to the contemporary use of language, and visions of the self and reality, is represented by the 'woodiness' of the poems in the collection – their opacity and exfoliations.

Fosfeni in many respects acts as a complement to *Il Galateo in bosco*. Whereas contemplation of the partially wooded Montello to the south of Zanzotto's region had induced processes of physical, historical and literary 'descent', the Dolomites to the north invite him towards a spiritual atemporality. There is a search for the *logos* which would reveal the meaning behind chaotic reality (characterized in the collection by contradiction) and which would throw light on the paradoxical make-up of the self – capable of bouts of depression and inactivity (non-being) and, conversely, high states of being, suffused by superhuman energies which find expression in great works of art. The woody and earthy lexicon of *Il Galateo in bosco* is now replaced by a scientific language, interspersed with logarithms, reflecting a search for the *logos* through the cultivation of a logical, clear-sighted vision.

Half the poems of *Idioma* are written in standard Italian, and half in the dialect of Pieve di Soligo – the 'idiom' to which the title refers. Dialect is therefore being put on a par with the official language in order to subvert the view of dialect as (what Zanzotto calls in a note) a 'deprived', 'idiotic' language. Social realities such as the mass media, terrorism and the arms race are dealt with in some of the Italian poems of the collection; while the self plays a minor role in these compositions, most of them being dedicated to other people, esteemed and/or held in great affection by the poet – celebrities (mostly literary ones) and ordinary, local inhabitants now passed away. The collection is exceptional in Zanzotto's *oeuvre* in that the majority of its poems are rudimentary and very accessible.

Overall, this study aims to highlight the great diversity present in the work of Zanzotto, where experimentalism and highly intellectual thought rest beside traditionalism and the expression of the simplest of feelings; where the culture and people of a peasant community are as important to the poet as some of the literary, philosophical and psychoanalytical adventures of the twentieth century.

Chapter 1

A Case for Poetry

Sul libro aperto della primavera
figura mezzodì per sempre,
è dipinto ch'io viva nell'isola,
nell'oceano, ch'io viva nell'amore

d'una luna che s'oppone al mondo
('A foglia ed a gemma', *DIP* 2)

On the open book of spring / where noon is forever depicted, / I have been
portrayed as one who lives on the island, / in the ocean, one who lives in love /
with a moon which is opposed to the world.

('By Leaf and by Bud')

Qui non resta che cingersi intorno il paesaggio
qui volgere le spalle
('Ormai', *DIP* 1)

Here all that remains is to wrap the landscape around oneself / here turn
one's back.

('By Now')

The first of these two quotations from *Dietro il paesaggio* (*DIP*) (*Behind the
Landscape*) suggests that Zanzotto had anticipated how his first three books would
be attacked, as they were, for their non-commitment to the historical and social
issues of the day (these collections being composed either during the Second World
War or immediately after it) (Giacheri 40–1; Frattini 273–8). Given this, and
read in the light of the second quotation, one is led to suspect that the poet's
anti-(historical) world or insulated position ('ch'io viva nell'amore / d'una luna *che
s'oppone al mondo*'; 'ch'io viva *nell'isola*') was something deliberately adopted
by him, something premeditated. Here he says that there is nothing left
for him to do but lock the landscape around himself, turn his back.

This detached, insulated position is one which is also highlighted in the titles of
DIP's three sections: 'Atollo' ('Atoll'), 'Sponda al sole' ('Bank in the Sun') (where
the 'bank' is perhaps that of the 'atoll', but in any case indicating a marginal area)
and 'Dietro il paesaggio', where 'paesaggio' works as an antithesis to 'man' and
historical reality. This Zanzotto himself explains when in a recent discussion
of his early verse he confirms the reader's suspicions that in these works he is
deliberately 'turning his back' on current social and political issues:

> In my first books, I had deliberately erased any human presence, out of a type
> of 'distaste' generated by historical events; I only wanted to talk of landscapes,
> return to a nature in which man had not been active. It was a psychological
> reflex-reaction to the devastations of war. (*Sulla poesia* 97)

A 'distaste' for historical issues is not, however, the only reason why Zanzotto
refuses to speak of them in his writing. Being deliberately uncommitted is also
part of his way of making a case for poetry – poetry as what he has called an
'*autre* world' (Allen 254), a 'power' which does not associate itself with political
power (as it does, he believes, for the Avant-garde writers ('Parole' 353)), which
does not even complement historical power (as it does, he believes, for Dante
('Petrarca' 1974, 96)), but which is diametrically opposed to it, as is the case
for Petrarch:

> Petrarch instead seems to display the 'desire' for a completely alternative
> power, . . . a power which is not in the same category as that which makes
> history . . . , it is he who sees in the poetic act a way of escaping the network
> of conditionings positioned by the 'powers' which manage history . . . It is
> precisely the tragic experience of frustration, of negation, of the 'no' which
> is at the foundation of his examination of poetry . . . which becomes a
> zero-point from which he can judge 'this' history as it is being made, in
> order to postulate, in conclusion, 'another' history. From this there is born
> the feeling of the inflexible autonomy of the poet (of the man of letters).
> ('Petrarca' 1974, 96)

It is this Petrarchan insistence upon the autonomy of poetry and of the poet
underlined by Zanzotto, not just here, but also in other articles and interviews
(Allen 254; 'Petrarca' 1976, 5, 8, 16), which is the essential issue of *A che valse?*
(*ACV*) (*What was the Point?*) and DIP. For a start, the landscape of these two books is
closely linked to the idea of poetry itself and the reader is made aware of this from
the beginning in the constant use of a 'tu' ('you'), which, much like Montale's
'tu' in *Occasioni*, is employed to address an anonymous feminine figure. In
Zanzotto this 'tu' is presented, as I shall show, as a personification of poetry who
is present among the elements of Nature. The landscape is used to reinforce the
concept of poetry. The major part of this chapter will attempt to illustrate how
in the first two books (I will, however, be dealing mostly with DIP), Zanzotto
does draw upon the visible landscape of Pieve di Soligo and the surrounding area,
but *poeticizes* it in a number of specific ways in the texts. That is to say,

the poet's presentation of the landscape is deliberately inventive as opposed
to matter-of-fact or prosaic.

It is perhaps this inventive treatment of reality that has led many critics to
observe how Zanzotto's early works seem to have been influenced by both
the Hermetic and the Surrealist traditions (Mengaldo; Milone; Agosti 1973;
Nuvoli). With regard to the Hermetic influence, it is, I believe, more specifically
the aesthetic ideas of Ungaretti that Zanzotto is reiterating. For Ungaretti, and
indeed the Surrealist school, proposed that poetry should not repeat real-
ity but subject it to an imaginative rearrangement. Ungaretti claimed that
this earthly world should be perceived as man's continual invention (Piccioni
lxiii) and that in order to represent things poetically, exterior, objective real-
ity should be cancelled and substituted by subjectively imaginative forms:

> This poetry is born from the feeling that one can only represent things
> poetically, that is to say, one can only seize them in their deepest reality
> when they do not exist; and it is only at that point that they are ours, and
> they have become ours through our inspiration. (Savanio 249)

The Surrealists, likewise, rebelled against the classical idea that art should
imitate exterior reality, as explained by Éluard, the most original poet of the
Surrealist school, in *Donner à voir*.

> The vanity of painters, which is immense, has for a long time driven them to
> sit down in front of a landscape, image, or text, as if in front of a wall, to copy
> them. They did not hunger after themselves. They applied themselves. The
> poet, he always thinks about 'something else'. He finds the unusual familiar,
> premeditation is something foreign to him. (Éluard 1939, 73)

Instead, reality should be defamiliarized by the artist's poetic imagination: the
poet should 'permit man to see different things differently' (147).

While the early Zanzotto shares the aesthetic ideas of Ungaretti and the
Surrealists, he also employs one of their techniques to achieve this imaginative
recreation of reality: the use of analogy and metaphor. Ungaretti has said

> Today's poet will try to juxtapose distant images with no linking threads.
> . . . When from the contact of images, light is born, poetry will exist, and the
> greater the distance which is brought into contact, . . . the greater the poetry
> will be. (Piccioni lxxiv)

Éluard voiced a similar opinion in the words 'Everything can be compared to
everything. Everything finds its echo, its reason, its resemblance, its contrast,
its becoming, everywhere' (*Éluard* 1939, 134). Zanzotto's various 'assimilations'
are something that will be dealt with in the main body of this chapter.

It is the absence of poetry in the contemporary world at large which would
seem to be the basic reason why Zanzotto is concerned with reinstating its
importance. This idea is intimated in six lines from 'Primavera di Santa Augusta'
('Saint Augusta's Spring'), (*DIP* 1 lines 22–6):

Le voci della vera
età chiara ti fanno
ma gli occhi restano spenti
su questa terra che di te s'estenua
e dal tuo volto vinto da morte
il mio conosco

Voices of the true / age make you bright / but eyes remain extinguished / on this land which grows weary of you / and from your death-defeated face / I recognize my own.

The reference here in lines 22 and 23 to the 'voices' of a certain 'true age' suggests that Zanzotto is talking about 'voices' of poets and literary 'ages'. The 'tu' which is linked to these 'voices' is used by Zanzotto to address a feminine presence in the land (hence the feminine adjective 'chiara'). But rather than talking about how other poets in other ages celebrated woman, Zanzotto would seem to be commenting here upon poetry in general as he appears to be doing in the majority of poems in the first section of DIP. If one accepts that the 'tu' is therefore coterminous with the concept of poetry (and I shall be supporting this argument again in the course of this chapter), the reference to the 'voices' which 'make you bright' can only be interpreted as a metaphor for 'voices' which lend value or importance to poetry. But which poets and which poetic age is Zanzotto referring to? In the context of the whole of DIP one can only make the broad assumption that they are poets from various former poetic ages. For firstly, the work is pervaded by an abundant use of rhetorical figures (examined by Guglielminetti) lending the writing a dignity and solemnity which comes from the association of rhetoric with the noble literary achievements of the past. Secondly, what has also been identified (Nuvoli 1979, 40–4; Guglielminetti 171; Agosti 1973, 8–9) as Zanzotto's imitations of Romanticism (Hölderlin, Leopardi), Symbolism (Poe, Rimbaud) and Surrealism (Lorca, Éluard) all conveyed in the strains of Hermeticism (and Zanzotto also, as I shall show, abundantly echoes Quasimodo, Ungaretti, and Montale) are surely to be read as implicit tributes to these established poets and schools.

The negation 'ma' which opens line 24 indicates that the rest of the sequence has an oppositional relationship to the first two lines. One can therefore presume that Zanzotto is still talking about poetry, but in this case, the absence of it in the present: the adjective 'spenti' ('extinguished') related to the 'eyes' on 'this land' works as an antithesis to the adjective 'chiara' ('bright') related to the poetry of the 'true age'. 'This land' is also said to be weary of poetry, and poetry itself has a death-defeated face.

The serious reality of a war or the memories left by it, could possibly be the reason why poetry with its less urgent concerns is felt to be missing in the

present. For although the subject of war is generally overlooked in the first two
books, in accordance with Zanzotto's desire to dissociate poetry and politics, it
tentatively raises its head on two occasions – in 'Adunata' ('Gathering') and in
'Atollo' (*DIP* 1). 'Adunata' begins:

> Indugia ancora la parvenza
> dei soldati selvaggi
> sulle porte, ed ostili
> insegne sui fortilizi
> alza la sera, chiama piazze a raccolta

There still lingers the appearance / of savage soldiers / by the doorways, and
hostile / banners over the small forts / are hoisted by the evening which calls
piazzas to assembly.

This is the nearest Zanzotto ever gets to mentioning the war directly. Lines 6
to 10 of the poem talk of how an 'arso astro distrusse questa terra', which is
possibly a metaphorical image for falling projectiles which crater the land. It is
the gravity of the tone which gives this impression: 'Un arso astro distrusse questa
terra / profonda in pozzi e tane / s'avventa l'ombra dell'estate / da vicoli e da
altane / e dai rotti teatri' ('A burned-out star destroyed this earth / deep in wells
and dens / the shadow of summer hurls itself / from alleys and roof-terraces /
and from damaged theatres'). The sequence is full of dark, accentuated vowels;
there is the jarring assonance ('arso astro'), the discordant near-rhyme ('estate'
'teatri') and the equally dissonant 'tane' 'altane' with its identical rhyme of two
syllables. The poem is pervaded, moreover, by the language of destruction,
disintegration and degeneration: 'distrusse' ('destroyed'), 'rotti teatri' ('damaged
theatres'), 'nelle crepe delle caserme' ('in the cracks of the barracks'), 'appassisce'
('withers'), 'traligna' ('degenerates'). (This method of referring to war in a coded,
oblique fashion makes one think of Montale – especially his 'Mottetto III' in
Occasioni).

In the poem 'Atollo', which directly precedes 'Adunata' in the collection, the
precariousness of sandcastles ('precari monumenti'), built, it would seem, on the
'atoll', their tiny grains at the mercy of salty waves, becomes a metaphor for
the precarious situation and the destruction of Italy in the present: the 'minute
segments' of 'fragile Italies' are 'faded' by 'greedy salt':

> Un sole che con oziosi giri
>
> . . .
>
> scruta le differenze d'ago
> della sabbia dei piccoli castelli
> e brilla da mille bandiere
> da scudi e da porte
> dagli angoli dei morti.
> Tra quei precari monumenti,
> io là vi collocai, fragili Italie

> i cui minuti segmenti
> avido sale stinse

A sun which with lazy rotations / . . . / scrutinizes the needle differences / in the sand of the little castles / and shines from a thousand banners / from shields and doors / from the corners of the dead. / Among those precarious monuments, / I placed you, fragile Italies / whose minute segments / a greedy salt has faded.

The metaphor is an effective one, for sandcastles, although built in the image of real castles, have none of the latter's attributes of strength and fortification. The poem continues:

> la brace là s'indovina
> dell'insetto e del libro,
> là tra giochi vuoti e pericoli
> al silenzio si appoggiano le clausole
> della mia memoria infelice
> e monti decrepiti affidano
> alla sabbia insensibili sfaceli,
> la sabbia senza parsimonia
> colma i volti e i sorrisi
> spegne l'oro dei suoni

there one can foretell the embers / of the insect and the book, / there among empty games and dangers / there leans towards silence the clausulae / of my unhappy memory / and decrepit mountains entrust / to the sand their indifferent decay, / the sand lavishly / fills up faces and smiles / and extinguishes the gold of sounds.

Although sandcastles lack the strength of real castles, they are still, however, images of power. By referring to them above as 'giochi vuoti' Zanzotto suggests a comparison between the children's game of building sandcastles, and the futile, power-playing 'games' of history (echoing the 'giocattoli di guerra' ('toys of war') of Montale's *Bufera* ('La primavera Hitleriana' line 13)). These games destroy everything ranging from small, insignificant life (hence the embers of the insect), to culture (the embers of the book), land (the mountains are suffering an indifferent decay), and humanity (there is an allusion, it would seem, to the silence of the dead buried within the land in the reference to the sand filling up faces and smiles and snuffing the gold of sounds).

   To the silence caused by such destruction the poet, we are told, leans the clausulae of his sad memory. Here Zanzotto (Agosti 1973, 9) suggests how he means to contest the discontinuity which historical issues incur with a type of continuity that can be achieved by writing. But since the phrase 'le clausole / della mia memoria infelice' links a *writing* theme to the *past*, one can possibly be a little more precise. Since culture is one of those things which has undergone destruction ('la brace . . . / . . . del libro'), Zanzotto can attempt to resurrect it by permeating his poetry with the voices of past poets lodged in his 'memory'; voices tinged with melancholy ('memoria infelice') in that they are seemingly no longer relevant, although, by reinstating them in the present Zanzotto is clearly asserting their relevance and, by extension, asserting the relevance of poetry in general in his contemporary world. This, I believe, is the reason why these works are so literary.

The poems which best serve to highlight Zanzotto's restoration of past poetry are 'Arse il motore' ('The Motor Burned'), 'Indizi e luna' ('Indications and Moon') from DIP and 'I bianchi vermi con occhi di sole' ('The White Worms with Sunny Eyes') from ACV. In the first two of these Zanzotto deliberately creates a modern setting in which he places allusions to poets of the past (in much the same way as Ungaretti had done in *Sentimento*); while in the third he fuses a relatively modern content with an old style of writing.

In 'Arse il motore' the modern setting is announced by a car intruding into the landscape, generating heat and dust, frightening children and disturbing the exterior elements:

> Arse il motore a lungo sulla via
> il suo sangue selvaggio ed atterrí
> fanciulli. Or basso trema all'agonia
> del fiume verso i moli ed i mari.
>
> Assetato di polvere e di fiamma
> aspro cavallo s'impennò nella sera;
> a insegne false, a svolte di paesi
> giacque e tentò le crepe dell'abisso

For a long time on the road the motor burned / its savage blood and terrified / children. Low down now it trembles at the agony / of the river by the piers and seas. / Athirst for dust and flame / in the evening the relentless horse reared up; / at false signs, at village bends / it lay and tested the clefts of the abyss.

Detaching himself from this scene which would seem to symbolize the fury of practical, modern living, the poet also undertakes a journey but one which is an 'abbandono del mondo' ('abandonment of the world'). But before this 'abandonment' is depicted, the emphasis falls, once again, upon the poet's marginality, his non-commitment to the type of world symbolized by the car. He is an unconvincing, impractical figure talking about seasons and elements:

> Figura non creduta di stagioni
> di creta, di neri tuoni precoci,
> di tramonti penetrati per fessure
> in case e stanze col vento che impaura,
>
> aspettai solo nella lunga sosta

Unbelieved figure of seasons / of clay, of black precocious thunders, / of
sunsets that have penetrated through cracks / into houses and rooms with a
frightening wind, / I waited alone in the long pause.

Consequently, one is lead to suspect that the world to which he is journeying is
his own *timeless* world of *poetry*:

> acuti ghiacci avvizziti di febbre
> alghe e fontane con me discesero
>
> nel fondo del mio viaggio:
> *e clessidre e quadranti mi esaltarono*
> *l'abbandono del mondo*

sharp ice withered by fever / seaweed and fountains with me they descended
/ into the depths of my journey: / and *hourglasses and dials magnified for me / the*
abandonment of the world.

It is precisely the timelessness of this poetical world which is accentuated in
the allusion to Ungaretti's 'L'isola' (*Sentimento*) where Ungaretti himself had
transformed a modern-day Latium into an Arcadian landscape (like that found
in Virgil's bucolic poetry) with nymphs, meadows, streams, sheep, and a shepherd
whose hands are depicted (in a startling Surrealist fashion which jars with the
classical echoes) as a '*vetro* levigato da fioca *febbre*' ('*glass* smoothed by weak *fever*')
(compare Zanzotto's 'acuti ghiacci avvizziti di febbre'). It is then, maybe, the
classical overtones in Ungaretti's 'L'isola' which prompt Zanzotto to echo Ovid
in the final lines of the poem:

> O ruote e carri alti come luna
> luna argento di sotterranei ceselli
> voci oscure come le mie ceneri
> e strade ch'io vidi precipizi,
>
> viaggiai solo in un pugno, in un seme
> di morte, colpito da un dio

O wheels and carts as high as the moon / silver moon of subterranean chisels /
voices as dark as my ashes / and streets which I saw to be ravines, / I journeyed
alone in a fist, in a seed / of death, struck down by a god.

The reference here to the poet's falling journey, 'struck down by a god', cannot
fail to evoke the Icarus myth; Zanzotto's 'wheels and carts' also recalling the
sun-chariots of Apollo (Ovid, *Metamorphoses* VIII, lines 211–49). But the Icarus
myth itself was appropriated by another writer in whom Zanzotto has always
taken a great interest – an interest which he indicates at various stages in his
poetical works: Hölderlin. A Hölderlin quotation, for example, is used as an
epigraph to section 2 of DIP. (See also 'La perfezione della neve' ('The Snow's
Perfection') and 'Possibili prefazi X' in *La Beltà* (LB) (*Beauty*)). Hölderlin, at the

end of his poetic career when he was becoming increasingly insane, interpreted his failing genius as a suffering inflicted on him by Apollo. Apollo had struck him down for his hubris in approaching too close to the gods. In one of his letters from this period he states, 'to repeat the words of heroes, I can indeed say that Apollo has struck me down' (*Sämtliche Werke* 432) (an idea taken up again in 'Mnemosyne', a poem which Zanzotto actually quotes from in 'La perfezione della neve').

I will be returning later to the exact implications of the Icarus myth and Hölderlin's appropriation of it, but for the time being, their presence in 'Arse il motore', together with the allusion to Ungaretti, can be seen to underscore Zanzotto's desire to be deliberately anachronistic. This deliberation is made even clearer by the fact that the first half of the poem relates a journey of descent undertaken by a car in the modern day and age, and the second half also deals with a descending journey – the poet's own – in which he alludes to the fate of Icarus and Hölderlin. Zanzotto, therefore, would seem to be assimilating both halves of the poem by the theme of the downward journey, thereby (like Ungaretti in 'L'isola') consciously placing echoes of past literature into a very modern setting.

The same procedure is carried out in 'Indizi e luna'. At first, the scene is relatively realistic. Zanzotto speaks of the city lights now lit at evening time (which introduces a modern context) and he imagines the 'star of spring' – probably the moon (and recalling thereby Montale's 'primavera lunare' ('lunar spring') (*Occasioni*, 'Cave d'autunno' line 1)) – causing sap to rise in the young trees:

> La stella della primavera
> il dolce succo
> trae negli alberi giovani.
> La verde sera al suo specchio s'adorna,
> ha grandi insegne ormai la città

The star of spring / draws up the sweet sap / in the young trees. / The green evening embellishes itself at its mirror, / by now the city has vast neon signs.

Then reality becomes surreal. Normal spatial dimensions are overthrown by an interrelation of the above and below:

> Cieli di giardino
> sorgete ancora dai vostri spazi

You still rise up from your spaces / skies of garden

while at the end of the poem the qualities of elements are reversed, 'leaves' being presented as an attribute of both 'water' and the 'moon' as opposed to the implied trees of the 'kitchen gardens' or plants of the 'greenhouses' (this technique of 'taking liberties' with natural phenomena (which also occurs elsewhere in the collection, see pages 21–6) has probably been partly inspired by Quasimodo whose early work is characterized by phrases such as 'l'acqua tramonta' ('the water sets') (*Subito*, 'Oboe sommerso' line 8); 'alata aria / amare fronde esala' ('winged air / exhales bitter leaves') (*Subito*, 'L'Eucalyptus' lines 8–9)):

> Negli orti e nelle serre piú lontane
> si sfogliano e si smarriscono
> le acque e la madre luna

In the kitchen gardens and farthest greenhouses / waters and mother-moon / shed their leaves and go astray.

While having, therefore, a certain Surrealist quality, the last three lines cannot fail to evoke Leopardi's moon in the orchard (or kitchen garden – 'l'orto' can mean both) in 'La sera del dì di festa' ('The Evening of the Festive Day'): 'e in mezzo agli orti / posa la luna' ('and amidst the orchards / lies the moon'). Indeed, there are other allusions to Leopardi's poem both on the level of lexicon and content. (One could also argue that 'Indizi e luna' contains echoes of Montale's 'Crisalide', *Ossi*, in that, for example, certain key words such as 'stringere' ('to make tight') and 'cuore' ('heart') occur in both poems; both are addressed to a 'voi' ('you' (plural)); and in each spring is the seasonal backdrop. Nevertheless, the allusions to Leopardi are much stronger.) Following the scene described at the beginning of the poem, Zanzotto proceeds to talk of a woman who gazes at the ice of the mountains, and in fear, 'si stringe al petto il cuore' ('clasps her heart to her breast'), a line which echoes Leopardi's 'mi si stringe il core' ('my heart wrings'). Immediately afterwards, 'Indizi e luna' speaks of a 'festival' which has also taken place that evening:

> indizi angosciosi di festa
> giacciono agli angoli delle piazze

distressing signs of the festival / lie at the corners of the piazzas

and just as the lady whom Leopardi addresses in 'La sera del dì di festa' is tired after the festivities of the day ('che t'accolse agevol sonno / nelle tue chete stanze'; 'or da' trastulli / prendi riposo' ('light sleep welcomed you / in your quiet rooms'; 'you rest / now from the amusements')), so too the people in Zanzotto's poem are blinded by sleep:

> Gli abitanti camminano
> abbagliati dal sonno

The inhabitants walk / dazzled by sleep.

The message itself of 'La sera del dì di festa' serves Zanzotto's artistic purposes in 'Indizi e luna'. The end of the festival symbolizes for Leopardi the transience

of all things in life, a transience which he laments (for Zanzotto too, the signs of
the departed festival are 'angosciosi' ('distressing')):

> e fieramente mi si stringe il core,
> a pensar come tutto al mondo passa,
> e quasi orma non lascia. Ecco è fuggito
> il dì festivo, ed al festivo il giorno
> volgar succede, e se ne porta il tempo
> ogni umano accidente

and cruelly my heart wrings, / to think how everything in the world passes
on, / and hardly leaves a trace of itself. Behold it has now fled / that festive
day, and after it the ordinary / day follows, and time carries off / every human
happening.

Zanzotto, by contrast, is asserting in 'Indizi e luna' the non-transience of poetry,
the feasibility of poetry in the modern age. He does this in two ways. The Surreal-
ist defamiliarization of reality which occurs at the beginning and towards the end
of the poem, underlines that the poem is not a direct transcription of reality but
a poetic recreation of it. Then, by placing verbal echoes of Leopardi's 'La sera del
dì di festa' both with this more modern Surrealist writing and in a contemporary
setting (in 'Indizi e luna' there are greenhouses as well as neon lights), Zanzotto
is implying the durability of Leopardi's poetry and, by extension, the possibility
of 'poetry' itself in the modern and contemporary world.

To the same end a modern, Absurdist content is juxtaposed with an outdated
style in 'I bianchi vermi con occhi di sole'. The poem speaks of an invasion
of grubs attacking nature, the poet himself, and the 'rooms', 'corridors' and
'windows' of his house. It has the nightmarish quality of Kafka's writing where
the individual appears crushed by exterior forces. (The poet himself, like Gregor
Samsa of Kafka's *Metamorphosis*, would also seem to have turned into some kind
of creature: 'e l'unico mio piede / osso di bestia e tenaglia' ('and my one and
only foot / bone of beast and pincers')). However, the structure of the poem
could possibly be said to work against its grotesquely Absurdist content, for
the obsessive repetition of the conjunction 'e' ('and') and the prepositions
'su' ('on') and 'di' ('of') which makes of the whole poem one long sentence
of twenty-one lines is a rhetorical schema (polysyndeton), associated with the
literary achievements of the past. One could equally claim, however, that this
repetitive schema does not jar with the content but gives the poem a tone of
fearful excitement, well-suited to its subject-matter.

Nevertheless, a certain dissonance *is* created at the end of the poem where
Zanzotto suddenly moves to an old romantic phraseology. The last twelve
lines are as follows, the shift to the 'romantic' occurring at line 17 ('which once
poured tears') and made all the more shocking from its juxtapositioning with the
preceding line which speaks of 'eyes plucked out':

e, fregi delle mie stanze,
dei miei corridoi, del nulla
delle mie finestre, le carni
mie insensibilmente ricercano
e l'unico mio piede
osso di bestia e tenaglia
e gli occhi sconficcati
che in lacrime si versarono
su abissi di scale
e la mia testa
piena di errori funesti
cui questa notte è diadema

and, forming a frieze in my rooms, / in my corridors, in the nothingness / of my windows, my flesh / they insensitively seek / and my one and only foot / bone of beast and pincers / and my plucked out eyes / which once poured tears / over abyssal stairways / and my head / full of sorrowful errors / like the diadem of errors which is this night.

Zanzotto's concern to assert the relevance of poetry in the present day and age is continued in his depiction of the landscape. For the landscape is deliberately poeticized in a number of different ways, and being a poetical object in itself, it lends itself to this operation. Just as the feminine personification of poetry is depicted as being present among the elements, quotations such as the following from DIP are meant to reinforce the fact that there is poetry 'behind' the landscape that Zanzotto wishes to place in the foreground: 'lei dal fittissimo alfabeto' ('she of the thickest alphabet') (in reference to the water of Dolle in the poem of that name, 'L'acqua di Dolle'); 'e fanno rime con le colline' ('and they make rhymes with the hills') (in reference, again, to 'water' and 'sand' in 'Nel mio paese' ('In My Village')); and 'il fico va sillabando dolcezza' ('the fig-tree syllabizes sweetness'), ('Con dolce curiosità') ('With Sweet Curiosity'). There is also a Heideggerian element at work here (a Heideggerian line of thought can be traced, as I shall show, from DIP up to and including *IX Ecloghe* (IXE) (*IX Eclogues*)). Heidegger in his 'Die Frage Nach der Technik' ('The Question Concerning Technology') claimed that Nature, for the Greeks, was considered *physis*, a word containing the Greek sense of 'coming into radiant being'. Since poetry–*poiēsis* – is a bringing into being, Nature and poetry were, for Heidegger, once inextricably linked (*Basic Writings* 293). It is precisely this pristine relationship between *physis* and *poiēsis* which Zanzotto is hankering after, and which he emphasizes by poeticizing the landscape, thereby allying poetry and Nature.

The poetic, that is the imaginative, rendering of the landscape means that the visual landscape is transcended; but what it does *not* mean is that the work displays any kind of Symbolist transcendentalism. I do not believe that Zanzotto is expressing any desire for an Absolute world (Manacorda 398). Zanzotto himself has assimilated writing with painting in his early poetry, calling it 'a poetry inclined towards "ut pictura"' (Listri 188), which suggests that to some extent he is 'drawing' his own landscape and his own surroundings.

There are also some further features in the poems which support this argument. Although 'Arse il motore' (examined earlier) speaks of the poet's 'abbandono del mondo', the allusion to the Icarus myth and Hölderlin's appropriation of it, suggests that what he is abandoning is not this world at large in favour of some higher, more perfect Absolute. Icarus, Hölderlin, and indeed the Symbolists themselves have shown how the climb to the 'idéal' is followed by a 'spleen', how any desire to transcend terrestrial reality and reach a supernatural realm of ideal forms and essences is doomed to failure. One must reiterate, therefore, that what Zanzotto is abandoning in this poem is merely the practical side of this world in favour of its poetical side.

One could, however, interpret the presence of the Icarus myth in 'Arse il motore' in a different way. One could claim that Zanzotto, irrespective of reason, is obstinately continuing the Symbolist quest, that *DIP* displays a desire for a higher, Absolute world which is negated a priori (Barberi-Squarotti 1966, 127–9). But in the context of another poem from the collection, this, once again, does not seem to be the case. 'Montana' ('Montane'), *DIP* 1, emphasizes how the poet's concern with this world as opposed to another is a completely natural choice. Here the feminine personification of poetry is depicted as belonging to two different worlds: the cold mountains above, and the grass below, which may be taken to symbolize the Absolute, and this earth, respectively. The poet is indeed tempted to turn his back on the second and aspire towards the first:

> e s'io cercassi dove cerca il monte
> da te non tornerei sarei la fronte
> che ignora, il passo che scade e finisce

and if I searched where the mountain searches / I would not come back to you I would be the brow / that ignores, the footstep that expires and ends.

But accepting his exclusion from the 'cold sphere of "her" paradise' he decides to seek out her presence in Nature below. The conversion of the negative 'da te non tornerei' ('I would not come back to you') in the extract above, into the positive 'No, tornerò' ('No, I will come back') in the following extract, has not a reluctant, but an affirmative, categorical tone:

> Da sé mi esclude il freddo paradiso
> dei tuoi monti trovati dal sole
>
> . . .
>
> E di là tanto mi tace
> dopo i prati e i freddi meli
> la fredda spera del tuo paradiso

No, tornerò nell'erba tua
ti vedrò col tuo nome di natura

The cold paradise of your mountains / discovered by the sun excludes me /
. . . / And from there the cold sphere of your paradise / falls so silent on me /
beyond the fields and the cold apple trees / *No, I will come back into your*
grass / I will see you with your nature name.

One could also claim that the recurrent 'cold' imagery emphasized on three
occasions in the sequence above and throughout a number of poems in ACV
and DIP, is to be interpreted as a deliberate desiccation of the landscape by
Zanzotto who wants to reinforce the fact that it regrettably refuses to reveal
'correspondences' with an ideal world of which the real world is a shadow
(Barberi-Squarotti, 1966, 127–9). But it is my view that the 'ice', 'snow'
and 'water' of these poems are natural features of Zanzotto's landscape, of a
poet who, as he himself reminds the reader, lives 'al di qua delle alpi' ('on
this side of the alps') ('Perché siamo' ('Because We Are'), DIP 3), and where
the neighbouring Dolomites and their associations with snow intensify, even in
summer, the impression of cold and winter. This is the reason why Zanzotto can
speak in 'Montana' (above) of 'il freddo paradiso / dei tuoi monti trovati dal sole',
and again in 'Là sul ponte' ('There on the Bridge'), DIP 3, of 'l'estate legata dalla
neve' ('the summer bound by snow'). In fact the first way in which Zanzotto
could be said to poeticize the landscape is by, in his own words, 'embroidering',
not 'repeating' this geographical feature, and in doing so he is adhering to a
personal theory of poetry:

> I believe that poetry should neither create worlds which are totally foreign
> to ours, nor repeat a reality which one presumes to be marble-hard and
> codified once and for all: for me poetry is rather like a continuous embroidery.
> (Camon 160–1)

Consequently, unless read in the context of the phenomenal reality of Zanzotto's
region, as explained above, the reader cannot understand why exactly Zanzotto
continually uses poetical images which sharply juxtapose sun and snow, hot
and cold:

i raggi del tuo sole
non maturano che neve
('Là sovente nell'alba', DIP 1)

the rays of your sun / ripen nothing but snow

('There Often in the Dawn')

. . . esce il sole
dal bocciolo di neve
('Serica', DIP 1)

. . . the sun comes out / from the bud of snow

('Silken')

> il fiato dei pianeti di fuoco
> arde sui monti e scopre
> gelate decadenze di materia
> ('Gli ornamenti sereni delle viti', ACV)

the breath of the fiery planets / burns on the mountains and discovers / frozen, decaying material

('The Serene Embellishments of the Grapevines').

On other occasions he interrelates these opposites as in the following example where the circle of the sun is said to be 'repeated' in the millions of 'circular' snowflakes, while the snow itself is referred to as 'shining infernos', a term which has immediate associations of heat but where the fusion of hot and cold is strengthened by evoking Dante's *Inferno* with its frozen lake of Cocytus instead of the expected fire of hell in the ninth and last circle:

> splendenti inferni crea la neve
> ripete l'anello del sole a milioni
> ('Per vuoti monti e strade come corde', ACV)

the snow creates shining infernos / repeats the ring of the sun by millions

('Through Empty Mountains and Cord-like Streets').

It is because of these juxtapositionings and blendings of hot and cold images that one cannot help feeling that some sort of relationship is being established between them and the abundance of poems in the first two collections which deal with autumn (two in ACV and six in DIP). In these poems Zanzotto emphasizes how autumn is a transitional time which (like the natural landscape) seems capable of combining a winter period with a summer period; cold, death and darkness, with a sense of life and warmth. It is almost as if Zanzotto is positing autumn as a poetical embodiment of the real landscape where neither summer nor winter seem to exist autonomously but are apparently synchronized. It is, as it were, always autumn in Pieve di Soligo. Thus 'Spegne il vento le sagre' ('The Wind Blows Out the Festivals'), from ACV combines the opulent image of wine overflowing from vats like thick blood, with that of deer in search of snow:

> Come un torbido sangue
> traboccherà dai tini
> altissimi l'autunno
> . . .
> come si sviano cervi
> cercando neve

Like a turbid blood / autumn will overflow / from the deepest vats / . . . / as deers go astray / in search of snow.

Similarly, 'Nei cimiteri fonti' ('In the Graveyard-Fountains') speaks of 'l'oro dei climi in rovina' ('the gold of climates in ruin'), and its references to exhausted grape-harvests, perishing game and the sacrificial land, present a picture of life and fruitfulness which is expiring:

> Alle affannate vendemmie
> gelide stelle donano conforto,
> le ignare selvaggine
> perirono tra i solchi
> e tra i giardini
> delle case gentili;
>
> . . .
>
> cibo santo ai suoi dolori
> s'offre la terra

To the breathless grape harvests / frozen stars give comfort, / the unknowing game / perished among the furrows / and among the gardens / of the noble houses; / . . . / the earth offers up / holy food to its sorrows.

In 'Assenzio' ('Absinth'), *DIP* 1, chilly images – autumn's cold regret for summer gone by, and a petrified dawn – are set against rich, sensuous images: the purple boast of grape-must and gardens, and the scented growth of a wood. The interrelation of these conflicting states is further emphasized by an alternating rhyme scheme in which those words or phrases which assume an oppositional meaning within the context of the poem, are given an identical rhyme: 'rimpianto', 'vanto'; 'che impietrisci l'aurora!', 'il chiuso bosco odora':

> E il tuo freddo rimpianto
> sta sui vacui confini
> contro il purpureo vanto
> dei mosti e dei giardini
>
> . . .
>
> delle tenebre alunno
> che impietrisci l'aurora!
> Nell'ombra dell'autunno
> il chiuso bosco odora

And your chilly desolation / is on the empty margins / against the purple ostentation / of the grape-musts and the gardens / a disciple of the penumbral / who petrifies the morn! / In the shadow of the autumnal / smells sweet the wood forlorn.

The arrival of the September equinox is in fact announced in 'Equinoziale' ('Equinoctial'), *DIP* 3, and this poem is followed by four others (the first three of them running in succession), which take as their theme the indeterminacy of the autumn period. In 'La fredda tromba' ('The Cold Trumpet') the combination of summer and winter is well conveyed in the presentation of hills as stinging, empty beehives: 'le colline / sono alveari pungenti e vuoti'. In 'In Basso' ('Low Down'), the rich memory of summer is rotting ('la ricca memoria marcisce'), the sun is exploring distant clouds ('e tenta il sole nuvole remote'), and streams have been reduced to a vitreous iciness ('Dei ruscelli fantasia / di bimbi ignari non resta / che una trasparenza di gelo') ('Of the streams – the fantasy / of young, unknowing children – nothing remains / but an icy transparency'). Similarly, the sunflower whose leaves the poet counts in 'Elianto' ('Helianthus') is a metaphor for the sun whose last days he counts in the latent freshness of the earth:

> Questo elianto mutato dall'acqua
> è il sole ch'io vado contando
> nelle riposte frescure della terra
> nelle botole dell'autunno

This helianthus changed by the water / is the sun that I go counting / in the secret cool of the earth / in the trapdoors of autumn.

And finally, in 'Al bivio' ('At the Crossroads'), there is the junction of the 'verde vivo' ('living green') on the mountains, and the 'dazzled cocks' who 'chiameranno domani / le ragioni eterne della neve' ('will call out tomorrow / the eternal reasons of the snow').

Besides that of heat and cold, there is another pair of opposites – fluidity and solidity – which pervade the poems of DIP. Here Zanzotto most probably has in mind the Piave river which with its constant floods transforms the flatlands of his Veneto region into lakes. However, this reality is made more poetic in the manner in which Zanzotto interrelates fluid and solid images in new and creative settings.

In 'Salva' ('Salvo'), DIP 3, the setting is a simple one of a field. Here, solidity and fluidity, land and sea, are brought together in an inextricable unity by the method of lending the properties of the second to the first:

> La terra . . .
> gonfia impetuosi pesci
> dalle sue vene
> e le correnti fanno i prati incerti
> sotto le ali delle colline

The earth . . . / swells with impulsive fish protruding / from its veins / and the currents make the fields unsteady / under the wings of the hills.

It is a method employed by Rimbaud in *Les Illuminations*. The 'currents' of what is probably a ploughed field in the extract above are reminiscent, for example, of 'Marine' ('Marine'), where one is uncertain as to which term of Rimbaud's metaphor is the tenor, and which, the vehicle: 'Les courants de la lande / Et les ornières immenses du reflux' ('The currents of the moor / And the huge ruts of the ebb-tide').

In 'Grido sul lago' ('Cry on the Lake') and 'Le carrozze gemmate' ('The Jewelled Carriages'), *DIP* 1, the settings are more intricate. The former depicts a number of pile-dwellings – 'palafitte'. A pile-dwelling technically denotes a prehistoric village built on beams driven vertically into the bed of a lake. However, Zanzotto's use of the term 'palafitta' cannot but evoke a more modern setting as well: Montale's description in *Occasioni* of the 'Bank Holiday' at Eastbourne where trumpets are playing 'God Save the King' from a 'padiglione erto su palafitte' ('Steep pavilion on piles') (there are 'padiglioni colmi della festa' ('pavilions thronged with festivities') in Zanzotto's poem too).

The environment in which Zanzotto places his pile-dwellings is also characterized by half-solid/half-liquid phenomena: the water of the lake in which, presumably, the pile-dwellings stand is *frozen* ('Costruzioni ed asili / della più sensibile rovina / si spalancano al lago / gelato') ('Buildings and shelters / in most perceptible ruins / open wide onto the frozen / lake'), overturned glasses on tables within one of the dwellings pour out *wax* ('sui tavoli i bicchieri rovesciati / versano cera'), and carts and cars have turned the nearby road to *mud* ('carri e macchine / resero fango la via'). A suspension of the movement associated with liquidity is also something that is emphasized: time has stopped still; vehicles using the mountain road have become choked up with earth; and boats could sail only in another age:

> Il grido d'uccello dell'inverno
> arrestò i quadranti degli orologi,
>
> . . .
>
> intorno al monte s'interrano
> bovi motori e ruote,
>
> . . .
>
> Chiamate all'altra riva
> in altro tempo
> volarono lungi le barche

The winter bird's cry / stopped the clock-faces, / . . . / oxen motors and wheels / clog up with earth around the mountain, / . . . / Called to another shore / in another time / boats flew far away.

Such images of liquid solidified and of movement arrested combine to produce an impressive still-life picture, made all the more striking in that the anachronistic pile-dwellings are placed against a modern background of cars and engines, thereby creating an incongruous imaginative vision of the sort often found in Rimbaud (see, for example, 'Fête d'hiver' ('Winter Festival'), *Illuminations*).

'Le carrozze gemmate', with its fairy-tale, and vaguely Rimbaldian title (cf.
Rimbaud's 'Fairy', 'Génie' ('Genie'), 'Bottom', 'Parade' ('Parade'), and 'Conte'
('Story')) is, by contrast, full of movement. Here, buildings and constructions
from fictional and technological worlds, and a land which reveals the mythical,
are all synchronized within one poem and are being demolished by torrential
rainfall. The poem opens with a storm scene where 'palaces' are flagging
beneath the weight of thunder, and a party and convoy of jewelled carriages
are departing madly to escape the deluge, their wheels rotting in the mud, so
that any relationship to factual reality is severed and the reader is plunged into
a fictional, fairy-tale world:

> Le carrozze gemmate
> disperatamente alle chine
> partono, cariche di rovina;
> sotto il peso dei tuoni
> i palazzi stentando si raccolgono
> e i convogli agitando
> i loro anelli marciti
> s'insinuano nel fango della terra

The jewelled carriages / tilting to one side frantically / leave, laden with
ruins; / under the weight of the thunder / the palaces are hardly able to
assemble / and the convoys shaking / their rotten rings / slide into the
earth's mud.

A sudden shift from this fictitious world to the modern and technological is
announced by the reference to aqueducts which then follows:

> i paramenti di cemento
> degli acquedotti scemano colpevoli
> verso fontane e croci,
> sorge il rischio dei ponti
> . . .
>
> gli ossuti parapetti
> attendono il trionfo dei torrenti

the cement faces / of the aqueducts decline guiltily / towards fountains and
crosses, / the bridges' risk rises / . . . / the bony parapets / await the torrents'
triumph.

These aqueducts, along with bridges and parapets, are being destroyed by the
water with which they are moreover associated: the aqueducts burst open, it
would seem, from an overflow of water to become 'fountains', the bridges are in
danger of collapsing, and the parapets too anticipate their demise by the deluge.
As well as the constructed landscape, the elemental landscape is also at the
mercy of these rains: they thrust the sun downwards so that it sinks, not naturally,

but like a stone in a whirlpool ('vortici di sasso del tramonto') ('the sunset's stony vortices'), and they dig into the land so that the earth collapses to reveal the mythical beneath the technological: statues of the most distant depths, and perhaps of ancient gods, given the reference to incense with its connotations of homage and adulation:

> E tutto è invaso dal passato
> dalla luce del tossico
> e dell'incenso;
> . . .
> e tutte le statue si liberano
> tutte le statue legate
> nei fondi lontanissimi

And everything is invaded by the past / by the light of toxic / and incense; / . . . / and all the statues free themselves / all the statues bound / in the most distant depths.

The fact that the destructive properties of water upon concrete material, as emphasized in this poem, are functioning as an inventive depiction of the floodings typical of Zanzotto's region is supported by three stories in Zanzotto's largely autobiographical *Sull'altopiano* (*SA*) (*On the Plateau*): 'Vagabondaggi notturni' ('Nocturnal Wanderings'), 'Mercato distante' ('Distant Market'), and 'Pagine dissepolte' ('Disinterred Pages'). In all three of these rain forms the climatic background. In 'Pagine dissepolte' it is said to be capable of lasting for 'dieci settimane consecutive' ('ten consecutive weeks'), and in 'Mercato distante' a deluge is presented as practically wiping out a whole community, giving rise thereby to an extended motif of disappearance (the section of it which reads 'L'Asia e l'Europa . . . spariscono a poco a poco' ('Asia and Europe . . . disappear little by little') – a phrase echoed in different ways throughout the whole of 'Mercato distante' – is, once again, of Rimbaldian descent ('Qu'est-ce pour nous, mon coeur', *Derniers vers*): 'Europe, Asie, Amérique, disparaissez' ('Europe, Asia, America, disappear')):

Everything solid *crumbles* under the force of the rain. The water rises, the birds fly far away . . . . Asia and Europe, closed in their crystal casings, *disappear little by little*. On the islands *nothing remains but* stands and kiosks . . . . Beneath the darkness the hills are infinite heaps of mud, furrowed by torrents which gush and descend precipitously from the individual peaks. *Only a few sections of street surface here and there* among the suctions of water . . . . Further and further behind the mountains and the plateaus, veils of rain cover other veils of rain, cataracts, other cataracts, sounds of thunder, other inaudible catastrophes. . . . The wheels mark out two furrows, like railway tracks which, forever visible, point straight towards the south, leaving aside *houses half buried or submerged*, with all of their shutters closed . . . on the piazza of the market place the water beats down like an ocean, and washes and *wears away* the windows of the 'Gran Caffè'. (*Sull'altopiano* 44–5)

Another of the ways in which Zanzotto recreates reality in a poetical way is by assimilating the real to something else. There are in fact three different types of comparisons – what I shall call, comparative projects – at work in ACV and DIP. The first of these consists of a systematic use of metaphor, combined, on some occasions, with what could be called a defamiliarization of common, verbal relationships. Again, unlike the French Symbolists who used metaphor as a means of severing the real in an attempt to probe the other-worldly, as Baudelaire himself acknowledges, using a metaphorical image in *Les fleurs du mal*, 'Le Voyage': Notre âme est un trois-mâts cherchant son Icarie' (Our soul is a three-masted ship searching for its land of Icarus), Zanzotto's figurative language merely marks the primacy of the imagination, announces poetic precedence in opposition to general acceptance. It is used, as it was for Ungaretti, only as a means of inventively recreating '*questo* mondo terreno' ('*this* earthly world').

The world recreated by metaphor in the first two books emerges as one where separate landscape elements are continually fusing. In the examples here from ACV the tenor of the metaphor (on all occasions, one element), is related to the vehicle (another element) by the verb 'essere' ('to be'); while in DIP, the noticeable absence of the word 'come' ('like') (which also makes of these examples, metaphors as opposed to similes) means that again one element is depicted as *being* another as opposed to being *like* another:

> Qui cicale grigie
> sono ormai tutte le erbe

By now all the grass is / grey cicadas here

> il vento si è rattrappito
> lucertola delle pietre

the wind is benumbed / – a lizard of stones

> ha (il vento) paura del sole ch'è un nido
> d'aspri falchi

(the wind) is afraid of the sun which is a nest / of harsh falcons

> le bufere oscurissime
> accecate negli occhi
> sono monti lontani e mai veduti
> ('Davvero soffici pennellate', ACV)

darkest storms / blinded in the eyes / are far-off mountains which have never been seen

> ('Really Soft Brush-Strokes')

. . . il sole
tranquillo baco di spinosi boschi
('Ormai', DIP 1)

the sun – a quiet grub of thorny woods

. . . la crisalide
intricata del sole
('Là sul ponte', DIP 3)

. . . the entangled / chrysalis of the sun

e della notte caverna di fango
('Serica', DIP 1)

and of the night, a cavern of mud

le lumache petali madidi
('Notte di guerra, a tramontana', DIP 1)

snails – moist petals

('Night of War, with a North Wind').

The poet too is involved in this harmonizing process and in startling Surrealist pictures he has actually become the space occupied by a deserted sun, his hair, branches of a wood merging with the sky, his bones, those of a bird, and his forehead, a feathery nest. (This tendency to refer to oneself in terms of Nature is, again, characteristic of Quasimodo's earlier period, for example, 'il mio cuore d'uragano' ('my hurricane heart') (*Subito*, 'Dormono selve' line 15); 'A te mi porgo / trebbiato senza seme' ('I give myself to you / threshed without seed') (*Subito*, 'Anellide ermafrodito' lines 6–7)):

Io sono spazio frequentato
dal tuo sole deserto
('Distanza', DIP 1)

I am space frequented / by your deserted sun

('Distance')

ch'ero guarito coi capelli a bosco
d'un cielo azzurro e prossimo
('Le case che camminano sulle acque', DIP 1)

that I was cured with my hair like a wood / of a blue, close sky
('The Houses which Walk on the Waters')

La febbre ha vuotato
le mie ossa d'uccello
un sonno sublime distrusse il mio volto
un'ala ha fatto grande nido

piumoso nido della mia fronte
('Quanta notte', *DIP* 1)

Fever has emptied / my bird bones / a sublime sleep destroyed my face / a
wing has made a huge nest / a feathery nest of my brow

('So Much Night').

However, the grounds for such syntheses are not readily apparent. Zanzotto's
metaphors are obscure, personal ones, 'Hermetic' in the original sense of the
word as applied by Francesco Flora. It could also be argued that, rather than
echoing Quasimodo, they are imitating Ungaretti's use of elliptical imagery,
and/or following the Surrealist doctrine of free association. One can, how-
ever, attempt to explain Zanzotto's metaphors by suggesting that on some
occasions the two elements involved in the metaphor are fused because of
their spatial proximity: cicadas and grass, falcons and sun, snails which leave
moist trails on petals (hence 'petali madidi'). On other occasions the relationship
between the two elements appears to be more impressionistic: one thinks of
a lizard's stiff, immobile stance among stones, and in that sense the lizard is
like the 'benumbed' wind. It is perhaps the idea of the black, weighty mass
of storm-clouds gathering in the distance, which allows for the comparison
between 'darkest storms' and 'far-off mountains' that have 'never been seen'.
The sun is described as a grub, maybe because the circular shape of the
first recalls the cyclical weaving of a chrysalis (which would also explain the
metaphor which follows it: 'la crisalide / intricata del sole'); and it is possibly
the mere concepts of darkness and dampness which link 'night' to a 'muddy
cavern'.

But whereas the meaning of these metaphors is obscure, their function is
somewhat less equivocal: in my view, they serve to present a new, interacting,
kaleidoscopic landscape as opposed to one characterized by an absence of
movement, of 'becoming', which the omission in *DIP* of any comparative link
between elements (the absence of 'come' ('like')) denoted for Barberi-Squarotti
(1961, 150).

Unlike the examples above, comprising both tenor and vehicle (the 'grass',
'wind', 'sun', and so on, constituting the first category, and the 'cicadas', 'lizard',
'harsh falcons', and so forth, the second), there is another use of metaphor in *DIP*
where one is presented only with the vehicle and left to posit what the tenor
might be from the context of the poem. Such is the case in the following example
where the poet speaks of being awakened by

il rombo lieve e il tremito
degli azzurri vulcani
('Là sovente nell'alba', *DIP* 1)

the light rumble and trembling / of the blue vulcanoes.

Here 'azzurri vulcani' is, in my opinion, referring to active volcanoes rather than to flashes of lightning (there is a reference to 'lava' in line 9). However, the allusion to active volcanoes is not to be taken literally, for there is nothing of the kind in Zanzotto's local region. So as the poem proceeds to talk of a 'deer born of snow' which has entangled its frail antlers among the mountains ('Tra i monti specchi eccelsi del primordio / impigliava le gracili corna / il cervo nato dalla neve' ('Among the mountains – lofty mirrors of the beginning – / the deer born of snow / entangled its delicate antlers')), one realizes that Zanzotto has found an inherent analogy between active volcanoes and snow-covered mountains, characterized by avalanches (the word 'neve' ('snow') occurs twice in the poem – lines 7 and 21). Both are apparently inanimate structures capable, however, of coming alive with thunderous noises and a pouring of liquid substance. The tenor of the metaphor, that is, the subject which the poet is really considering, is therefore a mountain avalanche, but this reality has undergone an imaginative recreation to become an active volcano (again with the object of highlighting a fusion of hot and cold features within the natural landscape).

Both these types of metaphor (the first comprising both tenor and vehicle, the second, leaving the tenor of the metaphor implied), are on occasions combined with phrases which defamiliarize normal, sometimes clichéd relationships between words. Such a practice reinforces Zanzotto's rejection of a rational, familiar reality, in favour of the novel and creative.

Conspicuous verbal defamiliarizations are to be found in some of those examples from ACV which have been given previously to illustrate Zanzotto's first type of metaphor (see translations on page 21):

> il vento si è rattrappito
> lucertola delle pietre
>
> le bufere oscurissime
> accecate negli occhi
> sono monti lontani e mai veduti.

In the first there is an inversion of the common relationship between the noun 'vento' ('wind') and the verb 'rattrappire' ('to benumb'). 'Vento' is made the passive element instead of the usual, active agent, so that here the wind does not 'benumb' but is 'benumbed'. In the second example it is the normal association between the noun 'occhi' ('eyes') and the verb 'accecare' ('to blind') which is overturned: eyes are usually blinded, things are not 'blinded in the eyes'. (This blindness theme, at first related to the tenor of the metaphor – 'le bufere oscurissime' ('darkest storms') – is then extended to the vehicle: 'sono monti . . . mai veduti' ('are mountains . . . never seen')).

Similar verbal displacements are combined with metaphors of the second type in 'Reliquia' ('Relic'), *DIP* 1:

1   Dolci, mansueti
       tra le zampe di vello
3   i colli celano il tepore,
       pende lungi l'autunno
5   erto dei monti.
       A stento un sole estraneo
7   si sottrae alle fauci
       dei sotterranei dei fortilizi,
9   la terra umida chiocciola
       bruca fiumi acuti di zucchero.
11 Glutine lussuoso
       germoglia e cresce verso il cielo
13 che l'acqua costrusse,
       con cupe foglie il mare
15 tenta il mio corpo.
       Illeggibili sono ormai le reliquie
17 dell'oro e della seta;
       nell'equivoca luce
19 degli uccelli e delle nubi
       sonnolenta si libera la luna
21 dal carro colmo del raccolto.

Sweet, docile / among the fleecy hooves / the hills conceal the warmth, / the steep autumn of the mountains / hangs far off. / An alien sun with difficulty / escapes from the jaws / of the small forts' dungeons, / the earth – a moist snail – / browses on sharp rivers of sugar. / A sumptuous gluten / buds and grows towards the sky / that the water created, / with dark leaves the sea / entices my body. / By now illegible are the relics / of the gold and silk; / in the equivocal light / of the birds and the clouds / the moon drowsily frees itself / from the cart brimming with the harvest.

'Zampe di vello' in line 2 reads like a precious metaphor for sheep, while 'mansueti' ('docile') in line 1 reinforces this impression since it is an adjective generally associated with sheep or lambs. Here, however, this common association is abolished and 'mansueti' refers directly to the 'colli' ('hills') of line 3. In the same way, the verbal relationship usually recognized as existing betweeen 'erto' ('steep') and 'monti' ('mountains') (line 5) is dislodged, 'erto' being used to describe 'l'autunno' ('autumn') as opposed to 'mountains'. This displacement is made all the more conspicuous by the manner in which 'erto' is placed alongside 'monti' within the same line, with the intention, it would seem, of reminding one of the normal relationship between the two words.

Line 9 contains a metaphor of the first type. The subject of this metaphor – 'terra' ('land') – and the use of the verb 'brucare' ('to graze') seem to highlight the sheep metaphor of line 2. But whereas these two terms 'terra' and 'brucare' are generally accepted as being related, their relationship here is not a generally acceptable one, for it is the land that is grazing off water as opposed to animals grazing off land.

In line 14 'mare' ('sea') is used as a metaphor for the 'cielo' ('sky') mentioned in line 12, although this relationship is only implied in the reference in line 13 to the sky 'che l'acqua costrusse' ('that the water created'). One assumes that it is probably the blue of the water and the blue of the sky which enable the poet to speak of the second in terms of the first: the 'cupe foglie' ('dark leaves') of the sea operating only as a metaphorical image for the 'sumptuous gluten, 'budding' and 'growing' towards the sky' (itself a metaphor for the sap and foliage of branches).

Finally, the moon 'freeing itself' from the cart – probably rising from behind the cart brimming with the day's harvest – would seem to be a figurative depiction of nightfall. This interpretation can be supported by lines 6 to 8 where the sun is said to be escaping from (underground) dungeons thereby suggesting that it is not high in the sky but close to the horizon, as it is at sunset. Consequently, the 'relics' of gold in lines 16 to 17 could refer to the feebler rays emitted by this setting sun (reinforced by the reference to the 'equivocal light' in line 18); while the 'silk' of line 17 possibly denotes the silkworm which only comes out at night-time.

The nature of Zanzotto's two other comparative projects in *ACV* and *DIP* have been indicated by him in an interview when he spoke about his early works as being 'founded on a particular feeling of *Eros* and "psychicism"' (Listri 188). I shall deal with these two concepts of Eros and 'psychicism' separately.

Eros is a term which becomes synonymous with woman, and images of women are superimposed upon the land. In this Zanzotto is consciously following in the footsteps of Éluard (his later collection, *LB*, speaks of the 'crismi eluardiani fortemente amorosi' ('strongly loving Éluardian chrisms') ('Possibili prefazi IV') to be found in these works). For Nature in Éluard is never presented as it really is, but eroticized to the extent that his landscape actually becomes the body of a woman as exemplified by the following quotations:

> . . . le soleil dans la forêt
> Est comme un ventre qui se donne dans un lit
> > (*Oeuvres* 2, 143)

. . . the sun in the forest / Is like a belly which gives itself in a bed

> sur l'herbe courbe comme un ventre
> > (*Oeuvres* 1, 591)

on the grass curved like a belly

> la langue sucrée des lilas
> > (*Oeuvres* 1, 1200)

the sugary tongue of the lilacs

> La nature s'est prise aux filets de ta vie
> l'arbre, ton ombre, montre sa chair nue: le ciel
> (*Oeuvres* 1, 173)

Nature is caught in the nets of your life / the tree, your shadow, shows its naked flesh: the sky.

Examples of this kind are innumerable in Éluard's poetry. But whereas Éluard's constant emphasis upon the physicality of woman makes the woman of his landscape a single idea, a concept, in Zanzotto's landscape there are many different types of women. The feminine presence is seen, as the poet himself explained, in 'a kind of continual multiplication, of refraction behind the scenes of nature' (*Sulla poesia* 103).

In 'Là sovente nell'alba', DIP 1, the woman is a protective mother, and Zanzotto's town, traversed by the Piave river, becomes the metaphor for a sheltering womb girded by water: 'freddo rifugio cui gl'insoliti / fiumi cingono il grembo' ('cold shelter whose unusual / rivers surround the womb'). This allows the poet to denote his affinity with it in terms of a symbiotic relationship evoking that of the child within the womb:

> Ma ancora negli abissi
> tuoi cercarti m'è caro,
> in ogni tua forma giaccio sepolto

But it is still dear for me to search for you / in your abysses, / I lie buried in all of your forms.

In 'Perché siamo', DIP 3, the protective mother now epitomizes the security of life in a domestic, country environment (portrayed also in 'Nella valle' ('In the Valley'), DIP 3) where one wakes each morning to see the customary snow on the same three mountains, where one is surrounded by valueless but cherished belongings, like the tiny kitchen garden that yields no produce, and where one takes pleasure in the small and apparently unimportant, such as the cultivation of chicory or the taste of an apple. (Zanzotto's pastoral nostalgia – which he shares with Rilke and Heidegger (see Heidegger, *Poetry*, 113) – his love for a rural life where man lives in intimate affinity with his natural surroundings, is much in evidence here, and will be developed in IXE):

> Nelle mattine, se è vero,
> di tre montagne trasparenti
> mi risveglia la neve;
> nelle mattine c'è l'orto
> che sta in una mano
> e non produce che conchiglie,
> c'è la cantina delle formiche
> c'è il radicchio, diletta risorsa

> profusa alle mie dita,
> a un vento che non osa disturbarci
>
> Ha sapore di brina
> la mela che mi diverte

In the mornings, if it is true, / I am awakened by the snow / of three transparent mountains; / in the mornings there is the kitchen garden / which would fit into your hand / and which only yields shells, / there is the ants' cellar / there is the chicory, beloved resource / lavished on my fingers, / beneath a wind that doesn't dare disturb us / The apple which amuses me / tastes of hoarfrost.

The warm assurance the poet feels within this environment is akin to that of a child consoled by its mother, as becomes obvious in a passage where the lexical repetition and balanced rhythm are reminiscent of a mother's *berceuse* (the sequence is also typical of a 'school' poem of the type composed by Zanella):

> O mamma, piccolo è il tuo tempo,
> tu mi vi porti perch'io mi consoli
> e là v'è l'erba di novembre,
> là v'è la franca salute dell'acqua,
> sani come acqua vi siamo noi

O mother, your time is small, / you bring me there so as to console me / and there there is November's grass, / there there is the water's pure health, / there we are as healthy as water.

In two other poems, it is not necessarily a mother, but a sensuous woman who is present within the rivers and canals. In the second quotation below, she is depicted as a kind of 'Ambra', the reference to the 'naked graces' of the woman and the 'sweet grasp' of the canal recalling Lorenzo de' Medici's poem where Ombrone, the river-god, desires to take 'quella bella ninfa in braccio . . . / e nudo il nudo e bel corpo tenere' ('that beautiful nymph in my arms . . . / and naked, hold her naked, beautiful body'). (The precise connection may be remote, but nevertheless, a tradition is evoked):

> ora viene quest'acqua ch'io sospiro
> perché traspare dalle tue
> membra gemelle
> ('L'acqua di Dolle', *DIP* 2)

Now comes this water that I sigh for / because it shines through your / twin limbs

> o tu che accetti la stretta dolce dei canali
> e che ti lasci guardare

in tutte le tue nude grazie
('Le case che camminano sulle acque', DIP 1)

oh you who accepts the canals' sweet embrace / and lets yourself be seen / in all of your naked grace'.

On another occasion, it is a young virgin girl (from 'a family of wild rains and leaves') who has waited patiently for her lover, now returned from a long absence, who is fused with the image of a ripening harvest, awakening from its 'shining indolence'. In other words, it is suggested that the lover's return infuses the girl with new life like the harvest 'enjoying good health again':

di minuto in minuto
quella messe riprende salute
e tu vergine vi ti dicevi
per aver tanto atteso,
ed eri d'una famiglia
di selvatiche piogge e foglie
ed eri schiava
d'una lettera in arrivo
('Con dolce curiosità', DIP 2)

minute by minute / that harvest enjoys good health again / and you called yourself a virgin there / for having waited so long, / and you came from a family / of wild rains and leaves / and you were a slave / for an arriving letter

('With Sweet Curiosity').

The last type of woman that can be detected in this landscape appears to come from another age. The speaker of 'Oro effimero e vetro' ('Ephemeral Gold and Glass'), DIP 2, is depicted as a kind of courtly lover who, revitalized by the enchantment and beauty of a snow-enveloped land, is now hopeful and expectant of his 'lady's' favour. The courtly love phraseology of the third stanza here intimates the medieval setting:

e cresce a meraviglia
del mio volto innocente
la neve che somiglia
alla luna recente.

Le mie vene febbrili
tanta linfa ristora
che l'oblio degli esili
gli affanni miei colora,

che del tuo bene il caro
segno attendo e i soccorsi
ed illudo l'amaro
pianto degli anni scorsi

and the snow which resembles / the recent moon / grows to the amazement / of my innocent face. / It brings back so much lymph / to my feverish veins / that my anxieties are coloured / by the oblivion of exiles / and I await the dear sign / of your happiness and help / and avoid the bitter / tears of the past years.

A more explicit medieval setting is created in 'Figura' ('Figure'), ACV, with its banquet scene and singing minstrels. And the 'figure' again resembles a medieval lady, her eyes, hair and lips (features celebrated in Provençal verse) appearing in the landscape through the windows of the 'illustrious house':

> Ma i commensali, raccolti
> i nobili dolori nel cuore,
> per le mirabili trifore
> guardano il lontano azzurro
> e l'oro dei capelli
> consuma le loro sembianze
> e gli occhi
> in cui sporge la perla
> e le rosse labbra di figura.

But the table-companions, having gathered up / their noble sorrows in their hearts, / watch the distant blue / through the wonderful three-light windows / and the golden hair / and the eyes / where the pearl protrudes / and the striking red lips / consume their features.

But regardless of the type of woman Zanzotto is depicting, she is, on all occasions, his poetic inspiration. If the feminine presence is not felt by the poet, although known to be there among the elements, then the landscape seems colourless and prosaic, and fails to move the poet:

> Tu sei: mi trascura
> e tutto brividi mi lascia la stagione;
> fragole a boschi e pomi a perdizione
> nelle miriadi delle piogge
> . . .
>
> e tutta un'altra fioritura
> che non significa e non pesa

You exist: the season ignores / me and leaves me all shivering; / woods of strawberries and apples rotting / in the myriad of rains / . . . / and a totally different blossoming / which neither weighs nor means anything.

This blossoming of Nature which, when his 'tu' is inaccessible, neither means nor counts for anything, is transformed into 'blinding richness' at the end of the poem when contact with the 'tu' is retrieved:

> Con te verde ora
> di caligini e raggi
> mi salvi, io vedo ancora
> tra accecanti ricchezze
> ('Tu sei, mi trascura', *DIP* 1)

Together with you, you now green / with mists and rays / you save me, I can
see again / among blinding richness

> ('You Exist, It Ignores Me').

Accordingly, it is never the prosaic reality of landscape phenomena such
as heat, cold, sun, snow and so on which one is confronted with in the
first two books. Rather, all of these things are presented as inducing and
therefore representing for the poet certain psychological states (Milone 208).
It is something, however, which I interpret as an attempt to embellish earthly
reality, rather than to circumscribe it, as Milone believes.

However, the symbolism of Zanzotto's landscape is not always constant. Just
as those metaphorical images dealt with on pages 21–2 presented landscape
phenomena that were continually moving and interacting with each other, in a
similar manner, landscape phenomena are continually changing their *significance*,
their *symbolic meaning* for the poet. It is a feature which, in fact, prefigures the
polysemic nature of Zanzotto's later writing (to be examined in Chapters 4 and
5) where signifiers will be infused with many different meanings as opposed to a
single specific one.

Generally, the symbolism that is given to an element of the landscape alternates
from being sometimes negative and sometimes positive (as is often the case in
Montale's *Ossi*). The negative symbolism of heat is emphasized in 'Quanto a
lungo' ('How Long'), *DIP* 1, where it represents, what Milone has called, the
poet's 'neurosis'. Here Zanzotto, across the two sections of the poem, makes a
comparison between the real attic of his house and the 'attic' of his mind ('il mio
tetto *incerto*' ('my *uncertain* roof')) with its 'comignoli *disorientati*' ('*disorientated*
chimney-tops') and its 'terrazze ove cammina impazzita la grandine' ('terraces
where the crazed hail treads'). Coterminous with this attic of the mind are the
poet's writings depicted in the first section as 'rischi *appassiti*' ('*withered* risks'). A
relationship is therefore established between the adjectives 'incerto', 'disorientati'
and 'appassiti', denoting a connection between mental uncertainty, confusion,
and the mind 'withered' or dried up by heat. Heat, in fact, is engendering
these negative qualities. For the main thrust of the poem deals with how
the poet has abandoned his writings (or attic of the mind) in the real attic
of his house so that they might be saved from the 'scalding light' of day, and
that something of their 'disorientated', 'withered' nature, the spilled 'blood'
which they symbolize, might be tempered by the 'cold lances' of Sagittarius
and Capricorn and the silence and 'transparencies' of Aquarius. Cold, therefore,

working as a counteracting, oppositional force to heat, is consequently attributed a positive symbolism:

> Quanto a lungo tra il grano e tra il vento
> di quelle soffitte
> piú alte, piú estese che il cielo,
> quanto a lungo vi ho lasciate
> mie scritture, miei rischi appassiti
> . . .
> vi ho lasciate lassú perché salvaste
> dalle ustioni della luce
> il mio tetto incerto
> i comignoli disorientati
> le terrazze ove cammina impazzita la grandine
> . . .
> su voi sagittario e capricorno
> inclinarono le fredde lance
> e l'acquario temperò nei suoi silenzi
> nelle sue trasparenze
> un anno stillante di sangue, una mia
> perdita inesplicabile

How long among the wheat and among the wind / of those attics / higher and broader than the sky, / how long I have left you, / my writings, my withered risks / . . . / I have left you up there so that you might save / from the scalding light of day / my uncertain roof / the disorientated chimney-tops / the terraces where the crazed hail treads / . . . / Sagittarius and Capricorn / tilted their cold lances on you / and Aquarius tempered in its silences / and transparencies / a year oozing with blood, one of my / inexplicable losses.

In 'Per vuoti monti', *ACV*, and 'Atollo', *DIP* 1, the heat of the sun works on the poet in the same damaging fashion – draining his body and mind, and severing the 'ties' of his 'substance' – thereby maintaining its negative symbolism:

> e il sole come un anello,
> . . .
> . . . assorbe e sugge il mio nudo corpo
> in ricerche mirabili
> in vite tortuosi labirinti di raggi
> > ('Per vuoti monti', *ACV*)

and the sun like a ring, / . . . / . . . soaks up and sucks my naked body / in admirable quests / in lives – tortuous labyrinths of rays

> Già il sole penetra per le
> cieche gallerie delle finestre
> sugge e scinde gli ultimi
> legami della mia sostanza
> > ('Atollo', *DIP* 1)

Already the sun penetrates through the / blind tunnels of the windows / sucks and severs the last / ties of my substance.

The alternation of heat with the positive effects of cold which took place in 'Quanto a lungo' is repeated in 'Arse il motore', DIP 1. For here, to escape the fever of modern living, symbolized, as will be remembered, by the dusty aridity generated by the car ('Arse il motore' ('The motor burned'), 'il suo sangue selvaggio' ('its savage blood'), 'Assetato di polvere e di fiamma' ('Athirst for dust and flame')), the poet brings with him on his retrogressive journey to his own personal poetic world, objects which are glassy and cool: sharp ice, even if shrivelled by fevers, seaweed and fountains (see translation on page 8):

> acuti ghiacci avvizziti di febbre
> alghe e fontane con me discesero
>
> nel fondo del mio viaggio.

Snow, like the cool elements above, is also an edifying feature capable, like them, of removing a 'feverishness' and revitalizing the spirit, as was seen to be the case in 'Oro effimero e vetro', DIP 1. In this poem when speaking of snow, Zanzotto says that it brings back blood to his feverish veins: 'Le mie vene febbrili / tanta linfa ristora'. Covering the land with a white uniformity, snow also achieves this salutary effect by inducing a state of peaceful 'enchantment' ('E lo smarrito sguardo / che quegl'incanti beve' ('And my bewildered gaze / which drinks up those charms')), a state reproduced in 'Oro effimero e vetro' by a method of coupling a hypnotic, alternate rhyme with a regular *settenario* (see page 29).

But all of the symbolism established so far is inverted elsewhere. The 'heat' of spring, along with the other attributes of the season, is welcomed in 'Ormai', DIP 1, encouraging the poet to embrace the landscape, to 'lock it around' himself. And whereas in previous examples heat was related to verbs like 'appassire' ('to wither'), 'avvizzire' ('to shrivel'), and 'suggere' ('to suck') (the first two verbs forming a motif in section 1 of DIP: for example, 'l'oro sui deschi appassisce' ('Adunata') ('the gold withers on the tables'); 'Palafitte avvizziscono' ('Grido sul lago') ('Pile-dwellings shrivel')), here it is actually instrumental in removing his 'male', in slaking his 'thirst':

> Ormai la primula e il calore
> ai piedi e il verde acume del mondo
>
> I tappeti scoperti
> le logge vibrate dal vento ed il sole
> tranquillo baco di spinosi boschi;
> il mio male lontano, la sete distinta
> come un'altra vita nel petto

Qui non resta che cingersi intorno il paesaggio
qui volgere le spalle

('Ormai', *DIP* 1)

By now the primrose and the warmth / at one's feet and the green sharpness
of the world / The uncovered carpets / the verandahs trembling in the wind,
and the sun / – a quiet grub of thorny woods; / my malaise far off, my thirst,
different, / like another life in my breast / Here all that remains is to wrap the
landscape around oneself / here turn one's back.

Cold, by extension, is sometimes depicted as a negative feature. In 'Montana'
it is representative of exclusion (see translation page 14):

Da sé mi esclude il freddo paradiso
dei tuoi monti

. . .

E di là tanto mi tace
dopo i prati e i freddi meli
la fredda spera del tuo paradiso.

Whereas in 'Oro effimero e vetro' snow stood for a revitalizing force (see
page 33), elsewhere in *DIP* it is symbolic of a devitalization of the senses, and
in *ACV*, of death. It assumes, thereby, a Lorcaesque symbolism (see, for example,
Bodas de sangre where dead individuals are frequently referred to in terms of
snow, for example 'montón de nieve' ('heap of snow'); 'dos puñados de nieve
endurecida' ('two fistfuls of hardened snow')):

La simmetria della morte
brilla nella neve
dei boschi
circoscritti di spine
('Alle scale del mondo', *ACV*)

The symmetry of death / shines in the snow / of the woods / circumscribed
by thorns

('At the World's Stairways')

la neve è qui nella sua bara
('A che valse l'attesa del gioco?', *ACV*)

the snow is here in its coffin

('What was the Point of Waiting on the Game?')

in questo luogo di legno
odoroso ed oscuro
dove le nevi luminosamente
ininterrottamente tremano
e i sensi languono feriti
('Quanta notte', *DIP* 1)

in this place of wood / fragrant and dark / where snows luminously / and unceasingly tremble / and senses languish, wounded.

In its negative context it is also a Lorcaesque symbolism that is attributed to the moon. As in the famous moon soliloquy from *Bodas de Sangre*, the moon in *DIP* represents a knife and, by implication, death. Thus in 'Notte di guerra, a tramontana', *DIP* 1, the moon is one of the honed 'lances' in the war-game of the night, a 'curved silver' which has cut the world off from light:

> La notte si è ridotta
> e acuminata in ogni sua lancia
> ma più nella luna
> che già dalla luce
> ha diviso le parti perdute del mondo
> e ha lasciato l'argento curvo
> e il diamante poroso
> alla mano dei morti

The night is shortened / and has sharpened all of its lances / but mostly that of the moon / which has already divided the lost pieces of the world / from light / and left the curved silver / and porous diamond / in the hands of the dead.

In *ACV* the moon is a tomb with a sepulchral light:

> già ogni casa è la più bianca
> tomba della luna
> ('Alle scale del mondo', *ACV*)

already every house is the whitest / tomb of the moon

> Vi chiamerà la luna
> che vi ha guardato tanto
> e con tanto lume di sepolcro?
> ('"Alla bella"', *ACV*)

Will the moon call you, / that moon who has watched you so much / and with so much sepulchral light?

                                                        ('"To the Beautiful One"').

But in its positive context, the moon is a consolatory element of Mother-Nature: 'la madre luna' ('mother-moon'), ('Indizi e luna', *DIP*, 1).

Oscillatory landscape symbolism is a feature which recurs in *SA*. Whereas in *ACV* and *DIP* psychic conditions are created basically by sun and snow, heat and cold, in *SA* other phenomena such as dusk and rain operate in the same way. A chapter devoted entirely to the latter, entitled 'Segreti della pioggia' ('Rain Secrets') (74–7), helps to explain why the symbolism of landscape phenomena should fluctuate in the poetic works in the way that it does.

The chapter is divided into various sections, separated by asterisks. In the first, the rain is presented in a positive light. The section opens, 'Una pioggia che ci sia amica' ('A rain that could be our friend'), and continues to picture a showery day in town, full of gaiety and animation: tower clocks ticking madly, girls in shiny wellingtons and plastic overcoats, shop-windows lowering their 'eyelids' to escape the cheery fury of the sky. The next two sections figure, by contrast, a dreary Sunday afternoon, suffocated by a much heavier, alluvial rain which brings all life to a standstill: men are tediously whiling away time, playing cards beneath an electric lamp; an old woman cannot see to continue her embroidery in the aquatic darkness of the room. These negative effects of rain run into the fourth and final section where a downpour plunges into darkness the compartment of the train in which the protagonist is travelling. Only some mist-enveloped rocks are visible through the streaming carriage windows. Given this atmosphere of gloom, created by the rain, the sun which returns to illuminate the compartment should be attributed a positive symbolism, inciting feelings of joy. But for the protagonist this is not the case. For at the precise moment when the sun returns, a beautiful, unknown girl seated opposite the narrator during the course of his journey, but then hidden by the shadows, leaves the compartment and descends from the train. It is darkness which the protagonist now desires, the light which heralded the girl's departure, paining and 'persecuting' him:

> . . . so free and luminous is the air, that if he breathes he can feel his breast ache. With eyes closed, he rests his head in his shady corner, but a ray of sun follows him, persecutes him. (*Sull'altopiano* 77)

This fourth story gives a new relevance to those which precede it. In the preceding sections, different types of rain are presented as inducing a positive or negative frame of mind, thereby independently dictating their own symbolism, as it were. But what Zanzotto is clearly emphasizing by the fourth story is that it is not so much the landscape which works upon the mind, as the mind which works upon the landscape.

This is a discovery one can bring to bear upon ACV and DIP. For although one can readily recognize that here Zanzotto is drawing a comparison between the visible, outer landscape and the inner, psychic one, in order to embellish the former and to give it a poetical significance which it does not normally have in everyday life, the reason why landscape phenomena should continually change their symbolic meaning for the poet still remains to be explained. They do so for the same reason that the rain in the last section of 'Segreti della pioggia' suddenly switches from being something negative to something positive. The fluctuating symbolism serves to re-emphasize the autonomy of mind over landscape, and to affirm that the foundation on which Zanzotto's aesthetic ideas are based in these poetical works is the concept of artistic creativity, a *mental reconditioning* of reality.

In section 2 of DIP reality is conditioned in a manner very different from the way in which it is in sections 1 and 3. Here, by contrast, there are none of the poetical images or settings which juxtapose or interrelate opposites such as sun and snow, fluidity and solidity. Simple analogies, using 'come', replace the intricate metaphors discussed before, and the landscape assumes no psychic symbolism. The depiction of a feminine 'tu' within the landscape elements does, however, prevail, and this 'tu' is both an infant girl and a suckling mother:

> al di là non è sazia
> mai la tua fame di bambina
> ('Al di là', DIP 2)

your baby's hunger / is never satiated, beyond
>
> ('Beyond')

> o tu dalla docile polpa,
> chiaro collo curioso
> seno caldo che nutre
> ('Declivio su Lorna', DIP 2)

oh you with the soft flesh, / bright curious neck / warm nourishing breast
> ('Slope on Lorna').

The protective mother image has already occurred in section 1 (in 'Là sovente nell'alba') and in section 3 (in 'Perché siamo'). But whereas in those poems the emphasis in the mother-land / child of the land relationship fell more upon the mother, section 2 concentrates upon the child. Also, the child theme is now developed in a different way. For Zanzotto is not so much depicting himself as a child of the mother-land (the infant here is, for example, not himself, but another, a female 'tu') as he is attempting to view, to experience the landscape through the eyes of an infant.

This is because poetry is something that comes naturally to the child (and one presumes that Zanzotto makes the child feminine only to highlight this association with poetry), not only in the sense that she takes pleasure in the musicality of words, which, as in the sequence below with its recurrent 'i' sounds, 'clink' for her 'like coins', but also in the sense that the child has a strong imaginative faculty. She is full of a creativity which allows her to make spontaneous analogies:

> colli piccoli come noci
> per i tuoi denti giocosi,
> soli come voli di vespe

e parole che suonano come monete
('Al di là', *DIP* 2)

hills as small as walnuts / for your playful teeth, / suns like wasp flights / and words which clink like coins.

Section 2 is in fact pervaded by Rimbaldian images such as that above in line 3 (the 'suns like wasp flights'), fresh and innocent visual images immediately evocative of children's picture-books where phenomena – above all, natural phenomena – are animated (see Rimbaud's 'Après le déluge', 'Aube' and 'Fleurs', *Illuminations*. Moreover, in 'Alchimie du verbe', *Une Saison*, Rimbaud gives an inventory of all the types of visual and verbal art forms which attract him, among which figure the 'petits livres de l'enfance' ('children's little books'). It is also noteworthy that Zanzotto himself has published one illustrated story for children– *La storia dello zio tonto* ('The story of the foolish uncle')). 'L'acqua di Dolle', for example, presents a fig-tree which stands on guard, a lamp in the shape of a snail, and stars as a hoard of little beings who plunder the Alps and return 'fat' with silver. (The subject of the verbs, and the 'lei' ('she') of these quotations, refer to the 'water' of Dolle):

> . . . a lungo
> indugiò nello scrigno d'ombra
> dove il fico s'affaccia guardiano
> . . .
> lasciatemela mia,
> per la mia lampadina di chiocciola
> per l'orto di che il nano è mezzadro,
> lei dal fittissimo alfabeto
> lei che ha i messaggi
> di nobili invasioni
> degli astri che ritornano dalle alpi
> ormai pingui d'argento
> ('L'acqua di Dolle', *DIP* 2)

. . . for a long time / it lingered in the shade's casket / where the fig-tree stands on guard / . . . / let it remain mine, / for my little snail-lamp / for the orchard which the dwarf share-crops, / she of the thickest alphabet / she who receives messages / about the noble invasions / of the stars which return from the Alps / by now fat with silver.

Coupled with these there are the more verbal, story-book images of 'Là cercando' ('There, Searching'), humorous, delicate, or predictable, as is the case respectively in the following examples: grass which is 'short-sighted' in that, one presumes, it is short, and unable to see much of the surrounding countryside!; evenings which uncoil their spirals to wash themselves in the rain; and stars swarming like ants:

Luci armate di falce che discendevano
per la miope foresta delle erbe,

. . .

sere verde-lume
si snodavano con tutte le spire
a lavarsi alla pioggia.
Lentamente sotto il paralume
dallo schema infranto delle tenebre
brulicavano astri
deboli come formiche
    ('Là cercando', *DIP* 2)

Lights armed with sickles which descended / through the short-sighted forest
of grass, (. . .) / green-light evenings / uncoiled with all of their spirals /
to wash themselves in the rain. / Slowly under the lampshade / from the
shattered sketch of the darkness / there swarmed stars / as feeble as ants.

The intuitive imagination of children is perhaps most prevalent in their 'let's
play at being . . .' games, which Zanzotto seems to imitate verbally in his use of
the jussive forms in the passage below. In this passage the child's game involves
the landscape. The poet-child assumes the role of authority, and in accordance
with her innate desire to own things (stressed elsewhere in a frequent use of the
possessive pronoun, common to children's vocabulary, for example 'io sto nel
mio paese' ('I am in *my* village'), 'Del *mio* ritorno scintillano i vetri / ed i pomi di
casa *mia*' ('Upon *my* return there shines the windows / and the apple trees of *my*
house') ('Nel mio paese' ('In My Village'), *DIP* 2)), the land becomes her personal
property, subject to the dictates of her will:

conduciamo la ghiaia a bere
a piccoli sorsi,
dissetiamoci alla notte,
inventiamo una fanciulla
educabile al vento alla frescura,
dissetiamoci all'ombra di giglio
della sua mente
    ('Con dolce curiosità', *DIP* 2)

let's lead the gravel to drink / in little sips, / let's quench our thirst in the
night, / let's invent a girl / who can be taught in the wind in the cool, / let's
quench our thirst in the lily shade / of her mind

settimana ingombrata dalle spine
e dalle zinnie, dovunque tu ospiti
miti mercati nelle tue radure

> e nelle tue piccole sere
> compero e vendo
> ('Lorna', *DIP* 2)

a week cluttered up with thorns / and zinnias, everywhere you accommodate / moderate markets in your clearings / and in your little evenings / I buy and sell

('Lorna').

Accordingly, whereas in section 1 there was sometimes an emphasis upon wide, open spaces, which created a feeling of insecurity:

> Or che mi cinge tutta la tua distanza
> sto inerme dentro un'unica sera
> ('Distanza', *DIP* 1)

Now that all of your distance surrounds me / I am defenceless within a single evening

> ho dolore di tanta
> vastità circondata
> da ombre remote di tuoni
> ('Balsamo, bufera', *DIP* 1)

I am distressed by so much / vastness surrounded / by distant shadows of thunder

('Balsam, Storm')

in this section there is a reduction both in spatial dimensions and in the size of objects, far-away things coming near, and large things becoming small, to emphasize what is now a close familiarity between Nature and the poet–child, generated by such feelings of ownership:

> teneri uccelli che si districano
> dai vischi della lontananza
> e che indugiano audacemente
> tra gli equilibri delle dita
> a illustrare le loro piume
> e le loro gioie minute,
> . . .
> aiole come mazzi improvvisati,
> laghi dallo stupore di goccia
> ('Declivio su Lorna', *DIP* 2)

soft birds who extricate themselves / from the bird-lime of distance / and linger boldly / between the equilibrium of fingers / to show off their feathers / and their tiny joys, / . . . / flower-beds like improvised bouquets, / lakes with the wonderment of rain drops

> Sole piú piccolo piú umile
> ('Lorna', *DIP* 2)

Smaller and more humble sun.

Even the 'earth' itself is a tiny and, consequently, securer planet:

> . . . questa terra non è
> che un mite minuto satellite
> che ben sa dove si dirige
> ('Al di là', *DIP* 2)

. . . this earth is just / a gentle, tiny satellite / which knows exactly where it's going.

It is also a realm of narcissistic pleasure where the poet takes the landscape to himself with the 'hunger' of a child, experiencing his harmony with his surroundings with the same sensual delight that a child takes in eating:

> . . . non è sazia
> mai la tua fame di bambina
> ed hai la mela e il ghiaccio vegetale
> ('Al di là', *DIP* 2)

. . . your baby's hunger / is never sated / and you have the apple and vegetable ice

> infanzia sapido racimolo
> ('Declivio su Lorna', *DIP* 2)

infancy, a small, sapid cluster of grapes

> da tutti amato
> con essi io sto nel mio paese,
> mi sento goloso di zucchero
> ('Nel mio paese', *DIP* 2)

loved by everyone / and with everyone I am in my village, / I'm greedy for sugar.

A simple directness, coupled with a tone of joy in statements such as those above, is a feature common to *DIP* 2. In the collection of poetry which follows – *Elegia e altri versi* (*EAV*) (*Elegy and Other Verses*) – and which I now go on to discuss, language is also plain and direct. But whereas in *DIP* 2 the simplicity of expression helps to transmit the unsophisticated nature of the child's vision that Zanzotto is attempting to recapture, in *EAV* it serves a different purpose. Rarely is it united with feelings of joy, almost all of the poems having a plaintive monotone conveying the 'death' that is implied in the title of the final poem, 'Elegia' (the same elegy as the one indicated in the name of the collection); or the sense of an 'end' communicated in the titles of three of the other 'altri versi' ('other verses') which are six in number: '*Partenza* per il Vaud' ('*Departure* for Vaud'), 'Ore *calanti*' (the '*Waning* hours' described are those of evening), and 'È un tuo *ricordo*' ('It's one of your *memories*'). It is the demise of poetic inspiration, or more precisely, of the poet's ability to feel the landscape in a poetic way, that is being lamented in this collection. This accounts for the simplicity of expression: he is incapable of transforming the reality of the land into something original and creative, and, consequently, it emerges in all of its immediacy across the direct, unelaborate language of the poems. Such is the case, for example, in 'Storie dell'arsura' ('Stories about the Drought'), where Zanzotto is depicting the dried-up Soligo river:

> Vuoto d'acque, misero scheletro
> lungo le case del mio paese,
> Soligo io ti guardo e non mi basta
> la Pasqua dell'Angelo, non piove da mesi.
> Hai sete, piccolo fiume imbavagliato
> nudo nudo e senza parola

Empty of water, wretched skeleton / running alongside the houses of my village, / Soligo I look at you and The Angel's Passover / is not enough for me, it hasn't rained in months. / You are thirsty, little gagged river / stark-naked and silent.

The lucidity here creates a type of writing very different from the obscure, Hermetic utterances of the poems in DIP 1 and 3, and indeed it is no less 'poetic' for that. Something of the barren desiccation of the landscape is reproduced in the bare precision of the lines – the factual 'non piove da mesi' and 'Hai sete'. The use of ordinary, everyday language also helps to communicate the poet's sympathetic affection for the suffering Soligo, an affection which becomes clear in his humanization of the river and his use of the endearing diminutive 'piccolo fiume'.

But that Zanzotto himself is seeing the parched Soligo as an emblem of his own poetical aridity is suggested at first in his emphasis upon its silence, its inability to 'speak', as it were: it is 'imbavagliato' and 'senza parola'; and the analogy is then made explicit a few lines later where he draws a direct comparison between himself and the Soligo, *his* thirst and that of the river:

> Da tanto a te, Soligo, mi conformo,
> la sete lunga lunga trassi come il tuo letto

I've conformed to you, Soligo, for such a long time / like your bed I've derived a long, drawn-out thirst.

Hence, the drought-stricken landscape of this poem becomes an objective correlative of the poet's feelings of desolation and 'nothingness':

Nulla per dorsi spenti
e per cavi torpori mattutini
nulla dietro il ventaglio del meriggio
che soffocate sere scopre
per tramiti gessosi e stecchi e brividi

Nothing on the lifeless ridges / and throughout the hollow morning torpors / *nothing* behind the fan of noontide / unveiling suffocated evenings / through chalky paths and brushwood twigs and shivers.

Rarely, however, does Zanzotto succumb to such feelings; rather he is constantly wrestling with them. In 'È un tuo ricordo' he tries to restore his faith in the land as a prelude to discovery and adventure, a faith now grown torpid:

sopita la fede oscura
ch'ebbi in tutta l'apertura del mondo
in tutti i nodi avventurosi
d'alberi crete e venti

Da acque ed acque comparse e scomparse
mi ristoro a fatica

it has been sent to sleep that dark faith / that I had in the whole opening of the world / in all the adventurous knots / of trees clays and winds / I refresh myself with difficulty / by waters and more waters which appeared and disappeared.

And in 'Contro monte' ('Against the mountain') the sight of the Soligo as it bravely winces in a struggle to free itself from the mud of autumn makes him feel that some escape from his own miry condition might still be possible, and momentarily infuses him with new life:

dove il fiume sussulta
e tenta col vano meandro
liberarsi dal melmoso autunno,

. . .

là mi riscuoto, là rovescio la vita
mia, sonno infetto di terra

where the river jumps / and tries with a vain meander / to free itself from muddy autumn, / . . . / there I rouse myself, there I turn upside-down my life – / a drowsiness infected by earth.

In the same way, the five sections of 'Ore calanti' contain some sporadic revivals of hope. On the one hand, there is a portrayal of the landscape which sums up the poet's condition – 'exhausted', 'waning', 'silent':

Quale lento riflesso, quale vitrea memoria
di sè ai prati *affranti* va tentando
questo scorcio di maggio *calante*?

. . .

Tace il fianco beato del colle,
guarda incerto il papavero
le dissolte forze delle erbe

Prati *affranti*, *affranti* di tante acque,
grilli residui dello spazio *vinto*,
e *non raggiungeranno* il crudo azzurro
né il felice giro dei monti

(section 1)

What slow reflection, what glassy memory / is this end of *waning* May /
attempting to give to the *exhausted* fields? / . . . / The blessed flank of the hill *is
silent*, / the poppy looks doubtfully at the / *dissolved forces* of the grass / *Exhausted*
fields, *exhausted* by so much water, / left over crickets of the *conquered* space, /
who *will not reach* the coarse blue / nor the happy curve of the mountains.

While on the other hand, there are unexpected returns of fantasy:

. . . e al verde umano al verde vano
delle chine la mia poca vita
si fa grande di tante
profonde fantasie di colline

(section 5)

and at the humane green, the vain green / of the slopes my little life / grows
big with so many / deep hill-fantasies.

But it is the 'Elegia' which brings the collection to a close, and the entire
poem is pervaded by the emphatically repeated negatives 'non', 'nè' and 'nulla'
('not', 'nor' and 'nothing'). Zanzotto's ability to infuse the landscape with that
inward-looking poetical charge has gone and, as a result, it is no longer the
lively, prolific reality it once used to be:

non puoi dirmi la grandine fresca
che in fuga volò dalla nube
a pettinare paesi frettolosi,
nè l'erba grande nei giardini
nè i grandi pomi dell'agosto,
nulla puoi dirmi nulla so nulla vedo

You *can't* talk to me of the fresh hail / that, escaping, flew from the cloud /
to comb hasty villages, / *nor* of the tall grass in the gardens, / *nor* of the
high, August apple-trees, / *you can't talk to me of anything, I know nothing, I
see nothing.*

The sense of crisis evident in these declamatory lines foreshadows the new
developments of Zanzotto's next collection of poetry. For in *Vocativo* (VCT)

(*Vocative*) Zanzotto questions the authenticity of his own poetic 'calling' and of poetry in general, as he begins to doubt the ability of the written word adequately to express subjectivity. To some extent, he also turns away from the landscape to take into account the historical reality that was deliberately excluded in his early poetry. It is these new developments that I shall examine in Chapter 2.

Problems of Poetry
Metalanguage in *Vocativo* (1949–56)

In an interview with Beverly Allen on 25 July 1978 Zanzotto gave some explanation of the title *VCT*:

> *Vocativo* is where the old theme of poetic invocation, of poetry as invocation of the gods that are there or the gods that are fleeing or whatever, becomes a pure and simple grammatical given, the vocative case.

He went on to explain how his aborted invocation to the gods was 'tragically traumatic' since it was

> an effect in which the word became a pure sign without a signified, in which the signified oscillated extremely, or in which the signified had to be sought in territories quite different from those indicated on the surface by the sign.

In other words, Zanzotto is questioning the traditional theory of language in which the signifier is seen to reflect or harness meaning. He remarks that in retrospect he recognizes this as an unconscious pre-Lacanianism. He found himself almost on the same ground as Lacan when Lacan's *Écrits* (*Writings*) had not yet been published, precisely because of his need 'to test the depth of this *manque*, this void, this barring, this fracture line existing right inside language', a 'fracture line' which he aimed to suggest in the title *VCT*. Nevertheless, not all of *VCT* is about the linguistic problem. In *Effetto Lacan* (*Lacan's Effect*) Zanzotto says that although there is 'something Lacanian' in the title, this is less true of the work in its totality.

Hence the title *VCT* refers first and foremost to a loss of faith in the proper functioning of language. Indeed there are addresses or vocatives in the text to a 'ponte' ('bridge') and a 'vortice' ('whirlpool') – metaphors, as I shall show, for poetry and language respectively (see pages 58 and 79–80) – as well as to a 'tu' ('you'), identifiable in the three books prior to *VCT* with a feminine presence who was seen as the poet's poetic inspiration, who acted, therefore, as a kind of Muse. But there are vocatives in the collection as a whole: vocatives to the landscape (on a recurrent basis to 'water' in section 1 and to the light of the 'sky' and the 'sun' in section 2, all of which assume particular symbolic values); vocatives to friends who have fought and sometimes died in the Second World War; vocatives to the self and the poet's mother; biblical vocatives; vocatives to people from Zanzotto's local region for whom dialect is becoming a language of the past; and vocatives to humble georgic bards, to name but a few.

This widespread use of the vocative case has been attributed to a number of different motivations: Zanzotto's desire to continue writing lyrical poetry – a 'vocative' tension – which his conscience, however, forbids (Forti 1963, 213–15); it indicates an unanswered call for communication with humanity (Barberi-Squarotti 1961, 153); the persistent use of the vocative (together with an emphasis upon the first person pronoun, 'io') is a feature of 'grammaticalism', a 'grammaticalism' which indicates how Zanzotto is encountering problems with language in *VCT* (Agosti 1973, 11–12; Allen 1984).

But it is much too reductive to give the vocative a single and exclusive significance. Each of the arguments presented above is valid on different occasions. For Zanzotto's use of the vocative case goes hand in hand with a general concern which comprises features such as those above – a suppression of the lyrical, a desire for communication, and the language problem. This general concern could be posited as Zanzotto's growing awareness of a division, of an incompatibility which exists between literature and reality.

The two sections of *VCT* contain sixteen and thirteen poems, respectively. The first section is entitled 'Come una bucolica' ('Like a Bucolic Poem'); and the second, 'Prima persona' ('First Person'). Then follow six poems (in the 1981 edition) which fall under the heading 'Appendice' ('Appendix'). In section 1 this problem of the separateness of literature and reality is investigated from three different angles. Zanzotto debates, firstly, what relevance the lyric, landscape poetry he has written up until now has had to the real world about him; secondly, the relationship between a practical and a romantic (in the literary sense) attitude towards life; and thirdly, the language problem, from which there emerges the question of whether literature is an effective and important means of communication. The first and third of these considerations are also carried over, with slight variations in treatment, into section 2 of the work. It is because of these variations in treatment that I shall deal with each section individually.

SECTION ONE

From Idealism to Realism; from Isolationism to Social Commitment:
a Time for Change

Roughly half of the sixteen poems in section 1 of *VCT* deal specifically with Zanzotto's new feelings toward the type of poetry he has written up until now. In two of them ('Epifania' ('Epiphany') and 'Se non fosse' ('If It Were Not')) it would appear that his conscience urges him to abandon his personal treatment of the landscape – those creative, imaginative visions of it that he had given in

ACV and *DIP* and coveted in *EAV* when his imaginative resourcefulness was felt to be lacking. Rather than reinterpret the landscape in a poetic way, he should be more true to life, present it as it is. The rest of the poems in the section contemplate moving away from the theme of the landscape altogether in favour of a poetry which will bear on human interests. Hence Zanzotto's disengagement from the landscape (Raboni 1976b, 77; Cambon xv–xvii; Milone 212–18) and his new need for social commitment (Pasolini 1960; Hainsworth 1984, 119; Cambon xx) which have already been observed in some manner or other by a number of critics. Indeed, a greater social awareness is eventually achieved when Zanzotto includes some of the harsh realities deliberately kept at bay in the earlier works, notably the issue of war (the First as well as the Second World War). In the process however he makes an anti-war plea, for all of these poems as well as being metapoetic are rooted in ambivalence, Zanzotto considering his ideas for change to be alternatively good and bad. The quotation from Éluard which forms the epigraph to the book underlines his ambiguous thinking: 'Ce qui est digne d'être aimé / contre ce qui s'anéantit' ('That which is worthy of being loved / against that which is destroying itself'). What is still worthy of being loved is the landscape. But the subject of the landscape as well as the old manner of treating that subject, in short, the whole ethos of Zanzotto's earlier works where 'paesaggio' ('landscape') stood as an opposite to 'man' and political history (see pages 1–2), is beginning to break down, due to the dictates of Zanzotto's conscience. But the poet frequently clings on desperately to his old poetic creeds. His conflicting emotions are never expressed directly in the poems, but rather in an oblique, mostly symbolic language, as for example in 'Epifania', the first poem of the collection.

'Epifania' presents a winter landscape. The initial eight lines are descriptive. Nevertheless, if read in the context of the preceding collection, *EAV*, the scene described here would appear to hold some symbolic significance for the poet, indicating his own present condition and a possible one of the future.

The poem opens with a picture of Nature covered in snow and ice:

> Punge il pino i candori dei colli
> e il Piave muscolo di gelo
> nei lacci s'agita, nel bosco

The pine pierces the hills' whiteness / and the Piave an icy muscle / stirs in its snares, in the wood.

Already the Piave is struggling to burst free from its ice-snares ('nei lacci s'agita'), and even though the image of the dark pine tree piercing the whiteness of the hills is a purely representational one, the verb 'pungere' is again suggestive of movement, of forcefulness. It is this combination of fixity and imminent movement in the scene before him which Zanzotto continues to emphasize in the rest of the eight-line sequence, and which allows him to hail the scene, for reasons which will soon become clear, as a 'mirifico disegno':

> Ecco il mirifico disegno
> la lucente ferma provvidenza
> la facondia che esprime
> e riannoda e sfila
> echi, gemme, correnti

Behold the marvellous design / the shining motionless providence / the eloquence which expresses / and re-ties and unthreads / echoes, buds, streams.

It is a 'design' in which phenomena are, as the poem says, shining and still ('lucente', 'ferma'). Yet there is an eloquence ('facondia') within this stillness: echoes, buds and streams are provisionally tightened up but will be released again with the thaw, like pearls, perhaps, strung tightly together ('e riannoda') and then released, unthreaded from the string ('e sfila'). (The enjambement reinforces the process of release: 'che esprime / e riannoda e sfila / echi, gemme, correnti'.)

The use of linguistic terms to describe this 'disegno' – 'la *facondia* che *esprime*' – certainly implies a correlation between it and Zanzotto's own poetic condition. 'Epifania' picks up where *EAV* left off. *EAV* ended with Zanzotto proclaiming a state of poetic aridity, as well as a severance of relationships between the landscape and woman/poetry. Here this frozen landscape conveys the poet's mental paralysis. However, just as the static condition of the landscape is only something provisional, so too the poet may be able to extricate himself in the near future from his present state of inertia.

But although the idea of being able to be productive again is a happy one, Zanzotto then seems to suggest the only possible road which is open to him, and initially he is loath to pursue it. What follows is a direct address to the landscape:

> Tra voi parvenze e valli appena
> sollecitate dal soffio del claxon,
> mormorate dall'alba,
> valgo come la foglia che riposa
> col vivo cardo col bozzolo e l'oro,
> valgo l'onda minuscola
> che fu tua sete scoiattolo un giorno

Among you appearances and valleys hardly / stimulated by the klaxon's breath, / hardly murmured by the dawn, / my worth is like that of the leaf which rests / with the live thistle with the cocoon and the gold, / my worth is like that of the tiny wave / that was one day your thirst, squirrel.

It is dawn, but as yet the valleys have hardly been stirred by the first signs of movement and noise indicated here by the car and the distant sound of its horn

– the 'klaxon's breath'. The word 'appena' is significant. In the first poem of *DIP*, 'Arse il motore', the journeying car acted as a symbol of practical, modern living and Zanzotto deliberately underscored his non-allegiance to the world it stood for by alluding to himself as an impractical, unconvincing figure talking about the landscape and positing in opposition his own journey into the fictitious world of poetry (see pages 7–9). Things have now changed. The landscape is *hardly* disturbed – indicating that it *will eventually* be disturbed – by the car. In other words, Zanzotto foresees the 'dawning' of a new creative practice: he realizes that he needs to abandon the deliberately poetic treatment of the landscape that he had given in *DIP* (as well as in *ACV*) in favour of one that will be more convincing, more realistic.

At first the realization is infused with remorse. Hence Zanzotto's passionate statement of attachment to the landscape as, presumably, he envisaged it before. He is at one with its smallest, apparently valueless and insignificant components: the leaf which rests with the thistle and the cocoon, the thirst of the squirrel.

But as the poem now draws to a close, quite suddenly the emphatic repetition which helps to convey this identification with the landscape ('valgo come', 'valgo') is used to support a different, indeed oppositional, feeling:

> valgo oltre il dubbio oltre l'inverno
> che s'attarda celeste ai tuoi balconi,
> valgo più che il tuo stesso
> venir meno con la neve
> che il motore per sempre, fuggendo
> dietro al sole, tralascia

I am worth more than the doubt more than the winter / which lingers sky-blue at your balconies, / I am worth more than your own / fainting away with the snow / which the car fleeing / behind the sun, puts aside, for ever.

This passage seems to relate back to the first eight lines of the poem. There Zanzotto focused upon the growth and movement that would be highlighted eventually by the thaw; the life that would remove the provisional death. Now comes the realization that for some things in the landscape death will be final. For the squirrel, winter (and his search for food) lingers on relentlessly as he peers hopelessly over the vast balconies of sky-blue snow ('l'inverno / che s'attarda celeste ai tuoi balconi'). The squirrel's death is inevitable and predictable ('il tuo stesso / venir meno con la neve'). Consequently, the initial identification with the landscape due to a regretful realization of the need to deal with it more realistically, turns into dissociation from it. For Zanzotto realizes that it can also symbolize not the provisional death which heralds a reinforcement of life that he had originally imagined, but a final demise which he is not prepared to identify with ('valgo oltre . . . oltre', 'valgo più'). Progression, continuing to be creative in some way, is the poet's primary concern. So that whereas before he lamented abandoning his former treatment of the landscape as a means of escaping his own inertia, now he pushes the landscape further behind him: he asserts his independence over and above it when he realizes that it can also represent a final death which contradicts his desire for progression. For this reason perhaps, the car which symbolizes the only manner in which he can continue to write, albeit a disagreeable one, returns in the final two lines of the poem, now not even slightly 'stimulating' phenomena but fleeing the landscape, this cold, lifeless scene in search of sun ('che il motore per sempre, fuggendo / dietro al sole, tralascia').

In this poem it appears that the winter landscape stands for the landscape in general. The theme of the landscape is defunct. It has been exhausted and the poet must move on to other concerns. Also, the more realistic elements which Zanzotto feels he must now include, and which the car symbolizes, cannot be included while still talking about the landscape, cannot be made to 'stimulate' it. The car is *fleeing the landscape*.

Zanzotto's decision to abandon the theme of the landscape is an epiphanic one. (The title of the poem could refer either to the Epiphany at Christmas time, concurring with the winter scene, or on a more figurative level to some other revelation.) The regret which initially infuses the expression of a need for change, resulting in that nostalgic reassertion of his affinity with the land, develops in the course of a climactic ten-line sentence into a joyful declaration of independence, of liberation, via the accumulative

> valgo come . . .
> . . .
> valgo . . .
> . . .
> valgo oltre . . .
> . . .
> valgo più . . . .

Reservations about Change

'Epifania' is however the most, perhaps the only truly, epiphanic poem in the collection. For the poems which follow serve to show that the split with the old theme has not been achieved. Zanzotto is not capable of making his 'exile' from the landscape something 'eternal', but is 'eternally' returning to the landscape theme: 'Da un eterno esilio / eternamente ritorno' ('Appendice' no. 2). Consequently, the ambivalence which he appears to rule out in 'Epifania', continues to make itself felt in other poems. This is particularly the case in 'Fiume all'alba' ('River at Dawn'), 'Piccola elegia' ('Little Elegy'), and 'Nuovi autunni' ('New Autumns'). I will deal with the first two of these poems.

In 'Fiume all'alba', the second poem in the collection, the enthusiasm which ended 'Epifania' has already disappeared. Here the river, perhaps the Piave of the preceding poem, has broken free from the ice and is flowing easily again. But whereas before the thaw was seen to be something positive – symbolizing a return of creativity –, here moving water (and the associations it is given with 'moving' – metamorphic larvae) has negative qualities, imparting Zanzotto's reservations with regard to those changes that must take place in his poetry if creativity is to be achieved.

The poem opens with a vocative in the form of an imperative to the river's water, asking it not to rob him of his 'sight', in other words, the vision of poetry that he had in his first two books: poetry as an autonomous, utopic space which precludes a realistic treatment of issues and pragmatic themes pertaining to the social or political world:

> Fiume all'alba
> acqua infeconda tenebrosa e lieve
> non rapirmi la vista
> non le cose che temo
> e per cui vivo
>
> Acqua inconsistente acqua incompiuta
> che odori di larva e trapassi
> che odori di menta e già t'ignoro
> acqua lucciola inquieta ai miei piedi

River at dawn / infertile dark and light water / do not rob me of my sight / nor of the things that I fear / and for which I live / Mobile water unfinished water / smelling of larvae and changes / smelling of mint and already I do not know you / water a restless firefly at my feet.

The treatment of such themes might turn out to be unfruitful ('infeconda'); or he might feel them to be dark and gloomy issues ('tenebrosa') which hold no weight or importance in poetry ('lieve'). His scepticism with regard to this type of writing is also reinforced by the negative prefix 'in' which is repeated three times in the sequence above ('infeconda', 'inconsistente', 'incompiuta'); while the repetition (in this case, anaphora) which pervades the whole poem conveys, as in 'Epifania', the poet's heightened feelings – feelings now, not of identification with the landscape nor of independence from it as before, but of tension.

The same tension is present in 'Esperimento' ('Experiment') when in an attempt to walk the 'bridge' linking one bank to another, the old set of themes to the new, the water which flows beneath – 'acri correnti / fredde che sempre mi turbano' ('acrid cold / currents which always perturb me') – becomes the water of the Acheron: 'Si sperpera gigante, si risucchia / e sfonda l'Acheronte' ('The gigantic Acheron wastes itself, swallows itself up / and crashes through'). The poet, hallucinating sensational images of crashing waters, a roaring engine and irreversible goodbyes, draws back, unable to make the crossing to the shores of this 'hell'.

But in spite of the misgivings of both poems, 'Fiume all'alba' ends by harking back to the decision arrived at in 'Epifania' – the break with the landscape must be achieved even for the simple reason that it has devoured too much of the poet's attention. Verandahs and flowers are 'troppo amati' ('loved too much'). His 'obsession' with the landscape, as he suggests in the fifth of the appendix poems, is a reductive thing which starves his creative potential and which induces a lack of variety in content and language ('la scena unica / la sillaba / sola' ('the one and only scene / the single / syllable')). Consequently, in the last five lines of 'Fiume all'alba', the river, the symbol of progressing in a new direction, is presented like the car of 'Epifania' as deserting the landscape – it 'unmoors' itself and 'flies' beyond the Montello:

> da digitate logge
> da fiori troppo amati ti disancori
> t'inclini e voli
> oltre il Montello e il caro acerbo volto
> perch'io dispero della primavera

from digitate verandahs / and flowers loved too much you unmoor yourself / tilt and fly / beyond the Montello and the dear unripe face / because I have no hope in the spring.

However, the river's gesture, unlike that of the car, does not gladden the poet. For his attachment to his area which was expressed and then repudiated in 'Epifania' is much more manifest in the lines above and in the poem as a whole. (The opening request to the river not to rob him of his 'sight' is then echoed right through the poem by his obsessive calling out to the water: 'acqua' as an address is repeated four times in the space of the first nine lines.) It is only Zanzotto's pressing need to turn away from the landscape that taints his love for it, to produce a love-hate, love-fear relationship: 'le cose che temo / e per cui vivo' (lines 4–5).

'Piccola elegia' to some extent marks the transitional point between the poet's 'talking about' change, and actually initiating a change. At first we are presented with a peaceful and rather harmonious picture of Nature:

> tra questi clivi dove nuziale
> s'apre la rosa ai pergolati
> e giugno appannato d'acque e funghi
> stillicidi insensibili protrae
> per la festa delle api e delle zinnie

among these slopes where the bridal / rose opens on the bowers / and June misted over with water and fungi / prolongs its imperceptible dripping / for bees and zinnias to feast on.

Only one element jars with these surroundings:

Ma perpetuo il torrente nel fondo si divora

But the torrent endlessly devours itself in the depths.

The 'Ma' introducing the torrent's presence, reinforces its difference. The river is drying up whereas the rest of Nature manages to find its imperceptible drops of water. And it is with the river that the poet identifies, for 'Piccola elegia' is, as the title puts it, a 'little *elegy*', a *lament* for the involuntary '*drying up*' of his lyrical voice:

Io sto solo e non parlo dell'amore

I am alone and not speaking of love

e nulla posso
e nulla posso dare

and nothing can I / nothing can I give.

Since the poet feels he must no longer write lyric, landscape poetry, but at the same time, is incapable of embarking upon a different sort of composition, he confesses to being 'senza meta / e senza inizio' ('without an aim / and without a beginning') – an aimlessness indicated by the suspension points which 'conclude' the poem.

However, one can feel a catharsis at work in the declamatory and rather impassioned statements such as the last two cited above, and indeed the four poems which follow 'Piccola elegia' – 'Se non fosse', 'La notte di Serravalle' ('Serravalle's Night'), 'Esperimento', and 'I compagni corsi avanti' ('Friends who have Hurried Ahead') – make more affirmative steps in a direction which is both realistic and socially aware, even though, as yet, this is not done with any real sense of conviction.

Attempts at Change

'Se non fosse' presents commonplace and recognizable features of a rural area that could well be the poet's: birds, flags and chimney-pots:

è il paese . . . dove premono
uccelli comignoli bandiere

it is the town . . . where crowd together / birds chimney-pots and flags.

More suggestive but equally realistic is the reference to

e gerani lassù
tra uccelli comignoli e vette

and geraniums up there / among birds chimney-pots and peaks

conjuring up an image of birds flitting among houses clustered together at different levels, their high balconies strewn with potted plants (hence the geraniums 'among' chimney-pots) and all set against a background of Alpine peaks.

Nevertheless, Zanzotto would still seem to be governed by the temptation to intercalate poetic, even rhapsodic visions of Nature. There are, for example, idyllic images of a freezing river which slaps your cheek, an apple tree veiled by the rain, conversing and reclining on his heart, and fruit-trees overflowing in a silken dusk (a silken dusk and chimney-pots – the incongruity is striking). Joined to these there is an abstract, surrealist picture of a blue sorrow disentangling fields from the sky, and a literary (Leopardian) association of the moon and unhappy youth:

> Frutti effusi a un crepuscolo di seta,
> prati che a forza districa dal cielo
> un azzurro dolore,
> e gerani lassù
> tra uccelli comignoli e vette
>
> Come incenso la stanza,
> trapassata
> la luna appena sul telaio e tutta
> accennata per lacrime per palpiti
> una gioventù sventurata
>
> . . .
>
> è il paese . . . dove premono
> uccelli comignoli bandiere,
> dove il fiume schiaffeggia la tua guancia
> algido e fabuloso
> e il dolcissimo melo già nel velo
> delle piogge conversa
> giustamente recline sul tuo cuore

Fruits poured out in a silken dusk, / fields which a blue sorrow unravels / by force from the sky, / and geraniums up there / among birds chimney-pots and peaks / The room is like incense, / the moon has just / passed by / the loom and / an unfortunate youth / is beckoned fully through tears and throbbings / . . . it is the town . . . where crowd together / birds chimney-pots and flags, / where a chilly and mythical / river slaps your face / and the sweetest apple tree already veiled / by the rains converses / rightly reclined on your heart.

Hence the commonplace is outweighed by the sublime, and what was suggested in 'Epifania' seems to demonstrate itself quite forcefully in this poem – that a greater realism cannot be achieved while pursuing the landscape theme. Perhaps here too there is a latent awareness of this, for in an emotional concluding sequence Zanzotto allows himself just one more touch, one more glance at this landscape. With an emphatic enumeration of all those features of his area which

are dear to him in a poeticized form ('torbide lamiere' ('turbid metal sheets')
works perhaps as a metaphor for thin, dark clouds, and the icy mountains *become*
glaciers), he wraps them around himself, as it were, for the last time:

> Ancora un tocco a gridii di ghirlande
> ancora a venti senza accordi
> a torbide lamiere
> a ghiacciai spalla a spalla
> qui sconfinati.
> Ancora uno sguardo al giardino
> al braciere di frane e di vette

Just one more touch of the calling garlands / one more touch of the dissonant
winds / of the turbid metal sheets / the back to back glaciers / boundless here. /
Just one more glance at the garden / at the brazier of landslides and peaks.

'La notte di Serravalle' displays an ever greater decision to evade and destroy
the past. Symbolizing his old poetic condition there is the Serravalle theatre – a
seat of art – derelict and dilapidated in an empty town. It is pictured in a storm
with furious mountain rains wringing and consuming its 'noble stone', eroding
its old festoons and stairs now exposed to the eye, and bursting open its worn
shutters. Zanzotto beseeches this rain to maintain its force, to contribute to the
theatre's destruction. (His repeated imperatives to the rain and to the 'echo'
(below) to wreak havoc recall Montale's imperatives to the north wind to do
the same in 'Notizie dall'Amiata', lines 33–9 ('News from Amiata', *Occasioni*)).
If the rain slackens in the least, he, among the gloomy hangings, and the dead
velvets of a world that *no longer sounds*, invokes its return:

> perch'io se appena trepida diradi,
> pioggia, ancora ti chiami
> tra le squallide tende, tra le grevi
> fibre del mondo che non dà più suono,
> tra i velluti defunti,
> vergine danza
> davanti ai ferrei monti

so that if you slacken in the least, / rain, I still call out to you / among the
dismal hangings, among the heavy / fibres of a world which no longer sounds, /
among the dead velvets, / virgin dance / in front of the iron mountains.

Without the earlier ambivalence, it seems as if he is now prepared to accept a
negative aesthetics more fitting to the times. The poem ends with an address to
an 'echo', synonymous perhaps with Zanzotto's inspirational 'tu', ordering it /
her to tell him of lamenting bodies and lost reasons for living:

> Sciogli il futuro, eludi il losco
> tergo, dimmi

i corpi tutti in pianto
il fragile fanale
lo scheletro
filiforme della luce,
poca eco
riecheggiami
da gole corrose di vicoli
dagli atri già mondati dalla luna

le perdute ragioni della vita

Release the future, elude the sinister / back, tell me / of bodies all weeping / of the fragile lamp / the thread-like / skeleton of light, / faint echo / re-echo for me / from corroded throats of alleys / from halls already cleansed by the moon / the lost reasons for living.

In 'Esperimento' Zanzotto concedes that he has overlooked a whole aspect of the landscape, failing to be true to it thereby. There may be poetry 'behind' it which previously he was concerned with illustrating, but there is war and death 'behind' it too:

Ma pure . . .
. . . vostra è l'ora
che stride di canzoni e di preghiere,
vostro il sangue premuto dalle nuche
uomo da uomo

And yet . . . / . . . it is still yours that hour / which screeches with songs and prayers, / yours the blood squeezed forth from necks / by man from man.

The Montello region saw some of the worst fighting in the First World War (and is in fact run through by, what Zanzotto calls in *Il Galateo in bosco* (*The Woodland Book of Manners*), a 'Linea degli ossari' ('Line of the ossuaries'), which stretches eastwards as far as the Adriatic sea, while on the west and north-west it continues across Italian and French territory until finally reaching the English Channel). The region has therefore been sullied by the unpoetic and factual intrusions of war and bloodshed which now form part of it, as it were, and which Zanzotto has overlooked in favour of 'torride finzioni' ('torrid pretences') and a slothful wallowing in the more agreeable aspects of the area: 'm'interro in fisiche verdi lentezze' ('I bury myself in green physical sloth'). In other words, Zanzotto in 'Esperimento' is acknowledging the idealism and 'narcissism' of his former self who wrongly dismissed 'the cosmic and human presences' (Cambon xx).

This mere recognition of his area's involvement in the war finally introduces a new social awareness into Zanzotto's poetry. But still it is present in a rather indirect way, the subject of war being introduced casually, in a reflective manner ('Ma pure'), giving the impression that Zanzotto did not start out with the intention of bringing it up. Indeed, a less personal treatment of the landscape which would speak of the dead, rather than the poetry, 'behind' it ('tenebrose onuste erbe' ('dark burdened grass'), 'armate ombre sul greto' ('armed shadows on the gravelly shore')) is set aside as a theme with which he will possibly deal more trenchantly and more rigorously in the future. This is implied in a vocative to a bridge – the bridge to which I have previously referred (see page 52) – or rather, a vocative to 'poetry', for the bridge is acting as a metaphor for his own poetry 'suspended' between two poetic possibilities. The similarity in the shape of a bridge and a scansion sign of poetry helps to create the metaphor (compare Montale's 'O ritmico scandire di piroghe' ('Oh rhythmical scansion of canoes') in the poem 'Barche sulla Marna', line 12 ('Boats on the Marne', *Occasioni*)):

> O scansione sospesa
> via vita verità
> ponte chi t'aprirà
> tra informi tenebrose onuste erbe,
> ponte chi ti darà
> alle armate ombre sul greto
> alle erte acque in rovina?

Oh suspended scansion / way life truth / who will open you, bridge, / among shapeless dark burdened grass, / who will give you, bridge, / to the armed shadows on the gravelly shore / to the steep ruined waters?

Nonetheless, it is obvious that there is no social commitment built into the greater social awareness which this poem tentatively displays and of which there is a suggestion of further development in the future. Realism is not as yet entirely capable of governing the poetic text. The lending of God-like qualities to poetry – 'via vita verità' – implies that it is something too sacred to be marred by the filth of war and violence, and it is exactly this idea which is reinforced in the image which concludes the poem, perhaps the most memorable and compendious one of the whole collection:

> E tu nel vuoto nel vortice del ponte,
> tu la cui bella fronte
> soggiace al verde squamoso del mondo . . .

And you in the void in the whirlpool of the bridge, / you whose beautiful brow / is subjected to the scaly green of the world . . . .

Zanzotto's 'tu', the feminine presence in his landscape and the inspirer and personification of poetry itself, is being sucked away by the symbolic waters and is subjecting her lovely forehead to the dross and squalor of the world. If in the future there is to be a more definite inclusion of the ugly aspects of reality, poetry itself will become tarnished and defiled.

A social awareness bereft of any social commitment, is even more forcefully demonstrated in 'I compagni corsi avanti'. Despite the fact that the poem must have been written at least four years after the Second World War and probably more – the lyrics of VCT being composed mostly between 1953 and 1956, though some go back to 1949 – Zanzotto places himself back in the war-years and addresses a friend who has left to fight in the Resistance. (The title, however, suggests that the poem is dedicated to all of his friends who have done the same.)

Here the subject of war is treated more directly than in 'Esperimento'. Hitler is even mentioned by name, and Zanzotto imagines his friend on hostile territory ('Ah perduto alle spalle, tra il nemico sole' (Ah lost behind me, among the enemy sun')), lying face-downwards in mud or water ('Dove, . . . nel remoto / gorgo, nel fango celi la tua fronte?' ('Where, . . . in the remote / whirlpool, in the mud do you hide your brow?')), or returning disillusioned to his native land ('Ah compagno, ma a quali spente rive / la disillusa vita riconduci? ('Ah my friend, but to which lifeless shores / do you bring back your disenchanted life?')).

But apart from these overt allusions to war, the poem still manifests a strong reluctance to speak about it directly. His friend is 'among the enemy *sun*' as opposed to 'among the *enemy*', and on other occasions too, the war is referred to indirectly, across the landscape. It is summer that is warring:

> E va, l'estate in guerra, muove al corso
> dei suoi dolori le grandi erbe e i fumi.
> Ah compagno, chi ti darà soccorso
> quando agosto deflagri e ti consumi?

And summer goes to war, it moves its tall grass / and smoke to the flow of its sorrows. / Ah my friend, who will help you / when August flares up and wears you out?

Similarly, it is not the poet himself but his heart which is 'exiled' or detached as he wanders in Petrarchan fashion from mountain to mountain:

> Esule il cuore, dentro il regno vuoto
> brancolo, è tardi, e monte io muto a monte

My heart an exile, within the empty realm / I grope, it is late, and I exchange mountain for mountain.

The Petrarchan echo (compare 'Di pensier in pensier, di monte in monte / mi guida Amor', *Canzoniere* 129 ('from thought to thought, from mountain to mountain / Love guides me')) is probably allied to an emphasis which the poem puts upon the idea of poetry itself. This emphasis is implicit in Zanzotto's uncharacteristic use of a more regular and organized poetic structure – a return to traditionalism on the level of style, noted already, although interpreted as Zanzotto's attempt to underline his resistance to contemporary experimentalism

(Frattini 275) – an explanation for which I can see no evidence, either in the context of the poem or in the book as a whole. The piece, if rhythmically irregular, is entirely in hendecasyllables. The first five stanzas are quatrains with alternate rhyme, with the last two lines of each quatrain taking the form of a question to his friend. Stanzas six and seven are both tercets with the rhyme ABC ABC. They are linked by enjambement and form an imperative to his friend.

Going hand in hand with this emphasis upon the idea of poetry, conveyed through Zanzotto's return to traditionalism, there is another emphasis upon Zanzotto's own particular conception of poetry as something which precludes the treatment of political issues such as war. The concluding imperative makes an ardent plea for imagination over reality, Zanzotto encouraging his friend to find some escape from the very real and ugly situation in which he is involved by using his 'fantasia':

> Oh stringiti alla terra, a terra premi
> tu la tua fantasia. Strugge la mite
> notte Hitler, di fosforo, e congiunta
>
> in alito di belva sugli estremi
> muschi dardeggia Diana le impietrite
> verità della mia mente defunta

Oh cling to the earth, upon the earth press / your fantasy. Hitler destroys / the mild night, with phosphorus, and joined / to the wild beast's breath on the farthest / mosses Diana shoots her darts into the petrified / truths of my dead mind.

Accordingly, while making his plea Zanzotto himself refers to Nature in imaginative terms – the moon is given her mythological name and role as Diana, the huntress, and placed alongside the breathing of a wild beast (possibly a metaphor for Hitler) to stress how poetry is still possible in the most insufferable conditions. Zanzotto also implies that Hitler and his war stands as an opposite to a propensity – which is, of course, his own propensity – for viewing things in a poetical way.

Nevertheless, Zanzotto's plea to his friend is an ironic one given the 'impietrite / verità' of his own 'mente defunta', and the fact that, notwithstanding his reluctance to do so, he has allowed his poetry to be profaned by the subject of war. The 'passaggio' ('crossing') that he spoke about two poems previous to 'I compagni corsi avanti', in 'Caso vocativo' ('Vocative Case') has now been made.

Society and the Romantic Attitude

This 'passaggio' was posited as being not only 'accorato' in that it would lead to a defilement of poetry, but also 'amoroso' ('Ah passaggio mio fervido, accorato /

amoroso passaggio' ('Ah my fervent, heartbroken crossing / amorous crossing')).
So far, I have considered one of the reasons why the inclusion of new themes
were to be welcomed – quite simply, the old landscape theme was suspected to
be exhausted. But there is another, fundamental reason for Zanzotto's desire to
break away from the theme of the landscape. It is first suggested in the third poem
of the collection: 'Piccola elegia', which I spoke about earlier and to which I
now return. In 'Piccola elegia' Zanzotto acknowledges that if he continues to
write metapoetic poetry of the kind we have largely met with up until now,
which *speaks about* the need to write poetry other than lyric, landscape poetry,
more than actually *doing* something about it, that same poetry will inevitably
display a romantic sentimentalism. There is in fact a strong romantic dimension
to the poem related to the involuntary 'drying up' of the poet's lyrical voice.
Romantic phraseology abounds: 'sto solo' ('I am alone'), 'aspro moto delle cose'
('the harsh movement of things'), 'cuore' ('heart'), 'pianto' ('weeping'), 'agonia'
('agony'). An emphasis upon the first person pronoun as well as the possessive
pronoun (both repeated three times) is a feature of 'grammaticalism' which
underscores the romantic preoccupation with the self (and not, in this instance,
the language problem (Agosti 1973, 11–12; Allen 1984)). In fact, in an elegiac
attitude reminiscent of Leopardi ('Alla luna' ('To the Moon')) the poet twice
depicts his soul as 'young' and 'unhappy':

> Giovane ed infelice
> qui torna l'anima mia,
>
> . . .
>
> Ah giovane ancora ed infelice io sono

Young and unhappy / my heart comes back here, / . . . / Ah still young and
unhappy am I.

Moreover, he suggests that his 'tears' and his invocations to the feminine,
inspirational 'tu' who inhabits the land, bear witness to a sentimental streak in
his personality of which he is not ashamed:

> e non ho pudore del mio pianto
> né dell'eco invocata

and I am not ashamed of my weeping / nor of the echo I've invoked.

Consequently, romantic sentimentalism would seem both accentuated and
defended. But not necessarily because the poet believes in it. On the contrary,
there are certain features in the poem which suggest that Zanzotto is belying his
true feelings; that he defends his romantic attitude precisely because deep down
he feels it to be unacceptable. The verb 'tornare' in the first reference to youth
and unhappiness already suggests that he is no longer young (here again there are

Leopardian overtones, for example 'che travagliosa / era mia vita: ed è, né cangia stile' ('Alla luna') ('for my life was one / of torment: and it still is, nor does it change its kind')), and preceding the second reference to the same, the point is reinforced:

> Io membra incerte
> occhi sfibrati
> dall'aspro moto delle cose

I with unsteady limbs / eyes weakened / by the harsh movement of things.

The 'harsh movement of things' – probably the passing of years and the endurance of adverse experiences – have taken their toll on the poet. The poet is therefore not young, and Zanzotto seems to be indirectly acknowledging that his emotional expression of unhappiness is something which does not befit his age. The 'pianto' of the elegy, the profession of love for the landscape, and the general concentration upon personal elements, are not adult, relevant issues. They are romantic issues which are no more justifiable from the point of view of a human and social function than the insular landscape poetry of DIP. 'Piccola elegia', in other words, sparks off a whole new debate on the question of Zanzotto's inherent romanticism *vis-à-vis* society. This issue comes to the fore in 'Per il mite dicembre' ('Through Mild December'), ('Appendice' no. 4), 'Elegia del venerdì' ('Friday's Elegy'), 'Altrui e mia' ('Another's and Mine'), and 'I paesaggi primi' ('The First Landscapes').

In the first of these Zanzotto reaches a conclusion which contradicts that of 'Piccola elegia'. 'Non adulti i dolori?' ('Are sorrows not adult?'), the poet reflects. Why should an expression of the pain of love be considered immature ('dolori' rhymes with 'amori' in the poem)? He looks around him at the 'love' displayed by the things of Nature, their processes of interacting as if wanting to animate each other before winter and their imminent death:

> . . . l'erba
> immune ridonda
> offerta ultima sui vecchi balconi,
> acque gentili a stimolare i tardi
> campi, sussurro fervido di venti
> felicemente giunti

The immune / grass abounds / a last offering on the old balconies, / graceful waters to stir the late / fields, the fervent whispering of winds / happily arrived.

This makes him ponder:

> intirizziti
> intirizziti amori?

benumbed / benumbed loves?

Is the profession of love for the landscape something immature when love is not frozen, but alive and demonstrative all around him?

'Elegia del venerdì' moves on to other aspects of Zanzotto's romantic sensibility and highlights as in 'Piccola elegia' their negative implications. His romanticism involves not only an unhappy love for the landscape which is something immature, but a general feeling of detachment from life. Again this idea is reinforced by the adoption of Leopardian attitudes, but now in order to highlight a regressive mentality resembling Leopardi's – a mentality which lives off memories, is divorced from the present and disillusioned by the future; is incapable, in short, of feeling involved.

The poem, in the form of a monologue, is a narrative divided into two parts. Part 1 contains memories of Zanzotto's adolescence (here he addresses his younger self in the second person) while in part 2 memories are dropped and there is a return to the present.

As in 'Piccola elegia' it is an unhappy youth that is portrayed in the first half of the poem. The sickly (asthmatic), adolescent poet lost in his 'povere scritture' ('poor writings') is full of mournful reflectiveness and reined-in emotions:

> Ma te distinguo ansimante di fieni,
> ti distinguo caduto con lo sguardo
> nel sole dei bicchieri,
>
> . . .
>
> . . . Ritorna il tuo sguardo
> e il grande pianto
>
> . . .
>
> nel non placato azzurro d'una notte
> scaturirai
> cometa soffocata.
> Ansimante di fieni ti rivedo
> ti rivedo perduto
> nelle tue povere scritture
> su cui piove equivoca la morte

But I can make you out gasping from the hay, / I can make you out fallen with your gaze / in the drinking-glasses' sun, / . . . / . . . Your gaze returns / and your bitter weeping / . . . / in the night's unalleviated blue / you will burst forth / – a stifled comet. / Gasping from the hay I can see you again / I see you lost / in your poor writings / on which ambiguous death rains down.

But these memories of sadness are all preceded by a question in which Zanzotto, addressing his younger self, laments the fact that he will never be reborn, will never live again those winters and summers of old:

> Mai più rinato, mai più conosciuto
> a quale fredda scala a quale estate
> mi riporti?

Never again reborn, never again known / to what cold staircase to what summer / you take me back?

Consequently it is suggested that the past, even if unhappy, becomes sweet again in memory, a notable Leopardian attitude: 'E pur mi giova / la ricordanza, e il noverar l'etate / del mio dolore' ('Alla luna') ('And yet I enjoy / the memory, and counting the summer / of my grief'). Zanzotto's question to his younger self contains 'un van desio / del passato, ancor tristo' ('Le ricordanze') ('a vain desire / for the past, albeit sad' ('Memories')).

Part 2 opens with Zanzotto juxtaposing a 'venerdì' ('Friday') and a 'sabato d'oro e di rame' which 'non sarà mai' ('a Saturday of gold and copper which will never come about'):

> Il venerdì è così stento che appena
> ci sta il tormento della formica,
> il sabato d'oro e di rame non sarà mai;
> ma tintinnano falci, trema azzurro ferrigno
> e l'erba mura il monte

Friday is so full of hardship that / the torment of the ant hardly appears in it, / the Saturday of gold and copper will never come about; / but scythes clink, an iron-like blue trembles / and grass walls up the mountain.

The juxtaposition echoes 'Il sabato del villaggio' ('Village Saturday'). Zanzotto's 'venerdì' is equivalent to Leopardi's 'sabato' on the evening of which the village people eagerly prepare for the 'dì di festa' ('festival day').

Similar preparations are being made in Zanzotto's poem. Like Leopardi's 'legnaiuol' ('carpenter'), there are those who are hurrying to finish their work so as to leave the morrow free for pleasure: 'ma tintinnano falci, trema azzurro ferrigno'. But whereas Leopardi can find hope and joy in the mere feeling of anticipation, thereby saying of his Saturday:

> Questo di sette è il più gradito giorno,
> pien di speme e di gioia

This of the seven is the most agreeable day, / full of hope and joy

Zanzotto's 'venerdì' is, by contrast, entirely darkened by the prospect of disillusion and as such it is unbearable:

> Sei, venerdì di cereo sole
> e di tetre lusinghe di vallate,

intorno alla mia mente come un gemito

You, Friday of waxen sun / and of huge valleys' gloomy delusions, / you exist around my mind like a groan.

It epitomizes for him a number of things. It is an 'ansia' ('anxiety') which 'spezza le mani delle ghirlande estive' ('breaks the hands of summer garlands') (an allusion, it would seem, to Leopardi's 'donzelletta' ('young girl') symbolizing the joy of anticipation, as she comes from the country carrying a bunch of roses and violets with which she means to adorn herself at the festival; while echoing on a purely verbal level Montale's 'vento del nord' ('north wind') in 'Notizie dall'Amiata' which 'spezza le antiche mani dell'arenaria' (line 34) ('breaks the ancient hands of the sandstone')). It has all the harshness of impossible love: 'vicinanza che gli occhi cauterizza / o silenzi che offendono' ('closeness which cauterizes eyes / or silences which offend'); or of an unvoiced love which gradually dies: 'informulati amori che si spengono' ('unexpressed loves which fade away'). In short, Friday, the here and now, is presented as a vocative without a response, a communicative impulse which is thwarted, or a feeling of love, impeded. Friday epitomizes life – a forsaken vocative.

'Altrui e mia' presents a similar idea: the poet's romantic sense of disengagement segregates him from society and his involvement with others. As in 'Piccola elegia', romantic vocabulary prevails: 'le mie pene' ('my afflictions'), 'il tormento' ('torment'), 'il dolore' ('sorrow'), 'dispera' ('despairs'), 'ho agonizzato' ('I have been in agony'), 'le lacrime' ('tears'); and the older poet is presented as having sustained the sentimentalism of his youth. A similarity with 'Elegia del venerdì' is also present in that the poem is in two parts and in the form of a narrative monologue.

In part 1 Zanzotto remembers an occasion when as a young boy he forgot his 'mother's' birthday and had nothing to offer her on the day: 'e nessun dono il mio cuore / dimentico t'ha offerto / . . . / nulla per te sul desco / di scintillante e amabile' ('and my forgetful heart / offered you no gift / . . . / nothing sparkling and sweet / for you on the dining table'). Part 2 is set in the present, and the past repeats itself – it is once again his mother's birthday and the occasion has slipped the poet's mind: 'Del tuo giorno nulla ho saputo o mamma / e tu me ne hai reso memoria tacendo' ('Oh mother I wasn't at all aware of your day / and you brought it to my mind by not mentioning it'). His forgetfulness on the second occasion as on the first is attributed to a melancholia, a vague sense of anxiety. A series of correspondences between parts 1 and 2 serve to highlight this sad and self-involved withdrawal of the young and older poet, an attitude conveyed by the metaphors of blindness and deafness:

Ma la mia mente fallisce e non parlo
non parlo a nessuno. Veloce

e *sordo* scendo dal frumento
arso a monti, mi distolgo
da cicli oscuri e porto
afa e *chiusi occhi*

(Part 1).

Dove madre *m'acceca*
l'estate, dove io sono?

. . .

Oggi così a lungo ho agonizzato
che *non ho udito* le cicale,
tempo mi ha tolto il cuore,
la strada s'inerba e *le lacrime*
s'assiepano al mio sguardo

(Part 2)

But my mind fails and I do not speak / I do not speak to anyone. *Deaf* / I quickly descend from burnt / wheat on the mountains, I withdraw / from dark cycles and bring / sultriness and *closed eyes* (Part 1).
Where, mother, does summer / *blind me*, where am I? / . . . / Today I have been in agony for so long / that *I did not hear* the cicadas, / time has taken my heart away, / the street grows grassy and *tears* / *hedge my sight* (Part 2).

In fact not only does such sombre brooding prevent the poet from remembering his mother, it also differentiates him from her. He is for ever attempting to 'return' to her, to communicate or identify with her in some way: 'sempre invano accenna, sempre torna / tuo figlio, o madre, per le curve / strade, per infiniti avvolgimenti' ('oh mother, your son always / beckons in vain, always returns / through twisting streets, through infinite windings'). The discordancy between himself and his mother is one of the things that the poem clearly aims to emphasize. It is done in a curious way across the metaphor of heat. The poem opens with the poet desiring this 'return' to his mother in order to escape an 'immondo calore' ('foul heat'), perhaps symbolizing a neurosis. Both parts of the poem, however, serve to highlight how an escape from 'calore' is not possible through a return to his mother, for since his mother's birthday is in July, he associates her with heat and light (and most notably with the 'cicada' ('cicada') – mentioned seven times in the poem). Accordingly, heat and light and things related to them are foregrounded in his depictions of those two separate birthdays of his mother and are most often presented as oppressive factors. (The phenomenon of 'light', however, acquires a different symbolism in section 2 of *VCT.* See pages 73–7):

bolle di cicalette la collina

the hill *is seething with little cicadas*

. . . la popolosa luce

e *la cicaletta* sul melo del cortile

. . . *the crowded light* / and *the little cicada* on the apple tree in the courtyard

> . . . Veloce
> e sordo scendo dal *frumento*
> *arso* a monti, mi distolgo
> da cicli oscuri e *porto*
> *afa* e chiusi occhi
> > (Part 1)

(See translation, page 66).

> Eri nata allora e su te, lieve
> ricamo di lini e vagiti,
> era *il sole*; oh tu non ti esaltavi
> o madre, *al sole*, allora. Eri bambina
> cercavi il latte *nella grande estate*

You were born then and upon you, a light / embroidery of linen and whimperings, / was *the sun*; oh you were not enraptured / *by the sun*, then, oh mother. You were a baby / looking for milk *in the great summer*

> *che sete e sete* di rugiade
> dovunque nel cielo in ogni cielo.
> Dove madre *m'acceca*
> *l'estate*, dove io sono?

what thirst and thirst of dews / everywhere in the sky in every sky. / Where does *summer* / *blind me*, oh mother, where am I?

> Sopra i dorsi di Lorna il frumento è trebbiato
> e *la stoppia patita va in canicola*
> > (Part 2)

On Lorna's crests the wheat is threshed / and *the sickly stubble undergoes the heatwave.*

Moreover, as the first sequence from part 2 above serves to illustrate, in contrast to himself, for his extrovert mother light and warmth are agreeable things. He imagines the original day of her birth and when as a child she was not *as yet* enraptured by the sun, implying that later in life she was. Similarly the poem presents pictures of her letting light into fragrant rooms in the house – 'Tu nella casa odorate stanze illumini' (there are echoes of Leopardi's 'A Silvia' here: 'quiete / *stanze*'; 'maggio *odoroso*' ('quiet / *rooms*'; '*fragrant* May') lines 7–8, 13) – and throwing open the windows to let in the July dawn, claiming herself reborn with all the seething life of the month (a painful gesture for the poet)

> 'Svégliati bimbo, la cicala ha cantato,
> io sono nata, è luglio'.
> Aprivi le finestre, io respiravo
> tutto il dolore dell'alba di luglio

'Waken up child, the cicada has sung, / I am born, it is July'. / You were opening the windows, I was breathing in / all the sorrow of the July dawn.

In short, the poet's romantic sensibility obstructs identification or involvement with his mother. In fact the point is that his 'dolore', 'tormento', 'lacrime', bear witness to an 'amore inquieto' ('restless love') which is something soulful, artistic, so to speak, and extrinsic to manifestations of love on familial and, presumably, social levels. I say this in the light of 'I paesaggi primi' where the equation between art and 'amore' is made more explicit.

'I paesaggi primi' acts as a counterpart to 'Altrui e mia' and parental identity is here achieved, but with the poet's 'father' as opposed to his mother. This, it seems, is for the simple reason that his father is presented as having a creative temperament similar to his own. 'I paesaggi primi' depicts Zanzotto's father as a painter (as indeed Giovanni Zanzotto was) whose work the poet finds seductive in that it 'draws' not upon the ugly aspects of reality nor a reality external to his region, but the sheltering and paradisean realm of Lorna:

> Dal tuo pennello fervido,
> . . .
> lavorano di luci
> e muschi i paradisi ed i presepi
> che tutt'intorno hai già, che sulla
> bianca parete a me seduci

From your fervent brush, / . . . / paradises and cribs / which you already have all around you, / and which you seduce me towards on the white wall / abound in lights and mosses.

This artistic side to his personality, this creative impulse, is equated with 'un mai sopito amore' ('a for ever implacable love') which Zanzotto has inherited, thereby making of his father, not only a creator in his own right but an 'arteficer' of his son as well:

> tu modesto signore
> di Lorna che creasti e che ti crea,
> tu artefice
> di me, di un mai sopito amore

you modest master / of Lorna which you created and which creates you, / you maker / of me, of an ever implacable love.

The word 'amore' has occurred in all of the five poems I have discussed in relation to the 'romantic' issue, and on each occasion it has occurred with slightly varying implications. But these different implications are all interrelated. In 'Piccola elegia' and 'Per il mite dicembre', 'amore' denotes a romantic love for the landscape which although defended in 'Per il mite dicembre', is obliquely acknowledged in 'Piccola elegia' as a puerile attitude with little social application. In 'Elegia del venerdì', 'amore' indicates the aborted vocative which, for the romantic sensibility at odds with living, epitomizes life. In these three poems, therefore, 'love' is related to a romantic disposition, and the echoes of Leopardi in 'Piccola elegia', 'Elegia del venerdì', and 'Altrui e mia' indicate that love and romanticism are also to be interpreted in literary terms. 'Altrui e mia' consolidates this idea: Zanzotto's 'amore inquieto' forms part of his romantic, artistic temperament and is incompatible with the demonstrative and interrelational love of the family or society. 'I paesaggi primi' then reinforces the equation between love and art but now with no reference to romanticism. Instead, the 'mai sopito amore' Zanzotto has inherited from his 'father' would seem to refer to the creative impulse in general. For although his 'father' is presented as having an artistic nature akin to that of his son, it is not in any way suggested that it is a romantic one. Nor is he engaged in the same type of art as his son. Zanzotto here is making the point that creativity in general, in his case, writing, is, like love, a vocative, communicative instinct that cannot be placated – it is 'inquieto' and 'mai sopito'. In fact, this is precisely what Zanzotto has said about poetry in an interview wherein he also used terms synonymous with those of 'I paesaggi primi' to qualify 'amore' (here 'eros'). Poetry, he said, receives its stimuli from things and events of everyday life 'in a circuit of emotiveness, of a restless love, that can never be sated' (Listri 191). (Compare this equation between poetry and love with Pavese's diary entry of 12 August 1940: 'Love and poetry are mysteriously linked, because both are a desire for expression, for talk, for communication. . . . It is an orgiastic desire which has no substitutes' (*Il mestiere di vivere* (*This Business of Living*).)

Consequently, in 'I paesaggi primi' there are intimations of a movement away from the consideration of romantic writing and its relationship to life, to a consideration of writing in general. This concern appears in two other poems in section 1 – 'Caso vocativo' ('Vocative Case') and 'Colloquio' ('Colloquy') – where Zanzotto focuses upon the relationship between words and their referents. How effective is the functioning of the written word? This is the question Zanzotto would seem to be contemplating in this, the third part of his consideration of the literature/reality divide.

Problems with Language

In 'Caso vocativo' it is denounced as being ineffective, since, as has been widely observed, language for Zanzotto is becoming a problem (Agosti 1973, 10–14; Ramat 1976, 608–12; Allen 1984; Conti-Bertini 1980, 207–9):

> O miei mozzi trastulli
> pensieri in cui mi credo e vedo,
> ingordo vocativo
> decerebrato anelito

Oh my broken playthings / thoughts in which I believe and see myself, / greedy vocative / decerebrated yearning.

Writing, like the 'mai sopito amore' of 'I paesaggi primi', is an 'ingordo vocativo', an insatiable feeling of an invocatory kind; an 'anelito', a yearning to express, but a crazy, 'decerebrated' one. The poet is foolish to 'believe' and 'see' himself in the thoughts he transcribes for they are betrayed by the very language he uses to express them. His words are 'broken playthings'. They impair, that is, his real thoughts and feelings, and given their inadequate functioning, they are not to be taken seriously. This makes of writing a mere pastime as opposed to an earnest *métier*. Indeed, Zanzotto would seem to reflect that the value of the written word has long since been depreciated by man at large, even if for reasons less intellectual than his own. One glance at the landscape suffices to convince him of this:

> Come i cavi s'ingranano a crinali
> i crinali a tranelli a gru ad antenne
> e ottuso mostro
> in un prima eterno capovolto
> il futuro diviene

As cables mesh onto ridges / the ridges onto snares onto cranes and aerials / and the future becomes / a dull monster / in an eternal capsized past.

There is construction work taking place. The ridges of hills and mountains are being meshed with cables (presumably telephone or telegraphic wires), cranes and aerials (presumably television aerials). Two closely related things are suggested here. First, the Heideggerian distinction between true knowledge (with which creative artists and scientists are endowed) as a 'vocation', a 'calling forth', and Western technology since seventeenth-century rationalism which, through its enslavement and harnessing of Nature to achieve its own ends, has misused this 'vocation' and set itself up as a 'provocation' of Nature (Heidegger 1978, 283–319). Second, Zanzotto is simply stressing how mass media go hand in hand with urbanization, making of the future what he calls a dull monster in an eternal capsized past. That is to say, the past is being turned upside down in the sense that the value of the written word has fallen into desuetude and been replaced by an emphasis upon the spoken word, dictated by technology. This holds out dull and monstrous prospects for the future. (It is interesting to note that Heidegger calls the destruction and enslavement of Nature by technology 'das Ungeheure', meaning 'the strangely monstrous', to which one may compare Zanzotto's use of the term 'ottuso mostro'.)

Hence while the poet himself is beginning to doubt the efficacy of the written word, all around him its importance is dying. As he goes on to suggest, literary writing in particular (for Zanzotto, one remembers, bound to the concept of love) 'softens into slaver, into a whim': 'l'amore s'ammollisce in bava / in fisima'. Indeed, given that on four previous occasions, 'amore', as I have shown, was more specifically linked to the creative impulse of a romantic, perhaps here the poet is acknowledging how by modern standards his romantic writing is this mere slaver.

However, in 'Colloquio' the negative thinking of 'Caso vocativo' is very much overturned by an unexpected incident. This incident helps to restore Zanzotto's faith in writing as a 'colloquy', as a vocative impulse which receives a response from the reader. Zanzotto now holds out the possibility that writing may be an effective means of communication, even if that communication operates only among poets or those with poetic temperaments.

While walking through the woods Zanzotto comes across a type of prose poem inscribed on a country wall, and he uses it as an epigraph to his own poem transcribing it as it is, along with its 'umili / lontanissimi errori' ('humble / most distant errors') – its scanty punctuation, its grammatical errors and spelling mistakes (in my translation I have left the punctuation as it is in the Italian, and italicized the erroneous grammar and spelling):

> 'Ora il sereno è ritornato le campane suonano per il vespero ed io le ascolto con grande dolcezza. Gli ucelli cantano festosi nel cielo perché? Tra poco e primavera i prati meteranno il suo manto verde, ed io come un fiore appasito guardo tutte queste meraviglie.'
> SCRITTO SU UN MURO IN CAMPAGNA

> 'Now serenity has returned the bells ring for vespers and I listen to them with great enchantment. Why do the *birds* sing cheerfully in the sky? Before long *it will be* spring the fields *will put on* their green coat, and I like a *withered* flower watch all of these marvels'.
> WRITTEN ON A WALL IN THE COUNTRYSIDE.

It is autumn when Zanzotto happens upon these lines celebrating the arrival of spring. But in spite of this, and in spite of the piece's solecisms, in a joyful, extended address to the anonymous 'poet' Zanzotto proclaims that this 'poet' has perpetuated that spring for him:

> . . . E tu
> in un marzo perpetuo le campane
> dei Vesperi, la meraviglia
> delle gemme e dei selvosi uccelli
> e del languore, nel ripido muro
> nella strofe scalfita ansimando m'accenni;
> nel muro aperto da piogge e da vermi
> il fortunato marzo
> mi spieghi tu con umili
> lontanissimi errori, a me nel vivo
> d'ottobre

> . . . And you / in a perpetual March / on the steep wall, in the scratched out
> strophe / gasping you point out to me the vesper / bells, the marvel / of buds
> and of wood-birds and languor; / on the wall cleft by rain and worms / the
> happy March / you explain to me with humble / most distant errors, to me
> in the height / of October.

Even though he is in full October, that scratched out 'strophe' which has
miraculously survived against the rain and the worms, in eagerly *indicating* the
marvel of spring ('ansimando *m'accenni*'), has managed to *explain* it to Zanzotto
('mi *spieghi* tu'). As he goes on to make clear, it is not just words which Zanzotto
sees on the wall, but March itself. And as if to show that this 'poet's' writing
has stirred in him an emotional response, Zanzotto repeats the final phrase of
the writing on the wall, and weaves a 'colloquy' with it by taking it out of its
context (correcting it!) and inserting it into his own poem proper:

> *Io come un fiore appassito*
> *guardo tutte queste meraviglie*
>
> *E marzo quasi verde quasi*
> *meriggio acceso di domenica*
> *marzo senza misteri*
>
> *inebetì nel muro*

*I like a withered flower / watch all of these marvels / And March almost green
almost / a bright Sunday noon / March with no mysteries / stunned in
the wall.*

Nevertheless, Zanzotto's misgivings about the effective functioning of lan-
guage are not totally eradicated for they return to trouble him in section 2 of
the collection.

SECTION TWO

There is, in fact, no sharp thematic division between section 1 and section 2 of
VCT. Not only does section 2 elaborate further on the linguistic problem, it also
offers additional views on the major preoccupation of section 1: the question of
the relevance of Zanzotto's earlier landscape poetry. What probably *does* account
for the structural division is the fact that the issues of language and landscape are
not dealt with in exactly the same way in the second section as they are in the
first. In fact, one discovers, initially with some alarm, that in spite of the *title* of
section 2 – 'Prima persona' – which refers, as I shall show, to the relationship
between language and subjectivity, there is only one poem within this section,
likewise entitled 'Prima persona', which deals specifically and exclusively with
that relationship. The vast majority of poems deal with Zanzotto's landscape
poetry which on some occasions he considers to be relevant, on other occasions,
irrelevant. Consequently, his feelings towards this type of poetry are again

ambivalent as in section 1 of the work. But ambivalence here is used to suggest something *about* subjectivity which Zanzotto is incapable of saying directly in words given the deficiency which exists in language. The 'Prima persona' issue, therefore, even though treated explicitly on only one occasion, is implicitly present in most of the other poems in section 2. But first we should consider Zanzotto's new ideas on the appropriateness of his landscape poetry.

A Natural Theologist View of the Landscape

In section 1 Zanzotto alluded to the fictitious idealism of his poetry which was intent upon poeticizing the landscape rather than presenting it as it really was. On other occasions he felt his landscape poetry to be of little human interest or practical value, and made attempts to write more socially orientated poetry – two arguments, therefore, reinforcing the futility of his early output, but both of which are frequently retracted. Now in section 2 Zanzotto begins to take into account something which, as I showed in Chapter 1, he had not as yet contemplated: he begins to debate the existence of what he calls in 'Io attesto' ('I Bear Witness To') an 'altrove' ('elsewhere'), an otherworldliness, or higher realm of being to which the landscape may be secretly attuned. It is not, however, quite certain whether the otherworldliness Zanzotto has in mind has a mythical or religious character. For the poems here combine allusions to pagan, classical deities such as Diana and Phoebus as well as to Christian personages such as Eve. Nevertheless, the abundance of biblical phraseology in the poems (a new feature of his style (Guglielminetti 172)) suggests that there is more of a Christian than pagan mentality at work here; that Zanzotto's reasoning is in fact akin to that of natural theology. But in spite of the ambiguity, Zanzotto would seem to think that if that otherworldliness does exist and if the landscape is attuned to it, then all the more reason why his earlier poetry intent upon presenting an idealistic vision of the landscape should be viewed to be relevant. For a landscape endowed with an unearthly significance should not be represented realistically. If, on the other hand, that otherworldliness does not exist, then his earlier poetry is indeed inconsequential.

'Ineptum, prorsus credibile' ('Stupid, But Utterly Credible') is the first of a series of poems on this subject, and just as its title (a verse from Tertullian – the Christian prose writer) takes the form of an open paradox, the poem itself presents a great number of antitheses all of which are attributed to 'light' – the light of the sky or the light of the sun. Three of the poems which follow 'Ineptum, prorsus credibile' ('Dal cielo' ('From the Sky'), 'Là nel cielo, là nel terrore' ('There in the Sky, There in Terror') and 'Io attesto') also focus upon this phenomenon. Arguing like a natural theologist and/or like Hölderlin and Heidegger, Zanzotto proposes that the existence of an otherworldliness is suggested by this light, that the light bears witness to it. On the other hand he recognizes this idea to be purely suppositional, and hence the antitheses: is the light a 'terribilmente pronta luce / o freddissimo sogno immenso' ('terribly ready light / or immense freezing dream') – does it indicate the reality of a more supernal existence, or is its unearthly significance a mere illusion created by the mind? Does the 'dazzling' light of morning provide a glimpse of the splendours of an 'al di là' ('beyond'), or is it a 'clotty', opaque light which prohibits clairvoyance – a 'grumoso abbagliante mattino' ('clotty dazzling morning')? Is it therefore 'squalid' or prodigious – a 'squallido prodigio'? ('squalid prodigy') (compare on a verbal level Montale's '*prodigio* fallito' ('failed *prodigy*') and 'limbo *squallido*' ('*squalid* limbo'), 'Crisalide' lines 37, 40, *Ossi*). Eventually the following conclusion is reached after the rest of part 1 of the poem juggles with similar antitheses:

> Ma freddissima e immensa
> sta la gloria in excelsis
> oltre il grigio spigolo del mondo;
> e gode di tutto il suo peso fulgente

> But the glory exists in the highest / freezing and immense / beyond the world's grey corner; / and delights in all its shining weight.

Tonally, this conclusion would seem to be positive: the insertion of the biblical exclamation in the second line suggests that Zanzotto attributes a religious, Christian significance to this light (to which we may compare Hölderlin, for whom the sky was a manifestation of Divinity: 'Ist unbekannt Gott? Ist er offenbar wie der Himmel? dieses glaub' ich eher. Des Menschen MaaB ist's' ('In Lieblicher BlÄue') ('Is God unknown? Is he manifest like the sky? I'd sooner believe the latter. It's the measure of man') ('In Lovely Blueness', *Selected Verse* 245)). However, the adjectives 'freddissima e immensa' although used here as predicates to the 'gloria', are *originally* used as predicates of an illusory light, thereby maintaining their negative overtones ('freddissimo sogno immenso').

'Dal cielo', by contrast, is purely affirmative. Indeed the poem is very much in the style of a laud, a hymn of praise to the sky (bringing to mind D'Annunzio's *Laudi del cielo*): there are nine lines which either begin with the phrase 'dal cielo è' or 'dal cielo', followed by a lengthy enumeration of all of the sky's life-giving qualities. It is hailed, among other things, as a brilliant and intransigent source in league with 'the truth'; a source which imposes certain laws which the things of the landscape understand and respect and follow with dauntless tenacity:

> conclusiva diafana ebrietà,
> intransigente e fulgida
> causa che stai nel vero.

> Dal cielo è questa penombra
> dove senza termine è la fede

> anche dell'insetto che procede
> dalla foglia invernale alla stella
> che ardendo gocciò nella valle,
> . . .
>
> dal cielo è l'ordine tenace e leggero
> delle viti sui colli

conclusive diaphanous drunkenness, / intransigent and shining / cause in league with the truth. / From the sky comes this half-light / where even the insect's faith / which proceeds from the winter leaf to the burning / star which dripped into the valley / is limitless, / . . . / from the sky comes the tenacious and light order / of the grape-vines on the hills.

But an appendix poem, 'Là nel cielo, là nel terrore', acts as a codicil to the above. Zanzotto admits that the words of 'Dal cielo' have become dark and foreign and his vision is being magnetized downwards toward earth:

> Dissi ieri 'dal cielo', ma remota nell'ora
> della notte, . . .
> . . .
> s'offuscò la parola, si pente la gola
> Dissi ieri 'dal cielo'
> come rivo di sangue
> dalle labbra –
> e l'oscuro cemento
> senza tregua dappresso mi guarda

Yesterday I said 'from the sky', but in the hour / of the night, . . . / . . . / the remote word became blurred, my throat repents / Yesterday I said 'from the sky' / like a stream of blood / from my lips – / and the dark cement / relentlessly watches me from close up.

The earthly and unearthly are then two things that are juxtaposed in 'Io attesto'. 'Deneb', a star from the Cygnus constellation is set alongside the 'Scandalo . . . / nella tetra città sotto monte' ('Scandal . . . / in the gloomy town under the mountain') – the provincial gossip of a local town. The mountain's 'weight' and 'song' are unheard and unlived in everyday life; its 'light', turned 'altrove', is incompatible with the pulsating traffic-lights below:

> la tua luce, di monte, luce volta
> altrove,
> il tuo peso il tuo canto
> non ascoltato
> non abitato.
> . . .
>
> Tu (monte) distinto dal palpito
> dei semafori incerti,
> dio di deserti e di pieghe e di sere . . ..

your mountain light, a light turned / elsewhere, / your weight your song is / not listened to / not lived in. / . . . / You (mountain) distinct from the throbbing / uncertain traffic-lights, / a god of deserts of folds and of evenings.

Zanzotto, lifting his vision away from the ground ('torpore, pavimento') ('torpor, floor'), and from the mundane and pedestrian, testifies again to this other-worldliness: 'Altrove / io sordamente attesto' ('I, turning a deaf ear, testify to / an elsewhere') just like the flower which closes at night but opens, 'resurrected' in the morning, responsive and spiritually attuned to the light: 'Vedi il fiore marcito in un riflesso / . . . / Vedi il fiore in un brivido, surrexit' ('See the flower spoiled in a reflex movement / . . . / See the flower in a shudder, it arose').

But it is the physical and not the spiritual side of the landscape that reasserts itself in 'Da un'altezza nuova' ('From a New Height'). Here there are no mountains or flowers in peaceful harmony with the extramundane, but an avid groping of beasts, of insects and flowers which he has hitherto ignored:

> Nulla dunque compresi
> del brancicare avido di bestie
> d'insetti e fiori

I understood nothing therefore / of the greedy groping of beasts / insects and flowers.

This has been ignored not only in Zanzotto's previous works but also in section 1 of *VCT*. Physical procreation – this perhaps is the only type of 'love' which Nature displays, a different type of offering and interacting than that which he contemplated in 'Per il mite dicembre' (see pages 62–3), and a love incompatible with his own romantic love for the land as professed in 'Epifania' and 'Se non fosse' (see pages 50, 55–6).

The idea is carried on into 'Esistere psichicamente' ('Existing Psychically'). The landscape is brute matter and nothing more, a murky and slimy struggle of algae and worms:

> . . . il conato
> torbido d'alghe e vermi,
> chiarore-uovo
> che nel morente muco fai parole
> e amori

. . . the muddy / effort of algae and worms, / egg-glow / which in the dying mucus makes words / and love.

This kind of 'love' is the only kind of 'poetry' it is 'making' ('parole' is linked to 'amori' above). There can be no unearthly significance within this brutish and pullulating force. Its light is not the diaphanous light of 'Dal cielo' but an 'egro spiraglio' ('sickly glimmer'), a 'chiarore-uovo' ('egg-glow'), 'Chiarore acido' ('sour gleam'), threatening to revoke the very existence of an 'altrove'.

But Phoebus is stubborn – 'pervicace Febo come una piaga' ('Colle di Giano') ('Phoebus, obstinate as a sore') ('Hill of Janus') (compare Montale's 'l'azzurro pervicace' ('obstinate blue'), 'Mottetto XVI', line 7, *Occasioni*) – and in 'Colle di Giano' and 'Prima del sole' ('Before the Sun') Zanzotto reasserts his belief in the spiritual, unearthly significance of the land, claiming that it is with his real voice that he speaks again:

> Giaccio nella mia vera
> voce, m'inoltro nella stasi
> prima, nella luce mai saziata.
> . . .
> Trovo il mio vero corpo
> le mie ossa e le lacrime,
> trovo l'amore che sottrassi
> alla violenta terra
> ('Colle di Giano III')

I lie out in my real / voice, I'm heading forth into my initial / stasis, in the never sated light. / . . . / I'm finding my real body / my bones and tears, / I'm finding the love I removed / from the violent earth.

Nature, after all, is animistic. It watches with its living soul as the poet watches it, but he is unable to define the otherworldly mysteries it locks within itself (the 'sun', the light, is in excess):

> quando occhi guardano guardati
> ma ancora eccederebbe il sole
> ('Prima del sole')

while eyes watch while being watched / but still the sun would be in excess.

As a consequence, Zanzotto's involvement with the land cannot be consummated, and wonder, 'stupore', is kept alive in a bitter-sweet relationship:

> Stupore che in sé e nelle cose
> dolorando, godendo s'instaura
> ('Prima del sole')

Wonder which in itself and in phenomena / establishes itself with grief, and delight.

Language and Subjectivity

So far I have examined eight poems in section 2 (including one from the appendix) where, on the subject of the unearthly quality of the landscape, Zanzotto hovers between affirmative and negative thinking. It would be true to say, therefore, that the poems here move along obscurely and contradict themselves

(Forti 1963, 214) even though they do not necessarily defy analysis. But do these contradictions serve any particular purpose? 'Campèa II' ('Campèa II') shows that they are by no means gratuitous:

> In fede evolve l'anima,
> tutto accoglie e allontana.

The soul, Zanzotto says, evolves in faith, 'accepting everything' and 'distancing everything'. That is to say, Zanzotto, at one point in time, may 'accept', or adhere, to certain opinions, which, at another point in time, he may 'distance' himself from, but not necessarily for an indefinite period:

> Antico e vivo è il ricamo che preme
> e carda il sonno
> delle mie tempie insoddisfatte

Ancient and alive is the embroidery which presses upon / and cards the sleep / of my unsatisfied temples.

Here Zanzotto talks about a past idea which has come alive again and is embroidering or working actively in his mind, helping to comb out his troubled thoughts and excite his thinking. The 'accepting' and 'distancing' of ideas, therefore, continually repeats itself. Thinking is, what Heidegger in his 'Letter on Humanism' defines as, a re-membering ('Denken ist Andenken' ('To think is to memorate')), an 'ingathering', a 'collecting and re-collecting of the dispersed vestiges of Being' (Steiner 124). What Zanzotto is highlighting is the inconsistency of subjectivity, how orderly or, what he calls in the interview with Allen, 'purely rational' thought (which he associates there with Hegel) is an 'old idealism', a 'dangerous illusion'. Indeed it is the predominance of irrational over rational thought which is emphasized more strongly by what follows in the poem:

> Tenui, tenaci architetture
> architetture di formiche,
> disarmonie d'alveari
> dove il miele si stringe
> in coerenza di raggi,
> apparite, strutture risibili
> ma forza senza grazia senza nome

Tenuous, tenacious architectures / architectures of ants, / disharmonies of beehives / where honey presses together / in a coherence of rays, / you look like, laughable structures / a graceless and nameless force.

The architectures of ants (possibly anthills) and the honeycombs of bees with their identical cells ('coerenza di raggi') are, Zanzotto proclaims, ridiculous, graceless structures. That is probably because both ants and bees (two of the most industrious of insects) exercise a methodical routine in the building of their structures, which are rigid and mathematical (hence 'graceless') in shape: the conical anthill, the hexagonal cells. Such systematized structures work (as Zanzotto goes on to say) 'contro il cuore', 'contro il grigio asilo della mente' ('against my heart, against the grey confusion of my mind').

The stating, unstating, and restating of views across the eight poems I have considered (from 'Ineptum, prorsus credibile' to 'Prima del sole') is therefore an unsystematic structural device through which Zanzotto attempts to imitate the inconsistency and vagrancy of subjectivity. For any attempt to explain this and other features of subjectivity directly in words is much less successful.

This is the point that is made in 'Prima persona'. Here there is a strong emphasis upon 'grammaticalism' – a recurrent use of the vocative case, and first person pronouns. The latter, in particular, are used by Zanzotto to indicate the difficulty of expressing subjectivity through language. The real I cannot be faithfully represented in language via the pronoun 'io':

> Io – in tremiti continui, – io – disperso
> e presente: mai giunge
> l'ora *tua*,
> mai suona il cielo del *tuo* vero nascere

I – in continual quiverings, – I – scattered / and present: *your* hour / never comes, / the sky never sounds with *your* real birth.

The 'hour' of the real self ('tu') never comes; subjectivity is never fully 'born' in language. The self when determined linguistically by the pronoun 'io' is scattered across the poem in a tremulous, unsteady existence. (The diary-writer of SA has exactly the same impression: see the story 'Vita di un diario' ('A Diary Life')). Pleasure, it follows, lies not so much in writing or in reading the finished product as in the impulse to express which precedes both of these. If the need to express is indeed an 'amore', – a desiring or loving impulse (an equivalence established in 'I paesaggi primi', see pages 68–9) – the actual act of writing wherein feelings and ideas are dispersed by the language which expresses them is more akin to the release and *loss* of desire through sexual intercourse:

> . . . cresce
> l'orgasmo, io cresco io cado

. . . the orgasm / grows, I grow I fall.

Language is a type of vortex which engulfs the poet's already doubtful attempts to be fully present in language, and the feeble urging of his heart which tries to make it possible:

> . . . o vortice a cui corrono
> i conati malcerti, il fioco

sospingermi del cuore

. . . oh whirlpool to which run / the uncertain attempts, the weak / goading of my heart.

The poet has only two options in the face of this 'humiliation'. Either he can accept the situation and concede that the real I will only brush the surface of the text: 'tu sempre umiliato lambisci' ('you for ever humiliated lick the surface'); or he can rebel against this indignity:

indomito incrini
l'essere macilento
o erompente in ustioni

unbeaten you crack / the being which is emaciated / or breaking out in burns.

In his search for a more authentic language associated with the self he can indignantly break the ice of language, can try to come to the fore by violating it. Hence a truthful representation of the self cannot be achieved through spontaneous expression but rather through a shaking up of language.

Subjectivity and the Landscape

The question which arises from all of this is: can the poet's subjectivity be represented at all? Is there anything external to mind and thought which is capable of evoking it? In 'Prima persona' Zanzotto denies this function to the written word, but he does suggest that there is another place where the 'tu' (the real, non-linguistically determined self) gushes forth in a fullness of being:

Ma tu scaturisci per lenti
boschi, per lucidi abissi,
per soli aperti come vive ventose

But you gush forth through idle / woods, through shiny abysses, / through spacious suns like living suckers.

Zanzotto's subjectivity is very much a part of this landscape, is stamped upon it, as it were.

This idea is also strongly present in 'Ineptum, prorsus credibile' and 'Dal cielo'. Here not only does Zanzotto debate the otherworldly significance of the phenomenon of light in relationship to the landscape, he also debates the same in relationship to himself, thereby giving thought to, what Heidegger calls, 'the simple oneness of the four', or, 'the fourfold' (sky, divinity, earth, and mortals) (Heidegger 1978, 319–41):

no non dici, ma stai nella luce
immodesta e pur vera

> nella luce inetta ma credibile,
> sospinto nella vita

no you do not speak, but you exist in the immodest / and yet truthful light /
in the inept but credible light, / driven on in life

> terribilmente pronta luce
> o freddissimo sogno immenso
> su cui trascende
> perpetuo vertice il sole,
> da cui trabocchi tu, tu nella vita?

a terribly ready light / or an immense freezing dream / which the sun, a
permanent vertex, / transcends / from which you, you overflow in life?

                                    ('Ineptum, prorsus credibile')

'No non dici, ma stai nella luce': even though the real self cannot be totally pres-
ent in writing (writing, it would seem, being indicated here by the verb 'dire') it
is to be found in the light from which it overflows: 'da cui trabocchi tu'.

'Dal cielo' then makes it clear that if the light does bear witness to the
unearthly, then the poet, like the land, has a special affinity with it: it represents
the spiritual, transcendental part of his being. When the 'gift' and 'blue'
of morning emerge in force from the 'death' of night, he transcends the
wretchedness of his physical, breathing body and becomes aware of a higher,
non-physical significance in himself:

> ecco il dono e l'azzurro
> usciti in forza dalla morte,
> ecco supero il corpo
> mio impoverito e il respiro
> e tutto da te riconosco,
> cielo

behold the gift and the blue / which have emerged in force from death, /
behold I overcome my impoverished / body and breath / and I acknowledge
everything as coming from you, / sky.

The morning light brings a 'fullness of love', and 'reproposed realities'; it makes
'seeing' and 'hearing' return anew, induces movement and allows him to 'be'
(lines 52, 63–4, 69–72).

As before, religious connotations would seem to be pertinent here. The light
symbolizes love, hope – life-affirmative instincts which keep returning to deflect
the negative ones (perhaps even 'oppression' is 'passion' in disguise: 'quando ogni
oppressione / già è velata passione che s'attende' ('when all oppression / is already
a veiled expected passion'), ('Prima del sole')). They are feelings which are not

so much cultivated by man, as instinctive and inherent in his make-up, divinely conferred.

And yet in 'Impossibilità della parola' ('The Impossible Word') Zanzotto calls himself 'reo di speranza e d'amore', guilty of precisely these two qualities of hope and love. For although they are indeed Christian virtues, would *his* conceptions of them still be considered Christian within a social context? In short, the ideas of 'Dal cielo' as presented above bring Zanzotto right back to the question of social commitment which he examines for one last time from a moral point of view.

Final Thoughts on Poetry and Social Commitment

He is guilty of 'speranza' because it was precisely hope which prevented him from feeling emotionally involved in the war (even though Zanzotto did in fact serve in it, although largely in the area of propaganda publications). Hope (given its association with 'fede' later in the poem) perhaps led him to believe in a non-violent solution to the war, and to maintain faith in humanity, thereby making him ill-prepared to share the purposeless 'sleep' or humble deification of his friends. But an optimism as great as this would border on escapism by normal standards and be denounced as a 'sporca speranza' ('shabby hope'):

> Che mi trattenne lungi
> da voi, dal vostro sonno
> sterile o dalla vostra
> umile apoteosi? Forse quella
> che dicono sporca speranza

What held me back far away / from you, from your sterile / sleep or your / humble apotheosis? Perhaps that / which they call shabby hope.

His 'amore' is equally culpable, perhaps also for its intellectual character – a love which believed in humaneness and expected it from humans, and which could not transform itself into a charitable act of self-sacrifice. For charity in the context of war was much less of a virtue than 'hope' and 'faith' (perhaps because in one sense it was involved in the perpetration of violence: those who died also fought and killed):

> Speranza e fede, virtù che dai cieli
> discendono, assai più che il fuoco offeso
> di carità

Hope and faith, virtues which descend / from the skies, much nore than the offended fire / of charity.

Charity was also, as Zanzotto says, 'offended'. The gesture of love by those who died – if it could be interpreted as such – was also a type of *vocative* which elicited a response ('attesa, eco, di testa / mozza' ('waiting, echo, of lopped off / head')), poorly and pathetically given by 'lo schema atono afoso delle lacrime' ('the toneless oppressive scheme of tears'). There is something blasphemous about the silence of the crowded sepulchre:

> Stipato avello, attesa, eco, di testa
> mozza: al più blasfemo
> dei silenzi equivale

Crowded tomb, waiting, echo, of lopped off / head: equivalent to the most / blasphemous of silences.

So whereas before in section 1 of the collection Zanzotto showed a degree of social awareness bereft, however, of social commitment, he now gives more precise reasons for that lack of commitment. Indeed in an article in *Poesia italiana contemporanea* (713–17) Zanzotto clearly makes the point that socially engaged art does very little to alter society. Poetry cannot be 'salvatrice' in the sense that it puts the wrongs of society right. It can only impinge upon society (or, as below, 'history') in so far as it can act as 'salute', 'verità', 'libertà' ('health', 'truth', 'liberty'):

> In reality poetry has never been redemptive in the form understood by the theorists of its most diverse functionalisms . . . . It was by itself, at all events, health; it has always been the most likely apparition of truth, liberty, and therefore of history: even poetry branded as uncommitted, that can boast in its honour to have been disliked by yesterday's leaders as much as by those of today.

'Impossibilità della parola' would seem to put the lid firmly on the question of commitment, so much a case of conscience in section 1 of *VCT*. The decision Zanzotto makes to reject committed writing would seem to be a conclusive one. Indeed in the penultimate poem of section 2 – 'Bucolica' – there is a reassertion of faith in a bucolic poetry which speaks of the countryside and its idyllic aspects. The world around the poet may be a stormy one but, as Zanzotto says, a rose will always hang at the edge of Arcady for the one he refers to as 'tu' – the female personage who for him personifies poetry:

> E se intorno la terra è tempestosa,
> se premono laggiù le rupi acerbe,
> oltre i secoli amica a te la rosa
> pende al lembo d'Arcadia pingue d'erbe

And if all around the land is raging, / if the bitter cliffs press down there, / for centuries to come your friend the rose / will hang for you on the edge of Arcady rich with grass.

In other words, the Arcadian world, which for Zanzotto was first created by Virgil in his *Georgics* and *Bucolics*, stands as a metaphor for poetry as it should be – a utopic space, free from civic and political engagement (a point made very clearly in Zanzotto's interview with Allen).

Ambivalence, it would seem, has finally been eradicated and Zanzotto will continue to write his landscape poetry with none of his previous remorse. But a problem remains to complicate issues and Zanzotto makes it known immediately after 'Bucolica' in 'Fuisse' ('To Have Been'), the final poem of section 2, thereby ending VCT on a precarious note. Here he voices the solemn recognition that it is becoming increasingly difficult to write the bucolic poem which attempts to perpetuate the Arcadian world when glimpses of that world are disappearing from the landscape ('Fuisse', a perfect infinitive in Latin reflects this loss). Although it is not actually stated in the poem, this is probably due (Hainsworth 1984, 120) to the movement of people towards the towns in the late 1950s and 1960s together with the new technological innovations which affected both the lives of those who remained in the peasant community and the landscape itself.

> Pace per voi per me
> buona gente senza più dialetto,
> senza pallide grandini
> di ieri, senza luce di vendemmie,
> pace propone e supremo torpore
> l'alone dei prati

Peace for you for me / good people now without dialect, / with none of yesterday's faint / hail, with none of the gleam of grape-harvests, / the halo of the fields / proposes peace and the utmost torpor

> Ah l'acqua troppo tenue che mi cola
> oltre la gola e gli occhi e di là di là s'invischia
> in tiepidi miseri specchi
> su cui l'ortica insuperbisce.
> Ed ah, ah soltanto, nei modi
> obsoleti di umili
> virgili, di pastori castamente
> avvizziti nei libri, nella conscia
> terrena polvere
>
>   ('Fuisse I')

Ah the excessively weak water which trickles through me / beyond my throat and my eyes and from there from away over there is snared / in lukewarm wretched mirrors / over which the nettle stands proudly. / And ah, ah only, in the obsolete / ways of humble / Virgils, of shepherds chastely / withered in books, in the conscious / earthly dust

> un nome avrò per quelle mani nude
> nel bollore dell'acqua nel nitore
> rodente della seta, per il volto
> che arse la falce,

per il corpo che brancica
scalfendo abissi di carbone?
('Fuisse II')

will I have a name for those bare hands / in the boiling water in the gnawing /
brightness of silk, for the face / burned by the sickle, / for the body which
gropes / as it scratches out abysses of coal?

Dialect is fading away, presumably being suppressed and replaced by the official
language; a lifeless torpor envelops the fields which no longer shine with as many
vineyards; and the waters have lost their idyllic attributes – they are weak, slimy
and warm (polluted, perhaps, by chemical waste). Humble lives such as those
of the housewife, the farmer, and the miner – a pre-scientific people relying
on their own spiritual and physical resourcefulness in the everyday task of living
and working – will soon have gone, and glimpses of Arcady will only be found
among the bards and shepherds of Virgil's withered pages.

To a certain extent the ideas of 'Fuisse' prefigure the content of *IXE*, Zanzotto's
next book of poetry. Its title obviously echoes once again the pastoral dialogues of
Virgil (to whom, Zanzotto tells us, the book was written in homage (Allen 255)).
But Zanzotto's attempted re-creation of a heroic Arcady in the appropriate
archaic and literary style is disturbed, as in 'Fuisse', by various aspects of the
present, modern age – most notably science and technology, as before, and the
language associated with each.

Chapter 3

Literature, Science, History
A Question of Culture in *IX Ecloghe* (1957–60)

> When I wrote a book entitled *IX Ecloghe*, it was in fact a homage (a presumptuous one, perhaps) to the great shadow of Virgil that reflects in itself all the contradictions of the meek man, the man far removed from any form of prevarication and violence who himself still gets pulled by circumstances to the centre of power. (Allen, 'Interview', 255)

The 'power' that Zanzotto refers to here would seem to be political power. Virgil, the 'meek man', was for Zanzotto the Virgil of the *Georgics* and the *Bucolics*, 'the Virgil who, taking up Theocritus' theme, created the Arcadian world' (Allen 255). The Virgil who 'gets pulled by circumstances to the centre of power' is the Virgil of the *Aeneid*, the Virgil who is the official poet of the Roman Empire. The comparison between Virgil and Zanzotto lies in the fact that Zanzotto too has had his 'bucolic' phase (the poems of *DIP*) where poetry was treated as a utopic space not to be sullied by a treatment of the contemporary Second World War. *VCT*, however, saw a violation of that conception of poetry when Zanzotto felt morally obliged to consider those who died during the First World War, and who now lie behind that bucolic landscape, and *IXE* will also, as we shall see, voice a similar political awareness.

But there is also another type of 'power' besides the political one which preoccupies Zanzotto in *IXE* and which, I believe, he also had in mind when he made the statement quoted above – the power of science, toward which he adopts an equivocal attitude. The poet or the 'meek man' is on the one hand 'removed' from the 'powerful' issues of politics and science, and on the other hand 'pulled' toward them, purely out of 'circumstance' in the case of history, more out of choice in the case of science (although, as will become apparent in the course of my chapter, certain scientific explorations in the late 1950s were of such vital concern to the poet that they 'demanded' comment).

Added to these two complicated viewpoints there is another that *IXE* displays – the poet's ambivalent attitude toward poetry. Consequently the areas of investigation which *IXE* offers can be posited as three: literature versus science, literature versus political history, and literature versus literature (the last two constituting a fuller inquiry into themes already treated in *VCT*). I shall examine these areas individually and in this order although there will be inevitable overlappings between the first and the third. In spite of the systematic nature of my approach, the book itself is multifaceted, and does not explore the themes of literature, science and history in an orderly, linear progression.

The term 'literature' is used here in a broad sense to comprise a number of related concepts, principally the literary tradition, lyric poetry, romanticism, and poetic inspiration. I shall specify during the course of my chapter to which of these individual concepts I am referring on different occasions. The areas of science that Zanzotto deals with are four: technological (most notably the phenomenon of space explorations), anatomical, medical and chemical. The historical theme that is most prevalent is that of war. Literature is generally associated with the 'human' element, science and history with the 'inhuman'.

LITERATURE VERSUS SCIENCE

There are five poems which fall under the first area of investigation – the relationship between literature and science: 'Ecloga I' ('Eclogue 1'), '13 settembre 1959 (Variante)' ('(Variant)'), 'Palpebra alzata' ('Raised Eyelid'), 'Appunti per un' Ecloga' ('Notes for an Eclogue'), and 'Ecloga VI'.

'Ecloga I', subtitled 'I lamenti dei poeti lirici' ('The Lyric Poets' Laments'), is one of the dialogue poems in the classical form of a debate between two personae – 'a' and 'b'. The identity of these two personae is not constant throughout all of the dialogue poems, but on this occasion 'a' generally equates with the poet and 'b' with lyric poetry.

'a''s discourse is divided into four sections separated by suspension points and the relationship between each of these sections is not readily apparent. In the first he expresses what does not seem to be a very positive view of lyric (landscape) poetry:

> a – Alberi, cespi, erbe, quasi
>   veri, quasi all'orlo del vero,
>   dal dominio del monte che la gran luce simula
>   sempre tornando, scendendo
>   a incristallirvi
>   in oniriche antologie

Trees, tufts, grasses, almost / real, almost on the edge of the real, / from the mountain's dominion which the great light feigns / always returning, descending / to crystallize yourselves / in oneiric anthologies.

The landscape – its trees, tufts and grasses – are 'almost real', almost on 'the edge of the real' in the sense that while being in this world they are endowed with an otherworldliness – an idea contemplated at length in *VCT* (see Chapter 2, pages 73–7).

This interpretation can be supported by lines 3 and 4 in the sequence above, for, as I illustrated in Chapter 2, Zanzotto proposes with a reasoning like that of natural theology (and Hölderlin) that the existence of an otherworldliness is suggested by 'light' – the light of the sun and the sky. Moreover, in the poem 'Io attesto' (*VCT*), the phenomenon of light turned 'altrove' is, as above, placed in direct relationship to a 'monte', and the mountain together with its light is inconsistent with the throbbing traffic-lights below ('la tua luce, di monte, luce volta / altrove, / . . . . / Tu (monte) distinto dal palpito / dei semafori incerti' (see translation, page 76.))

From the mountain's dominion, an otherwordly realm simulated by the vast light, landscape phenomena return – the poet says – and descend to crystallize themselves in oneiric anthologies. The verb 'incristallirvi' considered by itself does not necessarily have negative overtones, but through its association with the adjective 'oniriche' it seems to acquire them. The poetry of lyric anthologies is dreamy and removed from reality (an idea supported in the opening poem, 'Un libro di Ecloghe' ('A Book of Eclogues') where lyric poets are presented as astrologers, in other words, as star-gazers, or escapists: 'astrologi all'evasione intenti, / a liberar farfalle tra le rote superne?' ('astrologers intent on escape, / on freeing butterflies among the celestial wheels?')). The otherworldly qualities of the landscape are 'crystallized' in the sense of 'fossilized' in verses which grow old and mouldy on abandoned shelves (an idea reinforced later in the poem and to which I will return).

Because of these two negative factors involved in the writing of lyric poetry, the 'saying', the communicative gesture of the landscape which acts upon the poet's sense impressions inviting him to write poetry about the landscape, is in vain: the soft 'lament' which the wood whispers is a sad, obstinate but useless speech:

> mite selva un lamento
> mite bisbigliate un accorato
> ostinato non utile dire

gentle wood, you whisper / a soft lament a heartbroken / stubborn useless saying.

The question of sense impressions acquires more relevance as the poem proceeds:

> Significati allungano le dita,
> sensi le antenne filiformi

Fingers stretch out meanings, / thread-like antennae senses.

Semantically, the word 'Significati' could be considered as being equivalent to 'sensi' (which can also mean 'meanings') so that in one respect the second line here merely repeats the idea of the first – the notion of a text where there is an extension or multiplication of meaning (the implications of this idea will emerge later in the poem). However, given the reference to 'antenne filiformi', the feelers or sensory organs of crustaceans, it would seem that 'sensi' is also to be understood as referring to 'the senses'. Persona 'a' is juxtaposing two methods of writing – one where meanings ('Significati') are organized consciously by the poet's hand, and one where meanings are dictated more by the senses; an intellectual response to the world versus a more spontaneous and sensory response (an idea pursued as the poem develops).

Lyric poetry is undoubtedly involved with the sensory response, and as a further antithesis to the intellectual element, even with the emotional or romantic – a possible target for self-irony. This is reinforced in the lines which conclude the first section of 'a''s discourse:

> Sillabe labbra clausole
> unisono con l'ima terra.
> Perfettissimo pianto, perfettissimo

Syllables lips clauses / unite with the lowest earth. / Most perfect weeping, most perfect.

In contrast to the slow moving and contemplative tone of section 1 of 'a''s discourse, section 2 is speedy and agitated. This is in keeping with a sudden shift of emphasis from star-gazers to star-explorers, from lyric poets to scientists. The second are viewed partly in terms of what one has already been told of the first:

> E tenta di valere, accenna, avvampa
> l'altra mano dell'uomo.
> Da lei protesa
> rugge, accelera il razzo a dipanare
> il metallo totale dei cieli.
> Per lei fibrilla il silenzio, incellulisce.
> Oh aquiloni orientati
> piú su dell'infanzia, piú del punto che brilla,
> mano da un fuoco a un altro, mano bisturi

And man's other hand / tries to be of value, it beckons, blazes. / Impelled by that hand / the rocket roars and speeds off to unravel / all the metal of the skies. / It makes silence fibrillate, form cells. / Oh kites steered / higher than infancy, higher than the shining point, / hand from one fire to another, scalpel hand.

Whereas the hand of the lyric poet is involved in his oneiric anthologies, the 'other hand of man' – the hand of the scientist – tries to 'be of value'. 'a' is reinforcing a point already established in VCT but now seen in the context of the practicality of our modern and technological world: lyric poetry is considered to be of little social application (see Chapter 2, pages 70–1). The age of science is replacing the age of poetry.

The scientist's investigation of Nature is much more important than the poet's, although this is obviously not an attitude held by 'a' who compares the game of launching rockets to the children's game of flying kites. (Similarly, in 'Per la finestra nuova' ('Through the New Window') science is reduced to the level of science fiction and spurned as a game: 'gli squillanti satelliti / che il gioco umano ha lanciati, con lampi / di fantascienza' ('the shrill-sounding satellites / which human sport has launched, with science-fiction / flashes'). 'Lampi' in the sense of 'flashes of genius' is clearly ironic.) The scientist, far from being concerned with Nature's otherworldliness, sees Nature as nothing more than soulless matter– for him the skies are 'metal'. His investigation is authoritative and implicitly violent. The image of the rocket accelerating to investigate the 'metal of the skies' suggests an attempt to unravel the mysteries of Nature, to master it through reason and intellect. That 'a' regards this as a violation of its mystery is suggested in his description of the astronaut's hand burning upon the accelerator as it thrusts the rocket roaring into space – an attitude of aggressiveness being imputed to the astronaut – as well as in his reference to the hand which moves from 'one fire to another'. But it is even more forcefully underlined in his use of surgical terminology: 'fibrilla', 'incellulisce', 'mano bisturi'. The hand of the technological scientist is being equated with the 'scalpel hand' of the anatomist dissecting a human body ('a' is reinforcing that animism of Nature which the technological scientist ignores). The rocket splits the silence of Nature (and one recalls the 'soft', 'whispered' lament of the forest in section 1) like an anatomist splitting muscles into fibrils ('Per lei fibrilla il silenzio'). 'a' is acting as a mouthpiece for Zanzotto's rejection of modern day (here planetary) technology, already alluded to in VCT (see page 70), and as before, the line of thought would seem to be very Heideggerian. In *The Question Concerning Technology* Heidegger attacked twentieth-century technology (including the planetary technology of the United States and the Soviet Union) seeing in it not an authentic *techné* (technology) which brings into true being that which is already inherent in *physis* (Nature) (the philosopher's term for authentic *techné* was thus *zu entbergen*, meaning 'to reveal'). Rather, planetary technology was viewed by Heidegger as a provocation (*das Herausfordern*) of *physis*, forcing the elements of the natural world to become, what he called, *gegenstände*, which can mean two things: first, 'objects' (to which we may compare 'a''s view (above) of Nature as signifying nothing more than soulless, inanimate matter for the astronaut who sees the 'skies' as 'metal'); and second, 'that which stands against', thereby suggesting that technology's exploitation of Nature, its forcing of Nature to yield knowledge and energy has managed to turn the natural world against man.

It would seem, therefore, that whereas in section 1 of 'a''s discourse his attitude towards lyric, landscape poetry verged on the negative, he is now in section 2 beginning to retract that negative criticism when he considers the scientist's more violent 'treatment' of Nature. But what follows in the poem shows that the issue is not as clear-cut as this:

> mano da un fuoco a un altro, mano bisturi.
> Mano dove gli strati serpeggiano nel coma,
> dove il ventre della terra accampa
> profili irriferibili,
> funzioni insospettate, osceni segni,
> foglie e corpi di sofismi, il libro
> che non scrisse, la penna, non illustrò, il colore.
> Autopsie, autopsie.
> Mano da un fuoco a un altro, mano bisturi

hand from one fire to another, scalpel hand. / Hand where strata snake into the coma, / where earth's belly asserts / unrepeatable profiles, / unsuspected functions, obscene signs, / the book which the pen did not write, and the colour did not illustrate / contains leaves and bodies of sophisms. / Autopsies, autopsies. / Man from one fire to another, scalpel hand.

The landscape is not, perhaps, as gentle ('mite') or as otherworldly as the lyric poet believes. We are told that there are insidious activities and lewd goings on in the belly of the earth: 'a''s thought has now swung in an opposite direction, and he is is now contemplating the violent aspect of *Nature* – destruction caused by earthquakes, volcanic eruptions, floods, hurricanes and so on – and the possibility that Nature is nothing but a bestial, teeming force (an idea contemplated in 'Esistere psichicamente', *VCT*. See pages 76–7). The book of Nature which the pen did not write and the colour did not illustrate – the real, phenomenal landscape, not landscape poetry or paintings – contains ('a' proclaims in an attitude reminiscent of Leopardi) 'leaves and bodies of sophisms' – an element of falsehood, of deceit. Given this violence and given this deceit, 'a' comes to the conclusion that the scalpel hand even belongs to it. The technological scientist, and Nature, both in their own way are carrying out 'autopsies'. This is even now true of the poet himself who is performing an autopsy or critical dissection of lyric poetry in this cryptic discourse *about* lyric poetry (the scalpel – a small, light, straight knife – is, significantly, shaped for holding like a pen). This section displays that organized ambiguity that was juxtaposed in section 1 with a lyrical spontaneity.

However, in the final two sections of 'a''s discourse, his negative thinking both about the landscape and lyric, landscape poetry is retracted. (Contradictory attitudes toward poetry will characterize the collection as several critics have observed.) Ideas on lyric poetry already presented in section 1 are now re-established in a totally positive light:

insinui, selva,
tu molto umiliata,
tu quasi viva, piú che viva, quasi viva
– le tue foglie movendo
bagliori come d'insetto nel lago
albuminoso che fu notte fu giorno

you creep in, wood, / you who are so humiliated, / you who are almost alive, / more than alive, almost alive / – your leaves moving / flashes like those of an insect in the albuminous / lake that was night was day.

A link with section 1 is indicated here through the use of the terms 'insinui' and 'quasi viva', reminiscent of the earlier 'ostinato non utile dire' and 'quasi / veri'. The otherworldliness of the landscape ('quasi / veri') may be fossilized in lyric poetry. But the scientist's treatment of the landscape is a much more harmful one: it humiliates ('umiliata') and destroys ('quasi viva') the wood. The fact that in spite of this the wood obstinately continues to assert itself ('insinui, selva') is now seen as a positive gesture, and in this sense 'a' can claim that it is 'piú che viva' (compare Dante's 'selva', *Inferno* 1, 2; and 'la foresta spessa e viva', *Purgatorio* 28, 2). By means of the highly poetic image with which the section ends – the light sifting and shifting through the leaves of the wood like the flickering lights of insects on a white lake – 'a' seems to want to re-establish the relevance of the lyrical treatment of landscape, and this in spite of the problems facing the lyric poet in contemporary society, outlined in section 5:

Chiedono, implorano, i poeti,
li nutre Lazzaro alla sua mensa,
come cigni biancheggiano.
. . .
Nomi hanno, date con interrogativo,
schede, schemi,
cadaveri com'elitre
in oniriche antologie.
Perfettissimo pianto, perfettissimo.
I poeti tra cui
se tu volessi pormi
'cortese donna mia'
sidera feriam vertice

The poets ask, they implore, / Lazarus feeds them at his table, / they grow white like swans. / . . . / They have names, dates with question marks, / index-cards, outlines, / corpses like elytra / in oneiric anthologies. / Most perfect weeping, most perfect. / Poets among whom / if you would like to place me / 'my gracious lady' / I would walk so tall that I could touch the stars.

The question of lyric poetry's social irrelevance is resumed from section 2. The pale faced romantics, growing white like swans, plead in vain for recognition in the ruthless world of publishing, for lyric poetry does not sell. At best, they, with Lazarus, feed off the crumbs which fall from the rich man's table. Theirs are the obscure names on filing cards and their dates have question marks; their works are the museum pieces of libraries. Whereas before in section 1 the 'Perfettissimo pianto' was that *of* lyric poets, 'a' now voices one *for* lyric poets. Yet in spite of this lamentable condition, he, like Horace, if only honoured with the name of 'lyric poet' would soar to ethereal heights (see Horace, Ode 1, Book 1).

Having listened at length to 'a''s vacillating speech, lyric poetry ('b') now intervenes to sustain this euphoria. For his lyrical predecessors an 'immodest, loving confession' sufficed, and so it should be for him:

> b –   Come per essi, basterà la tua
>   confessione, immodesta, amorosa,
>   e quasi vera e piú che vera
>   come il canone detta

As for them, your immodest, / loving confession will suffice, / – a confession almost real and more than real / as the canon dictates.

Sincere sentimentality, though it may be considered otiose and not relevant to *this* world ('quasi vera' echoes the 'quasi / veri' of the opening lines of the poem), is still valid and important: it is 'piú che vera'.

'a' answers, suggesting that all the scepticism he has expressed with regard to lyric poetry bears little relevance in reality:

> 'Ma io non sono nulla
> nulla piú che il tuo fragile annuire'

'But I am nothing / nothing more than your frail assent'.

He is nothing but 'b''s (lyric poetry's) consent : 'b' dictates to him in the form of inspiration and he can only instinctively respond.

The conclusion arrived at in 'Ecloga I': that in spite of the greater social application of technological science, lyric poetry is still feasible and important today, is adhered to in the rest of the poems in the collection that focus upon lyricism and technological science.

In '13 settembre 1959 (Variante)' Zanzotto is concerned not so much with lyric poetry in particular as with literary language in general; and whereas technological science (again the phenomenon of space explorations) is once more seen in a negative light, anatomical science (linked here with medical science) is now viewed positively.

The date referred to in the title is significant. On 12 September 1959 the Russians launched 'Luna 2'. It was the first spacecraft ever actually to land on the moon, discovering how it was enveloped by a layer of low-energy ionized gas. '(Variante)' is a litany to the moon in which Zanzotto attempts to give it back its mystery, associating it in the course of the poem with the religious, the sacrilegious, witchcraft, literature, and above all with woman. Contrary to what Agosti believes (1973, 17) there is an emphasis on meaning as well as on sound in the poem.

The most striking characteristic of the poem is its language: Zanzotto is most interested in highlighting the influence of Latin and Greek on Italian – how Latin and Greek helped to form not only the Italian literary lexicon but also a non-literary lexicon, most notably here the language of anatomical and medical science: 'distonia' ('dystonia'), 'atonia' ('atony'), 'morula' ('morula'), 'paralisi' ('paralysis'), 'phiala' ('phial'), 'cariocinesi' ('karyokinesis'), and 'Vertigine' ('vertigo') are all terms either from the field of anatomy or the field of medical science. (For other views on the role of scientific vocabulary in *IXE* see Frattini 276; Agosti 1973, 15–16; Milone 222; Hainsworth 1982, 108; and Conti-Bertini 1980, 212.)

The subsequent link one presumes Zanzotto is making between the language of literature and the language of anatomical and medical science goes, however, further than this. Not only do both of these languages have a common etymological background. Zanzotto aims to show how anatomical and medical language can also be poetic. This scientific vocabulary rather than jarring with the literary context (Conti-Bertini) interacts and converges with the literary lexicon just as the majority of the words in the poem interact to reveal affinities and associations but also contradictions. It is a form of composition that Zanzotto has alluded to in a recent discussion of his poetry: 'the poet . . . links up ideas and images which usually are not associated with each other, and which in a specific situation, can reveal affinities and unexpected contiguities' (*Sulla poesia* 93) and it is such an important aspect of '(Variante)' that it merits some detailed attention.

> 1 Luna puella pallidula,
>   Luna flora eremitica,
> 3 Luna unica selenita,
>   distonia vita traviata,
> 5 atonia vita evitata,
>   mataia, matta morula,
> 7 vampirisma, paralisi,
>   glabro latte, polarizzato zucchero,
> 9 peste innocente, patrona inclemente,
>   protovergine, alfa privativo,
> 11 degravitante sughero,
>   pomo e potenza della polvere,
> 13 phiala e coscienza delle tenebre,
>   geyser, fase, cariocinesi,
> 15 Luna neve nevissima novissima,
>   Luna glacies–glaciei
> 17 Luna medulla cordis mei,

Vertigine
19 per secanti e tangenti fugitiva

La mole della mia fatica
21 già da me sgombri
la mia sostanza sgombri
23 a me cresci a me vieni a te vengo
. . . .

. . . .
24 (Luna puella pallidula)
. . . .

Moon pale little girl, / Moon hermitic flower, / Moon one and only inhabitant of the moon,/ dystonia life led astray, / atony avoided life, / wanton, mad morula, / vampirism, paralysis, / glabrous milk, polarized sugar, / innocent pestilence, merciless patroness, / protovirgin, privative alpha, / gravity-defying cork, / apple and power of dust, / phial and consciousness of darkness, / geyser, phase, karyokinesis, / Moon snow snowiest newest, / Moon ice–of ice / Moon marrow of my heart, / Vertigo / fleeting through secants and tangents / / Already you move away from me / the bulk of my toil /you move away my substance / you grow to me you come to me I come to you / ... / ... / (Moon pale little girl) / ... /.

The feminine personification of the moon in line 1 remains throughout the rest of the poem. Although '(Variante)' mainly echoes the *Litanies* of the Virgin (and to a lesser extent the Emperor Hadrian's 'Animula vagula blandula' ('Charming, wandering little soul')) line 2 contains other literary overtones – of Leopardi's 'La ginestra o il fiore del deserto' ('The Broom or the Desert Flower'); while sustaining the allusion to religion in the reference to the flower's hermitic existence. The antithetical address which follows would seem to bear an ironical reference to space explorations and their investigation of life on other planets: it is the moon who is the only hypothetical inhabitant of the moon!

'Distonia' provides the first example of an anatomical term used in a poetical sense. In the language of anatomy it refers to a lack or decrease of tonus, that is to say, of firmness or tension in the muscles. As such it evokes the waxing and waning process of the moon wherein the moon appears to lack rigidity, to be a malleable and elastic substance.

A certain malleability is implied on a figurative level in the term 'vita traviata' as well. The moon leads the 'corrupted life' of the 'courtesan' (*La traviata*).

'Atonia' means the same as 'distonia' but unlike the latter it can be used metaphorically to denote weakness or debility, reinforcing the 'pale girl' image of line 1.

'Vita evitata' (a similar form of which generally appears in litanies) also interacts with earlier terms. If the moon is an 'avoided life' it lives a solitary existence, shunned by humanity, underlining thereby its hermitical state (line 2) while contradicting the reference to space explorations suggested in line 3.

The Greek ματαία for which Zanzotto has created the Italian equivalent 'mataia' has a plethora of meanings: vain, idle, useless, wanton, rash, offensive and irreverent. Wantonness, another possible attribute of the 'courtesan', relates back to 'vita traviata'; the adjective 'matta' following 'mataia' has slender associations with rashness; and the notion of irreverence, while jarring with the religious overtones of 'flora eremitica' (line 2) and the appellative 'protovergine' used later in line 10, coincides to some extent with the moon's involvement in witchcraft alluded to in the line which follows (line 7).

'Morula' is the third anatomical term of the poem indicating the initial stage in the development of the embryo when the latter is constituted by a mass of cells in the shape of a mulberry (from 'morus', 'mulberry'). The image of the developing embryo, reminiscent again of the waxing stage of the moon, makes a new link between the moon and the mother who is of course attuned to moon cycles in a mysterious way.

'Vampirisma' – a form of necrophily in which the victim is violated after being killed – inverts the order of violence one associates with line 3 in the context of 'Ecloga I' with its reference to the 'autopsies' of astronauts. Relevant in this respect is a later address to the moon as 'cariocinesi' (line 14). Again, whereas in 'Ecloga I' the astronaut was compared to the anatomical scientist splitting muscles into fibrils ('Per lei fibrilla il silenzio'), the scalpel hand is now that of the moon – karyokinesis is the anatomical term for the process of dividing a cell nucleus, indicating the arrangement of protoplasmic fibres into definite figures.

'Paralisi' (the first medical term in the poem) following 'vampirisma' is a similarly contradictory address working against the implications of growth in both 'distonia' and 'morula'.

'Glabro latte', although predominantly a reference to the moon's texture and colour as it appears from earth, strengthens the mother associations of line 6 through the sheer sensuality of the image and its reference to milk. If 'zucchero' is extracted from its context (the playful portrayal of the moon as a rounded 'lump' of sugar) and seen in relationship to 'latte', the symbiotic relationship indicated in 'morula' is reinforced: milk is associated with the mother but also with the child; sugar is a food also related to childhood (and Zanzotto speaks of it in this context in SA (53–6) as he does there also of the 'apple' (54), another metaphor for the moon in line 12).

Further suggestiveness is achieved if in the same way one takes the adjective 'polarizzato' out of context and considers it alone. The verb 'polarizzare' in its figurative sense recalls the mythical ability of the moon to polarize one's gaze and induce madness. In this way it echoes the adjective 'matta' of line 6.

'Peste innocente, patrona inclemente', while presenting a rhyme form common to litanies, also reinforces the child-mother relationship suggested in the previous line through its juxtapositioning of innocent mischief and the implacable authority of the 'protectress'. The latter, it would seem, is also the Virgin, given the appellative 'protovergine' which follows. Together the two addresses 'patrona inclemente', 'protovergine', present, as before, a conscious clash of the profane and the religious: 'patrona' and 'protovergine' could easily find a place in an imaginary litany to the Virgin; the adjective 'inclemente' could not.

'Alfa privativo' has a tenuous link with this process of negating 'positive' terms with others that seem antithetical in nature. The first letter of the Greek alphabet is used as a negatory prefix (as, for example, in 'atonia', line 5). By itself, however, 'alfa' also denotes the principal star of every constellation and brings one's attention back to the moon.

The moon as a 'cork' or 'fishing float' ('sughero') invokes the idea of 'buoyancy'. 'Degravitante' implies a contradiction of the laws of gravity, a moving upwards instead of downwards. Together with 'sughero' – associated with trees ('sughero' meaning cork-oak in the language of botany) – the phrase recalls the manner in which the moon causes sap to rise upwards in trees. Cork also has the function of protecting trees against parasites, and a parasitic element has already been alluded to in lines 3 and 7: man as a parasite of the moon; the moon as a vampire.

Although inducing sap to rise, the moon holds no water vapour of its own (its gravity being much weaker than earth's) and 'potenza della polvere' suggests its bone-dry surface. Immediately, the image is contradicted by 'phiala' – a vessel for liquids (generally medical ones) – as well as by 'geyser' – a manifestation of vulcanism represented by emissions of hot, mineralized water. 'Geyser' then runs counter to the allusions of snow and ice which follow: 'Luna neve nevissima novissima', 'Luna glacies–glaciei'.

'Novissima', chosen probably for its phonic associations with 'nevissima', is, like the latter, a neologism of a sort, a superlative degree of 'luna nuova' – one of the four phases of the moon brought to mind through the reference to 'fase' in the previous line.

'Glacies–glaciei' has a tonal relationship with the rest of the poem, for the declension-reciting one associates with learning the Latin language reflects the incantatory, liturgical nature of the whole of this piece.

'Medulla' reinforces 'distonia' and 'atonia' for whether considered in its Latin meaning as marrow, or in its 'common' Italian meaning as pith, or pulp of fruit (although in a rare, literary sense it can also mean marrow) the emphasis is equally upon a spongy and pliable substance. As 'marrow' it also maintains the link with anatomy present in 'distonia' and 'atonia'.

'Cordis mei', directly following 'medulla', is another anatomical term although not used in the same register as the above: it combines the emotional with the physical: 'my heart' is also to be interpreted as 'my sweetheart'.

'Vertigine', the second medical term of the poem has, like 'polarizzato zucchero', a humorous effect: the earth spinning endlessly around the moon is causing the moon to suffer from vertigo.

The moon 'fleeing through secants and tangents' in line 19 emphasizes how the moon will always be out of reach and unfamiliar ('fleeing') in spite of the efforts of selenographers (evoked by the mathematical terminology); yet, paradoxically, Zanzotto seems to feel that his incantations have brought it nearer, have made it more familiar ('a me cresci a me vieni a te vengo'), so that in this sense it disappears and reappears like the waxing and waning process itself. It is almost as if by repeating the 'incantation' (and the poem ends with a return to the beginning) he will come even closer and closer to conjuring it up.

Meaning, therefore, in '(Variante)' is important, if not fixed. Its rhetorical style stands in sharp contrast with the ponderous debating of 'Ecloga I'. As in 'Ecloga I' technology is condemned: the bracketing of the penultimate line of the poem, as well as of part of the title, suggests how the moon is downgraded by science. However, what is new and important on the thematic level is Zanzotto's positive attitude towards anatomical science as opposed to the negative one of 'Ecloga I'. This positive attitude is suggested in the manner in which terminology from the field of anatomy and medicine interact with the literary lexicon to become literary or 'poetic' themselves.

The idea that there can be something poetic about science has in fact been presented by Zanzotto in *Sulla poesia* where he divides attitudes towards science into two separate areas: there are those who acknowledge its poetic element, its inventiveness, and the manner in which it avails itself of imagination; and there are those who interpret it in accordance with rigid and rational canons:

> You know that there is a dispute going on between those who would be inclined to codify the development of science in accordance with well-defined canons, even if they are too rigid and rational, and those who, on the other hand, can see in science a bit of an anarchic, 'poetic' spiritedness. It seems to me that the latter, even if they are perhaps exaggerating, are not altogether wrong; because certain scientific intuitions really do seem to be things that have come from out of the blue. (94)

As an example of such scientific intuition Zanzotto refers to Newton's use of the apple in his theory of gravitation, and continues:

> We can therefore say that the creativity of science, however much it has to do with the everyday hardness and concreteness of reality, nevertheless avails itself of fantasy, even if it doesn't pivot exclusively on fantasy, and it often bears a similarity to the inventiveness of poetry.

Science is also discussed in his interview with Camon where Zanzotto displayed his ambivalence towards the subject already suggested by the contradictory attitudes of 'Ecloga I' and '(Variante)'. What he rejects is the 'categoricalness' of science in respect of Nature and man: 'a certain conception of science as an absolute "categoricalness" in the face of, not only Nature, but also man' (and the phenomenon of space explorations is met again with special disapproval:

'human hideousness in its contact with spatial and temporal immensity'). The aspects of scientific research that interest him are its 'great propositions, and images and realities; its new words', and the possibility of superimposing the 'novelties' of science onto the familiar things of everyday life: 'we can try to bring . . . its innovations into contact with well-known human materials, carry out "iridescent" extrapolations' (158–9). The 'distonia', 'atonia', 'morula', 'paralisi', 'phiala', 'cariocinesi' and 'Vertigine' in '(Variante)' provide examples of this procedure: they are, I believe, '"iridescent" extrapolations'.

The link between poetry and science is tightened even further in 'Palpebra alzata'. Whereas in 'Ecloga I' 'a' condemned the technological scientist for his unemotional, intellectual treatment of Nature, now in 'Palpebra alzata' Zanzotto ironizes a school of literature likewise renowned for its scientific approach; one which in striking at '"le coeur romantique des choses"' (Robbe-Grillet 20) ('the romantic heart of things') repudiates subjectivism, promotes super-objectivity and presents detailed descriptions of phenomena devoid of intrinsic human values and qualities: the 'École du regard' (known also as the *nouveau roman* (new novel) writers) to whose followers the poem is dedicated.

> Essere un puro (unicamente un) raggio
> dunque è il destino
> cui ci ridusse il volere divino?

To be a pure (one and only) ray / is that therefore the destiny / to which divine will reduced us?

For them there is only one way of 'seeing', of registering reality ('(unicamente un) raggio'), for given their repudiation of the subjective point of reference it is never a *particular* mind that is being exposed nor a *particular* pair of eyes that is viewing the world. Reality chased and ransacked 'wrinkle' by 'wrinkle' ('Esser ciò che si / . . . / insegue fruga / la realtà ruga a ruga' ('To be that which one / . . . / pursues rummages / reality wrinkle by wrinkle')) – a reference, it would seem, to their meticulous, geometrical descriptions of reality (for which one needs fully opened eyes – one meaning of 'Palpebra alzata') – is defined as a 'campo dell'erosione' ('field of erosion'), an 'egro spiraglio / (dissi ieri)' ('sickly glimmer / (I said yesterday)'): not a celebration but an 'erosion' of reality, and this 'erosion' of reality reduces its significance. 'Egro spiraglio' – a quotation from 'Esistere psichicamente', *VCT*, (hence the 'dissi ieri') – was used there to indicate not the poetical or spiritual side of the landscape (its otherworldly qualities) but the landscape as brute, inanimate matter (see Chapter 2, pages 76–7). In the same way, the *nouveau roman* writers are not concerned with the spirit or poetry of things (anthropomorphism) but 'thingness' itself: 'chosisme'. 'Or le monde n'est ni signifiant ni absurde. Il est, tout simplement' ('Now the world is neither significant nor absurd. It, quite simply, exists') (Robbe-Grillet 18), and before such an attitude Zanzotto is quizzically raising an eyebrow (another meaning of 'Palpebra alzata').

For Zanzotto there is something flat and bloodless, indeed even sorrowful about this neutral perception of the world. It is one in which 'energy' is bled dry ('energia che si svena' ('energy which slashes its veins')); it is a 'pena' ('affliction') in comparison with his own manner of 'seeing' in which he aims to recapture 'il viso / lieto del mondo' ('the happy / face of the world').

His own manner of 'seeing', as Zanzotto goes on to suggest, may well function on the basis of a neurosis, at an opposite pole to the rationally objective perception of reality presented by the *nouveau romanciers*. Within the poet and without there are 'vertigine e tenebre' ('dizziness and darkness') – alternating periods of vertigo and depression (compare Steiner on Heidegger (146): 'Being . . . is 'everything'; but it is also indivisibly implicit in *nothingness* . . . all of us know Being in moments of anguish and of vertigo. We can write *Sein: Nichts*, says Heidegger'). And it is precisely these exceptional moments of excitability and depression, moments of Being which exist above and below the flat continuum of existence that are conducive to poetry ('tu') (an idea pursued in 'Riflesso' ('Reflection-Reflex') to be examined later). They reliably return to permeate the non-inspirational moments of everyday life (moments when the poet's head lies 'empty' on the page) and are characterized by a vitality (note the verb 'riarmi' ('you rearm me')) absent from the 'bloodless', mathematical exercise of the *nouveau roman*.

> Sí, in me, e fuori, vertigine e tenebre.
> Ma in me e fuori
> tanto frutto e vittoria di colori
> che, se anche vuoto
>
> il mio capo giace sulla pagina
> . . .
> anche se il cuore turbato ne sente
> le alte porte cadute, ah, tu, clemente
> di fontane, . . .
> . . .
> del tuo latte mi sazi, mai sazio,
> e mi riarmi di tutto il tuo spazio

Yes, in me, and without, dizziness and darkness. / But in me and without / so much fruit and victory of colours / that, even if my head / lies empty on the page / . . . / even if my disturbed heart feels / that its high doors have fallen, ah, you, merciful / of fountains, . . . / you satiate me with your milk, never satiated, / and you rearm me with all of your space.

'Appunti per un'Ecloga' re-establishes a definite distinction between literature and science. As in 'Ecloga I' science is anatomical, presented unfavourably and functions as a metaphor. Here, however, it also maintains its literal value. 'Literature' is less well defined than in previous poems. It is not a question of lyric poetry, literary language, or the *nouveau roman*, but the sensory, and emotional or spiritual response to the world – the human element – that was associated with the writing of lyric poetry in 'Ecloga I'. Spirituality is tied up with the notion of a metaphysical (and Utopian) poetry at the end of the poem.

The main thrust of the poem is the 'anancasma che si chiama vita' ('the anancasma one calls life'), that is to say, the automated nature of modern-day living ('anancasma', from the Greek meaning 'compulsion' denotes an obsessive repetition of thoughts and gestures). 'b', 'c', 'd' and 'e', indicated as 'personae' at the head of the poem are not actually personae in the body of the poem. 'b' is 'materia, macchie, pseudo-braille' ('matter, spots, pseudo-braille'), 'c', 'codici vari per tutti i suoni' ('various codes for all sounds'), 'd', a 'Catena di dattili, spondei etc.' ('chain of dactyls, spondees etc.'), and 'e', 'simboli matematici etc.' ('mathematical symbols etc.'). Zanzotto is attempting to suggest the dehumanization of the human: man has become just another symbol in a semiotic universe which is turning a subjective perception of the world through the senses into a thing of the past. We have now braille for fun ('pseudo-braille') and sounds can be represented by codes.

Equally operative in this battle against the human element is the increasing power and conventionalism of science (what Zanzotto called in his interview with Camon 'the excess of science-power'). 'a', the other persona of the poem identifiable as in 'Ecloga I' with lyric poetry, claims that what is important today is not the 'carme civile o intimo' ('civil or intimate poem') (a Carduccian or Hermetic poetry) but the 'retina o reticolo, / ma poi trama ed omento' ('retina or reticulum, / but then weft and omentum'): four phenomena the poet collectively calls a 'convenzione'.

The statement is ambiguous but begins to make sense when one considers the relationship between 'retina', 'reticolo', 'trama' and 'omento'. The first is derived from the Latin 'rete' because the blood veins in the eye are in the form of a 'network'. 'Reticolo' (also from 'rete') refers generally to any design or structure having the approximate form of a net. More specifically it denotes the second stomach of a ruminant. 'Trama', in the sense of 'weft', is also a kind of network; while 'omento' is the reticulated membrane which envelopes the small intestine.

All four terms therefore emphasize a net-like structure, and three of them ('retina', 'reticolo', and 'omento') bear references to anatomy. The point being made is that what is fashionable today is not an interest in the emotional responses of the body but rather the scientific study of bodily structure.

However much in this respect the science of anatomy is being condemned *per se*, it also seems to be functioning metaphorically. Anatomy epitomizes a modern-day preference for matter over spirit, the physical over the metaphysical. This is what is intimated in the remainder of the poem.

'a' proceeds to echo Dante:

> O quale e quanto in quella viva stella
> pur vinse, quale e quanto si sospinse
> oltre le soglie della sua stessa luce
> al di là del silenzio quale e quanto t'induce!

oh the quality and the magnitude in that living star / still conquered, the quality and the magnitude thrust themselves / beyond the thresholds of its own light / the quality and the magnitude induces you beyond silence!

The allusion is to lines 91–3 of *Paradiso* XXIII:

> E come ambo le luci mi dipinse
> il quale e il quanto della viva stella
> che là su vince, come qua giù vinse

And as the quality and the magnitude of the living star / who conquers there above, as she conquers here below / were depicted in both my eyes.

The 'viva stella' of Dante's quotation is a reference to the Virgin, operating in Zanzotto's quotation as a symbol of the spiritual. 'a' is contemplating, quite simply, the lack of importance now attached to the spiritual; the disappearance of the spiritual; and how its disappearance is conducive to poetic abdication, an absolute silence which cannot even be judged in terms of speech.

'a''s negative attitude does not last for long, however, and in the section which follows silence is rejected in favour of speech:

> Integrando, sul limite, sospinti
> solo minimamente sopra il suolo
> dell'impossibile, impossibilmente
> qui, e pure qui a dire l'impossibile
> e il possibile. E reversibilmente

Finding the integer, on the limit, driven / only minimally above the ground / of the impossible, impossibly / here, and yet here to talk about the impossible / and the possible. And reversibly.

The mathematical term 'integrando' (meaning to find the 'integer', the whole number) is being used ironically and in an abstract sense. Poetry has none of the rigidity and logic of mathematics. The 'integer' it searches for is a metaphysical one – a state of totality or plenitude. It searches for it on the 'limit', a word, for Zanzotto, synonymous with the sacred (as became apparent in his interview with Camon: 'The sacred (the limit), one must always have it before one's eyes, even when in danger of being blinded by it' (155)). Since 'limite' has associations with the sacred, the word recalls the 'viva stella' and her spiritual attributes, thereby re-emphasizing the metaphysical nature of poetry's search.

There is a Utopian element too in poetry of this kind (the link between poetry and Utopia is also recognized by Zanzotto elsewhere: 'Poetry then becomes the metaphor of another world . . ., a world where Utopia represents itself in embryo' (Allen 254)). Poets like 'a' are thrust 'above the ground / of the impossible, impossibly / here' (a contradiction like that involved in the word 'Utopia' itself: from the Greek, *ou* = not, *topos* = place). Their poetry aims to lay down new standards of possibilities (it talks about 'the impossible and the possible') but without fully realizing the nature of the Utopia it aims towards (Utopia is represented in embryo, as Zanzotto says). This is the idea behind 'a''s concluding remark:

> Avverbio in 'mente', lattea sicurezza

> Adverb in 'mind', milky security.

Any adverb he might use to qualify the Utopian state is kept in 'mind' rather than expressed (there is a play upon 'mente' as a common adverbial ending). To begin to talk about it in concrete terms would be to suggest that it were familiar. And it must remain unfamiliar, unknowable, so as to keep the desire to attain it alive. Nurturing it in the abstract provides a sense of 'milky security'.

The very subtitle of 'Ecloga VI' – 'Ravenna, Macromolecola, Ideologie' ('Ravenna, Macromolecule, Ideologies') – contains an allusion to the poetic and the scientific as two different 'ideologies'. Ravenna is the burial-place of Dante, the 'poeta-nume' ('numen-poet') to whom the narrator refers in the final section of the poem. 'Macromolecola', as Zanzotto's note explains, is a 'made-up word worthy of presiding over our reality', suggesting once again the power and conventionalism of science – this time, however, chemical science. Its presentation as an 'ideology' implies that, as with anatomical science in 'Appunti per un'Ecloga', chemical science is mainly operating as a metaphor, as a manner of thinking which is characteristic of the chemical scientist. This is also then the case with regard to poetry for the 'ideologies' are two in the poem. Indeed their metaphorical import is the same as before: the human versus the inhuman. The human (as also in 'Ecloga II') is now epitomized by the loving couple (and an equation between poetry, the human element, and love, is gradually established throughout the course of the poem). The inhuman is represented by political history as well as by science (technology, also present, is now considered as an industrial art). For this reason, 'Ecloga VI' provides a fitting transition to my second area of investigation: the literature –history area.

LITERATURE VERSUS HISTORY

'Ecloga VI' is prose-like and very direct in its message. The man presents the love of the two in terms of harmony and mutuality: 'fummo un amore fummo un'armonia / violenta fummo / il piú il vero l'offerta' ('we were a love we were a violent / harmony we were / the most the truth the offering'), and sets it against the background of Nature. The poem opens with an idyllic scene at Jesolo: 'un sole unico su / nevi marine / e deserti di spiagge vespertine di marzo' ('one sun alone on / sea-snows / and deserts of evening March beaches'), interpreted as a 'way' and a 'farewell', and shortly afterwards, as a metaphor for their own condition:

> Fummo la neve piú bella il mare
> piú nevoso
> il pino
> piú raggiante di rami
> fummo l'aroma del pinoso mare

We were the most beautiful snow the snowiest / sea / the pine tree / most radiant with branches / we were the aroma of the piney sea.

What the narrator is highlighting is the principle of reciprocity. It operates first and foremost between the couple, but also between the couple and the landscape in that the landscape symbolizes their love (an example of the anthropomorphism rejected by the *nouveau roman*). It even operates between the separate phenomena of the landscape itself: snow and sea come together in 'nevi marine' and 'il mare / piú nevoso'; pine and sea in 'pinoso mare'.

On the level of the couple, this method of relating – mutuality, reciprocity – explicitly identified as a 'human' element, is pitted against the disharmony which characterizes the external world:

> . . . fummo
> il piú il vero l'offerta,
> quanto d'umano
> può dare questo secolo di rictus,
> d'infarto, di fissile psiche

. . . we were / the most the truth the offering, / as much of the human / that this century of rictus, of infarct, / of cleavable psyche, can provide.

The present century is a horrific one, leaving man astounded and 'gaping' as it were. It damages him physically (the reference to heart attacks), as well as psychologically – his psyche is tending to split.

In the light of the discussion of technology and political history following later in the poem, one presumes that this degenerative state is seen to be induced by the same factors. In its immediate context, however, degeneracy is being attributed to science. The narrator exclaims that decline cannot conquer the couple if they hold onto their love and use it as their 'lance'; if they can stubbornly filter beyond the 'chemical idols' and the 'macromolecular' spirals:

> Nulla ci vincerà, nulla, se questo
> davanti al petto, nel pugno terremo,
> se tutto questo sarà nostra lancia,
> . . .
> se oltre i chimici idoli, oltre
> le spirali macromolecolari,
> ostinatamente filtreremo

Nothing will conquer us, nothing, if / we hold onto this in our fists, before our breasts, / if all this will be our lance, / . . . / if we can filter stubbornly / beyond the chemical idols, beyond / the macromolecular spirals.

Chemical science is being used as a metaphor in much the same way as anatomical science. The latter characterized a contemporary interest in bodily structure as opposed to spirit. Chemistry studies the laws of combination resulting from the *interactions* between *substances* in contact. The poet studies the *interactions* of *spirit*: the principle of reciprocity which is identified as love and which the narrator has depicted not only among humans, but also between humans and the landscape, and within the landscape itself in accordance with a neoplatonic doctrine of *anima mundi*.

There is a war developing between the two cultures. Scientific thought is beginning to monopolize the mentality of man and threaten a conception of the world in which the prime motivator is spirit and love. The narrator predicts that their love will remain only if the mind rises above the contemporary attitude (reminiscent of 'Ecloga II' where another self-regarding couple vows to cloister itself from the exterior world in a 'muta fedele difesa' ('mute, faithful defence')):

> Fino a te un varco
> sempre mi sarà aperto
> in ogni incubo in ogni inibizione,
> fino a me sempre tu potrai
> toccare, essere, dire:
> solo che un poco
> filtri la mente oltre, stilli oltre, colma resina

A passage will always be open / to me as far as you / in every nightmare in every inhibition, / you will always be able to / touch, exist, speak as far as me: / if only the mind filters / a little beyond, trickles beyond, like brimming resin.

In the following section there is a move from Jesolo to Ravenna and the narrator recalls a walk with his loved one along a Ravenna beach. The beach is attributed images of death acting as metaphors for the contemporary decline alluded to in section 1. It is described as a 'ben sicura soffocazione' ('very secure suffocation'), a 'satolla terrena mandibola' ('glutted earthly mandible') (probably a reference to organisms feeding off others), strewn with 'relitti e fatica' ('wreckage and toil'), 'livellati coacervi' ('levelled litter'), and 'colloidali depressioni' ('colloidal hollows') (colloid being a non-crystalline substance with very large molecules – the 'Macromolecole' of the title? – forming a gluey solution).

But it is also scattered with more 'positive' images: bright, crystalline substances spied by the narrator's talkative female companion. She does not see its images of death (she bears a slight resemblance to the 'Dora' of Montale's 'Dora Markus' (*Occasioni*). Compare the last five lines of the passage cited below, and lines 14–15 of Montale's poem: 'le tue parole iridavano come le scaglie / della triglia'. 'Dora Markus' also mentions Ravenna, and opens with a scene set by the sea):

> . . . tra
> colloidali depressioni
> che tu non vedevi, tu libera,
> tra occhiute gemme iridi
> di pietrischi collane
> per ogni istante nostro
> per la tua voce vagante narrante

> . . . among / colloidal hollows / which you did not see, you free, / among the precious stones you eyed, rainbowed / stony fragments and necklaces / for each of our moments / for your wandering narrating voice.

Likewise, the sea contains positive factors in spite of its dross ('mare di scorie nascite delizie' ('sea of dross births delights')). It has animated depths and is passionately involved in the creation of life ('mare dalle animose viscere' ('sea of spirited viscera'), 'febbricitante fabbro d'organismi' ('feverish maker of organisms')).

This shore and the seascape are used to reinforce the message of section 1. Just as the narrator's female companion is blind to the images of death on the sand, so too the narrator prefers to ignore them. As if in a gesture of defiance, the couple make love on the sand and the latter is hailed as a mother of love. As pledged in stanza one, love is used as a lance in the face of degeneracy:

> su quel mare di marzo
> . . .
> su quella sabbia che fu prodiga
> di conchiglie e miraggi alla tua dolce
> mano cogliente
> – e fu madre, col mare dalle animose viscere,

madre di tanto amore –
lottai con te, e pini all'orizzonte
furono e intorno al puro pino
all'aroma adriatico
del nostro amore

on that March sea / . . . / on that sand which lavished / shells and mirages on your sweet / gathering hand / – and it was a mother, together with the sea of spirited viscera, / a mother of so much love – / I struggled with you, and there were pine trees / on the horizon and around the pure pine / around the Adriatic aroma / of our love.

To the link already established between love and the human element, poetry is added at the beginning of section 3. The narrator urges his companion to 'believe' (that, presumably, they can conquer contemporary decline), but never to believe in any of his 'silences', in any of his 'absences', in any of his 'non-poems' ('tu mai non credere . . . ad alcuno / mio non-poema'). 'Silence' would designate a resignation to decline and as such is unacceptable. Even a minimal form of rejection will suffice:

– basta un sospiro –

. . .

. . . quel sospiro
forte che turba e orienta
la sapienza insipiente:
reticolati torri
e spirali macromolecolari
babeli esili innumeri
circúiti agguati triboli ove, vinta,
la piaga la distonia la tomba,
vinto, il drago letargico
arde in io–sono
anche se sotto il moggio

– a sigh is enough – / . . . that deep / sigh which disturbs and steers / foolish knowledge: / grids towers / and macromolecular spirals / slim Babels countless / circuits traps caltrops where, the wound / – the dystonia the tomb – is conquered, / where the lethargic dragon, once conquered / burns in I-am / even if under the bushel.

A mere sigh, expressive of sadness, weariness, or both, is capable of disturbing the 'foolish knowledge' of science and (industrial) technology: the positivistic thought typical of chemistry ('spirali macromolecolari'), the construction of sky-scrapers in urban development, and the 'electrification' of the world ('reticolati torri', 'innumeri / circúiti') – all 'Babels', all lofty structures by contemporary attitudes, but which the narrator considers as slight achievements ('babeli esili'). They are 'traps' and 'caltrops' ('agguati', 'triboli'). For whereas this 'foolish knowledge' thinks it heals the world – that it conquers pain, illness, death and lethargy – it has an alternative effect of self-apotheosis which is much less readily apparent ('vinto, il drago letargico / arde in io-sono / anche se sotto il moggio'). This view is, once again, matched perfectly by Heidegger who says of technological science:

> Technology is . . . posed by man's self-assertion . . . . What has long since been threatening man . . . with the death of his own nature, is . . . the sense of purposeful self-assertion in everything. What threatens man in his very nature is the willed view that man, by the . . . channelling of the energies of physical nature, could render the human condition, man's being, tolerable for everybody and happy in all respects. . . . What threatens man in his very nature is the view that technological production puts the world in order. (*Poetry, Language, Thought* 116–17)

And elaborating further on the link between science and apotheosis, Zanzotto remarked in his interview with Listri:

> In reality one has the impression that man feels all of his small acquisitions of scientific knowledge to be capable of producing euphoria, only because they fit once again into an unconfessed (repressed) plan of omniscience; man that is, ends by judging his new, slight ideas, as an increase in his own degree of omniscience, as a step towards a type of apotheosis. (190)

The final section of 'Ecloga VI' is a reflection of the second where love prevailed over death and decline. The latter is now specified as political history which is being associated with Ravenna – the capital of the western Roman Empire for two and a half centuries. The narrator speaks of the city's 'muddy wastes of mantles' and 'astonished salty kings'. But just as the beach at Ravenna combined images of death and life, united to its negative historical aspects, Ravenna stands for 'hope' – hope in the face of contemporary political history defined as a 'mud' and an 'alum', a 'dialectic flaring up of being' involved with blood and execution:

> E Ravenna di tenebre e di vento adriatico,
> che unisce
> ai cascami melmosi dei manti agli attoniti
> salini re le speranze
> in questa melma in questo allume in questo
> sanguigno effettuoso giustiziante
> impennarsi dialettico dell'essere

And Ravenna of darkness and Adriatic winds, / who unites / hopes to her muddy wastes of mantels and astonished / salty kings, hopes / in this mud in this alum in this / bloody effecting executing / dialectic flaring up of being.

This 'hope' is, however, personal to the narrator rather than collective, for the city prides itself not only on the part it has played in political history, but also on the significance it holds in literary history. It sees its 'loves' in terms of power and reputation:

> e Ravenna riflesso di re,
>
> . . .
>
> che crede sé i suoi spazi i suoi amori
> riflessi macromolecolari

and Ravenna reflexion of kings, / . . . / who believes herself her spaces her loves / to be macromolecular reflexions.

The allusion which follows shortly to Dante ('il poeta-nume') and the equation already established between 'love' and 'poetry' suggests how, since the fountainhead of Italian literature is buried at Ravenna, Ravenna interprets this as something which increases its historical self-esteem. Whereas the narrator separates poetry from power (Zanzotto once called poetry 'nonexistent power', 'utopic power', 'impotent power' (Allen 255)), Ravenna confuses them. Like the scientist's, its attitude is positivistic. Dante's metaphysics and theism are lost on the city which is only capable of appreciating realistic and factual data.

But poetry will prevail – this is the poet's 'hope' presented with faith. Although at present abandoned and buried with the 'numen-poet', she ('essa') will return as 'il nevoso marzo / che tra i pini s'ammalia a mutazioni / dei liquidi infiniti palinsesti' ('snowy March / which among the pine trees becomes enchanted by the mutations / of infinite liquid palimpsests') – a reflection with its interrelation of snow, sea and pines, of that idyllic scene at Jesolo used as a metaphor for the 'harmony' and 'violence' of the couple's love, the last sign of the human in this century of decline. Just like the 'liquid palimpsests' (the Adriatic waves) which erase sediment, and expose 'mysteries' (mysteries hiding truths) ('liquidi infiniti palinsesti / che azzurri azzurri si spogliano / d'ogni mistero, che ogni mistero tendono / nudo' ('infinite liquid palimpsests / which, intensely blue strip themselves / of all mysteries, and lay all mysteries / bare')), the dregs, so to speak, the inhuman, will be eventually washed away leaving what is valid and pure.

A similar juxtapositioning of poetry and political history is to be found again in 'Ecloga V', 'Miracolo a Milano' ('Miracle at Milan'), 'Sul Piave' ('On the Piave'), and 'Per la solenne commemorazione della morte del "Servus Dei" G.T.' ('In Solemn Commemoration of the Death of a "Servant of God", G.T.').

The subtitle of 'Ecloga V' is '"Lorna, gemma delle colline" (da un' epigrafe)' ('"Lorna, gem of the hills" (from an epigraph)'). According to the notes of Feldman and Swann, Zanzotto has transcribed with a minimal alteration a real inscription on a wall in a hill-town of his area – 'Lorna', a fictitious name, replaces 'Arfanta' (a hamlet near Tarzo which is a few miles north from Pieve di Soligo).

Zanzotto is using this epigraph to epitomize his early lyric, landscape poetry where poetry was personified by a woman, a 'tu', seen to be present within the landscape.

In section 3 of the poem, he contemplates how this landscape offered him an 'arida e pura morte' ('arid and pure death'): 'arida' in the sense that to focus only on the landscape and blinker himself from the outside world produced a shallow poetry; but 'pura' in the sense that neither eye nor mind was sullied by anything intruding upon 'la favolosa vita' ('the fable-like existence'):

> e tu, gemma, l'arida e pura morte
> – la favolosa vita –
> a me davanti stendevi, a fuoco, a punto,
> cosí che non la miseria non l'odio
> mi distraeva, né i maligni messeri
> i siri i golem i tarocchi,
> non il Baffetto non il Baffone non il Crapone
> non il Re dei Petroli o dei Rosoli
> non il Re dei Turiboli,
> 'non avea catenella, non corona':
> minimi, in te Lorna, si spettralizzavano, minime
> erano le loro frasi, le loro stragi,
> minima la strage di me ch'essi facevano

and you, gem, you spread out in front of me, / focused, exactly, an arid and pure death / – the fable-like existence – / so that I was not distracted by misery / or hate, nor by malicious masters / Sires golems tarots, / nor by Little Moustache Big Moustache Big Eater / nor by the King of Oil or Rosolios / nor by the King of Thuribles, / 'she had no chain, no crown': / their ghostly works were minimal in you, Lorna, minimal / were their clauses, their carnage, / minimal the way they massacred me.

No aspect of political history then intervened. He was not distracted by the adverse sentiments politics inflicts upon the mind, such as 'misery' or 'hate'. Nor by men of power from the low to the high: 'masters', 'sires', the war leaders themselves ('il Baffetto', 'il Baffone', and 'il Crapone' are caricatures for Hitler, Stalin and Mussolini respectively). The 'golems' escaped his attention then – those who followed the powerful figures, behaving machine-like with no active intelligence. And he overlooked the 'tarocchi' signifying money, swords, staffs and chalices – hence financial, military and ecclesiastical power. The latter is reinforced in the reference to the Pope as 'the King of the Thuribles', and by the quotation from Dante (*Paradiso* XV, 100) wherein Cacciaguida speaks of a former Florence, uncorrupted by church or state. While the remaining references to the wealthy kings of oil and Rosolios (an Italian liqueur) would seem to allude to the intrusion of neocapitalism upon provincial existence.

These spectral doings were, as Zanzotto says, reflected minimally in 'Lorna' and only damaged him minimally as a result. The psyche is affected by the issues it focuses on. For the hypersensitive it is wiser to turn a blind eye, so to speak, to reduce one's gaze to the size of a fly's.

Sections 4 and 5 of the poem qualify this 'fly's eye' – the eye on the landscape as opposed to the eye on the world. It is the multifaceted former and not the single beam of the latter which is considered all-embracing (thereby negating the previously stated idea that landscape poetry was 'shallow'):

> Gemma delle colline,
> mio mirifico occhio di mosca, icosaedro,
> arnia porosa d'umana sostanza,
>
> . . .
>
> da te ogni storia trae la sua fresca interezza

Gem of the hills, / my marvellous fly's eye, icosahedron, / a porous beehive of human substance, / . . . / from you every history draws its fresh wholeness.

Zanzotto is reinterpreting the concept of history. By definition a study of human affairs, it deals in effect with inhuman affairs. Since his poetry, by contrast, considers the 'human', it is more 'historical' and more embracing than history itself.

In 'Miracolo a Milano' (also the title of a neo-realist film by De Sica) Zanzotto plays again upon the erroneous connection between history and the 'human' (one of the messages of De Sica's film which examines the desperate attempts of working-class men to survive within the immense social, economic and political chaos of post-war Italy). Given Zanzotto's aversion for 'la storiale corrente' ('current historical phenomena') he must be below or above the human scale:

> io, infine: subumano? – Io forse trascendente?
> Io che abbandona al margine – la storiale corrente?

I, in short: subhuman? – I perhaps transcendent? / I whom the flow of history – leaves aside?

The neologism 'storiale' could be interpreted as a scornful condemnation of 'convenzionismo' ('conventionism'), implying that the discussion of current political affairs is a fashionable pursuit, and a must for the literary and cultured man. Zanzotto replies to this attitude with a mixture of sarcasm and humour:

> Piano: tre volte all'anno – milanese divengo,
> dunque storico, umano, – funzionale mi tengo

Hold on: three times a year – I become Milanese, / hence historical, human, – useful, I keep myself!

The rustic poet from the far-out province visits the big city three times a year. Since he is still in touch with the 'intellectual' scene he must still be in touch with the world!

'Sul Piave' is the most interesting of the poems in this group. The title immediately evokes the great importance the Piave river has in official national history in Italy, due to its constituting the main line of Italian defence in the First World War after the Austrian breakthrough at Caporetto in October 1917 which forced the Italians to retreat right down to behind the Piave. From there the Italians drew up artillery plans to meet a new enemy attack. This attack took place on 15 June 1918 with the Austrians crossing the Piave and reaching the last line of defence on the Montello. But the Italians held them and counter-attacked on 19 June. The final attack, known as the Battle of Vittorio Veneto, was launched from the mid-Piave sector on 24 October and ended with the Italians victoriously entering Vittorio Veneto on 30 October. The cost amounted to 39,000 killed and wounded Italians, and 30,000 killed and injured Austrians.

Undoubtedly Zanzotto's poem commemorates all these major historical events surrounding the Piave river. But since the subtitle of the poem explains that it was written on the fortieth anniversary of the 'Battaglia del Solstizio' ('Battle of the Solstice') it would seem to be the counter-attack of 19 June which Zanzotto has most in mind. This was a battle which lasted six days (concurring with the time of the solstice) – the Austrians withdrawing all of their troops back across the Piave river by 24 June.

The interest the poem generates lies largely in its difference from the other 'historical' poems in the collection. Whereas in the latter there was history on one side and poetry on the other together with its related concepts of love and the human element, Zanzotto in 'Sul Piave' tacitly acknowledges that there are elements in history that can be considered poetic.

The opening lines describe the river's itinerary as it descends from the mountains carrying and melting snow from the snowfields. One adjective and three nouns are attributed to it – 'fedele' ('faithful'), 'virtù' ('virtue'), 'rapina' ('robbery'), 'agnello' ('lamb') – which in the context of the battle assume ambiguous overtones: on the one hand, Italy can glorify those who died, for their 'virtuousness' and their 'faithfulness' to their country; but on the other hand, there is nothing glorious about a battle which 'robbed' men of their lives and lead them like 'lambs' to the slaughter.

There is ambivalence also in the act of commemorating the dead:

> Era ad era, minuzia a minuzia,
> crescesti questi sedimenti
> da cui prendemmo forma e forza a vivere

> (ah il tuo saluto dal
> palinsesto degli altri tuoi corsi
> in giovanile affanno abbandonati)

Era by era, petty detail by detail, / you grew these deposits / from which we took shape and strength to live / (ah your farewell to the / palimpsest of your other courses / abandoned in youthful grief).

From the sediment which settles when the turbulence has died, others can derive a reason for living. The details surrounding the events have been preserved and kept alive by the mere act of remembrance. Not even Zanzotto is exempt from this practice given the anniversary nature of the poem itself. But he does recognize it as a futile practice. The river bed is a 'palimpsest', a writing material or manuscript on which the original writing has been effaced to make room for a second: battles like this one have happened in the past and will continue to occur, with the importance of each being reduced by its successor. Even the river bids a romantic farewell to the palimpsest of its other courses. 'Giovanile affanno' when considered in the context of 'Piccola elegia', *VCT*, is indicative of romanticism (see Chapter 2, pages 61–2) and Zanzotto is suggesting that the very act of preserving the memory of a battle and its dead bears witness to the 'romantic' in man – the first of the poetic elements involved in history.

Another is presented in section 2 of the poem but retracted soon afterwards:

> vano forse non fu, forse fu santo
> scendere coi fratelli
> ad arrossarti, linfa senza fine

perhaps it was not vain, perhaps it was pious / to descend with brothers / to redden you, endless lymph.

Perhaps the death of his compatriots was not useless but saintly; the shedding of their blood an act of love or charity. However a charitable act such as this is not valid since it is intrinsically linked to the infliction of defeat. Section 3 serves to remind one of this as it moves quite suddenly to the concept of 'victory'.

On this anniversary day the river 'returns' 'tenacemente folle' ('tenaciously mad') and 'come a vittoria' ('as if in victory'), but the surrounding landscape is oblivious to its attitude: victory and heroism are engulfed by time and the ordinariness of everyday life. Wars would be forgotten were it not for anniversaries which represent an attempt to save them from oblivion.

As the poem continues Zanzotto's condemnations of the battle become much more fervent, and yet, paradoxically, it is through these condemnations that the most significant links between poetry and history begin to be established.

The term 'minuzia' is retrieved from the opening section and used along with 'inezia' ('trifle') in reference to the battle itself. Thinking about a specific

individual who has died in the battle Zanzotto reflects how today he has no
banners for adoration or hate; he cannot even take pride in his glory, nor
know of the

> ... l'orrida minuzia,
> l'orrida inezia,
> lo psichisma preterito, la fede
> d'automa: quanto
> forse in queste demoniche correnti
> di lui resiste

> ... the hideous petty detail, / the hideous trifle, / the dead psychism, the
> mechanical / faith: the amount / of him which perhaps / resists in these
> demoniac currents.

A 'psichisma preterito' has been conducive to the fighting. This term, I believe,
refers to a mentality, a way of thinking, which is 'dead' in the sense of
primitive and uncultured, and which goes hand in hand with a machine-like,
obstinate fidelity of 'automatons' (like that of the veterans in 'Per la solenne
commemorazione' who, paying their respects with their music and uniforms
by the graveside of a soldier, are called 'vecchi frivoli / e di malferma vista'
('poor-sighted / frivolous old men'), 'lo psichisma / sfatto da eccessi e ostinazioni'
('their psychism / undone by excesses and stubbornness')). Hence the nature of
the waters of the Piave – demoniac, possessed – in which the ghost of the dead
friend seems to persist.

The term 'demoniche' merits further attention. It can be used in reference to
poetic inspiration and perhaps it has infiltrated the poem subconsciously for in
'Riflesso' and 'Ecloga IV', two of the poems on poetry proper, Zanzotto talks
about poetry as being born of the same feelings that have been conducive to
his compatriots' fighting – an unpremeditated release of emotion, a reflex action
to an exterior stimulus (one of the meanings of 'Riflesso'). The man who writes
poetry may be an intelligent man but poetry in many ways is antithetical to
reason. The sensitivity of the poet versus the intellect of the scientist was one of
the themes of 'Ecloga I', and 'Palpebra alzata' offered a variation on this theme
condemning the 'mathematics' of the *nouveau roman*. In fact, I shall later argue
how in 'Ecloga IV' Zanzotto attempts to relax the controlling consciousness that
generally governs and constrains the writing of a poem.

If, as he says, the fighting of his compatriots displayed an unpremeditated
release of emotion, then a romantic element was also involved, since giving
preference to feeling over reason and logic is one aspect of the concept of
romanticism. But there are other aspects involved in fighting which are totally
un-romantic in character: the river which holds the dead man's ghost shows a
stubborn unwillingness to forgive and forget, and anniversaries betray the same
pertinacity. In future solstices which the poet may not 'see', the river will again

move 'viscere e monti' ('viscera and mountains'). If there is a sentimental element in commemorating the dead (and Zanzotto feels 'love' as he lies on the bank) it is also a perpetuation of pain and bitterness. Although the festival being held is in memory of the victorious, it must also commemorate the blood of the enemy. Zanzotto for these reasons wants an end to the tradition:

> Domani: ahi, non la stasi
> pallida del nemico, non la festa
> della patria salvata,
> non pure questo guasto spasimo
> e amore che sul tuo temuto fianco
> ora mi fa giacere

Tomorrow: ah, not the enemy's / pale stasis, nor the festival / of the saved fatherland, / not even this wasted spasm / and love which now makes me lie / on your dreaded slope.

Sustaining his distinction between history and the 'human', he calls to the river 'Resta, umano' ('Stay, human'); to be regarded as a part of the phenomenal landscape and no longer as a symbol for a historical event. Working-class man inherently desires a 'physical' (and 'foolish') solution to his grievances, but it is to be hoped that in the future it involves less 'error', and that the 'ridicule' – the insulting futility of war – may become more apparent to him:

> . . . stoltezza
> fisica che non falla, irrisione
> non più celata

. . . physical / foolishness which never fails, mockery / no longer hidden.

If impulsiveness is tempered by more intelligent reasoning, tragedies such as this one may begin to decrease. The poet's attitude is, quite simply, pious and humanist.

LITERATURE VERSUS LITERATURE

There is a commemoration of a different type in 'Un libro di Ecloghe' but the field of reference is now exclusively literature as it is for all the poems I now go on to discuss (with the exception of 'Scolastica' ('Scholastics') where the subject-matter is pedagogy, viewed, however, again in relationship to poetry). Although it was literature that inevitably won the day in the pitting of literature against science and history, the poems which deal with literature alone probe and scrutinize many aspects of writing and are characterized as before by ambivalence.

In fact, 'Un libro di Ecloghe' functions as a prologue or a 'parenthesis', as Zanzotto calls it, to the collection proper in its offering of an apology for the 'parentesi innumeri' ('innumerable parentheses') pervading the collection as a whole – the alternative thinking about science and history that break up the logic and continuity of the discourse.

The apology coincides with Zanzotto's self-depiction: he is Jacob's shortened ladder, unable to adopt a transcendental point of view, an elevated and exalted position:

> Faticosa parentesi che questo isoli e reggi
> come rovente ganglio che induri nell'uranico
> vacuo soma, parentesi tra parentesi innumeri,
> pronome che da sempre a farsi nome attende,
> mozza scala di Jacob, 'io': l'ultimo reso unico

Laborious parenthesis, you which isolates and supports this / like a scorching ganglion which you endure in the uranic / vacuous soma, parenthesis among innumerable parentheses, / a pronoun forever waiting to become a noun, / Jacob's lopped ladder, 'I': the last one made the one and only.

The nervous unsteadiness within the poem itself and which allows for its representation as a 'scorching ganglion' lies in its ambivalence towards the literary tradition. It opens with a send-up of the high-sounding lyricism and the lofty epic tones of Tasso and Ariosto:

> Non di dei non di príncipi e non di cose somme,
> non di te né d'alcuno, ipotesi leggente,
> né certo di me stesso (chi crederebbe?) parlo

Not of gods nor of princes nor of supreme matters, / nor of you nor of anyone, reading hypothesis, / nor certainly of myself (who would believe it?) do I speak.

Their singing (Tasso's 'Canto l'arme pietose' ('I sing of pious arms'); Ariosto's 'Le donne, i cavallier, l'arme, gli amori . . . io canto' ('Of women, knights, arms, and loves . . . do I sing')) is reduced to a 'speaking', reinforced by the jokey, conversational tone, the asides to the reader, and the deflation of the sustained crescendo effect with the placing of 'parlo' after the parenthesis.

But the joviality here is only superficial. There is a serious side to the literary 'rhythms'. A commemoration of norms is also to be intended and Zanzotto's 'speaking', or alternatively, his 'singing' 'out of tune', necessitates lying on the part of the poet (for this reason the epic parody is eventually retracted and line 1 of the poem is repeated in the affirmative: 'e dunque dei e príncipi e cose somme in te' ('and therefore there are gods, princes, and supreme matters in you')):

> Né indovino che voglia tanta menzogna, forte
> come il vero ed il santo, questo canto che stona

> ma commemora norme s'avvince a ritmi a stimoli:
> questo che ad altro modo non sa ancora fidarsi

Nor can I guess why so much lying is needed, strong / like truth and holiness, this song which sings off key / but commemorates norms clings to rhymes and stimuli: / this which cannot yet entrust itself to any other style.

The paradoxical description of the 'canto che stona' as a 'lie' which is 'strong like truth and holiness' permits two interpretations both closely related and emphasizing an allegiance to the literary norm. When Zanzotto sings 'out of tune' he is 'lying' to himself in the sense that he is being untrue to his feelings. But he realizes that traditional writing is no longer acceptable. Hence the 'truth' and the 'holiness' which exist in the 'lying'. Alternatively, he is satirizing a conventional attitude. For the writer and reader of poetry today there is 'truth' and 'holiness' in the poem which subverts traditions, and this subversion for Zanzotto is a 'lie'. But he must make a concession if his poems are to sell (an issue, one remembers, raised in 'Ecloga I'). While he is no longer writing in a purely traditional way, certain links and echoes are maintained in relation to the norms. This explains the homage Zanzotto intends to Virgil, *the man*, and the 'Virgilian', architectonic structure of the collection: the first poem 'Un libro di Ecloghe' acts as a type of prologue; then follow nine eclogues each accompanied by one lyric (with an 'Intermezzo', however, of seven poems between the lyric accompanying 'Ecloga IV' and the fifth eclogue proper); the last two components together form the epilogue. Yet it also explains how on the level of language and content Virgil's *Eclogues* exert no influence on the work except minimally as in the epigraph to 'Ecloga V'. While Zanzotto cannot altogether jettison tradition, neither can he be totally modern and innovatory ('questo che ad altro modo non sa ancora fidarsi').

This intermediate position between the old and the new, is apparent again in the clash of ideas between 'Ecloga III' and 'Ecloga IV'. The former (subtitled 'La vendemmia' ('The Grape Harvest')) juxtaposes the 'poesia pura' ('pure poetry') of the Arcadian past with the desecration of poetry in the present. Poetry today is a 'fonte imbarbarita' ('barbarized source'), 'difetto e perdizione' ('flaw and perdition'), a 'triviale slogan'. Advertising jingles and publicity slogans have become the new poetry of the twentieth century (they are also discussed and condemned by Zanzotto in *Sulla poesia* (98), and in Camon (155)), and however much the poet claims to be immune from this sacrilege – 'Ma io sono immune / e incolpevole: tanto oso dire' ('But I am free from fault / and innocent: I dare to say so much') – in 'Ecloga IV' he comes close to committing it in his use of catchy phrases from pop songs and signature tunes – slogans of a sort, although not related to advertising.

'Ecloga IV' is subtitled 'Polifemo, Bolla fenomenica, Primavera' ('Polyphemus, Phenomenal Bubble, Spring') and takes the form of a debate between

'Polifemo' and 'a'. 'a' can be identified as 'Ulysses' (Falchetta) but I believe he is also to be understood as a poet: Ulysses and poet combined.

The poem opens with an allusion to the biblical creation through a reference to the acquirement of life through breath (compare *Genesis* 2, 7–8):

> 'Dolce' fiato che muovi
> le nascite dal guscio, il coma, il muto;
> 'dolce' bruma che covi
> il ritorno del patto convenuto;
> uomo, termine vago

'Sweet' breath which moves / births from the shell, the coma, the mute; / 'sweet' mist which hatches / the return of the fixed agreement; / man, vague term.

The first two lines of this passage refer to birth ('che muovi / le nascite dal guscio') and a gaining of both consciousness and speech ('che muovi / . . . il coma, il muto'). The 'patto convenuto' is that of language. Language comes about with the birth of man and he enters into a 'pact', an agreement with it. Without language man is a 'termine vago', or to appropriate Ulysses, a 'no-Man'.

The allusion to Ulysses is strengthened shortly afterwards when 'a' makes a reference to a 'wandering about the world' (a 'wandering' element is also indicated in the epigraph, a quotation from the emperor Hadrian: 'Animula vagula blandula' (echoed before in '(Variante)', see pages 94–5)). Later there is a reference to a clinging onto wool, reminiscent of Ulysses's and his fellow mariners' escape from Polyphemus's cave: 'e premo alle lane' ('and I press against the wools'):

> Godono i prati acqua silenzio e viole;
> da fiale laghi, nevi si versano.
> Occhio, pullus nel guscio: ho veduto
> nell'errare del mondo errante il sole

The meadows enjoy water silence and violets; / lakes, snows pour forth from phials. / Eye, a chick in the shell: I saw / in the wandering of the world the wandering sun.

The 'eye' that is mentioned ('Occhio, pullus nel guscio') must be that of the Cyclops given that Polyphemus is the other protagonist of the poem. The blinding episode of the *Odyssey* comes immediately to mind (and when Polyphemus speaks it is to this that he refers). This episode is reinterpreted in the context of language, as will become shortly apparent.

Polyphemus's eye – a 'pullus nel guscio' – is related not only to the 'nascite dal guscio' but also to the spherical as well as generative images to be found in the rest of the poem: spherical bacteria, nits, seeds, bubbles, a spinning top, Spring, and even hope and thirst (for 'Sferica / è anche la speranza, anche la sete' ('Hope and thirst are / spherical too')). All of these images culminate in the eye of Polyphemus and epitomize a spawning creativity or 'coming-into-being' which is acting as a metaphor for the 'luteous, pliable wax of poetic afflatus': the rush of unstructured and inspirational energy which precedes the writing of a poem ('all'afflato / di lutea passibile cera'). Ulysses piercing Polyphemus's eye (which happens towards the end of Zanzotto's poem) is symbolic of the poet who kills the afflatus when the afflatus is transposed into the controlled consciousness of the poem. Hence the Ulysses of our poem wants to put off the blinding, and 'stay with the afflatus':

> Ancora un poco è giusto
> ch'io stia al gioco, stia al fiato,
> all'afflato,
> di lutea passibile cera,
> io, e mondo primavera

It's right that I stay for just a little while more / with the game, stay with the breath, / with the luteous and pliable wax / of afflatus, / I, and the spring world.

There is only one way in which he can do this: by relaxing controlling consciousness and releasing instinct and energy. Hence the breathlessness and ludic element in the rest of 'a''s speech:

> E vengo dritto, obliquo,
> vengo gibboso, liscio;
> come germe che abbonda
> di dente ammicco e striscio
> . . .
> M'adergo, prillo, come a musicale
> sferza la trottola. Poi che qui tutto è 'musica'.
> Non uomo, dico, ma bolla fenomenica.
> Ah, domenica è sempre domenica

And I come straight, then oblique, / I come humped, I come sleek; / like a seed rich / in toothmarks I wink and I creep / . . . / I lift myself up, I twirl myself round, like the spinning-top does / to a musical whip. Since here all is 'music'. / Not man, but phenomenal bubble, I say / Ah, Sunday is always a Sunday.

This writing could be symbolized by the 'musical top' – the movements described make one dizzy to read them and there is a much greater emphasis on sound than on sense (rhyme in particular is prominent and playful). 'Everything is "music"' as the poem itself says, appropriating the title of a signature tune ('Musichiere'), and showing how the section is partly composed of what jumps spontaneously into the mind. For example 'Ah, domenica è sempre domenica' (the signature tune of a television programme on football in the 1950s) is sparked off on account of its rhyme with 'fenomenica'. As before in '(Variante)' the links between ideas are not consciously organized, and 'a' derives so much pleasure from his game that he henceforth renounces his allegiance to the norm: 'Abiuro dalle lettere consuete' ('I renounce the normal type of literature').

Polyphemus seems to be enjoying it too. He wants 'a''s soliloquy / poem to go on and on ('No, qui non si dissoda, qui non si cambia testo' ('No, here one doesn't break fresh ground, here one doesn't change the text'), for its language, in its lack of conscious control, is very much 'drunk' like himself. Finally, however, 'a' plunges his stake in, and Polyphemus laments the 'most vicious rotation':

> *Po* No, qui non si dissoda, qui non si cambia testo,
> qui si ricade, qui
> frigge nel cavo fondo della vista
> il renitente trapano, la trista
> macchina, il giro viziosissimo

No, here one doesn't break fresh ground, here one doesn't change the text, / here one falls back, here / the reluctant drill, the wicked / contraption, the most vicious rotation / sizzles in the deep socket of my sight.

Immediately, a 'controlling consciousness' begins to take over and although Polyphemus is drunk with spring wine (the heady wine offered him by Ulysses in the myth), he humorously 'collects himself' in preparation for his own little soliloquy / poem where reason and logic prevail over the final, *parenthesized* rush of emotion: he knows who he is and he knows what he is: he, Polyphemus, drunk with spring wine, is one from whom life and debauchery dribbles:

> E qui su questo,
> assestandomi, giuro:
> io Polifemo sferico monocolo
> ebbro del vino d'Ismaro primavera,
> io donde cola, crapula, la vita
> (oh: vino d'Ismaro; oh: vita; oh: primavera!)

And here, as I collect myself, / on this I swear: / I spherical one-eyed Polyphemus / drunk with the spring wine of Ismarus, / I from whom there drips, gluttony, life / (oh: wine of Ismarus; oh: life; oh: spring!).

Four other poems hinge partly on the ideas of 'Ecloga IV'. 'Prova per un sonetto' in its '"Attempt" at a Sonnet' (it consists of one quatrain and the first line of the second) merely wants to emphasize that, according to convention, consciousness *should* control the material of poetry and a poem *should* be carefully organized. The sonnet which with its architectural structure is the epitome of such a conception is undermined in this poem in several ways. Firstly, poetry, if it is to accord with this world, can no longer be rigidly disciplined, for the contemporary world is a 'shapeless' one – not coherent and unified as of old. Secondly, the poet approaches this world with a 'sete / d'esistere' ('thirst / for existence') – a thrust and vitality which should not be controlled. And thirdly, the teeming life of natural phenomena ('ombra, monti, fiumi, verde' ('shade, mountains, rivers, green')) are 'forces' which would be suppressed or 'lost' in a closed and organic form:

> L'informe mondo, l'informale sete
> d'esistere, ombra, monti, fiumi, verde,
> sensi e occhi mai nati, orme inconcrete
> d'una forza che in sé chiusa si perde

Shapeless world, non-figurative thirst / for existence, shade, mountains, rivers, green, / senses and eyes that have never been born, / shaky traces / of a force which when closed in on itself is lost.

But as established already in 'Un libro di Ecloghe' Zanzotto is not totally attuned to the modern and links and echoes are maintained with the norms. This explains the inclusion of 'Notificazione di presenza' ('Notification of Presence'), a complete sonnet which complements the 'prova', and is modelled specifically on the example of Petrarch: in its subtitle ('Sui colli Euganei' ('On the Euganean Hills')), in its lexicon ('catene', 'dardo', 'tormenti', 'fuochi', 'geli' ('chains', 'dart', 'torments', 'fires', 'ice')), in its antonyms ('in opposti tormenti agghiaccio et ardo' ('in contrasting torments I freeze and I burn')), as well as in its subject-matter: Nature is presented as the mirror of a state of mind (Conti-Bertini 1984, 97–8).

Structurally speaking 'Appunti per un'Ecloga' combines both cultures: the old and the new. Presented in note form, like 'Prova per un sonetto' it is another deflation of a traditional composition. But importantly these notes are very carefully patterned. 'a', the only persona who does any talking, intercalates his remarks at regular intervals among the other personae – 'b', 'c', 'd' and 'e' (semiotic phenomena as I have already explained on page 101) which appear in alphabetical order. 'a' speaks four times in all: on the first and third occasions, for the duration of four lines; on the second and fourth occasions, for the duration of six lines. The 'notes' are consequently organized as follows: b–a (4 lines) – c–a (6 lines) – d–a (4 lines) – e–a (6 lines). In short, there is an organized structure at work notwithstanding the title implying the contrary.

Another idea from 'Ecloga IV' – the notion that man has no identity without language – is presented once again in 'Cosí siamo' ('That's How We Are'). Zanzotto and others are discussing what seems to be a dead person, and this dead individual during the course of the conversation is being referred to constantly by the third person pronoun:

Dicevano, a Padova, 'anch'io'
gli amici 'l'ho conosciuto'

My friends, at Padua, used say / 'I too knew him'

Zanzotto reflects upon the use of the pronoun (the phrase in inverted commas
is later repeated) and considers how this person is no part of language – neither
subject, object, usual speech nor jargon – given that the individual no longer
exists (he is also neither 'quiet' nor 'movement'):

Vitalmente ho pensato
a te che ora
non sei né soggetto né oggetto
né lingua usuale né gergo
né quiete né movimento
neppure il né che negava
e che per quanto s'affondino
gli occhi miei dentro la sua cruna
mai ti nega abbastanza

I did some clear thinking / about you who now / are neither subject nor
object / neither everyday speech nor jargon / neither quiet nor movement /
not even the not that negated / and however much my eyes / pierce the
needle-eye of the negation / it can never negate you enough.

Existence, it is suggested, is controlled by language which even continues to
govern non-existence. The dead individual is neither 'subject' nor 'object' yet
the poet cannot refer to him without using grammar: he is both an object
and a verb in the sequence above ('te', 'sei') which not even the negation is
enough to negate. As Zanzotto puts it again in 'Ecloga VII', to imagine 'cose
senza voce' ('things without a voice') is to imagine 'noi senza noi' ('us without
us'). Poetic language can only be a bringing-into-being, and, yet, as has been
shown in 'Ecloga IV', what is brought into being through the language of a poem
exists only as a result of negatively conditioning the afflatus, the metaphorical
coming-into-being, which gave birth to the poem in the first place. It now
becomes clear that language 'lies' in two ways: when it negates, it gives presence;
when it denotes presence, it negates.

But notwithstanding the contradictions, something of worth still persists in
poetry, more valid than 'jargon' or 'everyday speech' (Hainsworth 1982, 108).
('Ecloga VII' reinforces this position, as its subtitle suggests, 'Sul primato della
poesia' ('On the Primacy of Poetry')). Whereas Zanzotto is aware that he attains
being through language, allowing him to accept his intrinsic 'nothingness', he
cannot believe in the nothingness of poetry. The more it is threatened by his
logic and reasoning, and the more it is threatened by the filth of existence (in the
background there is the rumble of an 'acqua sporca / . . . e d'una sporca fabbrica'

('dirty water / . . . and a dirty factory') accompanying his thoughts) the more it 'comes close' to him, the more he can find it:

> E cosí sia: ma io
> credo con altrettanta
> forza in tutto il mio nulla,
> perciò non ti ho perduto
> o, piú ti perdo e piú ti perdi,
> piú mi sei simile, piú m'avvicini

And so be it: but I / believe with just as much / intensity in all of my nothingness, / consequently I haven't lost you / or, the more I lose you and you lose yourself, / the more like me you are, the more you draw me close to you.

In fact, the writing of poetry is an involuntary pursuit – the idea behind the cryptic 'Riflesso'. In different places and situations, and in various states of mind, the poet questions his relationship to reality:

> 1   Spesso nella morsa di gorgonici
>   autunni o in primavere
> 3   verdi di tabe
>   o nell'incubo che precede il sonno
>   . . .
> 9   o in attese piú estatiche
>   piú che nausee protratte,
> 11 qui sul colmo del viottolo
>   qui sul tenero fiume che s'intarla:
> 13 con ire di fanciullo o con disfatte
>   pause d'adulto,
> 15 che tu volessi, tu, da me, perché,
>   universa impresenza,
> 17 unicità e miriade,
>   chiesi;
> 19 tu, da me, perché,
>   semantico silenzio

Often in the vice of gorgonic / autumns or in springs / green with tabes / or in the nightmare which precedes sleep / . . . / or in waitings more ecstatic / more protracted than nausea, / here at the top of the lane / here on the soft and worm-ridden river: / with childish angers or with exhausted / adult pauses, / I asked / what you wanted, you, from me, and why, / universal non-presence, / oneness and myriad, / you, from me, and why, / semantic silence.

Reality is defined in paradoxical terms as a 'universal non-presence', a 'oneness and myriad', and reinforced by the contradictions of which the section is composed: for example the nightmares before sleep (line 4), and the waitings both ecstatic and nauseous (lines 9–10). The conjunction 'o' which characterizes the section changes to 'e' in the section which follows. The repetition of each conveys the 'non-presence' and 'myriad' of reality, for it is because of its myriad aspects (reinforced by the use of 'e') that reality eludes him (reinforced by the use of 'o').

Yet elusive reality demands that he 'be' (the answer to the question in lines 15–18), depending upon the poet for its own significance which emerges during moments of 'alapa' (Latin for a 'blow' or a 'box on the ear'):

> 21   E queste nubi e questi
>   spessi monti e i linguati
> 23   rivi e il sassoso sonno
>   e l'insonnia e i sospiri
>   . . .
> 26   solo questo da me, per me,
>   ch'io fossi
> 28   tu mi chiedevi. O nome
>   mai saputo abbastanza mai perduto
> 30   abbastanza, tenebra
>   che s'innamora, alapa
> 32   che disintegra e aggrega, tu, nell'ora
>   che tutto sulla fatiscente
> 34   anima
>   tutto sulla bocca inetta
> 36   ricadrà e sarò prossimo all'eco:
>   allora almeno

And these clouds and these / dense mountains and tongued / streams and stony sleep / and insomnia and sighs / . . . / you asked / only this from me, for me, / that I be. Oh name / never known enough never lost / enough, a darkness / which falls in love, a blow / which disintegrates and unites, you, in the hour / when everything will fall again on my crumbling / soul / everything on my inept mouth / and I will be close to the echo: / at least then.

Reality at times inflicts on him a 'blow', sparking off a reaction of psyche and soma, a 'riflesso' in the sense of a reflex action, making poetry either possible or impossible ('uniting' or 'disintegrating' the 'tu' (line 32)). As Zanzotto has remarked in his 'Autoritratto' (275) his poems are a means of overcoming hysteria; they are 'a type of fall-out, of minimal, secret explosions'. When the 'explosion' or 'blow' induces him to write, some contact is established with evasive reality, its 'silence' becoming meaningful ('semantico silenzio' (line 20)). Contact happens in an '"attimo fuggente"' (in the poem '"L'attimo fuggente"' ('The Fleeting Moment'); the other 'moments' in the ordinary continuum of life existing 'nell'incorposa / increante libertà' ('in incorporeal / uncreating freedom')). This is the second sense of 'riflesso': the poet's voice is a 'reflection' of the exterior world, and the echo between the two (reproduced in the poem in the question (lines 15–18) -cum-answer (lines 27–8)) is nearly complete:

'sarò prossimo all'eco' (line 36). That it is never totally complete is a guarantee of the fact that the process will continue and more poems will be written, for while the essence of reality can never be realized, the poet's efforts to realize it can never be 'lost': it is 'mai saputo abbastanza' and 'mai perduto / abbastanza' (lines 29–30). Hence the paradox of 'Sylva' where poetry is described as the presage of a beginning rather than a beginning itself: 'e ancora mai nell'inizio non sei / e sempre sei l'annuncio dell'inizio' ('and still you are never at the beginning / and you are always the announcement of the beginning').

Poetry as this self-perpetuating process, hailing the moments of *satori*, of enlightenment, is in itself an assertion of life. In his interview with Camon (156) Zanzotto compares it to the 'vera virtú "biologale"' ('real "bio-sacral" truth') of the child ('biologale' is a word coined by Zanzotto to express the biological with sacred overtones); the child's '"buona fede" nei riguardi della vita' ('"good faith" *vis-à-vis* life'). It is 'tensione all'essere e allo sviluppo' ('a reaching out toward being and development') which bursts forth from the 'no' which suffocates being. This is exactly the idea behind 'Ecloga VIII' and 'Ecloga IX', both written again in dialogue form.

In 'Ecloga VIII' which is subtitled 'Passaggio per l'informità, La voce e la sua ombra, Non temere' ('Passing Through Shapelessness, One Voice and its Shadow, Do Not Fear'), the 'shapelessness' denoted is a psychological one – it is the 'biologale frana' ('bio-sacral landslide') of 'Ecloga V' (note the use of 'biologale' (above) in the interview with Camon), a collapse of life-affirmative instincts.

Although 'a' and 'b' are denoted as 'personae' they are rather two aspects of a single personality: 'a', the pessimistic, and 'b', the optimistic; one voice and its 'shadow' as the subtitle puts it. 'b' makes a comment on contemporary life. Gone are the mystery and mythology of old, the 'fati d'un tempo' ('one-time fates') and their coexistent 'timore' ('fear'). Man no longer lives in abject fear of the gods, but controls his own destiny, is geared towards 'profit', and is contemptuous of 'death' (used in a figurative sense to denote lethargy or *taedium vitae*).

'a' proclaims his inability to adjust to this world. It is he who is suffering from the 'informità', and melodramatically lists all his problems of endurance such as the troubled shores of sleep and the blood of every dawn (lines 28–52).

'b' answers with a reproach, accusing him of indolence. While accepting that 'a''s is a 'human' reaction, he warns him of its shameful and self-humiliating aspects. Nevertheless he reassures him that this crisis will not crush him, for in the act of expressing it he has already overcome it:

> facendoti
> sanie informale, nigredo, liquame,
> fimo implorante, fimo
> muto, vincesti

by making yourself / shapeless poison, nigrescence, sewage, / imploring pus,
silent / pus, you won.

'a''s confession has been none other than a reflex-response, an instinctive reaction
to one of reality's 'blows' (the 'riflesso' and 'alapa' explained in 'Riflesso'). His
expression of despair (in the words of this poem) is a rejection of the same, a desire
for life in disguise.

'a' is now enthused by an awareness of this and reaches an objective and
philosophical conclusion. This assertion of life which epitomizes poetry is none
other than the 'art of existence' itself: the necessary surpassing of difficulties in life.
Since everything is involved in this 'art of existence', poetry is not something that
comes only from him. Life and living phenomena are poetical themselves ('dire',
below, has affiliations with the old Italian sense of 'to compose poetry')

> perché tutto conosce
> maestramente l'arte dell'esistere.
> Ora mi sarà inutile
> dirti e dire, poi che tutto dice
> di te, per me

because everything is an / expert on the art of existence. / Now it will be
useless for me / to speak to you and speak, since everything speaks / of you,
for me.

An analogy between poetry and the child occurs in 'Ecloga IX' ('Scolastica').
Here poetry is examined in relation to pedagogy. Again, rather than a dialogue,
the poem is a monologue wherein Zanzotto is examining his profession as a
teacher. He looks at its negative and positive aspects presented by 'a' and 'b'
respectively.

'a''s portrayal of the village school in the Montello region (where Zanzotto
lives) contains a strong picture-book element, reminiscent of 'la fola' ('the
fairy-tale') ('Ecloga VII'), and 'la favolosa vita' ('the fable-like life') ('Ecloga
V'), used previously in reference to life in the province:

> nella scuola povera e nuova
> tra candore di fogli,
> nel Montello, cesto muscoso, boccio
> di funghi multicolori, di prati,
> di querce clamorose
> per uccelli e per venti

in the poor and new school / among innocence of leaves, / in the Montello,
mossy tuft, bud / of multicoloured mushrooms, of meadows, / of noisy oaks /
for birds and winds.

The children emerging from the wools of autumn descend along the paths which lead to the school, and their contagious energy is related to poetry. The heart of poetry is 'englobed' by these children ('quel festante grappolo / che intorno al tuo cuore s'ingloba' ('that merry-making cluster / that englobes your heart')); poetry, tomorrow, will be in the classroom too ('nella scuola povera e nuova . . . / povera e nuova tu stessa, starai' ('in the poor and new school . . . / you poor and new, will also be')).

'a' now proceeds to make a distinction. There is this type of poetry in league with the child, and there is the poetry that is a part of the school curriculum:

> Ma che dirai a quelle anime di brina
>
> . . .
>
> Vengono i bimbi, ma nessuna parola
> troveranno, nessun segno del vero.
> Mentiremo. Mentirà il mondo in noi,
> anche in te, pura

> But what will you say to those souls of hoar-frost . . . ? / The children come, but they will find / no word, no sign of truth. / We will lie. The world will lie in us, / even in you, oh pure one.

The 'lying' exists with 'structured' knowledge. Teachers 'lie' but their lying is unwilful: the defectiveness is on the part of the pedagogical system. The active use of the verb 'mentire' manages to convey this idea: teachers do not intentionally lie about the world; rather, by teaching in accordance with the pedagogical rules, they transmit to children a false picture of the world, and even a false conception of poetry ('anche in te, pura'). One is eventually made aware, as the argument continues, of one such rule which 'a' has a grievance with (the inadequacies of the pedagogical system are explored in more depth in 'Misteri della Pedagogia' ('Mysteries of Pedagogy'), PSQ (see Chapter 5 pages 156–62)).

The child has an 'unlearned' knowledge of poetry and it is displayed in his questions, crayon drawings, and writings, his 'virgin writings' which poetry 'virginally' encourages:

> a domande, a pastelli, a scritture
> vergini, verginalmente
> darai forza

> you, virginally, / will give strength / to questions, to pastel drawings, to virginal writings.

'a''s teaching is merely a necessary pretence ('Necessità e finzione'). He carries out instruction in the conventional way, 'pretending' to teach poetry while being aware of the fact that the children 'know' more about poetry than him. And so it will be for ages to come for the system is old and not easily removed: 'nessun giusto rito / comincerà domani sulla terra' ('no just rite / will begin tomorrow on the earth').

'b' intervenes with a positive remark. He aims to teach that it is the question which is important; that the asking is more illuminating than the actual answer.

'a' quickly dismisses this as a Utopian attitude. Pedagogy has always laid emphasis on answers. 'b' probably only teaches because he knows the answers to his own questions, and it is the hierarchism involved in this attitude that he loathes. 'Sei poco' ('you are little'), he remarks, 'da fare grande / come l'iddio' ('to act as big / as a god') (an issue returned to in 'Misteri della Pedagogia', PSQ).

'b' continues to insist upon the question of enlightenment. Like the employer showing the workmen how bright the cut is in the wood, the teacher opens eyes to an appreciation of the world. He implies that there is no authority involved in this attitude. Rather, teaching involves an offering, a giving of oneself.

'b' is overlooking a paradox as far as 'a' is concerned (or perhaps the paradoxes are automatically engendered by the 'bruto / plasma' ('brute / plasma') which is language itself). If there is one who is giving the sign, the 'indizio', the hierarchism remains, since he who gives the signs or directions is not on a par with phenomena but places himself over and above phenomena. It is not only that he cannot agree with this set-up; he can no longer *assume* the authoritative role given his present 'scotoma' – the term for a blind spot in the visual field, used here by Zanzotto to refer to depression i.e. an eclipse of psychic vitality. 'a''s answer to 'b' in which he presents this argument is suffused with irony:

> io sia colui che 'io'
> 'io' dire, almeno, può, nel vuoto,
> può, nell'immenso scotoma,
> 'io', piú che la pietra, la foglia, il cielo, 'io':
> e, in questo, essere indizio, dono,
> dono tuo, agli altri donato

it is as though 'I' were the one / who can, at least, say 'I', in the emptiness, / can say 'I' in the vast scotoma, / 'I', more than the stone, the leaf, the sky, 'I': / and, in this, can be a sign, a gift, / your gift, given to others.

To attempt to be the linchpin, the one who sparks off awareness – the 'first element of a proposition', the 'breath' on children's eyes – is a 'rischio', a danger when one is pervaded by doubt. Yet in spite of these doubts he remains in the profession even though angrily so:

> Eppure tra questa che seppi menzogna,
> nella vita, rabbioso m'attardo

And yet amid this which I knew to be a lie, / I angrily linger, in life.

He discovers in his 'trembling' – his doubts and reservations – 'l'ostinazione, la brace, / l'ala di mosca superstite' ('obstinacy, the ember, / the wing of a surviving fly'). And even though his 'glances' are a 'casket' turned 'dull' (the jewels are not shining, his enthusiasm is gone), his 'looking' is 'rounded' like that of Polyphemus:

> . . . e guarda,
> tondo, torpido scrigno di sguardi,
> anche se ancora non sa
> né amore né insegnamento

and he looks, / rounded, a dull casket of glances, / even if he still does not know / either love or teaching.

If one considers how the Cyclops's eye epitomized energy and was related as I have shown to poetic inspiration (and the energy of the children was also a metaphor for poetry), 'a' would seem to be suggesting that the process of teaching regenerates vitality that is dormant or eclipsed. If one also considers how in the quotation above 'teaching' is being placed on an equal footing with 'love', and how 'love' in previous poems was used to symbolize poetry (in 'Ecloga VI' and again in 'Ecloga VII' where the poet is 'amando e parlando in un atto' ('loving and speaking in one gesture')), one must come to the conclusion that 'a' is intrinsically aware of how teaching and poetry have something in common.

It is in its combination of old and new cultures that *IXE* foreshadows *LB*. However, whereas in *IXE*, as I have attempted to show, Zanzotto's preference was ultimately for tradition, in *LB* conventions are breached in an effort to undermine traditional writing, to create 'outrage' ('oltraggio') on the part of the reader. Metapoeticism is present once again in the collection: some of the poems comment upon this procedure and debate the authenticity of an experimentalism of this sort, comparing and contrasting it with Hermeticism.

Chapter 4

Undermining Logocentric Thought
La Beltà (1961–7)

'Since the death of Eugenio Montale, Italy possesses once again a single "altissimo poeta"' ('very great poet'). This is how Thomas Harrison begins an article on Zanzotto in *The Empty Set* published in 1985, and statements of this sort, emphasizing the poet's singularity, are commonly found in critical studies of Zanzotto's later works, beginning with *LB*.

While it is easy to state that Zanzotto is original, it is a more difficult task to justify his originality. Critics, however, have attempted to do so when writing on *LB*. For two main reasons *LB* is posited as being like, but fundamentally very different from, Neo-Avant-garde poetry: Zanzotto's schizoid style is not programmatic, but rather the result of a neurosis; whereas the Neo-Avant-garde aimed at destroying all meaning, Zanzotto produced poetry with a plethora of meanings (see especially Corti 427; Forti 1971, 361; Agosti 1972, 211–12; and Bandini 1982, 9756).

These reasons, however, are not ones that I accept. *LB* is like Neo-Avant-garde poetry precisely in those areas where former critics draw distinctions: Zanzotto *is* attempting to destroy meaning, and he sets about doing it in a programmatic way.

Alfredo Giuliani in *I novissimi: poesie per gli anni '60* – the first major publication to draw attention to the group – outlined the main features of *Novissimi* poetry. He claimed that the effect of the new poetry would be shock and provocation, and that this was to be achieved in three ways: through an interruption of the imaginative process, an abandonment of traditional syntax, and a systematic use of violent images. The new poetry was also to have no definite meaning: the reader, rather than being traditionally 'entertained' was to assist in the process of lending meaning to the poem.

Except in one of these areas – the use of violent images – Giuliani's description of Neo-Avant-garde poetry could equally be applied to Zanzotto's *LB*. Radical distinctions between Zanzotto and the *Novissimi* can only be drawn in the field of declared intentions. The *Novissimi* movement was a politicized one. When Sanguineti, Curi, Balestrini and Giuliani established themselves in centres of cultural power – newspapers, radio, television, universities – they were intent upon destroying an institutionalized culture by attacking the linguistic norm through which it operated.

Zanzotto has never been a politicized writer. It is for personal reasons that he breaks linguistic rules in *LB* and these reasons, although serious, are not as aggressive as those of the *Novissimi*. In the light of his previous discoveries about language, and in view of contemporary theories of semiology, Zanzotto is questioning the functioning of language, and *inviting* his readers to do the same.

I emphasize 'inviting', for *LB* is also less dogmatic than the poetry of the *Novissimi*. Not only did the latter dismiss convention as a vice (seeming not to realize, as Zanzotto once observed, that their own poetry, through time, was destined to become conventional), they were also intolerant of contemporaries who did not conform to Neo-Avant-garde principles. An example in point was their *jeu de massacre* organized in *Il Verri* (their literary journal) against the *Officina* group that was lead by Pasolini. Pasolini, before the formation of the Neo-Avant-garde, had expounded a new form of poetry which he labelled *Neosperimentalismo* ('Neo-Experimentalism') – a movement born from the failure of Neo-Realist culture and which laid many of the foundations for the Neo-Avant-garde. It too was advocating the principle of innovation, yet the *Novissimi* attacked it because of its difference from their own ideology in one particular area: it operated within terms of moral and civil commitment, and was therefore still linked to immediate postwar tenets.

This intolerance of ideologies other than one's own is not typical of Zanzotto who partly for that reason has never identified himself with any literary movement. Broadly speaking, what Zanzotto has done is to set traditionalism against experimentalism. However, *LB*'s promotion of the second in favour of the first, which gives rise to its similarities with Neo-Avant-garde poetry, is accompanied by a *crise de conscience*, as it were, and a major part of the collection is concerned with the poet presenting reasons for the validity of both schools of thought. It is this obedience to his conscience which lends integrity to his poetry.

Agosti, writing on Zanzotto's *VCT* (1949–56), claimed that Zanzotto was anticipating Saussure's theory of the sign as presented in his *Cours de linguistique générale*. Agosti observed that the latter book only assumed a particular influence on European thought at the beginning of the 1960s. *LB* was written between 1961 and 1967 (mostly, as Zanzotto explains in a note to the collection, between 1964 and 1967) and by this time Zanzotto has obviously read Saussure. Indeed, I shall attempt to illustrate how *LB* not only displays an awareness of Saussurian thought, but is also to some extent prefiguring Derrida whose theory of language involves a re-reading of Saussure. I use the term 'prefiguring' since a question of influence is highly unlikely given that Derrida's work only began to be published in 1967.

Saussure, in his *Cours de linguistique générale* proposed that a linguistic sign consisted of two elements: a signifier (a sound or its written substitute) and a signified (a concept). The sign, composed of these two elements, is both 'arbitrary' and 'differential'. It is 'arbitrary' for two reasons. First, because there is no reason why a certain sound and its written substitute (for example, 'hat') should correspond to one particular concept (the concept of a "hat") and not to some other concept. Apart from special cases such as onomatopoeia, the relationship between the signifier and the signified is in no way motivated or natural or inevitable. Rather, it is the product of linguistic convention. Second, the sign is arbitrary because there is no necessary relationship between the sign as a whole (comprising signifier and signified) and the reality to which it refers. There is an essential division between the world of language and the world of reality.

The sign is differential because it acquires meaning only by virtue of its differences from other signs. In other words, a sound–image has meaning not 'in itself' but only because one differentiates it from other related sound–images (one differentiates 'hat' from 'cat' or 'mat'); just as one differentiates one concept from other related concepts (one differentiates "hat" from "coat" or "dress"). This shows how Saussure was aware of the chaotic continua of sound–images on the one hand, and concepts on the other. Nevertheless, he acknowledged that the linguistic system, by providing certain sound–images for certain concepts, sorted out the chaos. Within the linguistic system, signifier and signified are inseparably linked like the two sides of one sheet of paper.

It is this last idea about the linguistic system sorting out the chaotic continua of sound–images and concepts that is the point of contention for Derrida. In his *La Voix et le Phénomène (Speech and Phenomenon)* Derrida claims that if, as Saussure says, every sign is what it is only because it is not all the other signs, then every sign would seem to be made up of a potentially endless network of differences. In other words, if in the linguistic system, one sound–image has to ward off other related sound–images in order to be itself, then, according to Derrida, it is only true to say that the latter are contained within the former and form part of its identity. Consequently, signifiers refer only to other signifiers, not to things or entities beyond themselves; and meaning is a quality which is never free, never separable from the signifier which 'invokes' it. Derrida argues that language is self-referential, incapable of pointing beyond itself. He identifies Saussure with the *logocentric* tradition, that is, a tradition wherein writers and readers see the word and texts as *centred* by definite meaning in accordance with their belief in a *logos* – a God or some ultimate truth – which acts as a foundation for all of their language and thought. The logocentric tradition, Derrida then observes, is one which favours a system of hierarchies (the word being a derivative of the Word of God or some ultimate authority) which governs not only the linguistic system but also the whole of the cultural system. These ideas form the basic premises of Derrida's theory of *différance*.

Zanzotto's ideas in LB lean more toward Derridean than Saussurian thought. He does acknowledge the arbitrary and differential nature of the sign, and here his reasoning could be identified as Saussurian. Nevertheless, unlike Saussure, he never concedes that the linguistic system sorts out the chaotic continua of signifiers and signifieds. If anything, Zanzotto, like Derrida, is presenting the idea that the linguistic system is a false convention, and he attempts to undermine it by thwarting the reader's attempts to posit meaning. This subversion of meaning constitutes one of the ways in which Zanzotto tries to overthrow traditional, logocentric reading habits. Such a subversive practice is to be found in the majority of the poems in *LB* but there are a number of poems where Zanzotto debates the validity of his own revolutionary thought.

Toward the beginning of the collection, in 'Sí, ancora la neve' ('Yes, The Snow Again'), Zanzotto quotes from a variant of Hölderlin's 'Mnemosyne': '"siamo un segno senza significato"' ('"we are a sign without a signified"'). He then follows this quotation with a question of his own: 'ma dove le due serie entrano in contatto?' ('but where do the two series come into contact?'). Hölderlin was probably not even using the terms 'segno' and 'significato' with linguistic implications in mind: the line from 'Mnemosyne' in the original reads 'Ein Zeichen sind wir deutungslos' ('We are a sign without meaning').

However, given that *LB* is largely about language, and that its approach to the subject is a modern one, it would seem reasonable to assume that Hölderlin's line is being incorporated into a contemporary, Saussurian context. This is also implied by the question which Zanzotto directs at the citation from 'Mnemosyne'. Here he indicates two series of phenomena which do not 'come into contact'. The line is evocative of what Saussure called the arbitrariness of the linguistic sign. Zanzotto is suggesting one of two things: the disjunction between signifier and signified ('we are a sign without a signified'), or the disjunction between sign and reality – Saussure's two reasons for the sign's arbitrary nature.

But it is more likely the first of Saussure's reasons for the sign's arbitrariness which Zanzotto is alluding to in his quotation from Hölderlin: the essential disjunction between signifiers and signifieds or, to put it more simply, between words and concepts. If one were to choose between Saussure's two discoveries, this is, after all, the more far-reaching one in that from it developed the notion of differentiality, acknowledged, importantly, in some poems of *LB*, as I show later.

If words do not refer to the concepts that they are normally considered to refer to, then the poet who wants to conjure up concepts and say something about them, is a poet *malgré lui*. Such a poet must deal with the *impossibility* of writing. It is for this reason that in some of Zanzotto's poems one encounters the negation of words as soon as they are written on the page. It is a gesture which amounts to the erasing of the signifier because of its inability to signify:

storia – storiella

story – fib

. . . te ne vai; oh stagione.
Non sei la stagione

. . . you vanish; oh season. / You are not the season

e me e non-me

and me and non-me

vivi al superlativo
morti al superlativo
('Alla stagione')

superlatively alive / superlatively dead

('To The Season')

Là origini – Mai c'è stata origine

There beginnings – There never was a beginning

Nessuno si è qui soffermato – Anzi moltissimi

No one has lingered here – On the contrary too many have

L'assenza degli dèi, sta scritto, ricamato, ci aiuterà
– non ci aiuterà –
tanto l'assenza non è assenza gli dèi non dèi
l'aiuto non è aiuto

The gods' absence, it is written, embroidered, will help us / - will not help
us – / after all, absence is not absence gods not gods / help is not help

. . . storie storielle
('L'elegia in petèl')

. . . stories fibs

('The Elegy in Petèl').

It is obvious, however, that if the poet is to remain a poet and write something
productive, he must find a way out of his dilemma. Zanzotto, in the first poem
of the collection, 'Oltranza oltraggio' ('Outrance Outrage') reveals an attempt to
resolve his predicament. He suggests that the authentic poem may still be written,
but for the time being it is 'further ahead' not 'here'. The dominant motif of this
poem is 'ti fai piú in là' ('you move further ahead'), and the reflexive verb here
refers to poetry itself, for as has already become apparent in previous chapters, in
Zanzotto 'tu' and poetry are always coterminous, excepting two occasions: in the

'Prima persona' section of *VCT* where 'tu' referred to the 'real' self, as opposed to the linguistically determined self ('io'); and when the 'tu' occasionally refers to a person who is generally named in the poem.

A variant of the 'ti fai piú in là' motif is repeated in line 7: 'sei piú in là' ('you are further ahead'); and in line 13 it occurs again in the original: 'ti fai piú in là'. How Zanzotto may continue to write – and the repetition of the motif displays his urgency to do so – is suggested by the title of the piece: by going beyond all conventional conceptions of poetry, thereby creating outrage ('oltraggio') on the part of the reader.

Zanzotto's logic is quite clear. He feels it is untruthful to continue to write poetry where language aims to have a referential function. To write poems in that way is to conform to a logocentric and, consequently, false tradition. The authentic poem can only be one in which that tradition is subverted. However, the task of subversion is a difficult one, for Zanzotto knows that all readers conform to logocentrism: they will assume, for example, that words are referring to specific concepts even when, in the intentions of the poet, they are not; they will search for meaning and give meaning both to individual words and to the poem as a whole. The only manner, therefore, in which Zanzotto can subvert this tradition is by attempting to undermine some of the reader's logocentric reading habits, by attempting to dislodge his complacency. This is exactly what Zanzotto sets out to do in a number of poems in *LB*. His project is undoubtedly pursued with sincerity, although his attitude toward the reader is tongue-in-cheek.

Various methods are adopted: sometimes Zanzotto thwarts the reader's attempts to find *any* meaning in a poem; on other occasions he deliberately *confuses* the meaning of both individual words and poems as a whole; he also undermines the hierarchic structures regulating linguistic and cultural systems; and finally, he invalidates the reader's preconceptions of a poem as an artefact that is carefully constructed.

Each of these areas is explored individually here, and in the order in which they are presented above, although from such a systematic approach, one may get the impression that 'themes' are being examined. This impression derives from the fact that my critical method conforms to the tradition that the poet is subverting. Zanzotto does not inject his own writing with themes. This allows for a *comparison* with the Neo-Avant-garde rather than the distinction that is posited by Corti. Furthermore, since the aim of the collection is clearly subversive, Zanzotto's schizoid style *is* often programmatic, just as his point of departure *is* often destructive. Forti and Agosti present the opposite viewpoint (that Zanzotto's schizoid style is unprogrammatic and his point of departure is only creative), intending thereby to dissociate Zanzotto from the Neo-Avant-garde tradition. But *LB* is like that tradition precisely because of its subversive techniques.

There are a number of ways in which Zanzotto subverts the reader's attempts
to give meaning to a poem. In 'Adorazioni, richieste, acufeni' ('Adorations,
Requests, Buzzings in the Ears') he pokes fun at the reader who is attempting
to fix the traditional connection between title and content. Alluding to the first
he begins by asking

> . . . e che cosa
> è stato tutto questo chiedere?
> Questo voler adorare?

. . . and what / was all this asking? / This wanting to adore?

He then continues to suggest that he wants to clarify the connection, only to
interrupt these 'clarifications' with teasing and flippant remarks:

> Questo voler adorare? Ma che è questa storia dell'adorare?
> Adorate adorate. Fischi negli orecchi

This wanting to adore? But what is this story about adoring? / Adore adore.
Whistlings in the ears

> Eccomi, ben chiedere lungo chiedere,
> eccomi, bell'adorare
> – avevi un bell'adorare, tu! –

Here I am, asking in earnest asking at length, / here I am, fine adoration / – a
fine adoration you had! –

The poem ends by anticipating the reader's bewilderment:

> . . . Nonsense, pare?
> Nonsense e nottinere?

. . . Nonsense, it seems? / Nonsense and blacknights?

On other occasions Zanzotto places emphasis upon sound, and the pleasure
which sound and its oral articulation, irrespective of sense, can afford. He calls it
a 'Danza orale danza / del muscolío di tutta la bocca' ('Profezie *v*') ('Oral dance
a dance / of the muscles in the whole mouth') ('Prophecies *v*'), and it is prevalent
both in the 'petèl' monologues (to be considered later) and in sequences such as
the following:

> tutte sanissime e strette in solido

all very healthy and packed *in solido*

> mille linguine e a-lingue a-labbra
> argento neve nulla e anche meno
> oppure neve e poi a-neve a-nulla
>   ('Profezie v')

a thousand little tongues and non-tongues non-lips / silver snow nothing and
even less / or rather snow and then non-snow non-nothing

> . . . Là ero a perdifiato
> là. E tutta la mia fifa nel fifàus:
> tutto fronzuto trotterellante di verdi visioni

. . . There I was at breakneck speed / there. And all of my funk in the
frethouse: / all leafy trotting along with green visions

> e – oh i frutti, che frutti, fruttame

and – oh the fruits, what fruits, fruitage

> Perfidia, perfido, perfidamente
> ('Possibili prefazi II')

Malice, malicious, maliciously

> ('Possible prefaces II').

Here pleasure can be derived from abundant alliteration; from the creation of
compounds allowing two accents ('a-lingue a-labbra', 'a-neve a-nulla'); and from
the variety of stress present in a sequence of noun-adjective-adverb produced
from one stem ('Perfidia, perfido, perfidamente').

Zanzotto's intertextuality or, what previous critics have called, his
'culturalismo' (his allusions to and citations from other literary sources)
also hampers the reader who is looking for meaning – an idea not pursued
by the critics so far. If one has no knowledge of the literature evoked, one
cannot bring that knowledge to bear on the poems, and is left with the feeling
of having suffered a loss.

I am not concerned here with drawing up a list of Zanzotto's literary allusions
for such a list has been compiled by a number of critics (see Corti 427;
Rossi 1973, 115; Antonielli 628; Montale 339, who between them detect
echoes from Dante to Borges). Rather, using as examples the poems 'Possibili
prefazi *x*' and 'Profezie *IX*', I consider the *problems* these allusions create.

'Possibili prefazi *x*' opens with a translation of the title of an article by Lacan:
'1. – Lo stadio psicologico detto "dello specchio" / come costitutivo della
funzione dell'io' ('1. – The psychological phase called "The Mirror Stage" /
as a constituent of the function of the self'). Zanzotto gives the source of this
reference in his notes to the poem, but how he is using it only becomes clear
from an examination of the poem.

From a first reading it is obvious that the poem is an eulogy of Hölderlin –
a salute to a personal 'hero'. Zanzotto speaks of the 'homage' he feels, his
'imitation' of Hölderlin, his desire to reflect him, be a specular 'image':

Da qui basterebbe ora, in reattivo,
l'onesta imitazione l'omaggio convinto

From here the honest imitation the convinced homage / would suffice now,
as a psychological test

7 – Si fa degno, in quella lontananza,
anche questo speculare mancamento

7 – In that distance, even this / specular failing becomes worthy

10 – E divago, nel mancamento, alla ricerca di un'immagine

10 – And I stray, in the failing, looking for an image.

A quotation from Hölderlin – 'Mit Unterthänigkeit' ('With awe') – is cited
three times in the poem (twice in translation as 'Con soggezione'). It is the
phrase that Hölderlin placed before his signature ('Scardanelli') to the later poems
written during the period of his madness. Zanzotto's devotion to Hölderlin is
very much linked to his fixation with romantic eccentrics.

Where in all of this does Lacan fit? In his 'Mirror Stage' article Lacan argues that
a child, generally from the age of six months, can recognize as such his own image
in a mirror. Although still in a primordial form, the child's 'I', on the assumption
of this specular image, begins to take on its function as subject in the world.
The specular image becomes a 'je-idéal' ('ideal-I') and will later be the source
of *secondary* identifications. Lacan stresses the point that the 'je-idéal' situates
the ego in a *fictional* direction: the subject in its process of coming-into-being,
attempts to synthesize the real I with the 'je-idéal', but the synthesis can never
be fully achieved.

Hölderlin, it seems, is Zanzotto's 'je-idéal' in the form of a *secondary* iden-
tification. However, the allusion in the note to the article by Lacan points to
a strong element of irony in the poem: Zanzotto is acknowledging that his
identification with Hölderlin is only a *continuation* of the ego's first process of
situating itself in a *fictional* direction. His identification, in other words, is an
illusory one.

The poem is of greater interest when one examines how Zanzotto *uses* theories
of Lacan than when one attempts to decode it through Lacanian thought. Its
emphasis shifts from the greatness of Hölderlin to the impoverished figure of
Zanzotto himself. What is really being stressed is the I's inferiority, its inability to
synthesize with the 'je-idéal'. This idea is presented toward the end of the poem.
Here Zanzotto claims that if his coveted image were truly a reflection of himself,
it would have an ego, like his own, the size of a fly:

10 – E divago, nel mancamento, alla ricerca di un'immagine,
immaginina mia come una mosca, io

10 – And I stray, in the defect, looking for an image, / my little image like a fly, I.

A smaller intertextual problem is present in 'Profezie IX'. In his notes Zanzotto talks about the theme of the poem: '"L'Urkind", the original child (in a Husserlian sense too), tries to focus itself in an Ego that can never be fully specified'. The echo back to Lacan does not escape the attentive reader of 'Possibili prefazi X' who has consulted the 'Mirror Stage' article. However, this echo is less fertile than another which occurs at the end of the poem where Dante and baby-talk fuse:

> con tanta pappa-pappo,
> con tanti dindi-sissi,
> Ego-nepios, o Ego, miserrimo al centro del mondo tondo

with so much pap and chink, / with so many ting-a-ling collars with bells, / Ego-infant, oh Ego, most miserable at the centre of the round world.

The reader who misses the allusion to Dante ('Pappo e dindi', *Purgatorio* XI, 105) not indicated by Zanzotto in his notes to the poem, will only see in these lines Zanzotto's attempt to echo the language and cadence of nursery rhymes – indicated by him at the beginning of the poem (and also a feature of 'Sí, ancora la neve': 'bambucci-ucci', 'pini-ini' ('baby-wabies', 'piney-winies')):

> Bimbo, bimbo!
> Secondo cantilena, volta la carta, volta la carta

Baby, baby! / As in the lullaby, turn the page, turn the page.

The reader who sees the allusion to Dante can also recognize a mixture of high and low cultures, and go on to examine the reason behind it.

Earlier I observed that Zanzotto can hope to deflate, but not defeat the logocentric tradition. My own criticism so far has borne witness to this: I hunted for meaning (consulting Lacan, for example); or I arrived at the conclusion that the meaning of the poem is the *absence* of meaning (as in 'Adorazioni, richieste, acufeni') or again, that its meaning *is* the prevalence of sound over sense (as in 'Profezie V' and 'Possibili prefazi II'). What Zanzotto has succeeded in doing is to make me aware that I am being estranged from my logocentric reading habits.

A more interesting way in which Zanzotto does this is by suggesting differing interpretations for words and poems, thereby preventing the reader from seeing them as 'centred' by definite meaning.

Two methods are used to decentralize words. Sometimes Zanzotto in his notes to the poems indicates ambiguity in his use of certain terms: '"ninine": potrebbe essere un singolare friulano (fanciulla), sentito come plurale e conglobante ogni cosa piccola e graziosa' (note to 'Profezie XIII') ('"ninine": it could be a rare word from the Friuli area (meaning a little girl), felt as a plural here, and incorporating every small and graceful thing'); '"base": forse, secondo fantascienza, su un pianeta-exemplar' (note to 'Profezie XV') ('base': perhaps, in accordance with science fiction, on an exemplary planet').

On other occasions within the poems he uses polysemy as is the case in the following example where 'fonte' is meant in the sense of 'origin', but where the onomatopoeia underscores an allusion to Palazzeschi's 'La fontana malata' ('The Sick Fountain'):

> E che messaggi ha la fonte di messaggi?
> Ed esiste la fonte, o non sono
> che io–tu–questi–quaggiú
> questi cloffete clocchete ch ch
>
> ('Sí, ancora la neve')

And what messages does the source of messages have? / And does the source exist, or is it only / I–you–these–down here / these gutter splutter squirt spirt.

Here 'fonte' has not one meaning, but two: 'source' both in a literal and figurative sense – one related to the other through (Saussurian) 'difference'.

Zanzotto often plays with the Saussurian idea that language is a differential phenomenon: poems are constructed through a linking together of related sound-images and concepts. Generally the result is a variety of meanings. Such is the case in 'Possibili prefazi I', 'Profezie V', and 'La perfezione della neve' ('The Snow's Perfection'). 'La perfezione della neve' provides the best example. Here are the first sixteen lines of the poem, followed by my indication as to how they are 'structured'. I use the word 'structured' with some reservation since a sequence such as that quoted below has more of an extempore than a conscious construction (an issue I return to later). However, there seems little ground for accepting the opinions of some critics that psychoanalysis is involved in a sequence like this: to say that here one has an example of the Freudian preconscious (Corti 427), or the Lacanian unconscious (Siti 1973, 132; Milone 229) is to make shaky speculations that cannot be proven.

> Quante perfezioni, quante
> quante totalità. Pungendo aggiunge.
> E poi astrazioni astrificazioni formulazione d'astri
> assideramento, attraverso sidera e coelos
> assideramenti assimilazioni –
> nel perfezionato procederei
> piú in là del grande abbaglio, del pieno e del vuoto,
> ricercherei procedimenti
> risaltando, evitando
> dubbiose tenebrose; saprei direi.

Ma come ci soffolce, quanta è l'ubertà nivale
come vale: a valle del mattino a valle
a monte della luce plurifonte.
Mi sono messo di mezzo a questo movimento-mancamento radiale
ahi il primo brivido del salire, del capire,
partono in ordine, sfidano: ecco tutto

How many perfections, how many / how many totalities. Stinging it adds. / And then abstractions astrifications formulations of stars / frostbite, across stars and skies / frostbites assimilations – / I would proceed into the perfected / beyond the great dazzle, beyond the full and the empty, / I would search for proceedings / jumping once more, avoiding / the dubious the dark; I'd know I'd say. / But how it supports us, how great is the snowy fertility / how much it is worth: downstream from the morning downstream / upstream from the multi-sourced light. / I have placed myself in the midst of this radial movement-cum-defect / ah the first thrill of ascending, of understanding, / they fall into a sequence, they challenge: that's all there's to it.

The following relationships are at work in this sequence:

'perfezioni' ('perfections') 'totalità' ('totalities'): semantic contiguity

'astrazioni astrificazioni' ('abstractions astrifications'): phonic or orthographic relationship

'astri' ('stars') 'assideramento' ('frostbite'): semantic contiguity (Zanzotto in a note explains 'assideramento' as a neologism created from "'sideratus': colpito da un (maligno) influsso di un'astro' ("'sideratus": struck down by the evil influence of a star'))

'assideramento' ('frostbite') 'sidera' ('stars'): etymological relationship

'sidera e coelos' ('stars and skies'): same semantic field

'assideramenti assimilazioni' ('frostbites assimilations'): phonic relationship

'pieno' ('full') 'vuoto' ('empty'): antonyms

'dubbiose' ('dubious') 'tenebrose' ('dark'): semantic contiguity

'nivale' ('snowy') 'vale' ('it is worth') 'valle' ('valley'): phonic or orthographic relationships

'a valle' ('upstream') 'a monte' ('downstream'): antonyms.

As Zanzotto himself states in the final line of this section, the words of his poem fall into sequences and challenge the reader: 'partono in ordine, sfidano: ecco tutto'. They 'challenge' him to give a definite meaning to the poem, faced as he is by a number of meanings. For example, one could interpret the poem as a metapoetic discourse, dealing with the *fact* that words only function by virtue of their differences from other words. If one considers description to be more important than structure, the poem could be said to be depicting a snow scene, the 'Quante perfezioni' and 'astrazioni' referring to thousands of starry, molecular flakes. Yet again, the snow with its illusory presence (suggested in phrases such as 'del pieno e del vuoto', 'questo movimento-mancamento') could be said to be functioning as a symbol for the 'absence' inherent in words. One could even choose to pursue the poem's intertextual features – the words 'soffolce' and 'l'ubertà' of line 11 being taken directly from Dante (*Paradiso* xxiii, 130), and the 'grande abbaglio' of line 7 evoking the blinding light of *Paradiso*.

Rizzo thinks that Zanzotto authorizes the reader to paraphrase the poems in any way he wishes, but, in fact, a poem like 'La perfezione della neve' encourages the reader to discover a plethora of meanings (as in Mallarmé's poetry, as Hainsworth has noted (1982, 111)) which cannot be hierarchized in terms of importance.

The hierarchies involved in language and culture are also swept by the board. The following examples show Zanzotto inverting the hierarchies of grammatical law:

> Fa' di (ex-de-ob etc.) – sistere
> ('Al mondo')

Try to (ex-des-res etc.) – ist

('To The World')

> L'archi-, trans, iper, iper, (amore) (statuto del trauma)
> ('Possibili prefazi IV')

The archi-, trans, hyper, hyper (love) (the trauma statute).

In 'Al mondo' the morpheme '-sistere' is elevated to the role of a word *per se*, and expression is compressed to resemble a mathematical equation where prefixes within the parentheses are meant to be added to the morpheme outside. In 'Possibili prefazi IV' it is the prefix that is now raised to the status of a word, while 'real' words, by being placed in parentheses, have their importance reduced.

Culture in *LB* is to be understood in the sense of history and literature – two issues carried over from *IXE*. History is discussed in 'Retorica su: lo sbandamento, il principio "resistenza" (I-II-III-IV-V-VI)' ('Rhetoric on: Disbandment, the "Resistance" Principle (I-II-III-IV-V-VI)') (henceforth 'Retorica su'). Considering Italy's part in the Second World War, the poet audaciously remarks that the staple peasant diet – 'una zuppa gustosa' ('a tasty soup') – played a much greater part in keeping men alive and 'resistant' than did the rhetoric of politicians, called an 'opera-fascino' ('spell-work'):

E ho mangiato anche quel giorno
– dopo il sangue –
e mangio tutti i giorni
– dopo l'insegnamento –
una zuppa gustosa, fagioli.
Posso farlo e devo.
Tutti possono e devono.
Bello. Fagiolo. Fiore.

And even that day I ate / - after the blood – / and everyday I eat / - after teaching – / a tasty soup, of beans. / I can and must do it. / Everyone can and must. / Nice. Bean. Flower.

In other words, a small, unrecorded historical event – what Zanzotto calls in a note to the poem, a 'microstoria' or 'storiella' – is being elevated above the rhetoric of history.

'L'elegia in petèl' launches a simultaneous attack on hierarchical attitudes to language and literature. The title of the poem alludes to two contrasting 'languages' – an elegiac one and 'petèl'. The elegy has associations with death and an end, and it is the death of language that is being lamented in the poem, exemplified again (as Zanzotto explains in a note) by a fragment from the demented Hölderlin. This fragment comes significantly at the end of the poem: '"Una volta ho interrogato la Musa"' ('"Once I questioned my Muse"').

'Petèl' has associations with birth and beginnings. In another note to the poem Zanzotto explains it as the dialect word in Pieve di Soligo for the endearing nonsense talk used by mothers to their babies in which they try to approximate the language of the child. Examples from the poem are as follows:

'Mama e nona te dà ate e cuco e pepi e memela.
Bono ti, ca, co nona. Béi bumba bona. È fet foa e upi'.

Ta bon ciatu? Ada ciòl e úna e tée e mana papa.
Te bata cheto, te bata: e po mama e nana.

Hölderlin's alienated speech and the baby's 'petèl' are being highlighted by Zanzotto for the following reasons. Broadly speaking, both languages are unintelligible: Hölderlin's line, 'Once I questioned my Muse', makes *grammatical* sense, but given that it was uttered in a state of insanity, its import can never be fully ascertained. A primordial meaning may be present in 'petèl', but it is a meaning intuited only by mothers: 'petèl' is a 'lingua privata' ('private language') or 'lingua a due' ('language for two') (as Zanzotto underlines in another note to the poem) that does not even translate into standard Italian.

Moreover, Hölderlin's quotation and the 'petèl' sequences are marginal utterances with respect to the norm. The language of the child *precedes* the norm (displaying a freedom of speech as yet unconstrained by rules of grammar, syntax, or meaning); the language of the madman *goes beyond* it. Consequently,

Zanzotto, by using these languages, and by even highlighting them in the title, is attempting to raise what is generally considered to be nonsensical and marginal to the status of literature. 'Tutto fa brodo' ('Anything goes'), as he says in the poem using, as he explains in a note, a part of an advertisement jingle – 'non è vero che tutto fa brodo' ('it isn't true that anything goes' (literally, 'it isn't true that everything makes broth')) – to emphasize this process – recurrent in the collection – of including what the norm would 'normally' exclude. This is the reason for Zanzotto's much debated 'plurilinguismo'. By using many different lexical registers that are not normally considered to constitute the language of literature, Zanzotto is re-evaluating the notion of literature and deflating our traditional preconceptions of it.

The jingle above merits further attention. 'L'elegia in petèl' is claiming to be a 'brodo' ('broth'); 'Possibili prefazi x' calls itself a 'minestra' ('soup'). They are indelicate metaphors, and intentionally so. But they also reinforce the hotchpotch element that characterizes many of the poems in the collection. This is another of Zanzotto's revolutionary tactics, one which explodes the age-old notion of the poem as a perfected artefact. Many of his poems contain notes for poems: 'Dire, molte cose, di stagione, usando l'infinito' ('To say, many things, about the season, using the infinitive'); 'e l'uso dell'infinito' ('and the use of the infinitive') ('Alla stagione'). Others are presented as a series of notes, where lines are preceded by either arabic numerals or letters of the alphabet indicating point number one, point two, point a, point b, and so on. It is a 'modo piuttosto rozzo' ('rather rough method') in the words of the poet himself (see 'Possibili prefazi x' in which this quotation occurs, and 'Possibili prefazi viii', 'Possibili prefazi ix', and 'Profezie xviii').

The self-generating language that I emphasized earlier when discussing 'La perfezione della neve' brings an element of improvisation to the fore. Zanzotto, rather than choosing his own words and organizing them in a deliberate structure, lets words beget words by themselves. They precipitate forth, breeding off each other, and giving the impression that the main concern of some poems is to remain in a state of being born, as it were, – never to come to a literal 'end' ('Profezie ix' claims to be 'renitente all'omega' ('unwilling to reach the omega')). This is yet another reason why the collection displays an interest in baby-talk and nursery rhymes: there is echolalia in the first; and nursery rhymes, when recited, generally end with a return to the beginning. In both the repetition is gratuitous but pleasurable. (It is interesting to note that there is a reference to baby-talk in the canto from Dante's *Paradiso* that Zanzotto quoted from in 'La perfezione della neve' (see *Paradiso* xxiii, 121–2)).

'Sí, ancora la neve' is the best example of a poem which prolongs its duration by breeding off itself. Apart from cases of direct repetition (as in the examples below, under 1) this is achieved by a process of constantly modifying language in the following ways: by reversing the order of words (2), or changing the gender of adjectives (3); by adding prefixes or suffixes to a constant stem (4); and by repeating a sequence, with one or more words linked or added to the repetition (5).

> 1   e poi e poi . . . ma i pini, i pini   (4)
>   . . . – il mondo pinoso il mondo nevoso –   (7)
>   E il pino. E i pini-ini-ini per profili
>   e profili mai scissi mai cuciti   (100–1)

and then and then . . . but the pines, the pines / . . . – the piney world the snowy world – . . . / And the pine. And the piney-winey-inies by profiles / and the profiles never split never sewn

>   . . . bambucci-ucci, odore di cristianucci   (8)
>   . . . i bambucci-ucci   (42)

. . . waddler-toddlers, smell of wee Christian men / . . . waddler-toddlers

>   Buona neve, buone ombre, glissate glissate   (28)

Good snow, good shadows, glide glide

>   . . . sniff sniff
>   gnam gnam yum yum slurp slurp   (48–9)

>   E l'avanguardia ha trovato, ha trovato?   (90)

And the Avant-garde, has it found, has it found?

> 2   E tu perché, perché tu?   (15)

And you, why, why you?

>   . . . davanti
>   dietro . . .
>   dietro davanti   (102–4)

. . . in front / behind . . . / behind in front

> 3   . . . evaso o morto
>   evasa o morta (26–7)

. . . escaped or dead / escaped or dead

>   . . . piú o meno truffaldini   (52)
>   piú o meno truffaldine   (54)

. . . more or less swindling / more or less swindling

4   . . . in persona ed ex-persona
    un solo possibile ed ex-possibile?   (10–11)

. . . in person and ex-person / a one and only possible and ex-possible?

. . . – per una minima o semiminima
biscroma semibiscroma nanobiscroma
cose e cosine   (73–5)

. . . – for a minim or semi-minim / demisemiquaver semidemisemiquaver minidemisemiquaver / things and thingies

5   Che sarà della neve   (1)
    ma che sarà della neve dei pini   (22)

What will become of the snow / but what will become of the snow of the pines

E perché si è . . .
perché si è fatto . . .
perché si è fatto noi, roba per noi?   (7–9)

And why has it . . . / why has it become . . . / why has it become us, stuff for us?

However, there is a more constant method employed by Zanzotto to defer the conclusion of a poem – the stringing together of words or phrases by means of simple conjunctions: 'agganciare catene di e, di o' ('Possibili prefazi v') ('to hook together chains of ands, of ors'). Sometimes this phrase is to be interpreted literally – in 'Sí, ancora la neve' where there is an abundance of 'e's, and in 'Profezie IX' where there is an abundance of 'o's. Mostly, however, it has a figurative meaning, for the 'catene di e' (also called 'innesti' ('graftings')) denote verbal repetition (where words, ideas, but also sound, are repeated); and the 'catene di o' (also called 'clivaggi' ('cleavages')) denote verbal opposition – the use of antitheses.

Repetition and opposition of this verbal kind also help to defer the conclusion of a poem: when Zanzotto uses the first, the poem moves *forward* by repeating the words, ideas, or sounds that have come *before*, so that *progression* is really a form of *regression*. When Zanzotto uses the second, the juxtapositioning of opposites prevents the poem from attaining a linear discourse or, what he himself calls, an 'andatura rettilinea' ('straight walk') ('Profezie v'). 'Profezie v' and 'Profezie x' show the 'innesti' and 'clivaggi' simultaneously at work. They become much more readily apparent if isolated in the form of the charts that follow.

SEMANTIC

'Profezie v'
('Chiamarlo giro o andatura rettilinea')
('To Call it a Circle or a Straight Walk')

Repetition ('innesti')	Opposition ('clivaggi')
abbacina . . . sfavillanti (11) dazzles . . . sparkling	giro o andatura rettilinea (1) circle or straight walk
leccano l'idillio succhiano dall'idillio (12–13) they lick the idyll / they suck from the idyll	lievi o grosse (7) light or large
l'idillia la piccola cosa la cosina (14–15) the idyll the little thing / the thingy	seduzioni censure (9) seductions censorships
Danza orale danza del muscolío di tutta la bocca (16–17) Oral dance dance / of the muscles in the whole mouth	innesti clivaggi (9) graftings cleavages
	in stagione o fuori stagione (10) in season or out of season
	mille linguine e a-lingue (20) a thousand little tongues and non-tongues
	neve nulla e poi a-neve a-nulla (21–2) snow nothing / and then non-snow non-nothing

'Profezie x'
('Ammirata, eminente erba di Dolle')
('Dolle's admired, eminent grass')

Repetition ('innesti')	Opposition ('clivaggi')
luna nuova o mondata appieno (6–7) new moon / or fully cleansed	sereno o follia di piove (7–8) fine weather/ or madness of rain
equivale corrisponde consuona (10) is equivalent to corresponds harmonizes	Eccitavi, addormivi? (8) Were you excited, falling asleep?

Repetition ('innesti')   Opposition ('clivaggi')

E come oso rivolger(mi) a (te),
metter(ti) in rapporto con (me)   (25)
And how do I dare turn (myself)
to (you), put (you) in relation
to (me)

                                    Salire o scendere muovere
                                    o giacere con te   (9)
                                    Ascending or descending moving / or
                                    lying with you

                                    di realtà e di fantasma?   (15)
                                    real and fantastic?

                                    Ostensione immediata e rapina   (16)
                                    Immediate showing and robbery

                                    sulla via che da tutto svia   (19)
                                    on the road which leads astray from
                                    everything

                                    muta . . . sai il dicibile
                                    e . . . lo fai   (20)
                                    silent . . . you know the sayable
                                    and . . . you say it

                                    crittogamie fanerogamie   (23)
                                    crytogamia phanerogamia

Earlier I emphasized the point that although Zanzotto's attitude is often facetious, his revolutionary tactics are pursued with sincerity. This sincerity is reinforced by the attacks that he launches (especially in the sequence 'Possibili prefazi') on one of his earlier collections of landscape poetry – DIP. DIP (as demonstrated in Chapter 1) adhered to a tradition – Hermeticism – and never doubted or even questioned the logocentrism of words, so that consequently it was full of the themes and messages that one expects in traditional poetry. It is precisely these themes and the language of the collection that Zanzotto now ruthlessly ironizes. This, I believe, is the target, not exterior powers – consumerist society and an industrial civilization – that have made lyricism no longer possible (Forti 1971, 360).

Zanzotto now calls his love of the rustic a 'perfidious' one, full of green visions and a childish enthusiasm ('e – oh i frutti'; 'e – oh i collicelli'):

Quell'io che già tra selve e tra pastori.
Perfido, perfido

That I who already among woods and shepherds. / Malicious, malicious

tutto fronzuto trotterellante di verdi visioni
e le debolezze e la grazia di fioretti e germogli
e – oh i frutti, che frutti, fruttame
e – oh i collicelli, morbido da portare al naso da fiutare
assimilare come faceva quel vecchio: io
                    ('Possibili prefazi II')

all leafy and trotting along with green visions / and the frailties and the
gracefulness of florets and buds / and – oh the fruits, what fruits, fruitage /
and – oh the little hills, soft to bring to one's nose to smell / to assimilate as
that old I did.

He ridicules the way in which, in the vein of Éluard, the landscape was assimilated
to woman and love, suggested by the terms 'assimilare' above and 'similitudini'
and 'similitudine' below:

. . . un pleonastico straboccante
canzoniere epistolario d'amore

. . . a pleonastic overflowing / collection of love lyrics love letters

grande libro verissimo verosimile e simile,
grembo di tutte le similitudini: gremito di una sola similitudine

great most true book likely and alike, / womb of all similitudes: packed with
one single similitude

non le chantage mais le chant des choses,
con crismi eluardiani fortemente amorosi
            ('Possibili prefazi IV')

not the singing but the song of things, / with strongly loving Éluardian
chrisms.

Whereas in DIP a love for the moon indicated a romantic commitment
to Nature (see page 1), the poem 'Profezie III' is in praise of Nino, an
eighty-year-old selenographer of Zanzotto's region who holds sessions at his
home during which he and his friends study the moon in a *practical* way:

Nino, la piú bella profezia
non può mettere boccio che nei clinami di Dolle,
dove tu, duca per diritto divino
e per universa investitura,
frughi gli arcani del tempo e della natura,
. . .

> . . . nelle tue cantine
> presto ci troveremo in compagnia – che summit! –
> sceltissima e con cento e cento 'ombre'
> conosceremo sempre piú profonde
> le profondità del tuo valore
>
> ('Profezie III')

Nino, the loveliest prophecy / can only bud on the slopes of Dolle, / where you, duke by divine right / and by universal investiture, / search the mysteries of time and nature, / . . . / . . . in your cellars / we will soon find ourselves in the most select company / – what a summit! – and with hundreds and hundreds of glasses of wine / we will more profoundly acquire an ever deepening knowledge / of the depths of your worth.

'Possibili prefazi IX' actually quotes from *DIP* where Zanzotto was expressing his communion with the land – a feeling now dismissed as pretentious and laughable. Leopardi's 'A Silvia' ('To Sylvia') is sacrilegiously echoed, whereas in *DIP* the poet was fervently imitated as part of an attempt to restore the importance of past poetry:

> Nel risibile giaccio, nella pretesa.
> Astuzia di far posto al pretendente
> al promesso: 'non sa parlare – che per conoscere –
> il proprio oscuro matrimonio – con il cielo e le selve'.
> Natura natura che non realizzi poi
> quel che prospetti allor, quale puzzo, purezza di natura

How ludicrous, how pretentious I am. / How cunning to make room for what was expected / and promised: 'he cannot speak – but to acknowledge – / his own dark marriage – with the sky and the woods'. / Oh Nature nature, you who afterwards does not carry out / what you previously advance, what a stink, the purity of nature.

Attention is now diverted from the beauty of the landscape and focused instead upon the beauty of language: the archaic title, *La Beltà* is a reference to the first as something now obsolete, and an allusion simultaneously to the second. Beautiful effects can, as Zanzotto says, 'perhaps' issue from the word if it is used, as I have shown it to be used in this collection, as a many-sided crystal, a 'lingua-rubino' ('ruby-language') generating more words and a number of meanings:

> non sta il punto di equilibrio mai là: non apporsi accingersi
> a te bella, beltà

the point of equilibrium never lies there: not in an affixing a wrapping of oneself / around you, oh lovely, oh beautiful one

> non sta nel cammino esemplare
> di un Soligo

it doesn't lie in the exemplary path / of a Soligo

> non sta in quell'apprensione superante
> fumi e refoulements favori e guizzi

it's not to be found in that overwhelming apprehension / mists and repressions
favours and flickers

> ma forse sta nel rubino

but perhaps it's to be found in the ruby

> lingua-rubino
> ('Possibili prefazi VII')

ruby-language.

The qualifying 'forse' in the quotation above surprisingly implies that Zanzotto has doubts. And the doubts are not limited to doubts about whether his self-generating language is a 'beautiful' one. The very fact that Zanzotto writes not one poem but five denouncing the values of DIP makes the reader suspect that he cannot completely discredit his early Hermeticism. These suspicions are well-founded for there are intermittent suggestions in the 'Possibili prefazi' sequence and sometimes elsewhere that Zanzotto has not severed his links with Hermeticism; that he cannot help feeling in spite of himself that DIP's poems were authentic and relevant.

Some poems display a loving closeness to Nature:

> B – Petali verzure oro Asolo ovunque:
> intanto per questa sera
> non turbare l'assetto.
> ('Possibili prefazi IX')

B – Petals greenery gold Asolo everywhere: / in the meantime just for this evening / do not disturb the order.

And DIP's Éluardian woman who was part of the landscape (epitomizing the poetry 'behind' or within it) and over which Zanzotto once sentimentally 'drooled', is now pursued and invoked when in danger of vanishing:

> azzurro
> piú azzurro sui monti, ricche
> d'infinito le colline dove
> cercavo te sbavavo scalciavo.
> E mi torni con spessori
> di nascite e d'amori, nel terrore
> del tuo svanire, che non è terrore
> ('Profezie XI')

blue / more blue on the mountains, the hills / are rich with the infinite where /
I used search drool and kick for you. / And you come back to me with the
thickness / of births and loves, amidst the terror / which isn't terror, of your
vanishing.

Indeed in 'Retorica su' Zanzotto finds fault with some of *LB*'s revolutionary
poems for he sees them draw near to the forbidding area of politics. Part 3 of
this poem condemns political rhetoric: it has a dangerous ability to arouse heated
emotion, and to bewitch. It confuses reality with its contradictory arguments, and
it signifies nothing while pouring out words:

> Oh retorico amore
> opera-fascino

Oh rhetorical love / spell-work

> Ardeva il fascino e la realtà
> conversando convergendo
> horeb ardevi tutto d'arbusti
> tutto arbusto horeb il mondo ardeva

The spell burned and reality / conversing converging / horeb you burned full
of burning bushes / all a bush horeb the world burned

> questa espressione è la punta di diamante
> del retorizzamento, lo scolice della
> sacramentale contraddizione

this expression is the diamond point / of rhetorical speech, the scolex of /
sacramental contradiction

> una sola parola che diceva
> e diceva il dire
> e diceva il che. E. Congiungere. Con.
>   ('Retorica su')

one word alone which spoke / and it spoke the speaking / and it spoke the
why and the wherefore. And. To join up. With.

The passage, as indicated, ends with the words 'E. Congiungere. Con.'
Zanzotto is tacitly acknowledging that his revolutionary poems bear an affinity
with political rhetoric. They too have often functioned on the rhetorical
principles of 'contradiction' and 'addition'. The language of these poems was
called a 'lingua-rubino' ('Possibili prefazi VII'); now political rhetoric is called
a 'punta di diamante'. In the section above Zanzotto is condemning political
rhetoric for its ability to fascinate; in the sixth and final section of 'Retorica su'
he avows to his own use of language for the very same purpose:

> Quelle sarebbero state le parole finali
> ma . . . Ancora il fascino?
> Il fascino e il principio

Those would have been the last words / but . . . Fascination still? / Fascination and the beginning.

The poem ends with an indication that it has not ended as such, reinforcing thereby this principle of fascination:

> L'azione sbanda si riprende
> sbanda glissa e

The action scatters picks itself up again / scatters glides and.

Zanzotto, it would seem, is accusing himself of a degree of untruthful sensationalism. This sensationalism undoubtedly had a large part to play in his provocation of 'outrage' in the logocentric reader, as is testified by a line from 'Profezie I': 'non mancare allo show, né poi allo show dei piccoli oltraggi' ('Do not miss the show, nor the show of the little outrages').

The use of paradox and contradiction in LB is therefore not limited to individual poems. The poet's impudent parody of a logocentric tradition is occasionally beset with recantations and doubts. The fact that these doubts are strewn through the work and not bundled together into one of its sequences, helps only to intensify the impression of conflict. This conflict of ideas then intentionally jars with the architectural structure of the work as a whole (Agosti 1972, 217), to create yet another form of paradox.

Paradox is what is upheld in the end. Zanzotto refuses to make sense of his contrary allegiances to a traditional poetry with logocentric persuasions and to a revolutionary poetry destroying the concept of a logos. The variance is left in Zanzotto's mind in just the same manner as it is left in the book – in the disparate form of a 'collage':

> No, non respingo, non accetto.
> Lo sottopongo come tanti a
> un – creduto possibile – collage
> ('Possibili prefazi IX')

No, I do not reject, I do not accept. / I submit it like so many others for / a – believed to be possible – collage.

The last poem in the collection reinforces this idea:

> . . . torno
> senza arte né parte: ma attivante
> ('E la madre-norma')

. . . I return / with neither art nor part: but activating

('And the Mother-Norm').

To adhere exclusively to one school of thought necessarily implies the rejection of another. Zanzotto is 'attivante' because he refuses to be biased: more creatively 'free' on account of his tolerance. Paradox, in the collection, points toward poetical freedom.

All the same, paradox, of its nature, is opposed to logocentrism, since a serious commitment to it must necessarily include a paradoxical sense of the paradoxical. The doubter cannot be sure even of his doubt, of the validity of his word doubting his word. In this sense Zanzotto is paradoxically consistent.

Chapter 5

Deconstruction in *Pasque* (1968–73)

The most fundamental link between *Pasque* PSQ (*Easters*) and LB is Zanzotto's continued questioning of logocentrism. Zanzotto is once again concerned with undermining logocentrism, but whereas in LB his criticisms were directed exclusively against the logocentric reader, he now condemns two institutions which are responsible, in his opinion, for encouraging one to read and think in the logocentric tradition. The institutions in question are the school and the church, and in PSQ Zanzotto attempts to deconstruct some of the ideas underlying them, dealing mostly with the school system in the first section of the book ('Misteri della Pedagogia' ('Mysteries of Pedagogy')), and the church in the second ('Pasque' ('Easters')). However, in the process of his critique, Zanzotto, as in LB, is ready to acknowledge the inadequacies of parts of his arguments and in the final analysis, as will be shown, he deconstructs many of his own opinions and much of his own method of writing in PSQ.

Deconstruction, therefore, in PSQ is to be understood in a general sense. But the more theoretical use of the term 'deconstruction' comes into play, for the main reason why Zanzotto objects to the school and the church is because he sees them as being closely related to the concept of logocentrism in language: schooling can only operate on the assumption that words have specific meanings, and to believe in a God or a logos is to give a centre and meaning to all of one's language and thought.

In Chapter 4 I explained how Derrida's theory of language evolved from a criticism of Saussure: Derrida proposed that the sign is a container of innumerable meanings as opposed to a vehicle for conveying some specific meaning outside itself, arguing that there is no logos which stabilizes one's language and thought. The term invented by Derrida to describe this instability of language is 'différance' (a word created from the French verb 'différer' meaning both 'to be different from' and 'to defer'), and the philosopher himself throughout his work explores the instability of those concepts which serve as the axioms or rules for a period of thought.

Zanzotto too undertakes what might be called experiments with 'différance' in PSQ. He had prepared the ground in LB when he defied the reader to think in the logocentric tradition while reading the poems. He was, moreover, actually indicating 'différance' when he pointed to the numerous possible meanings of the signifier in his notes to the poems (see Chapter 4, pages 139–40) and when he allowed the signifier's 'differential' qualities to play a large part in the construction of a poem (see Chapter 4, pages 140–2). Experiments such as these are repeated on a much larger scale in PSQ, for whereas in LB Zanzotto was to a certain extent anticipating Derrida, now, by 1968, Zanzotto is familiar with Derrida's thought given that Derrida's work began to be published in 1967.

'MISTERI DELLA PEDAGOGIA'

In the poem which opens the book and has the same title as the first section, Zanzotto describes and comments upon an occasion when he was giving a lecture on Dante in the local 'Centro di Lettura', attended by people of various ages and occupations. It is through the use of irony that Zanzotto's basic objections to pedagogy become apparent. He objects to three things. First, the manner in which the pedagogical system promotes knowledge as something both personally and socially profitable, the social benefits being responsible, in Zanzotto's opinion, for reinforcing hierarchic systems of power within society. Second, he objects to the systems of power involved in pedagogy itself. And third, he opposes pedagogy's unquestioning faith in the undifferentiated meaning of signifiers.

It is the first of the above objections – the conception of knowledge as something personally profitable, as a kind of spiritual food which will enrich one's understanding and appreciation of life – which is ironized in the opening lines of the poem where Zanzotto continually plays upon the 'food' metaphor:

> Qui si somministra la dolcissima linfa del sapere
> . . .
> e i fanciulli e i vecchi suggono
> è certo che apprendono al Centro di Lettura:
> e si imparte e comparte la vivanda
> . . .
> si premia e castiga con frutto
> . . . ; si offre più d'un documento
> a bene pregiare la vita e tutto

Here one administers the sweetest lymph of knowledge / . . . / and the young and the old suck / they certainly learn things at the Reading Centre: / and one gives and shares the victuals / . . . / one rewards and punishes fruitfully / . . . ; one offers more than one document / to appreciate life and everything to the full.

This process of enriching the spirit (the 'inside') in order to appreciate life (the 'outside') ('a bene pregiare la vita') is also parodied in a recurring motif which operates as a metaphor for the spirit / life relationship: inside the 'Centro di Lettura' / outside the 'Centro di Lettura'. In the following passage, for example, Zanzotto underlines the disparity as opposed to the desired assimilation between the 'inside' and the 'outside', a disparity announced by the adverb 'invece':

> E i bachi li hai visti serificare
> da tutto il loro immenso ghiotto?
>
> . . .
>
> Primavera baco e natura
> da troppo in ambage
> fuori del Centro di Lettura
> vanno al bosco vanno in muda
> vanno in vacca dormono della quarta
> e noi del Centro invece – oh notte –
> siamo con Dante e la maestra
> e il maestro reggente e gli uditori
> alla questua dei valori
> siamo tesoro non turbato

And have you seen the silkworms satiate / their enormous gluttony on everything? / . . . / Spring silkworm and nature / deviating for too long / outside the Reading Centre / they go into the wood they moult / they go to pot they sleep like logs / and we in the Centre on the other hand – oh night– we're here with Dante and the schoolmistress / and the schoolmaster regent and the listeners / on the quest for values / we are undisturbed treasure.

This division between the 'inside' and the 'outside', or, in commonplace language, the illusion of learning about life through literature, will be highlighted again in 'Proteine, proteine' ('Proteins, proteins') (to be dealt with shortly). But in 'Misteri della Pedagogia' Zanzotto is even more concerned with undermining the idea that knowledge procures great social benefits.

Education, he ironically concedes, can help one to achieve status, to progress socially by means of the examination system:

> Capito? Attenti, vero? Ai comportamenti
> del mondo, a come si ottiene il frutto,
> a come abbondi il prodotto all'esame;
> esaminare dunque, e poi avanti

Understood? You're taking note, aren't you? Of the world's / ways, of how you obtain the fruit, / of how the product may abound on examination; / to examine therefore, and then on you go.

Nevertheless, it thereby divides society into the successful and the unsuccessful ('magagna sangue e tempo gramo / sulla pagina caso pone' ('fate places on the page / infirmity blood and wretched times')). In other words, that which claims to be acting for the progress and welfare of society both on an individual level, as indicated above, and by extension, on a universal level:

> e che successi perfino su guerre pesti
> e folgori otterresti   otterremmo
> grazie al nostro metodo

> and what successes even over wars plagues / and thunderbolts you would obtain
> we would obtain / thanks to our method

is, in fact, instrumental in creating systems of class and power within society which, far from combating war and pestilence, can be responsible for producing the latter. Zanzotto goes on to suggest this in a section of very passionate language:

> Fuori pedagogia   out out, contro i meli e le maestre,
> le potenze . . . i prìncipi . . . li scruti dalla finestrina dall'oblò
> (trafiggono imprendono gestiscono
> non conoscono le sazietà gesticolano impalano
> si fanno razzi scoppiano
> in corolle di scintille lassù . . .)

> Get out pedagogy out out, against apple-trees and schoolmistresses, / powers
> . . . princes . . . you scrutinize them from your little window from your
> porthole / (they pierce undertake administrate / they don't know when
> they're full they gesticulate impale / they become rockets which explode /
> into corollas of sparks up there . . .).

Here he condemns pedagogy (using rally-vocabulary: 'Fuori pedagogia out out') for the part it plays in establishing 'princes' or people in places of supremacy (in this particular passage he would seem to be referring to politicians whom he condemns elsewhere for other reasons (Allen, 'Interview' 256–7)). These people cultivate a desire for power which knows no limits ('non conoscono le sazietà') and their government must in some way involve the perpetration of violence – an idea conveyed not only by the reference to exploding rockets, but also by the manner in which Zanzotto juxtaposes verbs suggesting administration and organization ('imprendono', 'gestiscono') with verbs referring to murder ('trafiggono', 'impalano').

It is precisely this ability of pedagogy to divide society, and to generate class wars and violence on account of this division, which Zanzotto emphasizes in an article on Pasolini entitled 'Pedagogy'. Here he claims that Pasolini had always presented the problem of power in terms of education, and to illustrate this opinion which, as becomes apparent from the tone of the article, is very much shared by Zanzotto, he quotes from an interview given by Pasolini and released a few hours before his assassination:

> Power is an educational system which divides us into the repressed and the repressors. And, pay heed. It's the same educational system which moulds all of us, from the so called ruling classes, even down to the poor. . . . The first tragedy is this: a common, obligatory and mistaken education which thrusts us all into the arena of wanting to have everything at all costs. In this arena we are driven like a strange and dark army in which someone has the cannons and someone else the crossbars. . . . In a certain sense everyone is weak, because everyone is a victim. And everyone is to blame, because everyone is ready for the massacre game.

The 'massacre game' is of course one which operates in two directions: 'repressors' against 'repressed' and vice versa. Indeed in 'Misteri della Pedagogia' Zanzotto captures the mutuality of such violence through the image of his seventy-year-old and bluestocking colleague, 'la signorina Morchet' ('Miss Morchet') assuming her authoritative (repressive) role as teacher, as seated beside him she quotes Dante line after line, but symbolizing, as Zanzotto remarks in his notes to the poem, the (repressed) 'tricoteuse rivoluzionaria' ('revolutionary knitter') (the use of the French word for 'knitter' seems to indicate a reference to a knitter from the French Revolution):

> maestra Morchet assenziente tricotante
> e citando citando Dante
> sù verso a verso scalante

schoolmistress Morchet nodding knitting / and quoting and quoting Dante / climbing upwards and upwards line by line.

This authoritative role of the teacher is something that is heavily accentuated throughout the whole of the poem in the use of words and expressions such as 'onniveggenza' ('all-seeingness'), 'la signorina Morchet, medaglia d'oro alla P.I.' ('Miss Morchet, Public Education gold medallist'), 'le potenze' ('the powers') and 'il maestro reggente' ('the schoolmaster regent'). By means of such phrases Zanzotto's second objection to the school system becomes apparent. He is emphasizing how school itself is a power-based institution. The pupil, that is, is governed by the authoritative teacher, but the teacher is also subservient to those who administer the educational system, and who expect the teacher to assume an authoritative role. It is this aspect of pedagogy which Zanzotto alludes to when, with humour and self-directed irony, he presents himself as an incompetent lecturer, who is incapable of projecting authority ('e imito a gogò le potenze' ('and I imitate non-stop the powers')), who loses his train of thought (indicated by frequent ellipses), whose words are mere 'glossolalìe' (that is, connected by sound as opposed to sense), who prays to Dante himself for inspiration ('Se Dante aiutando . . .' ('If with Dante's help')), or for an intervening joke from the audience ('Ma non sapevi . . . / . . . che attendevo il tuo intervento / di dantista desmàt?' ('But didn't you know . . . / . . . that I expected you to be present as a Dante-joker'), 'desmàt' being the dialect word for a game without money stakes, hence, a not very serious game), and concludes that after such a disastrous performance he is liable to be 'castrated' by pedagogy:

> . . . Avrò un voto
> basso, di annientamento,
> sarò castrato dalla pedagogia

> . . . I'll get a low / annihilating score, / I'll be castrated by pedagogy.

Zanzotto's third and last objection to school is bound up with his second objection. In a reasoning which may be anachronistic today (at least, one hopes, among teachers of contemporary poetry), the poet claims that the hierarchical relationship between student and teacher is largely maintained through the latter's obligation to provide the 'right answers', or, in the context of literature-teaching, the 'correct interpretations'. This idea goes back to *IXE* where, in the poem 'Scolastica', a disillusioned teacher, denoted by 'a', tells teacher 'b' that 'b' probably only teaches because he knows the answers to his own questions, and it is the God-like omnipotence of this attitude that 'a' rejects: 'Oh, una sola risposta: e tutto / insegnerò, sed tantum dic verbo!' ('Oh, only one answer: and I'll teach / everything, but only speak the word!') (see Chapter 3, pages 126–9 where I examine 'Scolastica'). Providing correct interpretations of literature presupposes that words have *determinate* meanings. Pedagogy, in other words, operates under the assumption that language is a logocentric phenomenon. Consequently it is language itself which is underpinning pedagogy's ascending gradations of position and power. This point is reinforced in 'Frammento di un poemetto "Pigmalione '70" non più ritrovato' ('Fragment of a short poem "Pygmalion '70", never found again') – another poem in the first section of *PSQ*. Here Zanzotto indicates a possible 'teaching' which avoids the hierarchical relationship between teacher and student:

> Qui tra discente e docente il divario
> si conclude, tra chi guidi e chi segua

> Here the gap between learner and teacher / between the one who guides and the one who follows, closes.

The two elements involved in this reciprocal relationship are represented symbolically in the poem by what would seem to be the moon and the sun:

>Quieta luce, favola di spuma –
>luna albeggiante

Quiet light, fable of dawning / froth-moon

>. . .; il magistero cede
>là all'orlo, al varco. E cederà alla statua
>materica, simile suo, erede

>suo.

. . .; mastery yields / there at the edge, at the opening. And it will yield to the material / statue, its fellow, its / heir.

The reason why these two elements can have this special, mutual relationship in which each can simultaneously 'teach' and be 'taught' by the other is because their 'teaching' is a silent one where language does not intervene: '*Quieta* luce', '*Muta* statua docente' ('*Mute* teaching statue'). In pointing to this non-hierarchic system of 'instruction' operating between the silent elements of Nature (which is, admittedly, more a question of communication than instruction, although Zanzotto does apply the 'teaching' metaphor) the poet is attempting to emphasize how hierarchic systems of power occur only when the teaching is verbalized, only when it functions by means of language, and where that language is seen to consist of words with unequivocal meanings.

One presumes that Miss Morchet, a natural authoritarian, would never undertake to teach the poetry of Zanzotto: 'Le poesie di suo nipote si capiscono poco' ('Your nephew's poems are not easily understood'), she once remarked to the poet's aunt, and in this, Zanzotto declares, she symbolizes pedagogy itself: 'un po' dura, un po' tonta, un po' sorda' ('a little harsh, a little stupid, a little deaf'). Indeed Miss Morchet interrupts Zanzotto's lecture with what she thinks is an enlightening quotation from Dante:

>. . . 'Lume non è se non vien dal sereno
>che non si turba mai'

. . . 'There is no light unless it comes from heaven / which is never disturbed'

and the quotation itself allows Zanzotto to ironize that logocentric dependence upon a logos or a God (the 'Lume' of the quotation) who gives to words their 'serene', unambiguous meanings. The two lines are echoed at various stages in the poem to emphasize the complacency involved in this theory of language ('siamo tesoro non turbato' ('we are undisturbed treasure')), Zanzotto's rejection of it ('Turbato è il significato' ('The meaning is disturbed')) and his attempts, therefore, to disturb the 'serenity' of Miss Morchet's maxim by cutting it up in various ways, and by distorting its original sense:

'luce non è che non venga da quella'

'no light exists which does not come from that'

'Lume non è che non venga'

'No light exists which does not come'

'Lume non è se non vien
                                    si turba mai'

'There is no light unless it comes / it is never disturbed'.

To teach according to a theory which would deny the logocentrism of language, and would therefore emphasize the differential meanings of words and texts, would be to encourage the doubts in interpretation which pedagogy deceitfully wishes to avoid:

– oh cieli della pedagogia –
per andare avanti
indenne attraverso 'i dubbi eccessivi le negazioni
che feriscono i bambini'

– oh skies of pedagogy – / to go forward / unharmed through 'excessive doubts and negations / that wound children'.

'PROTEINE, PROTEINE'

Parts of Zanzotto's three objections to pedagogy as illustrated in 'Misteri della Pedagogia' are then highlighted in different ways in all of the poems which follow in the first section. On a very playful note, 'Proteine, proteine' once again ridicules the assumption that the ideas of books can be applied to reality. Here the poet has left the Teaching Centre and his serious discourse on Dante, and is really 'learning' about life, not through literature, but on the busy, fouled streets of town!:

E tu t'inoltri per entro la città e schiacci
entri col piede, così apprendi a fondo, nel vivissimo

And you head off into town and squelch / your foot sinks right in, that way you learn thoroughly, amidst that which is truly alive.

Zanzotto has slipped on dog-dirt which emphasizes how the 'food' of this poem is material as opposed to spiritual. Indeed the poet has gone into town to purchase some dog-food whose 'protein' and energy-value – in contrast to the sterile food of knowledge – is conveyed in the lively rhythm and exuberant internal rhyme of the following passage:

> 'Proteine in quantità – per la Sua felicità,
> mille vasi di Loyal – e di Kik e Ciappi e Pal;
> pieno colmo vo' che sia – ogni étage giardino o via
> della kukka del mio Lassi – che a ciascun suggelli i passi,
> vo' che il cantico di Fido – nelle psichi faccia nido;
> proteine proteine – bilanciate, sopraffine' –

'Proteins in big measure – for His happiness, / a thousand tins of Loyal – and of Kick, Chappie and Pal; / I want them brimming over – every floor garden or street / with the shit of my Lassie – so that it prints everyone's footsteps, / I want Fido's canticle – to make its nest in psyches; / proteins proteins – balanced, extra-lean'.

'LA PACE DI OLIVA'

In 'La pace di Oliva' ('Oliva's peace-treaty') Zanzotto is back in the class-room and it is the systems of power in which pedagogy is fixed which are shown again to be largely precarious. The light-hearted note is maintained. Here a memory lapse on the part of both student and teacher, neither of whom can recall the date of the 'Oliva' peace-treaty:

> Eh   dopo   mi pare
> que   e in   v v v
> dunque, nel Riss nel Mindel o nel Würm?

Emm . . . afterwards I think / th and in vvv . . . / hence, in Riss in Mindel or in Würm?

produces an embarrassing situation for the teacher whose supremacy is suddenly invalidated, and a humorous situation for the students who are aware of this. While the system demands that he, as teacher, must continue nevertheless to maintain the authoritative role, inwardly he recognizes that teacher and pupil now occupy a position of equality. Such an attitude is indicated in the poem by the first person plural verbs and by the mirror image announced by the adverb 'specularmente' which follow the initial imperatives for order:

> 'Voi là, in fondo. Fermi!
> La smettete?' Smettiamo
> riponiamo smorziamo
> specularmente fermi nel mattutino dolcore
> in un portento ⌣ in un
> equilibrio del terrore

'You there, at the back. Keep still! / Will you stop it?' We stop / we
consider the question again we quieten down / specularly still in the morning
sweetness / in wonder ∿ in an / equilibrium of terror.

Once again it is not only the power-based 'docente / discente' relationship which
is being highlighted here but that which also operates between the teacher and his
superiors. The poet can sense the students' glee that he, the teacher, is uncertain,
and expresses his fears (albeit somewhat tongue-in-cheek) that the incident might
be disclosed to the local educational authority:

> Sottoporre il docente a un test di accertamento.
> Segnalarlo al provveditore

Subjecting the teacher to an assessment test. / Pointing him out to the local
authority.

The point being criticized is the generally accepted belief that if teaching is
to operate successfully there must be a disciplining, on the part of everyone
involved, of thoughts, words, and deeds, and it is in opposition to this emphasis
upon discipline that Zanzotto in both sections of PSQ emphasizes a number of
states which convey mental and verbal disarray. These comprise not only dream
states and those effected by drugs and alcohol, but also memory lapses and certain
medical disorders. Memory lapses are often indicated in the poems by means
of blank spaces as above in 'La pace di Oliva', and again in 'Sovraesistenze'
('Supraexistences'):

> si rinsanguava   così   per difetto   con
> ogni deliziosa omissione ammanco addio
> oh rinnovatevi memorie come erboso spessore
> sagra vuota colonnina lampeggiatore
> ecco un   ecco un
> un misero pochino

got new blood thus for lack of with / every delightful omission shortage
farewell / oh renew yourselves memories like grassy thickness / empty festival
little pillar blinker / behold a behold a / a wretched little bit.

'Biglia (Pasqua e antidoti)' ('Marble (Easter and antidotes)') speaks of 'fosfeni' –
phosphenes, or the spots which appear before the eyes in a pathological situation;
as well as 'acufeni' – an incessant humming in the ears. 'Misteri della Pedagogia'
and 'Xenoglossie' ('Xenoglossies') indicate symptoms of psychological abnormal-
ity: 'xenoglossia' – a phenomenon whereby the subject expresses himself in one
or more languages unknown to him in normal conditions; and 'glossolalia' – a

pathological symptom where the subject speaks words with syllabic associations deprived of sense. Zanzotto even goes so far as to suggest that not only in the poems of PSQ, but also in literature in general, there is often a deliberate cultivation of mental disorder. This, it is implied, contradicts *a priori* the orderly structures which didactic readings attempt to impose upon literature:

> Così comincerebbe la poesia.
> Nell'ondeggiare, oscillare. Osteria.
> E strofinarsi gli occhi: buttate all'aria
> foglie montagnole
> stagnole
>
> ('Chele')

And so poetry would begin. / In wavering, oscillating. Tavern. / And rubbing one's eyes: throw into the air / leaves mountains / tinfoils   .

('Chelae').

'QUALCUNO C'ERA'

There are also two poems in the collection which aim to show how the mind by its nature defies the rational codifications which pedagogy would like to place upon it. Both 'Microfilm' and 'Qualcuno c'era' ('Someone was There') transcribe a dream, and, therefore, the workings of the unconscious or the more 'real' self. In 'Microfilm' (to be examined in more detail later) the dream actually contains its own interpretation which indicates the *impossibility* of rationally interpreting another part of the dream. In 'Qualcuno c'era' (where the poet dreams that the child who accompanies him on a walk is suddenly transformed into a mother rabbit; and the two dolls she carries, into two young rabbits), the transcriber of the dream, now in a state of consciousness, can easily recall all of its physical sensations – the things which he smelled: 'Fermento di legna odore in più' ('Wood-ferment added scent'); and which he heard: 'e udii: / nitriti guaiti mugugni' ('and I heard: / whinnies yelps mutterings'); or saw:

> E tutto è quasi senza colori, lo guardano,
> fieno a fili denteggiano e guardano: se piove?
> . . .
> Mamina-coniglia due bambi e – goccia a goccia –
> nello sfollato nel perso.   Sfocato

And everything is almost colourless, they watch it, / they munch through blades of hay and watch: if it's raining? / . . . / Little-mummy-rabbit two young ones and – drop by drop – / in the empty area in the dark. Out of focus.

But he cannot sensibly analyze the meaning of the dream although he is aware that its contents are operating as signifiers ('segni' ('signs')) of some deeper reality of the self:

> . . . E non avanzo nulla più
> che la fasciola di sera, che la tendina acquata,
> che il fieno impigliato tra i segni

> . . . And I don't leave behind anything more / than the little strip of evening,
> than the curtain of rain, / than the hay entangled among the signs.

By his use of the word 'segni' Zanzotto is relating the dream-work of the unconscious to language. In this he has been influenced by Lacan (in his interview with Allen he spoke of Lacan as being a 'decisive influence' on his work). Lacan in his 'L'instance de la lettre dans l'inconscient' claims that the unconscious is structured like a language because it is composed less of stable meanings (and Zanzotto cannot find one in his dream) than of signifiers. Just as in language, the signified 'slides beneath' the signifier because of the signifier's relationship to other signifiers, so that meaning can never be pinned down, so too in the unconscious. This is exactly what is illustrated in the poem 'Microfilm' where Zanzotto is actually dreaming about *theories* of language, and his dream reveals a metonymic movement of words and highlights the impossibility of pinning down meaning. In 'Qualcuno c'era', however, Zanzotto is only pointing to the relationship between the unconscious and language by using the word 'segni'. He then goes on to emphasize that relationship by making the words of the poem which describe the dream undergo the same transformation process that has taken place *within* the dream (the changing of the young girl into a 'Mamina-coniglia'). Hence the transformation of the word 'coniglio' ('rabbit') into the neologisms 'conigliazione' ('rabbiting'), 'sconigliare' ('to disrabbit'), 'legna-coniglia' ('wood-rabbit'), and 'Mamina-coniglia'.

The last two compounds 'legna-coniglia' and 'Mamina-coniglia' can be taken as examples of words which each refer to two concepts as opposed to one. In that sense they are connected to Zanzotto's third objection to pedagogy – pedagogy's belief in the undifferentiated meaning of signifiers – which was illustrated in 'Misteri della Pedagogia' but which is also illustrated in a much more exciting way in four other poems, three of which are in the first section of PSQ.

In contrast to pedagogy, these poems are not logocentrically oriented. Different features in them reveal that here Zanzotto is experimenting with Derrida's theory of 'différance'. This theory, as I explained in Chapter 4, proposes that a signifier is not a complete entity in itself, but is related to other *different* signifiers through phonic similarities and semantic associations (including antithetical ones). Consequently, an individual signifier *defers* the full presence of the concept which our linguistic system normally attributes to it, since it contains within itself not one, but a number of concepts.

The four poems in which Zanzotto experiments with this theory of language are 'Frammento di un poemetto "Pigmalione '70" non più ritrovato', 'Semine del Mazzaról' ('The Mazzaról's Sowings'), 'Per lumina, per limina' ('Through Lights, Through Thresholds'), and 'Microfilm'. Whereas the first three of these belong to section 1 of the book, the last divides the collection into two equal halves of eleven poems each, and acts as a transition to section 2 in that it attempts to deconstruct some of the premises of the church.

'FRAMMENTO DI UN POEMETTO'

Here Zanzotto presents the reader with a poem constructed entirely around a single term where, to apply some of the words of the poem itself, 'l'ambiguo ed il precario / cinge e irida il certo, gli si adegua' ('the ambiguous and the precarious / surrounds and colours the certain like a rainbow, conforms to it'). This ambiguity issues from the fact that it is a term which contains within it, not one signified, but a number of them, each of which relates in some way to the theme of pedagogy. Zanzotto is therefore playing with the concept of 'différance'. The term in question has been referred to earlier: 'Muta statua docente' ('Mute teaching statue') and one of its possible signifieds has already been suggested: the moon ('statua') involved in a reciprocal, non-linguistic 'teaching' relationship with the sun. This interpretation can be supported by three other lines of the poem where Zanzotto would seem to be juxtaposing the non-violent 'pedagogy' of the moon with the violence of man's pedagogical instincts – his 'rending' of the moon for the benefit of knowledge and science, his desire to 'humanize' the moon, to demystify, that is, its texture and operations, and make them accessible to the human intellect:

> . . . Machina squarciata
> che ostenta i suoi dolenti impasti:
> o già-umana, o ad essere umana destinata!

> . . . Rended machine / which flaunts its painful mixtures: / either you are already human, or destined to be human!

The last line of this quotation refers one, however, to another possible signified of the term 'Muta statua docente', one in fact emphasized by the reference to 'Pigmalione' in the title of the poem. According to the ancient Greek myth as recorded by Ovid, Pygmalion, the King of Cyprus and a very celebrated sculptor, fashioned a life-like statue of a woman (possibly Zanzotto's 'Muta statua') embodying his ideal of beauty (the phrase which complements the term in question reads 'che in beltà ti deponi' ('who lays yourself down in beauty')) because he could find no living woman who met that ideal. As it happened, the statue turned out to be so beautiful that he fell in love with it, and begged Aphrodite to bring it to life, which she did (Zanzotto's statue is 'destinata' 'ad essere umana'). Again in the story the emphasis falls upon man's pedagogical instincts – his desire for improvement, for perfection – which would justify Zanzotto's use of the adjective 'docente' in the term in question. The statue 'teaches' in that it is intended to represent perfect beauty.

It was the pedagogical aspect of the myth that led George Bernard Shaw to write *Pygmalion*. In this play, while focusing upon the theme of pedagogy in his story of a flower-girl trained by a phonetician to pass as a lady, Shaw simultaneously produced an effective satire on the English class system. This linking of pedagogy and class systems encourages one to think that Zanzotto is alluding to Shaw's *Pygmalion* as well, especially since, as I have shown earlier, he considers pedagogy and class systems to be intimately related (see pages 157–9). The 'Muta statua docente', in this case, could be taken as referring to Pygmalion, Eliza Doolittle's phonetician: the 'statua' reinforcing the inhuman, mechanical method of learning by repetition that he makes Eliza adopt, and the 'muta' being used ironically since Pygmalion's teaching falls on deaf ears. The epigraph to the poem which speaks of a 'Design for a Brain' reinforces the allusion to Shaw's *Pygmalion*, while at the same time the word 'Design' helps to maintain an allusion to the exemplary model created by the Pygmalion of the myth.

'SEMINE DEL MAZZARÓL'

A similar experiment with 'différance' is carried out in 'Semine del Mazzaról'. Here it is the word 'Mazzaról' which is charged with diverse meanings which are then, as the title suggests, 'disseminated' or scattered across the poem in a Derridean 'play of differences'. Taking his information from the *Dizionario del Feltrino Rustico* by Migliorini and Pellegrini, Zanzotto explains in his notes that 'Mazzaról' is the equivalent of an 'omenét salvàrek' which denotes a 'folletto vestito di rosso capace di portar via cavalli e persino ragazze. Ai cavalli intrecciava i crini e ci metteva degli aghi d'argento' ('an elf dressed in red and capable of carrying away horses and even young girls. He would plait the horses' manes and put silver needles in them'). Zanzotto observes that this 'mazzaról' must have spoken Italian, for the dictionary records him as saying of his mischievous behaviour 'ghi ghi ghi che bel gioco' ('hee hee hee what a fine game').

However, already in the first section of the poem, Zanzotto uses, not the concept of the 'folletto' itself, but its particular quality to 'portar via', to construct another signified for the word 'Mazzaròl': what is referred to later as an 'alkohol mazzaról':

> Quanto vero semini   in quante
> menti disattutite concimate aizzate –
> oh più ulissemente più lacciolo più gancetto e amo

> (e là il crollame dei vigneti
> che mi teneva a galla, a mamma,
> che mi teneva al soleggiato, in solecchio)

How much truth you sew in how many / unmitigated fertilized incited minds – / oh more like Ulysses more snare more little hook and fish-hook / (and there the felling of the vineyards / which kept me afloat, kept me with mummy, / kept me exposed to the sun, shading my eyes from the sun).

'Mazzaról', therefore, becomes a word to denote alcohol and, more specifically, the ability of alcohol to alter or 'carry away' the mind (the 'lacciolo', 'gancetto' and 'amo' of the section are all variations of the 'aghi d'argento' of the note, and operate as metaphors for this). It carries away the mind in that it 'unattenuates' ('disattutite') or incites ('aizzate') the thinking process. This second meaning of 'Mazzaról' as alcohol is also reinforced by the reference to the cutting down of vineyards.

In the second section, the two meanings of 'Mazzaról' which have now been established – 'folletto' and 'alkohol' – are fused to form a third meaning: the poet himself as a 'Mazzaról':

> anch'io
>   campanellini
> campanule   minimosaici
> molecolelle alcoolizzatamente
> lepide,
> o Algol-stella, alkohol mazzaról

me too / little bells / bellflowers minimosaics / little molecules alcoholically / witty, / oh Algol-star, alcohol mazzaról.

He is pictured as a mischievous 'folletto' or court-jester with bells ('anch'io / campanellini') writing poems which are light-hearted ('lepide') as opposed to sober-sided, and which fuddle the reader's mind ('alcoolizzatamente / lepide') in that meaning is scattered and needs to be fitted together like the pieces of a mosaic ('minimosaici') (and in this way, one could add, they 'carry' the reader 'più in qua o più in là / del giusto significato' ('Pasqua di Maggio') ('more behind or more beyond / the right meaning') ('May Easter')).

The third section begins with a return to the second meaning of 'Mazzaról' as 'alkohol':

> sei il mio vinello
> di una cantina canterina
> in bottigliette da sorcio da putto da mazzaról

you are my nice light wine / of a singing cellar / in little mice bottles cherub bottles mazzaról bottles.

In the course of writing, however, a fourth meaning of 'Mazzaról' has been casually introduced: 'Mazzaròl' as 'putto', a word which in itself carries two meanings since it is capable of referring both to a little boy and to a sculptured Cupid or cherub.

The section ends with another example of combining certain meanings which have already been created – the second ('Mazzaról' as 'alkohol') to the third ('Mazzaról' as poet-jester) – for the latter is now playfully depicted as being 'under the influence' of the former. An inebriated poet-jester is therefore the fifth meaning of 'Mazzaról':

> Oh mi è tolto mi è tolto il pallore
> nel prossimo giro do sullo stinco
> do nell'igneo nell'issimo

Oh my pallor is gone, it's been taken from me / on my next lap I'll be close to the shin-bone / close to the igneous to the superlative.

Finally, a sixth meaning occurs in the last section: the signified spoken of in Zanzotto's notes (the mischievous 'folletto') is now identified with the Cupid-'putto' of section 3, to create the last meaning of 'Mazzaról' as an elfin-Cupid:

> quanti teatri tutti da ripetere
> ai signori pòsteri ai signori majores
> quanti allestimenti incontri intenti
> ma più quando al suo amore (il bello scherzo)
> restituire qualcuno ci è permesso

how many performances all to be repeated / for the gentlemen descendants and the gentlemen ancestors / how many stagings meetings intentions / but it's best (the classic joke) when we're allowed / to give back someone to his love.

The poem then concludes by referring to the method by which it has been constructed: through a continual procreation of signifieds, an 'inanellarsi di tutti tra tutti e inoltre tutti' ('a linking up of everything among everything and beyond everything').

'PER LUMINA, PER LIMINA'

Before examining 'Per lumina, per limina' in detail, it would be beneficial to illustrate through diagrams the similarity and difference in construction between both 'Frammento di un poemetto' and 'Semine del Mazzaról' on the one hand, and 'Per lumina, per limina' on the other. The 'Per lumina, per limina' diagram illustrates at a glance the 'elaborate verbal architectures' of this poem (Agosti 1973, 23).

Just as in (a) and (b) where a specific term, and a word, respectively, radiated a number of different meanings, so too in (c) the initial signifier 'lumina' ('lights') is not fixed in unequivocal meaning, for it has two meanings: 'alba' ('dawn') and 'luna' ('moon'). But in (c) the discourse on 'différance' is much more extended than in (a) and (b) for the signifier 'alba' is shown to contain within itself different, oppositional qualities which then combine to create another signifier, 'napalm', which like 'lumina' has not one meaning but explodes into

(a) 'Frammento di un poemetto'.

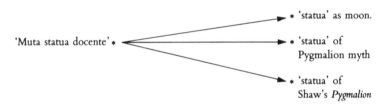

(b) 'Semine del Mazzaról'.

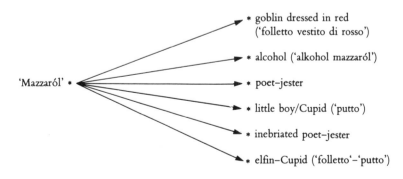

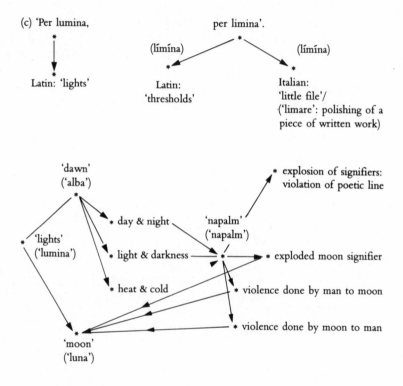

(c) 'Per lumina,   per limina'.

a number of related meanings some of which have associations with the earlier signified 'luna'.

The second noun of the poem's title, meanwhile, is also pervaded by 'différance'. With a change of stress, which from the point of view of 'différance' is insignificant, 'limina' can be considered both as an Italian word and as a Latin neuter plural. 'Limína' in Italian is the diminutive of 'lima', a file (recalling the verb 'limare' which in its figurative sense refers to the polishing of a piece of written work); 'límina' in Latin means 'thresholds'. Therefore, while the signifier 'limina' is itself pervaded by 'différance' since it refers to more than one concept, if taken to mean 'thresholds' it has a relationship of similarity with the other noun of the title – 'lumina' – one of whose meanings is the 'little light' of 'dawn', dawn being a threshold between night and day.

While illustrating along with 'Frammento di un poemetto' and 'Semine del Mazzaról' the concept of 'différance' in language, 'Per lumina, per limina', by lengthening the discourse on 'différance' also helps to exemplify the constant deferral of meaning in the poem – the deferral of, what Derrida calls, a 'transcendental signifier', that is, a signifier which would have a single signified (with unambiguous qualities) as opposed to a number of them. I shall now look more closely at the poem itself to show how an autonomous signifier is continually delayed.

The scene is that of dawn, but a dawn in which the moon is still present, so that the 'lights' of which the title speaks refer to both of these things: the light of dawn and the light of the moon:

> . . . e il venire
> all'impatto del levissimo col levissimo
> del freschissimo con l'altro astrale

and the coming / to a point of impact of the lightest with the lightest / of the freshest with the other astral one.

Two phenomena, 'dawn' and 'moon', which are normally related to two opposing times, day and night respectively, are therefore combined within one signifier ('lumina'). But 'dawn' also contains within itself these two opposing times in that it links day to night and the qualities of day to those of night. The signifier 'alba', therefore, is also run through by 'différance': it combines the light of day and the darkness of night to produce an attenuated light in which both are 'reconciled' or 'balanced':

> pruriti aurei di seccume   notturne e
> . . .
> mah eh per quanti e quali equilibri
> per quale concilio di lumi equilibri

golden itches of nocturnal dry branches and leaves / . . . / but ah for how many and which equilibria / for which meeting of lights equilibria.

Similarly, the heat of day and the cold of night are also fused to produce a warmth ('tepore') which is both a 'fragile freddo' ('fragile cold') and a 'sottile del fuoco' ('keenness of the fire'):

> tutto è roso da un fuoco sottile fragile freddo
> — il tepore —

everything is eroded by a thin fire fragile cold / — warmth —

> nel sottile del fuoco   foco
> nell'esile del fuoco esile
> nel frivolo nel freschissimo del fuoco
> — il tepore —

in the keenness of the fire flame / in the frailty of the frail fire / in the frivolous in the freshest of the fire / — warmth —.

This attenuated light and warmth are like those left by an explosion – the explosion (or, as Zanzotto puts it, 'hollowing out') of night with its cold and darkness, which has laid the foundation for (or 'hatched' the new foundation of) day and its accompanying light:

> è covato e incavato a un fuoco

it is hatched and hollowed out at a fire

> tutto è coinvolto precipite a darsi
> in filiazioni di napalm d'alba

everything is involved in haste to offer itself / in filiations of dawn-napalms.

I said earlier that 'lumina' refers both to dawn and the moon and is closely related to the Latin meaning of 'limina' – 'thresholds'. In fact, it also has a relationship with the Italian figurative meaning of 'lima' or 'limare' – the polishing of written work.

'Alba' is related to 'limina' in its Italian figurative meaning by its oppositional 'difference' to it. For the explosion that takes place at dawn becomes a metaphor for the violation as opposed to the meticulous polishing of the poetic line, a violation achieved precisely by the explosion of signifiers to form one or more signifieds. Individual signifiers operate as 'thresholds' for the new realities which can emerge if the signifier is made to burst open:

> vado di soglia in soglia – attraversato risaputo –
> effrangendo e violando

I go from threshold to threshold – crossed over banal – / breaking the rules and violating.

There are a number of phrases in the poem which like that quoted above actually refer to this violation of language which is operating in other parts of the poem:

> e il procedere violando intuendo

and proceeding violating intuiting

> . . . in tua letizia aberrante a diamante

. . . in your diamond aberrant delight

> e allora spezzettare e spruzzare

and then to divide into fragments and sprinkle.

The second and third of these quotations provide metaphors which help to clarify the kind of violation that is being operated on the signifier and the poetic line. The metaphor of the second quotation is one which has already been met in 'Possibili prefazi VII', *LB* (see Chapter 4, pages 150–1): the signifier is like a diamond radiating a number of meanings, a radiation process which the diagrams (a), (b), and (c) on pages 171–2 attempt to demonstrate visually. The third quotation emphasizes how the linearity of the normal poetic line is distorted by a process of 'spezzettare' – of cutting words into smaller parts, as it were, ('lumina', for example, divided into 'alba' and 'luna'). These parts are then 'watered', so to speak ('spruzzare'), or made to grow, to produce other meanings, so that the poem is being compared to a flourishing plant and its lines to the stems or branches of the plant continually spreading in different directions.

Having established this relationship between language and violence in the poem, one can now understand how language is related to 'lumina' in its meaning as 'luna'. For the moon of the poem is also attached to the theme of violence. From one point of view it is a symbol of calm, as in poems already discussed. But from another, it inflicts violence upon man, in that mythologically it has been considered to make him mad:

> . . . restando violati
> in luna e da luna

. . . remaining violated / in moon and by moon

and, inversely, it undergoes the violence of man's space explorations (one of the themes of *IXE*. See pages 89–90, 93–5):

> . . . cartocci spade
> scrigni lunari di noi-biade
> noi secco ma convalidato incontaminato raccolto

. . . powder charges swords / lunar caskets of us-fodder / us desiccated but corroborated uncontaminated harvest.

To tighten even further this relationship between language and the moon, the latter, as was the case with dawn, becomes at the end of the poem a metaphor for the exploded word, and the stars which accompany it are poetically seen by the poet to be the numerous signifieds which have erupted from the moon-signifier:

> mine di luna in fuga

moon-mines in flight

> nel fulgido sparso sagrato di segni di luna

in the shining sprinkled churchyard of moon-signs.

Finally, the poem ends with a phrase where Zanzotto takes the word 'insegnamento' ('teaching') out of its usual class-room context and applies the 'teaching' metaphor to the mutual relationships that exist between words. He does this in order to emphasize that the extensive play of 'difference' which has taken place between words and within individual words in this poem has been operated against the pedagogical system which gives undifferentiated meaning to them:

> – e l'insegnamento
> mutuo di tutto a tutto –

– and the mutual / teaching of everything to everything – .

It is a phrase which recalls the 'inanellarsi di tutti tra tutti e inoltre tutti' of 'Semine del Mazzaról', thereby reinforcing the point that language has operated in a similar fashion in both of these poems.

'MICROFILM'

The last and highly interesting poem which strongly exemplifies Derridean 'différance' is 'Microfilm'. It exemplifies it, but to a large extent it also plays with Derrida's theory of language as even the appearance of the poem suggests. Consequently, it combines something quite serious, even mechanical, with a ludic element.

'Microfilm', as indicated in a note to the poem, is a hieroglyph which Zanzotto claims to have dreamt, and afterwards transcribed: 'Not an invention . . . but the simple transcription (supposing that it is possible) of a dream, in which the commentary was also included'. Part of Zanzotto's dream – the comments outside the triangle – attempts to interpret the section of the dream within the triangle. It is interesting that this interpretation is carried out not in Italian but in French

– the language of Derrida and Lacan – through which Zanzotto has become acquainted with the theories of language and being which are activated here.

The content of the triangle is built around three graphic signs – I O D – which combine to produce different words. The comments outside the triangle serve to show how these words not only contain other *different* words and related concepts, but sometimes their own opposites. Consequently, each of the five words in Zanzotto's triangle *defers* the absolute presence of the one and only signified attached to it by our linguistic system.

The dictionary definition of the first word in the triangle, 'IODIO' is, as Zanzotto indicates, 'iodine' ('l'iode'). But iodine, because of its corrosive powers ('corrosion'), is related to a removal of stability (hence 'Unruhe' meaning 'restlessness' in German, and 'instabilité'). Zanzotto's next observation is that the word 'iodine' is derived from the Greek 'iōdēs', meaning violet-like ('"violet" en grec'). This etymological tracing of the word then reminds the poet of a quotation from Rimbaud's 'Voyelles' ('Vowels'): '(O l'Oméga,) rayon violet de ses yeux' ('[Oh the Omega,] purple ray of his eyes') (a quotation which takes on more significance as the poem proceeds). The Rimbaldian echoes in the word 'IODIO' go even further, for 'IODIO', in fact, contains

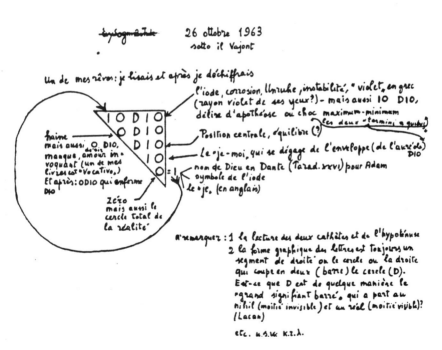

two words: 'IO', meaning 'I', and 'DIO', meaning 'God', which together in their 'choc maximum-minimum' ('clash of maximum-minimum') are suggestive of Rimbaud's attempts at self-deification ('délire d'apothéose' ('delirium of apotheosis')) announced in his 'Lettre du voyant' ('The Seer's Letter') of 15 May 1871.

The normal meaning of the second word 'ODIO' is hate ('haine'). 'ODIO', however, encapsulates 'DIO' ('God') ('ODIO qui enferme DIO'), and God is traditionally associated with love, not hate. Splitting 'ODIO', one arrives at the common exclamation 'O DIO' ('Oh God!') with its suggestion of appeal. It is this notion of an appeal, of *needing* or *desiring* something which Zanzotto highlights through his use of the words 'manque' ('lack') and 'désir' ('desire'). (There are also Lacanian overtones in 'manque' and 'désir', as I illustrate later). The words 'O DIO' invoke God in his omnipotence and love (hence 'amour invoquant' ('invoking love') – an antithesis to 'haine'), and, as an *invocation*, the phrase recalls Zanzotto's *VCT*. *VCT* (see Chapter 2) was the first collection to indicate a radical shift in Zanzottian thought. Whereas in preceding collections – especially in *DIP* – Zanzotto *promoted* the concept of poetry and poetic language in response to what he perceived (in war-time Italy) as a dying culture, in *VCT* he began, conversely, to examine the problems involved in writing poetry, and announced a scepticism *vis-à-vis* language similar to that shown in 'Microfilm'. Indeed, the terms 'désir' and 'amour invoquant', followed immediately by Zanzotto's reference to *VCT*, recall the ideas of a number of poems in that collection, where, albeit in the context of negative attitudes towards language and writing, Zanzotto presented the idea that writing is, like love or *desire*, a *vocative*, communicative instinct that keeps renewing itself. Such was the case, for example, in 'Caso vocativo' and 'Prima persona' (see pages 69–71, 79–80). In the first, the writing of poetry was denoted as an 'ingordo vocativo' – a passionate feeling of an invocatory kind, involving an 'anelito' – a longing to express. To these two terms, 'ingordo vocativo' and 'anelito' can be compared 'Microfilm''s 'amour invoquant' and 'désir' respectively. However, in 'Caso vocativo' Zanzotto then went on to modify the positive terms he had used to describe poetry, claiming that his thoughts and feelings when transferred into writing were impaired by the inadequate functioning of language. 'Prima persona' took up this idea, commenting on the failure of language adequately to express subjectivity (see translation on page 79):

> Io – in tremiti continui, – io – disperso
> e presente

and it is exactly this point which is reinforced in Zanzotto's comment on the last graphic symbol of the poem, 'I', to which I shall return.

In his comments on the third word of the triangle – 'DIO' – , Zanzotto, through the use of a question mark, both states and unstates the idea of 'DIO' as the point of balance at the centre of the triangle ('Position centrale, équilibre (?)' ('Central position, equilibrium (?)')), thus making that balance precarious. To affirm the balance would be to attribute to the poem a *structure* (which presupposes a centre, that is, a fixed principle, and a hierarchy of meanings) and the continual spilling and diffusing of meaning which the words of the triangle display cannot be easily contained within the categories of structure. Zanzotto is also clearly debating the metaphysical idea that 'God' gives a centre and meaning to language and thought, for 'DIO' itself is contained in the 'instabilité' ('instability') of the first word 'IODIO'.

The penultimate word of the triangle, 'IO' (which operates as a personal and emphatic pronoun – hence 'le "je-moi"' ('the "I-me"')) is, as Zanzotto observes, contained or 'enveloped' within the word 'DIO', and can therefore be considered as a breakaway from that word ('qui se dégage de l'enveloppe . . . DIO' ('which extricates itself from the enclosure . . . GOD')). This observation harks back (as is indicated by arrows) to discoveries pertaining to the first word of the triangle 'IODIO' . . . 'choc maximum-minimum'. Moreover, through a synonymic relationship, the notion of enveloping (enclosing, encircling) leads on to the idea of the halo of God ('(de l'auréole)'), and an echo back to Rimbaud would seem to be intended, for the 'O' which draws a halo recalls the 'O l'Oméga' of 'Voyelles' (Zanzotto omitted these two words when quoting Rimbaud, but undoubtedly knew them). This Rimbaldian echo then serves to reinforce the concepts of 'deux termini' ('two termini') and 'choc maximum-minimum', and links the 'délire d'apothéose' to the God of the Book of Revelation: 'Alpha and Omega, the beginning and the ending' (Revelation 1. 7).

Locked within the graphic 'O' there are again two contrasting ideas which reiterate Zanzotto's scepticism about God as a metaphysical 'centre'. 'O', while symbolizing God as the nucleus and meaning of reality ('le cercle total de la réalité' ('the whole circle of reality')) can also, in its function as an arithmetical symbol ('zéro') denote no quantity or number, and, by extension, non-entity. As a cipher, the word 'zéro' also serves to suggest the 'mathematical' (mechanical) element in the composition of 'Microfilm' (reinforced by its arrows and equals mark ('O=I')); while 'cipher', in its other meaning as disguised or secret writing, leads back to the idea of the poem as a hieroglyph which Zanzotto himself is attempting to 'decipher' ('et après je déchiffrais' ('and afterwards I deciphered')).

The three meanings that Zanzotto finds inherent in the symbol 'I' compare and contrast with each other. According to Dante's *Paradiso*, 'I' was the name of God in Adam's time ('nom de Dieu en Dante (*Paradiso* xxvi) pour Adam'), but 'I' also operates as the chemical symbol for iodine which earlier has been highlighted for its associations with corrosion and instability – not the traditionally positive attributes of God.

If one considers together only the second and third meanings given to 'I': 'I' as the 'symbole de l'iode' and hence indicating 'restlessness' and 'instability' ('Unruhe, instabilité'); and 'I' as the English personal pronoun, one has here a summary of the ideas of 'Prima persona' (*VCT*), which presents subjectivity as an unstable and 'restless' phenomenon when defined by the simple, personal pronoun ('Io – in tremiti continui' ('I – in continual quiverings')).

Since 'O' displayed an 'all' or 'nothing' antithesis ('zéro' / 'cercle total'), similar to the polarity inherent in 'I' (connoting God and standing at the same time for the corrosiveness of iodine), Zanzotto can therefore create the equation 'O=I'. The large sweeping arrow then pointing from 'I' as a symbol of iodine to the first word of the triangle – the word *for* iodine – suggests that 'Microfilm' has a circular composition. The dissemination of meaning that the poem displays is a phenomenon that cannot be arrested: one signifier implies another, and that another, and so on *ad infinitum*. The combination of letters preceding Zanzotto's signature – 'etc. u.s.w. κ.τ.λ', the last two standing for the German and Greek equivalents of 'et cetera': *und so weiter* and καὶ τὰ λιπά – allude, in the same way, to an endless movement from one signifier to another, while offering another instance of the poet skating across languages – or looking for a network connecting them.

So far I have considered 'Microfilm' as a very general exposition of Derridean thought, but the poem also suggests that Zanzotto was familiar with some of the more detailed aspects of 'différance', as well as with Lacan's use of Post-Structuralist theories in his writings on psychoanalysis.

Derrida's theory of 'différance' involves an undermining of the concepts of 'self-presence' and 'Absolute Presence' (I and God, respectively). Zanzotto's last graphic does exactly the same when it relates both of these concepts to the corrosiveness of iodine. The logic Derrida uses to discredit the notions of 'self' and 'Absolute' presence would also seem to be upheld by certain aspects of 'Microfilm'. Derrida pointed out that the idea of 'self-presence' goes hand in hand with the logocentric tradition, for logocentrism is phonocentric. As he explains in *La Voix et le Phénomène*, speech in the logocentric tradition is seen as being in direct contact with meaning:

> When I speak, it belongs to the phenomenological essence of this operation that I hear myself/understand myself (je m'entende) at the same time that I speak (*Speech and Phenomena* 77)

while writing is seen to be a parasitic mode of representation added to speech: the physical marks of writing are considered to be cut off from the thoughts that produced them. Logocentrism, therefore, raises the 'phoné' (the spoken word) over the 'graphie' (the written word), and Derrida inverts this hierarchy (drawing special attention to the spelling of the word 'différance' whose 'a' is 'discreet like a tomb' for it is noticeable only in writing; not heard). He claims that a subject, when he speaks, must make his speech conform to the linguistic system which is composed only of differences. Hence, rather than speaking language, he is *spoken* by language, and, consequently, there can be no grounds for claiming that he understands himself as he hears himself speak.

To invalidate, in this way, the notion of 'self-presence' is to discredit, simultaneously, the concept of 'Absolute Presence', since, in the metaphysical tendency which has dominated Western culture since Plato,

> The determination of Absolute Presence is constituted as self-presence, as subjectivity . . . Self-presence . . . simultaneously carries in itself the inscription of divine law. (*Of Grammatology* 16–17)

'Microfilm' also inverts the importance that logocentrism gives to spoken language over written language, for, unlike traditional poems, 'Microfilm' cannot be read aloud. In this, it too is undermining the self-presence of phonocentrism in which one understands oneself as one hears oneself speak. Furthermore, Derrida's statement that the 'a' of 'différance' which, because it cannot be heard in speech, is 'discreet like a tomb' and 'signals the death of a King' (he borrows the metaphor of the tomb from Hegel who in his *Encyclopaedia* compares the body of a sign to an Egyptian pyramid) leads one to suspect that the triangle of 'Microfilm' is actually drawing that tomb: the triangular A of 'différAnce' which pervades language and confuses being in a manner of which phonocentrism is unaware.

The 'death of a King' is clearly announced in Zanzotto's poem not only through its destabilization of the word 'DIO', but also through its use of the three graphic symbols that go to make up the word 'DIO' to illustrate the concept of 'différance' in language.

The two disciplines – Post-Structuralism and psychoanalysis – are brought closely together through 'Microfilm''s presentation as a *dream*. And as a dream 'Microfilm' illustrates *à la lettre* the famous proposition by Lacan that 'the dream-work follows the laws of the signifier'; that 'the unconscious is a writing system' (*Écrits: A Selection* 161). Lacan maintains that, like language for the Post-Structuralists, the unconscious works by a continual movement and activity of signifiers whose signifieds are often inaccessible because they are repressed. To this 'dissemination' of meaning in language and the unconscious, Lacan attributes the term 'desire' (compare Zanzotto's 'désir'). All desire presupposes a 'lack' which it attempts to fill (compare Zanzotto's 'manque') and language works by such lack in that every word indicates the *absence* of the object it stands for; and individual words take on meaning only by virtue of the *absence* and *exclusion* of others. To enter language, Lacan claims, is to become a prey to desire – desire for a (non-existent) 'transcendental' signifier which would have a stable, undivided meaning, and which, in that, would belong either to the 'imaginary' – a pre-linguistic state of being; or to the 'real' – an inaccessible realm lying outside language and signification (see *Écrits: A Selection* 30–107).

These are the ideas underlying Zanzotto's second note to 'Microfilm' ('À remarquer' ('To be noted')), where the graphic 'D' is used to symbolize 'le "grand signifiant barré"' ('the "great, crossed out signifier"') belonging both to a 'nihil' (which presumably designates Lacan's field of the 'imaginary', and which is denoted by the invisible part of the circle in 'D') and to the 'réel' (Lacan's field of the 'real', designated by the visible part of the circle). In metaphysical thinking, it is, of course, the word 'DIO' which assumes the role of transcendental signifier. Zanzotto's 'D' cuts the 'halo' ('l'auréole') associated with that signifier in half, and that Zanzotto intends his '"grand signifiant barré"' to be interpreted as a 'crossing out' of the signifier, 'God', is reinforced in 'La Pasqua a Pieve di Soligo' ('Easter in Pieve di Soligo') (in section 2 of *PSQ*, and to be dealt with later) where, describing the commemoration of the events of Holy Week by the people of Pieve di Soligo, Zanzotto claims (amid a number of other sacrilegious comments): 'sbarrato è il significante che è leader feroce del mondo' ('the signifier who is the world's fierce leader is crossed out'). (Interestingly, in the same poem he alludes, with a degree of self-irony, to his reading of Lacan: 'oui, je lis SCILICET, la revue paraissant trois fois l'an / à Paris, sous la direction du docteur J. Lacan' ('yes, I read SCILICET, the journal which comes out three times a year / in Paris, under the directorship of Dr J. Lacan')).

One important point needs to be made concerning the date of 'Microfilm'. At first sight it would seem that Zanzotto is leaving the poem open to two interpretations: it could be considered (as I have considered it) as a serious exposition of a linguistic theory, or, given its ludic appearance, it could even be seen as a playful form of scrabble. But a third interpretation, based on documentary evidence, is suggested by the date and location of the poem ('26 ottobre 1963' 'sotto il Vajont' ('26 October 1963'; 'below the Vajont')). On 9 October 1963 a landslide from the peak overlooking the Vajont dam (near Longarone) brought down a vast amount of earth and mud, causing a gigantic wave to overflow the dam. The flood submerged five villages to the north of Zanzotto's in the Piave valley, killing more than three thousand people. Zanzotto dreamt his dream somewhere close to the Vajont dam seventeen days after the incident when, perhaps, he was visiting the disaster areas.

In the light of this information certain words and phrases in 'Microfilm' take on a greater resonance: 'corrosion', 'Unruhe' and 'instabilité' evoke the landslide; 'ODIO''s relationship to 'DIO' suggests that the 'God' who has allowed this disaster to occur is a God, not of love, but of hate; while the appeal/exclamation 'O DIO' acquires dark and tragic overtones.

The date of the composition of 'Microfilm' helps, therefore, to confirm the validity of Zanzotto's dream. However, it could be said that the implausible complexity of the 'commentary' throws an element of doubt on the dream's authenticity, and points toward the fact that the poem has more of a conscious construction than the poet would have us believe. This is my view. And I believe that the poem has an element of conscious construction precisely because it intends to *draw attention* to the workings of the unconscious and language *in general*, as well as to the weavings of language in Zanzotto's unconscious in particular.

I underline the phrase 'draw attention to', for although the visual element of poetry is very important for Zanzotto: 'poetry has many aspects . . . the visual aspect is also very important' (*Sulla poesia* 78), and becomes increasingly important especially in the two collections following PSQ (*Il Galateo in bosco* (1975–8) and *Fosfeni* (1975–81)) there is no other poem in Zanzotto's *oeuvre* which is as distinctively visual as 'Microfilm'. The name of the poem itself indicates a visual element, but some doubt remains as to whether the title 'Microfilm' has actually any relationship to the content of the poem. For 'Microfilm', before being published as part of the collection PSQ, first appeared without a title in *Strumenti critici* (no. 5, February 1971, page 97). *Strumenti critici* has a section called 'Microfilm', and Zanzotto's poem, in the 1971 edition, happened to be the first piece in that section, and hence appeared with the name of the section written on top. Zanzotto subsequently appropriated the title 'Microfilm' for PSQ, or rather, he merely reproduced the poem exactly as it had appeared in *Strumenti critici*.

However, it may have been that Zanzotto thought the title appropriate for PSQ, and, that being the case, the title 'Microfilm' could provide a clue to solving the question of why Zanzotto places this anomalous piece exactly at the centre of the collection, occupying a 'Position centrale, équilibre (?)'. Just as a 'microfilm' is a book or a manuscript reproduced onto a very small film, the poem 'Microfilm' is a synoptic, visual representation of ideas pertaining to section 1 of the collection (Zanzotto's challenging of the concept of logocentrism in language) as well as of ideas pertaining to section 2 of the collection, as I now go on to illustrate.

SECTION 2: 'PASQUE'

Zanzotto's deconstruction of the word 'DIO' in 'Microfilm' is similar to that which is carried out on the word 'Pasque' in section 2 of the collection. Besides acting as an appropriate transition to section 2 in its introduction of issues pertaining to religion, 'Microfilm' also provides the reader with some indication as to what the poet is actually 'doing' with, or 'saying about' 'Easter' in the complex poems of the second section.

The word 'Pasque' is traced back to its origins, and in its origins Zanzotto discovers a semantic 'difference'. Quoting from a textbook of Latin etymology, Zanzotto remarks in his notes that 'Pasque' are 'Easters', but the word 'pasqua' comes from the Latin *pascha*, itself from the Greek *páskha*, which in turn comes from the Hebrew *pésah*, meaning 'passage', but crossed with the Latin *pascua*, meaning 'pasture'. Hence, it is discovered that 'pasqua' contains within it two other concepts: those of 'passage' ('passaggio'), and 'pasturage' or nourishment ('pascolo'). What Zanzotto actually does in the poems of this section (although this is not indicated in his notes) is to show how although the Easter festival is related to both of these concepts ('passage' and 'pasturage'), it is also related to their opposites – opposites which contradict all that the festival is normally considered to stand for. However, whereas Zanzotto's deconstruction of the word 'DIO' is confined to one individual poem, the deconstruction of the word 'Pasque' operates across three poems in section 2: 'Pasqua di maggio', 'Biglia (Pasqua e antidoti)', and 'La Pasqua a Pieve di Soligo'.

'PASQUA DI MAGGIO'

In 'Pasqua di maggio' Zanzotto activates the 'passaggio' part of 'Pasque''s etymology: 'Pasqua è Pasqua non è che un passa e va' ('Easter is Easter is only a pass and go'). Easter, in the title, has actually undergone a 'passage', or rather, a displacement – it has been moved forward from April to May. (In 'Lanternina cieca' ('Little Blind Lantern') it is moved forward to the Epiphany: '(a Epifania, pasquetta, mezz'oretta)' ('(at the Epiphany, little easter, about half an hour)')). The poem itself deals with the traditional symbol of Easter – the egg – indicative of 'passaggio' in the sense of 'movement forward', since the egg symbolizes the prospect of new life (the Resurrection) and proliferation. Zanzotto highlights this theme of 'passaggio' or 'movement forward' by writing a poem where the lines rush forward in what he calls 'lingue / appassionatamente uoviche' ('passionately / eggy languages'). There are many different types of eggs in the poem: chocolate Easter eggs ('e srotolare fasce' ('and unrolling wrapping paper'); '"Colori d'uova e di rosei regali"' ('"Colours of eggs and rose-coloured presents"')); eggs put on to boil ('uova s'accaniscono liete e leni . . . / si acuiscono in iridi, nel paiolo' ('eggs furiously collide with each other happy and light . . . / forming rainbow colours they become excited, in the pot')); and the stone egg – 'pondést' – placed in the coop where the hen has laid to remind it where its eggs are (hens being notoriously stupid birds) ('Avete deposto uova scodellato pondést?' ('Have you laid your eggs popped out a *pondést*?')). There are also a myriad things which because of their shape remind the poet of eggs: a door-handle ('pomolo'), the head of a pin ('capocchia'), eye-sockets ('Occhiaie-uova'), hailstones ('grappoli d'uovi di grandine'), maize-corn ('pannocchiette d'uova'), a bunch of grapes ('grappolini d'uovi'), the Pill ('anovular') which is also directly associated with the procreative practice, as are the nipple ('capezzolo') and dummy ('succhiotto'). Finally, there is the mother ('lei-MILO') who produces the eggs ('fessure donde cede uove donde lei-MILO / si fa fluido' ('slits where she yields the eggs where she-MILO / becomes fluid')); as well as the baby and baby-language. The latter (the 'petèl' we have already encountered in Chapter 4; see page 143) is made to pullulate with new forms, emphasizing the notion of coming-into-being: the 'petèl' for 'mummy' thus changes from its correct form, 'TAIU', to 'MIMO SAIU', to 'MILOMIMO', to 'MILO', to 'MILU', and finally to 'MAMIMIMO'. Similarly, various spellings are used to denote 'eggs' (all of which are, however, possible in *veneto*): 'uova' changes to 'ovi', 'uovi', 'uove', and 'ova'; and some strange adjectival and verb forms appear: 'uovoso' ('eggy'), 'inuovire' ('to egg'), and 'disuovare' ('to unegg').

All of this egg-language is in no way as organized as I have presented it above, for the sake of precision. Rather, the poem moves haphazardly from talking about one type of egg, to one of the 'petèl' variations, to something which resembles an egg, and so on. In these 'scivoli d'uovo in uovo' ('slippings from egg to egg') or 'uovo-vertigine' ('egg-vertigo') as the poem itself puts it, 'Pasqua di maggio' is, moreover, attempting to imitate the Easter game which in Zanzotto's local dialect is called 'rodolét'. In 'rodolét', as Zanzotto explains in his notes, coloured eggs are rolled from the raised part of a circular platform made of mud, to hit against other eggs already dispersed on the platform. In both the game, therefore, and the poem, the sliding forward of eggs emphasizes the connection between 'passaggio' and Easter:

> che slittare d'uova in giuù più in giùu

what a skidding of eggs downdownwards further downdownwards

> slittare da uovo a uovo

to skid from egg to egg

> ma sei sullo scivolo ormai
> scivoli d'uovo in uovo

but you're on the chute by now / you're slipping from egg to egg

> sto battendo le mani al passaggio
> irridendo e godendo ai passaggi

I'm clapping my hands at the passage / deriding and enjoying the passages.

The poem is also strikingly visual, for the O's of certain words have been deliberately shaped as ovals so as to resemble eggs, such as in 'sgiolθ' – the dialect word for a rotten egg; and 'θopàl' – the dialect word for the raised part of the 'rodolét' platform. This visual element, combined with abundant onomatopoeia (and Zanzotto tells the reader that here everything is 'auditivo' ('auditory') and 'orale' ('oral')), helps to create the impression that the poem itself is a large egg, cracking and bursting open before the reader's eyes:

> non vedi
> che cresci, non ti accorgi, che cricchi e scoppi
> pus piccinini gorgoglini d'uova
> tuorli goffi e fittissimi

can't you see / that you're growing, don't you realize, that you're cracking and
bursting / pus little chicks little gurglings of eggs / clumsy and thickest yolks

in giù in gluglu nell'acquaio nel rivolo

downwards glug glug in the kitchen sink in the streamlet.

However, while indulging in this 'uovo-vertigine', Zanzotto has come across
two egg images which negate the traditional idea that the egg is symbolic of
movement, growth, the emergence of being. These images are the 'anovular'
– the Pill (whose formula is actually reproduced in the poem) and the 'pondést'
or 'ovo di pietra' ('stone egg'). The first is used to prevent life and the second is
cold, impenetrable and lifeless.

The 'ovo di pietra' prefigures the marble or 'biglia' of 'Biglia (Pasqua e
antidoti)', a poem, as Zanzotto indicates in a note, 'Dedicated to certain
hermeticisms and, today, to the hermeticism of hill destroyers, encapsulated in
their horrible modern weekend houses, in the utmost hermetic privacy'. 'Biglia'
is thus a metaphor for weekend villas where holiday-makers shut themselves off
from the outside world during the Easter vacation. It is a common activity which,
as Zanzotto sees it, is 'antipasqua' ('anti-Easter') in that it celebrates death and
regression rather than new life and movement forward:

Ci s'intuorla all'uovo / sepolcro

There they slump like grumous yolks in their egg / grave

Recesso nell'   Regresso nell'

Recesso nell'abisso dei regressi
ermetica gabbiuzza tabernacolo

Recess in the Regression into the / Recess in the abyss of regressions /
hermetic coop tabernacle.

'LA PASQUA A PIEVE DI SOLIGO'

In contrast to these Easter holiday-makers, there are those who, like the people
of 'La Pasqua a Pieve di Soligo', stay in their native town to commemorate the
events of Holy-week. But even this commemoration, this attempt to relive the
events of the *past* ('Ricomincia il *vecchio* happening a cui t'hanno costretto, /
salita trave spugna lancia che squarcia il petto' ('The *old* happening to which they
subjected you restarts, / hill beam sponge spear which rips open the breast')),
works in opposition to the movement forward which 'passaggio' indicates.
Easter, therefore, exists in the '*vecchio* futuro' ('*old* future') ('Pasqua di Maggio')
and to emphasize the anachronism of the Holy-week rituals as described in 'La

Pasqua a Pieve di Soligo' (the rituals themselves are dealt with shortly), Zanzotto deliberately uses a rhyming couplet throughout all of this poem since it is an old-fashioned form identified with a literature of the past:

> E mi sfuggono intanto questi pseudoalessandrini
> – demodizzati, a gradini, da Cendrars a Pasolini –

> Meanwhile these pseudoalexandrines evade me / – gone gradually out of fashion, from Cendrars to Pasolini –

> l'alessandrino baciato non va più
> nemmeno per snobbarti non che per sviolinarti Gesù

> the alexandrine rhyming couplet will no longer do / not even to snub never mind to fawn on you, Jesus.

For the same reason he also prefigures some of these rhyming couplets with the letter-names of the Hebrew alphabet ('ALEPH', 'BETH', 'GIMEL', 'DALETH' for example) used in the Old Testament to distinguish the different verses of the lamentations of Jeremiah, the Israeli prophet of the ancient world.

In the description of the rituals in 'La Pasqua a Pieve di Soligo' and of the Easter celebrations which follow them, it becomes obvious that the nourishment or 'pascolo' part of 'Pasque''s etymology is being activated. The poem, in part, recounts how the people of Pieve have gathered in the local countryside to hold a service which commemorates the Stations of the Cross. The aim of the service is to provide *spiritual nourishment*, to try to make the congregation experience as intensely as possible the whole traumatic atmosphere of the Passion. Certain instruments are employed to this end. The poet describes, with some elucidation provided in his notes, how each of the children has been given a 'ràcola', the dialect name for a rebeck (a medieval instrument) which makes a harsh, croaking noise; while amplified recordings of heartbeats and their alterations (recordings normally used in the medical profession) attempt to convey the reactions of the body subjected to torture:

> 　　　　　　　　　　　　　　　　　　. . . mentre bistra
> gli orli dello spesso fulgore la ràcola, le sue stecche registra

> while the rebeck / blackens the edges of the thick brilliance, registers its slats

> e il ministro bada al disco sui toni cardiaci che propone
> il modello secundum scientiam della Passione:

> HETH così reagisce l'organismo sotto tortura, questi urti scosse tossi
> sono i toni cardiaci di que quei che ora, quanta　　ora, percossi

> folgorati tacciono　　e in urlo　　sotto l'abbacinante, e si fanno
> addosso: vomitano e tacciono: sotto la lorgnette del　　[tiranno]

and the minister looks after the record of the cardiac tones which proposes / the model according to science of the Passion: / HETH thus reacts the organism when subject to torture, / these blows jolts coughs / they are the cardiac tones of those those who now, so much now, are beaten / electrocuted they fall silent and in a roar beneath he who blinds them, and they / wet themselves: they vomit and fall silent: under the lorgnette of the [tyrant].

Zanzotto sees a contradiction between such spiritual indulgences (obviously, however, exaggerated in the poem) and the indulgences in actual *material* food which follow on Easter day. It is almost as if the first is an excuse for the second, so that, as he says below, one 'feeds off communion hosts' in order to 'feed off cakes and buns' (and it is noteworthy that the verb 'pascolare' ('to pasture') is related here to both spiritual and material food). Similarly, one drinks red wine supposedly to commemorate the blood of the Passion, and white, the Resurrection:

> e Pieve di Soligo ai nostri piedi formicola,
> pascola comunioni e focacce, per campi e selve svicola,
>
> e Pieve di Soligo vuota boccali di bianco e di rosso così
> che rosso-passio e bianco-surrexit sarà presto voto D.C.

and Pieve di Soligo swarms at our feet, / pastures on hosts and cakes, through fields and forests it sneaks, / and Pieve di Soligo empties tankards of white and red so / that red-passion and white-Resurrection / the vote will soon go to the Christian Democrats.

The poem, in fact, implies that the spirituality of Easter is all a fake and that as soon as the 'stone' is 'rolled back' Christ is literally no longer on earth ('non è qui' ('he isn't here')). Man, through material possessions, is seeking his own glory and his own apotheosis:

> per questo scatto, schizo, tic, rovesciata è la pietra,
> scinde le sue mascelle, grida, la terra e l'etra:
>
> gloria gloria, roar roar, tigre tigre, scoreggiano i cori
> di cars, di jets, di rockets: *omnes sicut dii, coi motori!*

for this trigger, schizo, nervous twitch, the stone is overturned, / the earth and sky separates its jaws, cries: / glory glory, roar, roar, tiger tiger, fart the choirs / of cars, of jets, of rockets: *all like gods, with their engines!*

> gloria gloria, schizo schizo, scrash scrash, *non è qui*, bau bau
> da polo a polo sopra l'ecumene già per passione esausta

glory glory, schizo schizo, crash crash, *he isn't here*, bow-wow / from pole to pole above the ecumene already exhausted from passion.

'Canine' man, whose concerns are not spiritual but material and physical (a note to the poem reads: 'dogs: accomplices in fostering man's dreams of apotheosis?

And in any case, accomplices of many human perversions') is, as it were, rolling the stone back on Christ's tomb during other times of the year:

> non è qui, caì, caì, bog bog, i cani dei sempre-più-ricchi
> abbaiano grassamente . . .

he isn't here, caì caì, bog bog, the dogs of the richer and richer / lewdly bark . . .

> la terra e l'etra ti abbaia il suo consenso, la tua gloria
> quae non est hic, la sua, qui, canina e classista, la sua storia

the earth and sky bark for you their assent, your glory / is not here, yours, here, canine is your history, and its politics for the classes

> . . . s'affretta s'adopra
> intorno alla pietra da te, Signore, rimossa, gliela rovescia sopra

. . . one hastens and one strives / around the stone by you, Lord, removed, and turns it over again.

Much of the content of 'La Pasqua a Pieve di Soligo' is highly sacrilegious. Zanzotto openly declares his faithlessness:

> anche se, mulo, non fido: né in te né in lui né in chimaisisia,
> perché ciascuno ha il suo
> עֵגֶל personale, la sua propria eresia

even though, a mule, I've no faith: neither in you nor in him nor in whom it may be, / because each man has his own personal עֵגֶל, his own heresy.

He also includes Christ's death as only one heroic example among a history of many: 'il tuo esempio sprofonda in mezzo agli altri esempi' ('your example collapses midst the other examples'). He insinuates that Christ could have been a neurotic: 'che vuoi? Va' in analisi, chiunque tu sia, prima di morire per me' ('what do you want? Go get yourself analysed, whoever you might be, before dying for me'). And he identifies with Christ's accusers: 'E chi trascinerò davanti al tribunale . . . ?' ('And who will I drag before the tribunal?'), 'ha sbavato già e mal seminato' ('he has already slavered and sewn bad seed'). This sacrilege, however, is partly induced by Zanzotto's desire to dissociate himself from what he considers to be the masochism of the rituals and the insincerity of spiritual indulgences at Easter time. He is also, of course, repudiating more forcefully than anywhere else in the book the transcendental signified of logocentric, metaphysical thought.

To summarize the ideas of PSQ one could say that Zanzotto has been concerned with establishing an a-pedagogical and an a-theological position. Since his main objection to both is that they are logocentrically orientated, he has attempted to undermine them by using post-logocentric, deconstructionist theories in the writing of some of his poems.

The critic Pedullà in a derisive, deconstructionist critique of PSQ claims that the work defeats its own purpose, and that Zanzotto is setting up his own

revolutionary attitude as a 'nuova pedagogia' ('new pedagogy'). It is an obser-
vation that does not escape any attentive reader. And least of all Zanzotto
himself who is generally his own best critic. This is what Pedullà fails to
observe. Zanzotto shows that he is aware of seeming to adopt a pedagogical
stance in his condemnations of religion and pedagogy when he complements
two tongue-in-cheek lines from 'Biglia (Pasqua e antidoti)'

> sono una didascalia di me stesso
> 'anzi didascalia apposta a dio, oh Dio mio

I'm a caption of myself / or rather a caption affixed to god, oh dear God!

with a note to the lines which reads: 'È uno dei miti pedagogici' ('It's one of
the pedagogical myths'). Similarly, in his article on Pasolini mentioned earlier
(see pages 158–9) he refers to the latter's anti-pedagogical ethics, with which he
identifies, as a 'tanto cercata *pedagogia* apedagogica' ('a long awaited non-
pedagogical *pedagogy*'). Moreover, in an interview with Listri where Zanzotto
once again voices objections to pedagogy similar to those made in section 1
of *PSQ*, he precedes these objections with an introductory statement wherein
he acknowledges the necessity and the beneficial aspects of culture in general
(in 'Scolastica', IX, teaching is also called a '*Necessità* e finzione' ('*Necessity* and
pretence'):

> Never as in these years has culture appeared so necessary, having introduced
> fundamental acquisitions in every field: it's an irreversible fact which everyone
> is obliged to recognize. And yet never as today has it assumed contradictory
> or ambiguous aspects, as if something spurious, something useless were
> contaminating it.

'Microfilm', moreover, makes an interesting allusion to the subject of dog-
maticism. At the head of the poem, the crossed-out word which is somewhat
difficult to decipher (a 'hieroglyph' in itself – in the jocular sense of the word)
seems to be a half Greek, half Roman alphabet version of 'ἀγδογματιχ[ος]'
meaning 'undogmatic'. It would seem that Zanzotto's original intention (before
cancelling the word) was to indicate that the ideas about language and religion
displayed by 'Microfilm' were not to be interpreted dogmatically. By extension,
it is implied that he had initially conceived of the poem as having a more ludic
than serious orientation. The fact that he then cancelled the word 'undogmatic'
suggests that he revised his intentions, and was inviting the reader to consider
the poem as a serious indictment of the logocentric tradition – if the reader so
wished. Just as the words in the poem have more than one meaning, so the poem
is left open to two interpretations: one can read it as a playful form of literary
scrabble, or as a more serious exposition of a theory of language. Zanzotto is
being undogmatic by giving the reader this choice, and, paradoxically, could only
have indicated the choice by writing and then cancelling the word 'undogmatic'.

Alternatively, or even simultaneously, by writing 'ἀγδογματιx[oς]' and then crossing it out, Zanzotto is reinforcing the main message of the poem: how words are a mixture of presence and absence.

There are also a number of poems or parts of poems in PSQ where Zanzotto himself 'deconstructs', as it were, much of his own thinking or manner of writing in the collection. The sacrilegious 'La Pasqua a Pieve di Soligo' is followed directly by the poem 'Codicillo' ('Codicil') which, as its title suggests, acts as a supplement to the former and negates its ideas. Here the poet suggests that he has been too harsh in his condemnations of the local celebration of Easter, for the community spirit which the celebration serves to emphasize is ultimately a positive and healing force:

> conciliazione che in tutto prevarrebbe
> congruità embricazione di sanerà
> con sanerà

reconciliation which would prevail in everything / congruity overlapping of it will heal / with it will heal.

He also suggests that the sincerity of these people's feelings is not to be questioned for it is founded upon simplicity:

> No, non è vero, più semplice e amico è l'impegno
> qui con umani con divinità

No, it isn't true, the commitment with humans with divinity / is simpler and more friendly here

> . . . Degno
> rapporto di placata amante memoria

. . . Worthy / relationship of soothed and loving memory.

Zanzotto tempers not only his anti-religious views, but also those pertaining to language. 'Sovraesistenze' which is structured like 'Per lumina, per limina' takes the reactions of a reader like Miss Morchet into account. The method of writing a poem where the line is 'broken' ('e la linea spezzata' ('and the broken line') ('Sovraesistenze')) is compared to the technique of a pointillist painter where the flowing line is cut up into small dots of colour which are then blended by the spectator's eye to produce a picture: 'tutto il pointillé la pre-esistenza com'è in linfa' ('all the pointillé the pre-existence as it exists as lymph'). This picture, however, may not be perceived by all – for some the reality of the picture-poem might come into being with difficulty:

> O com'è   è/   Ⓔ
>
> . . . che c'è   ed   è → essere

Oh how it is is / (is) / . . . that there is and it is → to be.

and the picture that emerges might be as blurred as in an over-exposed photograph:

> No, non–certo . . .
> . . . sovraesporre –

No, uncertain . . . / . . . over-exposing –.

Zanzotto acknowledges that while one set of readers might enjoy those of his poems where words are attributed more than one meaning, seeing them to be 'bursting' with 'possible' meanings:

> gronde e gronde   scorrimenti di vero
> . . . crepa nel possibile

eaves and eaves flowings of truth / . . . it bursts with possibility

for another set of readers (the Miss Morchet type) the same poems, although seeming to be highly profound ('sapientissimi'), might signify nothing from beginning to end ('sapientissimi in niente'):

> . . . spinti dal recto al verso ma
> per mano a tutto
> connessi a tutto dal niente
> sapientissimi in niente che glisa, glissa

. . . thrust from the right-hand page to the left-hand page but / led by the hand in it all / connected to all by nothing / highly knowledgeable in a nothingness which slips, slides.

There are also two poems in which Zanzotto allows for the authenticity of his earlier, Hermetic, logocentric vision, instead of rejecting it as he had done in 'Biglia (Pasqua e antidoti)'. In 'Xenoglossie' Zanzotto reflects on his two poetic phases – the Hermetic, logocentric one, and the post-logocentric one. Part 3 of the poem is largely concerned with the post-logocentric phase. The fact that the signifier in the poems of this period can embody a multitude of reality ('mille realismi' ('a thousand realities')) is now seen to be a productive thing:

> egli s'illustra in mille realismi in
> pupille (ora) credibilissime egli
> si deduce da ogni   da ogni punto stimolo soffio
> s'industria e colma di profitti
>   maravigliosi / ati
>   . . .
>   che birbi chimismi in diamante!

it illustrates itself in a thousand realisms in / pupils (now) most credible it / draws from every from every point stimulus breath / it strives so hard and fills to the brim with astonishing / ished / profits / . . . / what roguish diamond-shaped chemisms!

Parts 1 and 2 are largely concerned with his Hermetic poetry:

> Ritorna, egli, con media voglia con lieve
> foga al suo gusto per la centralità

He returns, half desiring with a slight / enthusiasm, to his liking for centrality

> . . . ed è bella
> questa convinta centrale crepuscolarità

. . . and how lovely it is / this convinced central crepuscularism

> . . . vieni Orfeo vieni con lei
> al piccolo cimitero di campagna

. . . come Orpheus come with her / to the little country cemetery.

Although there are no specific references to Hermeticism here, the invocations to Orpheus indicate how Zanzotto is referring to that poetic mode, since in an article on poetry in *Il Verri* (September 1976, 112) he speaks of his first poetic phase as being 'Orfico-ermetica' ('Orphic-Hermetic'). The poet now feels attracted again to the 'centre' or 'logos' of Hermeticism (there is a 'gusto per la centralità). Consequently, toward the end of the poem Zanzotto speaks of 'multiple double visions' ('multipli diplopici'), his willingness, that is, to recognize both these types of poetry.

In 'Chele' too, Zanzotto rewelcomes his 'spraticato vedere' ('unpractised vision'). He recognizes that even a logocentric vision can 'teach' in some way, and that if one wants to avoid being dogmatic, one's voice must be 'onnivoca' ('omnivocal'), and one's vision, an omnivorous one which feeds off everything:

> la didassi totale che   è anche
> terapia totale
>   onnivoca
>   onnivora
>   ehi!
>   sic!

total instruction which is also / total therapy / omnivocal / omnivorous /
hey! / just that!

In withdrawing some of his criticisms of pedagogy, theology, and logocentric writing, Zanzotto, in fact, is still not departing from Derridean thought. These three phenomena belong to a metaphysical tradition which, as Derrida himself admits, one cannot do without. 'There is no sense', Derrida says, 'in doing without the concepts of metaphysics in order to shake metaphysics. We have no language, no syntax and no lexicon which is foreign to this history. We can pronounce not a single destructive proposition which has not already had to slip into the form, the logic, and the implicit postulations of precisely what it seeks to contest' (*L'Écriture* 280–1).

What Derrida suggests that the honest writer of the twentieth century should do is exactly what Zanzotto has done in *PSQ*: he has '"posed" this problem'.

Conclusion

Filò (1976) and the 'trilogy' (1975–84)

Since *PSQ*, Zanzotto has written four more collections of poetry: *Filò* (1976), *Il Galateo in bosco* (1975–8), *Fosfeni* (*Phosphenes*) (1975–81), and *Idioma* (*Idiom*) (1975–84), the last three forming what the poet has called a 'pseudo-trilogy'. *Filò* marks a significant development in Zanzotto's work in that it is written entirely in dialect (which had previously only been used for individual words and phrases (as in *LB* and *PSQ*)).

The collection is divided into two sections. Section 1 is entitled 'Per il Casanova di Fellini' ('For Fellini's *Casanova*') and is composed of two pieces: a 'Recitativo veneziano' ('Venetian Recitative'), and a 'Cantilena londinese' ('London Lullaby'), both of which are written in a pseudo-archaic Venetian dialect. The second section takes the title of the collection, 'Filò', and is composed in the dialect of the Soligo valley. Section 1 is preceded by a letter addressed to Zanzotto from Federico Fellini, dated July 1976, which explains how the 'Recitative' and the 'Lullaby' came to be written. In it Fellini asks Zanzotto to consider composing for him some verse in a Venetian dialect (somewhere between that used by Ruzzante and Goldoni) for the Italian version of his film, *Casanova*. This verse was to accompany two scenes in the film: the opening scene of an (invented) ritual which takes place at night and at which the Chief Magistrate, the local authorities, and the people of Venice are present. The ritual involves an attempt to raise the gigantic head of a black goddess from the murky depths of the Grand Canal. It is an attempt which fails, for when the head is partially visible, the stakes break in two and the cables rip, so that the huge head sinks again to the bottom of the Canal and remains down there for ever, unknown and unreachable. Fellini explains how this black goddess is a type of 'lagoonal divinity', the 'great Mediterranean mother, the mysterious feminine presence which lives in each of us'; while the ritual involving her is the ideological metaphor of the entire film (*Filò* 8).

The second scene is set in London where a seven-foot-tall Venetian circus woman is taking a bath with two Neapolitan dwarfs. For this Fellini required a nursery-rhyme, somewhere between a rigmarole and a lullaby, to be sung by the bathing giantess.

Fellini explains how, with Zanzotto's help, he hoped to break through the opaque conventions of the Venetian dialect, and make it more alive, penetrating, mercurial. Better still, he wanted to rediscover archaic forms and invent new combinations of sound and meaning so that the language of the film would reflect the visionary madness that he had attempted to graft onto it.

Zanzotto, of course, agreed to Fellini's request, for various reasons, most of which were elucidated in his interview on *Filò* conducted by Sillanpoa. Here he explained how Fellini's proposal was not a daunting one given that dialect is his daily means of expression (as it is for most people in the Veneto region), and, indeed, speaking standard Italian is 'rather a chore' (Sillanpoa 298). Then again, he had always liked Fellini as a director because of his unique interest in the sound track, in 'euphonic data both as linguistic and musical facts' (Sillanpoa 301). Indeed Fellini had discussed his ideas about a film on Casanova long before sending Zanzotto his 'letter of intent' so that Zanzotto was aware of the linguistic problems such a film would encounter and was curious as to how Fellini would solve them. When invited to join forces with Fellini in tackling such problems, he found himself to be a willing participant.

Nevertheless, in spite of all of these reasons for complying, Zanzotto explains that his attitude toward the project was still an ambivalent one. He confesses to feeling a great reluctance to having any contact whatsoever with the film industry. This reluctance is clarified elsewhere in an interview with Camon where Zanzotto spoke of the 'osmosis between cinematography and the literary ambience (which) works to the detriment of the latter' (Camon 150). Consequently he told Sillanpoa that 'it would have taken very little for me to say no to Fellini' (Sillanpoa 303). Perhaps in an attempt to set the record straight, the actual 'Filò' section of the book opens by hurling a torrent of abuse at the cinema! This, in fact, is the only link between section 1 and section 2 of the work.

In spite of the occasional nature of the composition of *Filò*, Zanzotto claims that the verses of the 'Recitative' which accompany the opening ritual in *Casanova* were for the most part already written before Fellini's request. I would venture to suggest that they had already existed as part of Zanzotto's notes for the composition of IXE's '(Variante)'. In his letter Fellini explains how he wished the entire opening ceremony to be immersed in 'a vortex of sound, in an audible web of the sacred and the profane', a description which could function as a perfect word-painting of '(Variante)' (see pages 93–9). In a feverish attempt to exorcize the possible failure of the attempt to rescue the black goddess's head, the participants in the ceremony were to utter 'propitiatory orisons, repetitious supplications, seductive euphonies, evocative litanies, irreverences, challenges, insults, goadings, sneers' (*Filò* 8), many of which are to be found addressed to the moon in '(Variante)'. Besides, '(Variante)''s moon is, like the head of Fellini's goddess, associated with a mysterious female presence, and at one point in the 'Recitative' the head is addressed as a 'luna degli abissi profondi' ('moon of deep abysses').

The ceremony is officially opened by the Doge who invokes the black goddess not in dialect, but in a biblical Latin rich in sexual images of lips, placenta, and breasts sweeter than wine:

> DOGE:
> *Veni amica mea, columba mea,*
> *veni sponsa, veni –*
> *Osculabor labia tua, ubera tua,*
> *ubera tua dulciora vino –*
>
> *Veni, consurge nobis*
>
> (tagliando il nastro)
> *Resecabo ligamina placentae tuae*
> *ut fulgidior nobis nascaris*

Come my friend, my dove, / come bride, come – / I will kiss your lips, your breasts, / your breasts sweeter than wine – / Come, raise yourself toward us / (cutting the ribbon) / I will cut the bonds of your placenta / so that you might be born to us more resplendently.

With regard to this use of Latin (employed also in '(Variante)'), Zanzotto told Sillanpoa how Fortini in a review of *Filò* had claimed that the Latin phrases in it were rather like 'cream on a pudding', a bit forced and out of place beside the rest of the 'Recitative', which apart from a couple of phrases in French and German, is entirely in dialect (Sillanpoa 300). Zanzotto disagrees with this view. He explained how many expressions in the dialect of the Veneto region are very often charged with the lower Latin of the church, or with references to the Bible or Gospels. He went on to observe how sometimes the expressions that emerge from this fusion (researched by Spitzer and others) are very rich in creative effects – for instance, a woman from his area used to refer to a skiny person as a 'resurresi' ('resurrexit' in Latin, and an obvious reference to the resurrected, 'transparent' Christ). In short, Zanzotto is emphasizing how the Latin is not out of place in his poem since learned elements can and *do* exist in popular speech. The point is exemplified in the poem when the goddess is invoked for the third time, and her eyes are called 'Oci de bissa, de basilissa' ('Eyes of snake, of queen'). A note to 'basilissa' explains how it is the Greek for 'queen', while also containing a reference to the figures of mosaics, as well as to the mysterious 'basilisk' – a fabulous reptile hatched by a serpent from a cock's egg, and having a lethal breath and look. The dialect word 'basilissa' is still used in Venice today to indicate a 'bad woman, a woman with a bit of the serpentine inside' (Sillanpoa 299), thereby showing how the Byzantine Greek world, with which Venice had many ties, has left its mark on the dialect of the region.

In the course of the 'Recitative' Zanzotto even coins from Greek some nonexistent dialect words, thereby grafting archaic forms onto popular speech. He explains in his notes how the word 'baba' in the address 'baba catàba' designates an old woman or a grandmother in a pejorative sense. 'Catàba', on the other hand, is a made-up word which came to him subconsciously for it seemed to capture for him the sense of the Greek 'κϑτϑβϑι᾽ νειν', meaning 'to sink'. The context in which this insult is set provides a fine example of Fellini's desired 'seductive euphonies':

> Ma cossa xélo che zó te striga
> ma cossa xélo che zó te intriga;
> mona ciavona, cula cagona,
> baba catàba, vecia spussona,
> nu te ordinemo, in suór e in laór,
> che sù ti sboci a chi te sa tór –

But what is it that bewitches you down there / but what is it that entangles you down there; / *mona ciavona, cula cagona,* / old, sinking hag, old smelly, / we order you, in sweat and in work, / that up here you flower for whoever knows how to take you – .

The sexual connotations of the last line above are evident, and run right through the poem. Indeed at one stage the participants imagine themselves to be shackling the goddess with irons, and forcing her to drink and eat to excess:

> Metéghe i feri, metéghe i pai,
> butéghe in gola 'l vin a bocai,
> incoconéla de bon e de megio;
> la xé inbriagona, la xé magnona

Shackle her with irons, shackle her with stakes, / throw wine down her throat in bottlefuls, / stuff her with every good, better thing; / she's a drunkard, she's a glutton.

The head, rhythmically goaded with both flattery and insults, also seems to function metaphorically as the build up to an orgasm, which then, of course, fails when the cables break and the head sinks again to the bottom of the canal, accompanied by panicking voices screaming rage and disappointment in dialect, German and French:

> (crollo del simulacro, sprofondamento, smarrimento – voci varie)
>
> – Ciò, la crepa   – Schrecklisch!
> – Odìo, la smama

> – Odìo, s'ciòpa soto, tuto quanto
> > – Malheur, malheur!
>
> – La sbrissa
> – La smona
> – Se scavessa, se destrude, se désfa   – Ça crève
> – Dio, cossa nasse   – Gefährlich!
> – Stòrzela   – Ciàpela   – Inpirela

(collapse of simulacrum, sinking, bewilderment – various voices) / - Look, she's cracking – Terrible! / - Oh God, she's escaping / - Oh God, everything is exploding underneath / - Misfortune, misfortune! / - She's slipping / - We can't hold out any longer / - She's breaking, she's destroying, wrecking herself – She's dying / - God, what's happening – Dangerous! / - Twist her – Take her – Run her through.

In this sense Zanzotto's verses (although sounding in the film like mere gibberish – 'as much noise as discourse' (Almansi)) are, at least in their written form, a lot more erotic than the actual sexual activities of 'Casanova' in the film, which, according to Zanzotto, are deliberately meant to seem 'more anti-erotic than provocatory', for it was Fellini's intention for them to function as a repudiation of the consumer sex of contemporary cinema, which, in Zanzotto's view too, is 'a lot of smoke and no roast'! (Sillanpoa 304).

Sexual nuances are also strongly present in the 'London Lullaby'. The Venetian giantess who, after an unhappy marriage finds employment at a fairground, sings as she bathes, a childish, sorrowful little song which Fellini asked to be composed in the vein of the 'petèl' language Zanzotto had used in LB. ('"Mama e nona te dà ate e cuco e pepi e memela"', and so on; see page 143). What struck Fellini about these lines was their 'liquid sonority . . . the syllables which melt in your mouth, that sweet and broken singsong of babies in a mixture of milk and dribbled matter'(Filò 9). The lines for him had a soporific, lapping quality which suggested the underwater iconography of the film, the image of the placenta, and of a Venice heaving and surging with algae, moss, mould and damp darkness.

After long walks in the marshlands around Venice, Zanzotto claims that certain 'phonic-rhythmic suggestions' came to him, built around the phrase 'piè-piedino', to which he gave the variants 'pin penin' (close to Venetian dialect) and 'pin pidin' (more associated with the terra firma), both of which have strong sexual overtones, but in the form of 'a glorious euphemism' (Sillanpoa 301):

> Pin penin
> valentin
> pena bianca
> mi quaranta

mi un mi dói mi trèi mi quatro
mi sinque mi sie mi sète mi òto

Foot-little foot / valentine / white feather / I forty / I one I two I three I
four / I five I six I seven I eight

Pin penin
fureghin
perle e filo par inpirar
e pètena par petenar
e po' codini e nastrini e cordèa –

le xé le comedie i zoghessi de chéa
che jeri la jera putèa

Foot-little foot / little Nosey Parker / pearls and string to thread / and combs
to comb / and then pigtails and little ribbons and fine string / they are the games
the little games of her / who yesterday was a little girl.

Sexual euphemisms are continued in phrases such as "ste suchete 'sta sfeseta'
('these little pumpkins this little crack'), and are mixed up with elements
common to children's fairy-tales ('le xé le belesse da portar a nosse' ('they
are the beautiful things to bring to the wedding'); 'chi me descanta / chi me
desgàtia' ('who will free me from my spell who will untangle me')) and echoes
of eighteenth-century ariettas ('o mio ben, / te serco intel'l fogo inte'l giasso' ('oh
my beloved, / I search for you in the fire in the ice')).

The beauty of the lullaby lies not, of course, in the meaning of the words which
must be elementary if they are to evoke a nursery rhyme, but in its hypnotic and
mellifluous sonority, and the fact that such delicate sounds are produced by a
woman so huge, whose very size is meant to symbolize Casanova's neurotic
relationship with the female sex – with an overpowering, overwhelming force.

In contrast to the sweet-sounding strains of the Venetian *koiné* in which the
lullaby is written, the dialect of the Soligo valley in which the 'Filò' section is
composed, sounds, with its abundant consonant clusters, much more earthy and
rugged. It therefore comes as no great surprise to hear Zanzotto say (in 'Filò') that
to write in this dialect is a tremendous chore, that it almost dislocates the tendons
in his hands:

Élo vero che scriverte,
parlar vecio, l'é massa un sforzh, l'é un mal
anca par mi, cofà . . . / . . . far 'ndar fora le corde de le man.

He also confesses to it being a frightening experience ('e che scriver me à fat
senpre paura') for, as explained in an essay appended to *Filò* (henceforth 'Essay')
dialect has within it a 'pulsion and somatic gurgling', it is a bodily language in tune
with the biological make-up of those who speak it, and as such, does not lend
itself to being transcribed.

The actual title, *Filò*, is, according to Zanzotto, the dialect word for a 'peasant evening in the cowsheds in winter, but also an interminable discourse which serves to pass the time and nothing else'. Zanzotto's discourse opens by cursing the cinema in general which fills people's brains with 'bubbles' and 'poisoned colours'. The type of cinema that can be equated in some ways with poetry in that it gives access to strange paths ('trói stranbi') and new skies ('zhiéi del tut nóvi') is unfortunately only produced by a rare few ('Ma ben i é rari quei che pól far 'sto cine'). Presumably Fellini is to be included among the latter, for the 'Filò' then goes on to describe the film's opening ritual, and to comment upon the dialect invented for the 'Recitative', calling it

> . . . 'n parlar
> che no l'é qua né là, venizhian sì o no,
> lontan vizhin sì e no, ma ligà al me parlar
> vecio

a speech / which is neither here nor there, Venetian yes or no, / far off near yes and no, but bound to my old / speech.

It would seem that Zanzotto saw a correlation between this 'parlar vecio' and the black goddess's head of the film which could be taken to symbolize a type of primordial mother-earth:

> . . . 'l parlar vecio . . .
> quel che par mi l'é de la testa-tera,
> creda aqua piera léda

the old speech . . . / that which for me belongs to the head-earth / clay water stone mire

> Vecio parlar che tu à inte 'l tó saór
> un s'cip de lat de la Eva

Old speech who has in your savour / a drop of Eve's milk.

But the mother-earth of his own region which before had never 'assassinated' has now fallen prey to a 'crammed and cloudy madness' ('matìo bónbo e turbido'). Hence, from a discussion of cinema and dialect, Zanzotto proceeds, in the rambling style which characterizes a 'filò', to a consideration of the earth as a destroyer, giving special mention to the Friuli earthquake of September 1976, and (later) to the Vajont dam tragedy (treated already in 'Microfilm', *PSQ* (see page 182)), although in a note Zanzotto concedes that the latter disaster was mainly the fault of humans:

> ne vien l'ingóssa al cór par i fradei
> qua darente, cari fradei furlani,

. . .
se sa che quel che qua ne sgórla e basta
póch lontan schinzha copa désfa tra–dó;
se sa che tu sé furia pèdo che miér e miér de furie,
salvàrega tremenda irata sphynx

we are attacked by spasms of pain for our brothers / nearby here, dear Friulian brothers, / . . . / we know that that which only stirs us here / not far away crushes kills undoes demolishes; / we know you are fury worse than thousands and thousands of furies, / wild terrible angry sphinx.

He contemplates how perhaps Nature has turned against man because man has failed to 'court' or love her sufficiently; perhaps she is repaying mankind at large for the sins of a greedy few who have poisoned and contaminated her; or perhaps Leopardi ('quel . . . de la Ginestra') was correct when he posited Nature as uncaring and indifferent toward man, in which case we should unite forces and rise up against her.

'Filò' concludes by returning to the theme of dialect, highlighting some of its paradoxical features. Whereas on the one hand it does not suffice as a language, but for reasons unknown to Zanzotto ('(e no tu me basta)'; '(parché no bàstetu?)'), on the other hand, he feels it to be rich and prolific (as the 'Essay' puts it, it is both a stagnant water and an abundant stream): 'ma fis, ma tóch cofà 'na branca / de fien 'pena segà dal faldìn' ('but thick, but dense like a handful / of hay just cut by the scythe'). This is partly because ('Essay' 91) 'it is laden with the vertigo of the past, of the mega-centuries in which it has extended, infiltrated, subdivided and re-composed itself'. It is 'felt as coming from a place where neither writing . . . nor grammar exists', from a time of 'oracularity, minimal oratory'. Something of this enduring quality of dialect is emphasized in the lines 'noni e pupà i é 'ndati, quei che te cognosséa, / none e mame le é 'ndate, quele che te inventéa' ('grandfathers and fathers have gone, those who knew you, / grandmothers and mothers have gone, those who invented you'), and it is interesting to note that in keeping with Zanzotto's association of dialect with the mother-figure, it is posited here as having been invented by women. However, this 'parlar de néne–none–mame' ('speech of nurses–grannies–mothers') is in danger of becoming extinct, repressed as it is by the upholders of the 'grande lingua' (the 'school masters' who 'warn against it'; those who claim 'petèl' is 'bad for babies') even though ('Essay' 90) this 'grande lingua' came after dialect, superimposed itself upon dialect. And whereas standard Italian, the 'imperial language', is the language of official (and impersonal) history ('Essay' 92), dialect – the language of the poor and the humble, neglected by that history ('a girar pa'i marcà, / . . . / da juste boche se te sent' ('going around the markets, / . . . / one hears you spoken by just mouths')) – can, nevertheless, be considered the 'repository of real history'

(Hainsworth, 1984). This is because, as Zanzotto highlighted in 'Retorica su' (*LB*), it is precisely the 'microstorie' of ordinary, unassuming individuals which constitute authentic, human history.

But in spite of all the arguments that can be put forward in support of the preservations and cultivation of dialect, 'Filò' concludes with the acknowledgement that men might, without even being aware of it, begin to forget how to speak it. If this should happen, dialect will, however, somehow mysteriously persist as a primeval force within the landscape, within Nature, if only to be spoken by a couple of birds who have escaped from gunshots and slaughter:

> osèi che te à inparà da tant
> te parlarà inte 'l sol, inte l'onbría

birds which have learned you for so long / will speak you in the sun, in the shade.

Dialectal words and phrases reoccur in Zanzotto's next book, *Galateo*, scattered throughout the collection as in *LB* and *PSQ*. There is, however, one poem which is written entirely in dialect, '(*E pò, mucì*)' ('(*And then, Silence*)'). The title of this collection harks back to the original *Galateo* by Giovanni della Casa – a sixteenth-century book of manners, outlining the modes of speech and comportment befitting a courtly society. Della Casa wrote it while he resided at the monastery of Nervesa, near the Montello wood. Zanzotto's *Galateo* offers a literal (even, through unusual typographical devices, 'pictorial'), and metaphorical presentation of this same wood, attempting to embrace all of the events surrounding it in time, in a 'photographic vision taken with a wide-angle lens' (*Sulla poesia* 76). But the main comparison lies between the wood as it was in the sixteenth century, and as it now exists today. Whereas in Della Casa's time it was a 'frondoso mare' (*Galateo* 21) ('leafy sea'), dotted with fine Venetian villas housing great humanists and painters, it is now traversed by the 'Linea degli ossari' ('Line of the ossuaries') of the tens of thousands who died in the battles against Austria-Hungary in 1918 (see page 57). In the Montello region the line lies on top of the Peri-Adriatic fault in the earth's crust, as if to symbolize a major fracture, an irreversible rift which has occurred in the history of mankind. Gone is that symbiosis of society promoted by the sixteenth-century *galateo*.

As well as dealing with the part which the wood had to play in a political past, Zanzotto also treats of the role of the Montello wood and other woods in general in a literary, historical, and mythical past. The second poem of the collection begins with an extract from the 'Oda Rusticale' ('Rustic Ode') of Cecco Ceccogiato da Torreggia (a pseudonym for Nicolò Zotti) which was discovered in the municipial library in Treviso, and which, according to

Zanzotto, conjurs up with great immediacy the wood as it was in 1683 when the verses were written. On other occasions the Montello wood becomes fused with Tasso's 'Selva Incantata / della Gerusalemme Liberata' (*Galateo* 31) ('Enchanted Wood / of Delivered Jerusalem'), and with Dante's 'selva dei suicidi o / delle arpie' (*Galateo* 82) ('Wood of suicides or / of harpies'). 'Diffrazioni, Eritemi' ('Defractions, Erythemae') refers to a real, historical event of the 1600s when an abbot became a ringleader for some brigands taking refuge in his abbey in the Montello wood, but was saved from imprisonment by the Venetian courts by the Pope who insisted that priests had the right to be judged only by priests, giving rise to a dispute between the republic and the church, and the so called 'Questione Giurisdizionale' ('Question of Jurisdiction'). This historical personnage is placed alongside the legendary inhabitants of the wood: the magician 'Barba Zhucón' who was treated as an object of fun by his god-daughters; and the old hag, 'la vecia', a usurer who was robbed and throttled by a group of delinquents to whom she lent money to enable them to carry out their criminal deeds.

But it is the political past of the wood which is given most weight, as suggested by Zanzotto's anti-war declaration in a note appendixed to the collection, where he refers to the need to found a party of '"continual vomiting"' in protest at the 'squalid uselessness' of 'all massacres, wars and human sacrifices'. It is significant that Zanzotto's simple hand-drawn map, tracing the line of the ossuaries crossing the Montello heath, lies adjacent in the collection to a fragment of a lyric ('Canzone Montelliana') written in the style of D'Annunzio by a poet, now dead, called Carlo Moretti, who fought in the First World War and lost a brother in it. Zanzotto reproduces the old text as it was first published in 1926, but (as he explains in *Sulla poesia* 105–6) with some of the words and the phrase 'sospinto o re' ('driven along oh king') either partially visible or obliterated altogether, as if the text had been nibbled by mice. He emphasizes that his reasons for doing this were anything but ironical – he simply wanted to stress how one no longer remembers who the Italian King was in 1918, just as one no longer remembers the six hundred thousand who died in the war.

Another poem '(Maestà) (Supremo)' ('(Majesty) (Supreme)') takes the title from the 'Victory Bulletin', distributed to the victorious Italian side after their defeat of Austria-Hungary. The parenthesizing of the words of the title is an obvious attempt to deflate the suggestion that those who fought and/or died for their country achieved dignity thereby, an idea supported by the poem itself where the voice of a soldier who speaks in a type of Beckettian monologue from his coffin underground, denounces his very status as a human being: 'Non fui. Non sono. Non ne so nulla. Non mi riguarda' ('I did not exist. I do not exist. I know nothing about it. It doesn't concern me') – words which, as a note explains, are the translation of an epigraph on the tomb of an unknown Roman soldier. Zanzotto's soldier displays indifference to the hostile elements above his grave – the oppressive trees ('ogni albero è . . . sopraffazione'), the crackling sound of the acacias ('E crak crak acacie'), and the crows which peak away at his scalp and skull reducing them to the size of a thimble ('corvi / mi beccate lo scalpo o il netto cranio / rendendolo qual ditale da cucire'). He scorns those who come to pray over his grave with their 'clumsy', 'whining' words, to which he answers with 'gurglings of choked catarrh'.

This rather gothic monologue continues in the next two poems, 'Sono gli stessi' ('They are the Same Ones'), and '(*Sono gli stessi*)'. In the first the same frustrated voice protests at how, with the passing of years, his dead descendants are buried on top of him in the same plot of land, pushing him and his 'identity' further and further into the bowels of the earth. His furious 'I' which demands to exist:

eppur *(io)* furiosamente intimo qua e là di esistere –

and yet I furiously demand to exist here and there

becomes, because of its relationship to the dead descendants, swallowed up into a collective 'we': 'nell'identità del nostro noi' ('in the identity of our we'). It is as if he is being 'belched against time' ('mi ruttano controtempo'), and metaphorically eaten away by his own descendants, as well as (in '(*Sono gli stessi*)') literally devoured by the myriad life forms surrounding him in the earth: 'Chele chele di transferasi / ancora pressanti' ('Chelae chelae of enzymes / pressing still').

Indeed the 'biological interdependence of plant, animal, and human matter' (Welle 45) is one of the major themes in the collection, giving rise to a motif of 'eating, digestion, and defecation' (Welle 45) which can sometimes be vulgar as in '(*E pò, muci*)', and sometimes humorous: lines which seem to refer to the demonical powers and surreal effects present in Tasso's wood, also allude to a windy and rumbling, upset stomach: 'demoni ventosi, ventriloque / promesse e minacce' (*Galateo* 29) ('windy demons, ventriloquist / promises and threats'). Insects and animals feed off the bodies of the dead in the land ('certi pazzi-di-guerra, ancora vivi / allevano maiali; traffici con gli ossari' (*Galateo* 28) ('certain madmen-of-war, still alive / raise pigs; tradings with the bones')), and animals feed off other animals ('il gufo / giusto si tuffa, becca e trangugia lucciole' (*Galateo* 30) ('the owl / justly dives, peaks and gulps down glow-worms')), and in this respect the Montello is acknowledged as a violent wood where 'war', as it were, is still being waged:

> nidi, allora, di resistenze,
> di pericolosi mitraglianti rametti-raggio
> (*Galateo* 25)

nests, then, of resistances / of dangerous machine-gunning little branches-ray.

Even the acid rains beat down on the landscape and the gravestones with a military-like precision:

> militarmente precisa nell'andatura di
> lluvias **ıllıllılllı** chuvas
> *(Galateo* 29)

militarily precise in the pace of / rains **ıllıllılllı** rains.

Indeed, in many respects the people from the Montello region can be seen to be war-profiteers, turning the charnel-houses into a tourist attraction:

> Rivolgersi agli ossari. Non occorre biglietto.
> . . .
> Rivolgersi alle osterie. Dove elementi paradisiaci aspettano
> *(Galateo* 27)

Apply to the ossuaries. You don't need a ticket. / . . . / Apply to the taverns. Where heavenly elements await.

The upkeep of the ossuaries and the cataloguing of all those bones provide jobs for the locals who are therefore metaphorically living off the dead:

> Hanno come un fervore di fabbrica gli ossari

The ossuaries have a factory-like fever

> os–ossa, ben catalogate
> *(Galateo* 28)

bone-bones, well catalogued.

Whether this kind of 'living off the dead' is justifiable or intrinsically immoral is one of the questions which the text seems to pose. And it poses it within the wider framework of the theme of delving down into the 'woodiness' of the self: of reaching into the potholes, the 'buchi senza fondo' (*Galateo* 24) of the mind; of attempting to plough up its darkest recesses ('E troppo ⌒ avanzare ‿ impossibile ⌒ nulla ‿ regredire' (*Galateo* 43) ('It's too much ⌒ advancing ‿ impossible ⌒ nothing ‿ regressing')); of 'testing' one's own personal terrain as if 'with a divining rod' ('assaggi . . . rabdomantici' (*Galateo* 24)). Even the suspension points in the text which curl in upon themselves (' ·· . ·. .·˙·˙·. .·˙·. .·˙·. ˙·. .·˙·. .·˙·. ·. ' (*Galateo* 19)) represent this self-reflective process; and some of the signs to be found in the actual wood stand for an attempt to sound out the areas of the self which one has subconsciously repressed, and which therefore refuse to yield to investigation:

          DIVIETO DI
          CIRCOLAZIONE (*Galateo* 36)

As the quotation above serves to emphasize, there is also a strong visual element in *Galateo* where various notices pinned to trees ('indizi-alberi') are dispersed throughout the text, as they are throughout the wood:

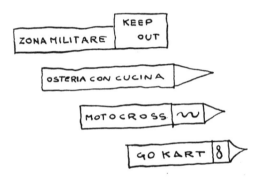

Very often the typographical layout of the poems attempts to reflect the topography of the wood. Parts of the poem 'Pericoli d'incendi' ('Dangers of fires'), for example, can be read vertically and/or horizontally:

Zirlii di princìpi
passato a crivello babil di chicchi
sèmi

un qualche suono
alberi indizi-alberi là e qua
chicchi a picco nel cavo
e non mai brulla
la betulla dal favo

Voci a strada ‖ la folla
la folla guada

sosta netta anche se
sopra vi posa la mano il crepuscolo

(Whistlings of beginnings
passed through a sieve confusion of
(grains

some sort of sound
trees signs-trees there and here

seeds   grains on the summit in the
                                               hollow
                                               and the birch of the honeycomb
                                               never bare
Voices on the street ‖ the crowd
the crowd fords   clean-cut pause even if
                                               the dusk places its hand upon you).

While vertical and horizontal readings tend to reinforce the 'Fili / vivi d'alberi' ('Living / threads of trees'), the meanderings the readers make in experimenting with horizontal and vertical readings, indeed the leaps they are encouraged to make from one part of the poem to another part which seems related to the first in sound or in meaning (for example the phrase 'Spini in pupille' ('Thorns in pupils') occurs at the top of page 36; 'i vostri occhi spinati' ('your barbed eyes') occurs at the bottom of the same page) reflect the (Heideggerian) 'Holzwege' –the paths through the wood which lead nowhere.

And just as man-made signs are attached to the trees, so too the wood itself is a hive of natural signs – of coded behaviours and sounds: 'i lóghia dei bisset' (*Galateo* 77) ('the insects's little discourses'); 'aminoacidi che i bala' (*Galateo* 78) ('amino-acids which dance'); the onomatopoeic 'Zirlii' (*Galateo* 35) and 'cerececè' (*Galateo* 82) of the birds – an endless chatter, apparently meaningless (which is meant to be confronted with the silence of the dead, pregnant with meaning), but in which there could exist (as contemplated in 'Subnarcosi', *PSQ*) 'un chiuso si-si-significare' – a primordial 'meaning' which is 'closed' to us. In this sense the wood possesses its own 'galateo'.

Whereas on the one hand Zanzotto tries, in the vein of Pascoli, to imitate the noisy chatter of the birds (as in the predominance of 'i' sounds at the beginning of 'Pericoli d'incendi'), on the other hand his language can be opaque to the point of seeming well-nigh incomprehensible (as in *LB* there is a hotchpotch of different lexical registers) and / or crude and vulgar: 'Ma ti, scagazha, scagazha, / e pò nètete 'l bèro' (*Galateo* 78) ('But you, crap, crap, / and then clean up your arse'). As such this language lies at an opposite pole to that promoted by Della Casa in his *Galateo* (XXII) which stipulates that words, no matter what their context, should be 'chiare' and 'belle in quanto al suono e in quanto al significato' ('clear [and] beautiful as much in sound as in meaning'). The use of language in contemporary society can no longer be codified in such stringent terms. A sonnet on the subject matter of 'decreasing' (in the sense of loosing weight) and 'nourishment' ('Sonetto del decremento e dell'alimento') – just one of the fourteen to be found in Zanzotto's *Galateo* would have been unthinkable in Della Casa's day.

Zanzotto's fourteen sonnets, which he calls an 'Ipersonetto' ('Hypersonnet'), were, in spite of their burlesque, parodic nature, written in homage to poets like

Della Casa and Gaspara Stampa who wrote sonnets in the Montello wood. They operate as a kind of 'parodic homage' to the Petrarchan tradition (Welle 71); an attempt to yoke experimentation with tradition (Welle 86). Each individual sonnet, we are told in a note, is meant to stand for one line in a traditional sonnet, or to put it another way, one sonnet has ramified, has exfoliated, so to speak, into fourteen sonnets, plus a 'Premessa' ('Preface') and a 'Postilla' ('Postil').

In these sonnets Petrarchan conventions are employed to the full: there are traditional Petrarchan rhyme schemes – the octaves for the most part rhyming ABBA ABBA, and the sestets CDE CDE, or in other possible combinations; Petrarchan vocabulary abounds: 'aureo' (*Galateo* 63) ('golden'), 'fiamma' (*Galateo* 66) ('flame'), 'gentil' (*Galateo* 67) ('courteous'), 'fronde' (*Galateo* 69) ('leafy branches'), 'pensier' (*Galateo* 70) ('thought'); as do typical Petrarchan devices such as the use of antitheses ('troppo radi / o fitti' ('too thin / or thick')); 'imprese lente o / più rapide' (*Galateo* 62) ('undertakings slow or / quicker')) and word-plays (as in the phrase 'non mondo o immondo io; né mai pur mondo' (*Galateo* 68) where 'mondo' can mean both 'clean' (as an adjective) and 'world' (as a noun); 'stili steli stami' (*Galateo* 71) ('styles, stems, stamens')). There is even a Petrarchan structure in the collection as a whole (Welle 73) in that it contains fifty-two poems, thereby offering one poem for each week of the year, just as Petrarch's *Canzoniere* contains one poem for each day of the year.

But in spite of the adoption of Petrarchan codes, the content of the sonnets is very contemporary, and sends up the Petrarchan tradition through the use of wit, irony, and vulgarity. Thus there are sonnets on the subject of false teeth (Sonnet II); the poet as a snouting pig, clawing the ground (I); and jaws salivating at the trough and releasing 'fury' in 'golden dung' (IV). Sonnet VII presents Zanzotto wandering in Petrarchan fashion through the wood pierced not by Cupid's arrows but by those of brambles and insects. Sonnet IX talks about Linnaeus, who founded an international system of classifying plants by new Latin names which are sharper than 'to a tongue the sweetness of clitoris'. Then there are metapoems: in the 'Preface' Zanzotto 'bows' ironically to the 'egregio codice' ('distinguished code') of the sonnet form; sonnet III refers to the 'sophistic' 'belle maniere' ('beautiful manners') posited in Della Casa's *Galateo*; and the 'Postil' points to Zanzotto's falseness in using the now outdated sonnet conventions in order to parody them:

> Falso pur io, clone di tanto falso

> Phoney even I, a clone of such fake

> > così ancora di te mi sono avvalso,
> > di te sonetto, righe infami e ladre –
> > mandala in cui di frusto in frusto accatto

thus I availed myself yet again / of you sonnet, infamous and thieving lines – /
mandala in which I borrow from shabby to shabby.

Whereas the emphasis in *Galateo* is all upon descent – Zanzotto delves into a
literary and historical past; he assumes a pig-like closeness to the earth, 'digging
up' the bones, rotting flesh, and multiple life-forms which lie behind it; he adopts,
on the one hand, a difficult, 'woody' language, and on the other hand, a vulgar,
'earthy' language – in *Fosfeni* he turns his attention away from the Montello,
which lies to the south of his region, and looks upwards to contemplate the cold,
rarified, icy world of the Dolomites, which lie to the north. The emphasis is now,
as Zanzotto states in a note, upon 'snow and abstractions', 'mists and frosts'. The
journey from the Montello to the Dolomites is Dantesque in orientation, for the
Alpine ascent testifies to a search for a 'logos', for a meaning which can only be
pursued after contemplation of the darkness of the self and of human history.
But whereas the ice imagery of the collection symbolizes a desire for 'intellectual
clear-sightedness' (Luperini), the title of the collection, 'Fosfeni', indicates the
difficulty of achieving this: 'Phosphenes' are the luminous spots which appear
before the eyes when the eyeballs are pressed, and which, therefore, impede clear
vision.

This desire for clear vision, and the difficulty of achieving it, is the first
in a long, abounding series of antitheses in the collection, for finding the
logos is posited as being akin to finding the centre, the point of contact, the
'non-scissioni' (*Fosfeni* 15) ('non-splits') between polar opposites.

The first poem of the collection, 'Come ultime cene' ('Like Last Suppers')
juxtaposes the notion of spirituality (implied in the title) and symbolized by
the 'chastity' and 'dignity' of the 'campagne rasoiate a freddo' ('countrysides
shaven to cold'), with the theme of physicality, especially (as in *Galateo*) physical
nourishment. The Alpine 'osterie' ('taverns') with their lavish menus ('meats
viande vivande e latte e cappuccino' ('meats dishes foods and milk and white
coffee')) offer sensual indulgences, and sexual attractions ('ragazza-osteria che
sgonna via' ('girl-tavern who 'skirts' away')) which highlight the beast in man –
his 'circuiti circèi' ('circean circuits'). The composed, lack of assertiveness in the
icy, Christ-like landscape, 'eccelsamente contento nel suo abessere' ('sublimely
content in its non-being') is set against the noisy, self-assertiveness of 'barking'
man, who moves and makes noise even when asleep ('zzz di sonni' ('zzz of sleep');
'sobbalzare nella notte' ('jerking in the night')), whose very sneezing (because of
the cold) operates as a 'miniorgasmo in etcì' ('mini-orgasm in achoo') (a note
to the poem refers to the relationship between sneezing and erotic orgasms,
as mentioned by certain analysts). Various word-plays in the poem also serve
to emphasize the disparity between this peaceful landscape, and consumerist
and destructive man: the word 'gelo' ('ice'), symbolizing 'intellectual clear-
sightedness', is played off against the word 'gel', to be interpreted, as a note

explains, as a 'frigida gelatina' ('frigid gelatine'), gelatine being a colourless and transparent water-soluble substance (and in that sense like ice) but derived from animal parts such as skin, ligaments, tendons, and used in food preparation, as well as, of course, in the making of explosives. 'Chiometta', the diminutive of 'chioma', is, on the one hand, used to depict the rays of a star (as in the literature of writers such as Pulci, Boiardo, and Bembo), and a feature of the natural and beautiful Alpine landscape. But on the other hand, it denotes a head of hair and leads Zanzotto to contemplate those banal products in our consumerist society which, however, are attributed great importance and meaning (logos) in everyday life, such as hair-colourings (the '"cachet . . . per i capelli"'), and other cosmetics and unnatural embellishments endulged in by women, especially on romantic, 'star-lit' occasions:

> 'Che lacca per unghie?'

What lacquer for nails?

> 'Che detergente che assorbente per le intimità, quelle fuori
> sotto le stelle . . . ?'

What cleansing cream what absorbent for intimacies, those out / under the stars . . . ?

But the polar opposites don't just exist between the landscape and man; they are present within the landscape itself and cannot be reconciled by the poet. Thus in 'Amori impossibili' ('Impossible Loves') Zanzotto finds it impossible that so much love is openly 'given' and at the same time 'hidden' by the hills:

> Non è possibile che tanto amore
> in esse venga apertamente
> dato
> e al tempo stesso dissimulato, anzi
> reso inaccessibile

It isn't possible that so much love / in them is openly / given / and at the same time hidden, or rather/ made inaccessible.

They are 'rich with a thousand deadly dangers', yet (as contemplated in 'Silicio, Carbonio, Castellieri' ('Silicon, Carbon, Fortified Villages')) their minerals contain chemical elements which are used in technology either to sustain life, or improve living standards: 'silicon' is widely used in industry, especially (as a note explains) in the making of computers ('"*logos in silicio*" nei calcolatori'), and in its function as something which assists calculation, it stands (as do the various indications of logarithms scattered throughout the poem 'Righe nello spettro' ('Lines in the Spectrum')) as a symbol of Zanzotto's desire to 'calculate' reality, to 'solve the problem' of the logos. The light present within the rocks of the hills:

'pietre da acciarino' ('flints for lighters'), 'un colpo di lucente selce' ('a blow of shining flintstone'); or those chemicals in the rocks, such as 'carbon' which (as an electrode) can be used in the generation of electricity and light, also function as symbols of Zanzotto's quest for the logos through the cultivation of 'intellectual *clear-sightedness*':

> logos in carbonio   logos in silicio
>
> logos in carbon   logos in silicon.

However, it is precisely intellect and 'stabilizing logic' ('stabilizzante / logica') which is rejected in 'Varietà del rosa e joni' ('Varieties of Pink and Joni') with Zanzotto proposing that perhaps the logos – the 'dio-raggio' ('god-ray') of the poem exists 'fuori . . . ragione' ('outside . . . reason'). Consequently, the 'pseudo-knowledge' of science and of 'crystallography' is denounced; the poet asserts that he will abandon all attempts to see clearly: 'iridi senza più collirii' ('irises with no more eyewashes'), that he will slacken the reins (in calesse . . . / a pugni rilassati' ('in a gig . . . / with relaxed fists'), and that revelation is more likely to be achieved in this unthinking, trance-like state:

> Così scongetturandosi il corpo
> forse che ti affratella
> all'altro bello

Thus dis-conjecturing the body / perhaps you will unite in comradeship with / the other beautiful one.

It is also in defiance of logic and reason that the poem opens with an alogical, surreal interpretation of reality where 'bees make wood' and 'a hen pecks at petals and makes honey of feather and eggs'.

'Periscopi' ('Periscopes') too emphasizes this notion of allowing oneself to be pervaded by understanding, rather than attempting to understand:

> lasciarsi invadere dell'inaudibile
> dagli extrasuoni

letting oneself be invaded by the inaudible / by the extra-sounds,

while the very title 'Periscopes' highlights the upward gaze and direction which characterizes the collection ('slalom in ascesa' ('ascending slaloms')), and the attempt to see and understand things which from earth are out of sight and comprehension.

Indeed the 'high state' of the boundless 'skies' ('alto stato / dei cieli' (*Fosfeni* 20); 'quanto blu dentro il blu' (*Fosfeni* 46) ('how much blue within the blue')), and the unfathomable mysteries they hide ('Ben disposti silenzi /

indisseppellibili / . . . Silenzi sottratti / ad ogni speculazione' (*Fosfeni* 45) ('Well disposed unexhumable / silences / . . . Silences removed / from any speculation')) are juxtaposed with the mysteries of minute, apparently unimportant life on earth, as if in an attempt to glimpse the hierarchic organization which lies behind them, and the point of contact between them. The poem '(*Loghion*)' (a dialect word which, as Zanzotto explains, has overtones suggesting something minor, almost non-existent) playfully presents a group of centipedes constructing ephemeral 'bricolages', falling over themselves because of their 'too many feet'. The poem also features a glow-worm trying to blind the poet with a fireworks display, posing as a blow-lamp flame or a dragon when a child's breath would be enough to snuff out his light.

The industriousness of such minor life forms are then set against the frequent dejection and morbidity suffered by modern man (in 'Collassare e pomerio' ('Collapse and Pomerium')) – a state of non-being which in turn is juxtaposed with great achievements in music, art and literature, composed by artists who, as if fired by the logos of a higher state of being, can manage to create a thing of beauty even out of the most sordid aspects of existence ('divine latrine' (*Fosfeni* 20) ('divine lavatories')). Yet here too a paradox exists, for it is recognized that such works of art are not the product of afflatus alone; rather 'intuizione e disperazione' ('intuition and desperation') are 'così strette gemelle' (*Fosfeni* 38) ('so close twins'). The poem 'Diffidare gola, corpo, movimenti, teatro' ('To be Suspicious of Throat, Body, Movements, Theatre') is partially about the difficulties of composing poetry – about moments of wanting to abandon writing, moments of wanting to succeed ('Vorrei desistere vorrei rivincere' ('I would like to desist I would like to win again')), and moments of hoping that something magical will intervene in the creative process, and that works, abandoned in the 'storehouse', when resurrected for revision (and Zanzotto has frequently spoken about his method of locking a poem, once written, in a drawer, and unearthing it at a much later date) will reveal an elegance and coherence not originally thought to be there:

> Immagazzinare avvicinarle fino a immagazzinarle
> e poi trovi invece parola-lustro d'ordine

To store to approach them until you can store them / and then you find instead a polished orderly word.

The same poem warns us against those poets (cryptically indicated as 'Ch. M., J. M. L.') who, rather than conceiving of poetry as an expression of meaning (logos), place emphasis (as indicated in a note) upon the 'phonic-somatic' aspects of verse, upon poetry as a 'performance'. But ironically this warning is conveyed in a poem which indulges in the style it condemns (and it is a style, moreover, not uncommon to Zanzotto):

vorrei intuirmi a strami a stormi a sciami

I would like to know myself intuitively by hay by flocks by swarms

E colare in calore e colore

And to drip in heat and colour

as if, paradoxically, to parody the concept of poetry as an expression of meaning –
for meaning is always scattered in language, given the metonymic chains of sound
and meaning carried by individual words.

If *Fosfeni* presents the reader with abundant paradoxes and antitheses of this
sort, an even greater one is in store. For *Fosfeni*, perhaps the most difficult and
abstract text of Zanzotto to date is followed by *Idioma*, the third book of the poet's
'pseudo-trilogy', which contains some of his most simple poems.

Roughly half of the fifty-two poems in *Idioma* are written in dialect, and it is
these dialect poems which are the most approachable, and to which the title of
the collection refers. 'Idioma', as a note explains, is meant to denote a language
(dialect) which is irrepressibly alive, and still in the process of being born; and yet,
at one and the same time, a language which is closed, private, even deprived, and
in a sense idiotic. But it is precisely in an attempt to subvert this view of dialect
as a deprived, idiotic language *vis-à-vis* standard Italian that Zanzotto intermingles
twenty-five elementary dialect poems with twenty-six Italian, and for the most
part, difficult poems, and writes one poem half in dialect and half in standard
Italian. This placing of dialect on an equal footing with standard Italian goes hand
in hand with other assimilations of superior and apparently inferior phenomena
in the collection, in an attempt (practised already in *LB*) to undermine systems of
power.

Hence the opening poem of the collection, 'GLI ARTICOLI DI G. M. O.'
('THE ARTICLES OF G. M. O.'), celebrates in a teasing, good-humoured
manner, a local, now veteran journalist, G. M. O., who in articles on his
own region, written in the high-blown style of D'Annunzio, would attribute
exotic names to plain, local spots – 'Riviera delle Rose' ('Coast of Roses'),
'Eremo di Giotto' ('Giotto's Hermitage') – thereby making them 'vertiginously
unidentifiable'; and give extensive, enthusiastic coverage to visits from famous
people, such as when D'Annunzio himself arrived 'in his red car' to dine at the
villa of Toti Dal Monte, an operatic soprano from the region who achieved
international fame in the period between the two wars. In short, G. M. O. put
his small, provincial Veneto region on a par with Australia and Canada:

come egli dava a questa zona minuscola
a questo giochetto di colline
spazi quanto meno australiani
grazie a soffi-di-vetraio dannunziani!

o quanto meno canadesi
grazie a tourbillons di linguaggio dannunziesi!

how he gave to this minute zone / to this little game of hills / spaces at least
Australian / thanks to d'Annunzian glassmaker blows! / or at least Canadian /
thanks to d'Annunzian linguistic whirlwinds!

Two birthday poems are even more indicative of this procedure of assimilating
the important and the apparently unimportant – one is dedicated to Montale on
his eightieth birthday, and the other to the eightieth birthday of Nino (the same
Nino of *LB*), a local inhabitant who dabbles in selenography. The tone of both
poems is the same – intimate and conversational – in spite of the fact that, in a
curious, but obviously intentional inversion, the poem to the noble prize-winner
of literature is composed in dialect, while that to Nino, the speaker of dialect, is
in Italian.

The only vaguely 'intellectual' element in the poem to Montale is the few
allusions it makes to Montalian imagery (such as the 'sbari de s'ciòp . . . inte 'l
pi raro vodo dei canp' ('gun shots . . . in the rarest emptiness of countrysides') –
a clear reference to Montale's 'gun shot' 'in the silence of the countryside' in 'Mia
vita, a te non chiedo lineamenti fissi', *Ossi*). Otherwise the poem is totally artless
and unaffected, with Zanzotto speaking of the 'risk' he is taking of 'embarrassing'
himself, of how it would have been wiser to have kept silent on this day, and read
some of Montale's poems; but how he is nevertheless sure that the sincerity of his
birthday wishes will be appreciated by the poet:

Ris'ce cussì 'sta òlta de intrigarme
e de inverigolarme pèdo che par al solito;
quant mèjo un taser fondo, taser e lèderte

Thus I risk embarrassing myself this time / and gimletting myself worse than
usual; / how much better a deep silence, to be silent and read you

Ma son siguro che ti tu vét quant lanpido
l'é l'agurar che mi – co tanti altri – te fae
par i tó otanta de 'sta umana vita

But I am sure that you see how limpid / is this greeting from me – and from
so many others – / for your eighty years of this human life.

The poem to Nino is slightly less sentimental, with Zanzotto emphasizing the
eccentricity of this character (an 'outlandish widower of hares and pheasants'
('vedovo di lepri e fagiani, strampolato')), and his amazing resilience: whereas
summer saw him limping, panting, and supporting himself with difficulty, the
glory of January had taken Nino to itself, and now immune from illnesses, he
appeared without an overcoat and with a sprightly step, leaving the poet to
suspect that he would go on

> . . . pedalando
> tra i novanta e i cento anni quasi volage

. . . pedalling / between ninety and a hundred years almost fickle.

Mirroring these two poems, there is another entitled '*Sarlòt e Jijeto*', celebrating the real Charlie Chaplin who died on Christmas night in 1977, and a certain 'Jijeto' – the Chaplin of Zanzotto's town who attempted to look like and imitate his hero, and who with his 'good-natured art' 'brought the best of 'Chaplin' everywhere'. Addressing the real Chaplin, a 'poor king' ('pore sovran'), a 'god of youthfulness' ('dèo fresch'), who 'slipped off very silently in a light bubble' on that Christmas night to where 'arms of galaxies and decalcomanias of mysteries' were 'ready to put on a great party' for him, Zanzotto asks him to reach out his hand to Jijeto, and to all the Jijeti of the past, and transform their journey into 'one big burst of laughter', into 'the most beautiful farce that has ever been seen in the cosmorama'.

Two other celebrities of literature are commemorated – Edmond Jabès and Pasolini. In the poem to the latter Zanzotto reflects upon his similar origins to Pasolini, but also upon how life laid 'different traps' for them: Zanzotto was to remain 'fermo, inpetolà 'nte i versi' ('immobile, smeared in poetry'); Pasolini, 'dapartut co la tó passion de tut' ('everywhere with 'his' passion for everything'). But in spite of their differences, we are told that what bound them together was their sharing of similar ideas on things which mattered most. Now, in old age, Zanzotto can only offer to the murdered Pasolini a few 'muttering' words, in an agonizing attempt to

> . . . pontar-sù, justar-sù in qualche modo
> – par un momento sol, par saludarte –
> quel che i à fat dei tó os e del tó cor

re-stitch, re-connect in some way / – for just a moment, to say goodbye – / what they have done with your bones and your heart.

But in keeping with the pattern already established of celebrating the humble as well as the renowned, complementing the poems dedicated to Montale, Chaplin, Jabès, and Pasolini, there is a spate of 'Where are they now?' poems in dialect about ordinary, local individuals who have passed away: Pina, always as black as a chimney from selling coal and newspapers in the brightly painted shop behind the square; Zanzotto's dearest aunt who composed poems for carnivals, some even containing Latin words, but who reputedly took to drinking and brought about her own ruin; the widow, Bres, from Belluno who won the lottery and squandered all the money merry-making with her friends; Aurora who after Vespers used to sell sweets and carobs to kids for ten *centesimi*; and Marietta Tamòda who was obsessed by the novels of Alexandre Dumas, and while washing mountains of clothes in the Soligo would be dreaming of Montecristo, or the king's good musketeers in hot pursuit of ruffians and mountebanks.

Similarly there is a series of dialect poems gathered together under the title, *Mistieròi* (already published separately in 1979, although Zanzotto in a note explains how these poems were originally conceived as an integral part of the present collection). 'Mistieròi' is the dialect word for 'piccoli, poveri mestieri' ('small, poor trades'), and the 'poor trades' celebrated, but now in danger of becoming extinct include those of the cartwright, whose carts are 'securely built' with 'solid rims of iron' and 'wheels that spray mud', and 'jump on stones'; the shepherds who for some resemble beasts, always dirty with lambs and goats, but who are really 'men' and 'poets', 'kings of Arcady'; the blacksmith with his frightening dark and fiery workshop; the umberella maker whose belly is always hungry when it does not rain enough; and the chair-menders (a secret society) who, when mending a chair purposely put a herring in the straw, so that a cat will rip open the stuffing, and a job will thereby be secured for another chair-mender.

Besides such rudimentary, but colourful images, there are poems on more 'sophisticated' matters. 'ALTRO, ALTRO LINGUAGGIO, FUORI IDIOMA?' ('OTHER, OTHER LANGUAGE, OUTSIDE IDIOM?') contains hermetically compressed images which try to conjur up the nature of dialect – a 'circuito chiuso che pulsa' ('closed, pulsating circuit'); a 'gesto ingessato' ('gesture encased in plaster'). 'VERSO IL 25 APRILE' ('TOWARDS THE 25 APRIL') is in the vein of 'Sul Piave' (*VCT*) and calls, as in the latter, for an end to the anniversaries of 'human sacrifices' such as the Feast of Liberation in Italy. And 'Corsa non affaticata' ('Race not Wearied') discusses the arms race – a race which never gets tired of running, and yet is running nowhere ('Corsa non affaticata a qui, a dove mai' ('Race not wearied, to here, to nowhere at all')) – a paradox like the clichéd paradox of arms as a threat and arms as a deterrent ('irrequietezze e calma' ('restlessness and calm')). As if to reinforce the absurdities of such paradoxes, the poem itself rambles on meaninglessly with something of the hysteria of a man who has come face to face with his killer (a note at the end of the poem claims that it was written '*sotto la mira di armi orientali, tra mucchi di armi occidentali*' ('*under the aim of eastern arms, among piles of western arms*')):

> Corsa non affaticata, a qui, a dove mai,
>   dei colori, disinnescata cangianza
>   che pur non abbandona
>   mai nessuno abbandona –
>   E autorizza chiunque, oltre ogni chiunque,
>   a parlare con vivi e alterati
>   Aprite, colori, le dolcezze
>   del percorso che non è affatto percorso

> perché è al futuro di tutti i percorsi
> . . .
> Indulgenza, clemenza dintorno!

Race not wearied, to here, to nowhere at all, / defused changefulness of colours / which still does not abandon / no one ever abandons – / and it authorizes whoever, beyond every whoever, / to speak with the living and those in a changed state / Open, colours, the sweetnesses / of the course which is not at all run / because it is at the future of all courses / . . . / Indulgence, mercy around!

At an opposite pole to this poem where a political issue is considered in the abstract, there is a poem to a certain Maria Fresu, the innocent victim of a political incident. As a note explains, she was literally pulverized by a bomb at the station of Bologna so that people were lead to wonder whether she had ever been there in the first place. All that remains of her is her name. Her death is commemorated in a tragicomic manner, with Zanzotto reflecting how the name, Maria Fresu, still crops up at mealtimes; how she explodes all over again, as it were, in every burp and belch since (presumably) her dust could have settled on the food being consumed:

> E il nome di Maria Fresu
> continua a scoppiare
> all'ora dei pranzi
> in ogni casseruola
> in ogni pentola
> in ogni boccone
> in ogni
> rutto – scoppiato e disseminato –
> in milioni di
> dimenticanze, di comi, bburp

And the name of Maria Fresu / continues to explode / at mealtimes / in every saucepan / in every pot / in every mouthful / in every / belch – exploded and disseminated – / in millions of / forgettings, revelries, bburps.

Idioma may strike many readers as being less intellectually engaging than Zanzotto's previous works. But the beauty of many of the poems in this collection, especially those in dialect, lies in their almost naive simplicity, and in the warm affection they display toward the culture and inhabitants of a closely-knit community. A poem to an old seamstress, Maria Carpèla, provides the best example of such qualities; its limpid sincerity making all attempts at 'commentary' superfluous:

> Si no 'l te fèsse 'n paradiso
> aposta par ti, anca si paradisi no ghe n'é,
> al saràe da méter a l'inferno

l'istesso Padreterno –
la saràe da méter a l'inferno
tuta, tuta quanta 'la realtà',
si par ti no la fèsse 'n paradiso
pien de bontà come la tó bontà,
gnentaltro che 'l paradiso
come che ti tu l'à pensà

If he did not make a paradise for you / especially for you, even if paradises do
not exist, / the Eternal Father himself / should be sent to hell – / all, all reality /
should be sent to hell, / if for you he did not make it a paradise / full of goodness
like your goodness, / nothing else but the paradise / as you imagined it.

But the question remains to be asked: what links *Galateo, Fosfeni,* and *Idioma*?;
indeed, is there a link between them? Welle refers to the 'non-sequential
correlations among the individual volumes in Zanzotto's trilogy' (Welle 13);
and Zanzotto himself has spoken about the 'impregnable autonomy' of all of
his individual texts ('Autoritratto' 172). Each of the three book does, of course,
focus exclusively upon the Veneto region (the Montello wood, the Dolomites,
Pieve di Soligo), but apart from the nexus of 'place', it would seem that there is
nothing substantially cohesive between the three volumes, and the poet himself
seems to indicate this by referring to the works as a '*pseudo*-trilogy'.

Furthermore, what is the poetic necessity of the 'trilogy'? While it is true to say
that it contains some very distinctive elements, unlike any of the poet's previous
work (such as the 'Petrarchan' sonnets of 'Ipersonetto', and *Idioma*'s dialect poems
to people and trades which are less contrived than the dialectal compositions of
Filò) the 'trilogy' does return, for the most part, to familiar subjects: *Galateo* to the
theme of political history, as in *VCT; Fosfeni* to the question of the logos, already
debated in *LB;* and *Idioma* to the message of *IXE:* Zanzotto's promotion of the
human aspects of life, and his rejection of all systems of power. Nevertheless there
are a few indications within *Idioma* which seem to point to the fact that Zanzotto
himself felt it necessary to re-examine for the last time some of those issues which
had been of major importance to him up until then. We are told in a note that the
poem 'E S'CIAO' which speaks of Cecco Ceccogiato, the eighteenth-century
poet who wrote about the Montello wood in Paduan dialect, and from whom
Zanzotto quoted in '*Chive, chive à l'ombria*', *Galateo,* functions as an 'addio', a
final farewell to the whole collection, *Galateo.* 'VERSO IL 25 APRILE' also
speaks in a conclusive manner of one of the issues raised in *Galateo:* the poet is
thankful for having 'lived' and 'passed beyond' the Montello wood and the blood
of the dead:

con mano assodo i pregi dell'essere vissuto,
      e passato a un millimetro da dove
   la selva e il vostro sangue
si sfiniscono

and with my hand I ascertain the merits of having lived,/ and passed a milli-
metre away from where / the wood and your blood / exhaust themselves.

The necessity of the trilogy would seem therefore to be a need on Zanzotto's
part to rework his major preoccupations, putting them in the specific context of
his own region, in an attempt to solder the links between himself and his area, and
find his right place within the latter. One could say that Zanzotto's vision in the
first two books of the 'trilogy' had fluctuated between inner realities (the delving
down into the self of *Galateo*) and transcendent realities (the reaching and looking
upwards to 'superhuman' heights in *Fosfeni*) and that finally in *Idioma* he begins to
register the field in between, emphasizing the concepts of communication (most
of the poems in *Idioma* talk about *other people*, not the hitherto persistent theme
of the self and subjectivity) and of feeling at one with humble, commonplace,
and *very human* people. Perhaps this is the strongest, but disguised link between
the three books of the 'trilogy'.

And indeed there is, for the most part, an atmosphere of calm and contentment
in *Idioma* which derives from the poet's new found equilibrium, his sense of
having discovered his true self amid the 'non-violenza' ('non-violence') and
'bonarietà qualche volta sonnolenta' ('sometimes drowsy good-naturedness')
of his local '*Genti*' ('*People*'):

> e sono partecipe, finalmente, delle azioni
> da cui mi distoglieva il deliquio amoroso e pauroso
> ('VERSO IL 25 APRILE')

and I participate, finally, in the actions / from which the loving and fearful
swoon removed me

> . . e mi adagio nel giusto
> essere uno coi tanti di qui
> ('*Genti*')

and I settle down in the right / being of one with the many from here.

Montale once said that 'Zanzotto's metronome is perhaps the heartbeat'
(Montale 339), and indeed a visual representation of the pull and direction
of the three books of the 'trilogy' is reminiscent of a cardiograph – pointing
downwards in *Galateo*, shooting upwards in *Fosfeni*, and finally achieving a level
and regular plain in *Idioma* (the 'guizzi in un monitor' ('quivers in a monitor') of
'ALTRO, ALTRO LINGUAGGIO, FUORI IDIOMA?'?).

It will be interesting to see if, in future works, Zanzotto will prolong his
dialectal phase, or re-embark on the plurilinguistic adventures for which he is
more renowned. What matters most, however, is that, in the realm of poetry,
he will go on 'pedalando / . . . / quasi volage'.

Select Bibliography

EDITIONS OF ZANZOTTO'S WORKS

Poetry

Dietro il paesaggio (Milan: Mondadori, 1951).
Elegia e altri versi (Milan: La Meridiana, 1954).
Vocativo (Milan: Mondadori, 1957).
IX Ecloghe (Milan: Mondadori, 1962).
La Beltà (Milan: Mondadori, 1968).
Gli sguardi i fatti e senhal (Pieve di Soligo: Tipografia Bernardi, 1969), republished,
    Milan: Mondadori, 1990.
A che valse? (Milan: Scheiwiller, 1970).
Pasque (Milan: Mondadori, 1973).
Filò (Venice: Edizioni del Ruzante, 1976).
Il Galateo in bosco (Milan: Mondadori, 1978).
Mistieròi (Feltre: Castaldi, 1979), now included in *Idioma*.
Fosfeni (Milan: Mondadori, 1983).
Idioma (Milan: Mondadori, 1986).

Prose

Sull'altopiano (prose 1942–54) (Venice: Neri-Pozza, 1964), now included in *Racconti
    e prose*.
Racconti e prose (Milan: Mondadori, 1990).

Selected Editions

Poesie (1938–1972), ed. S. Agosti (Milan: Mondadori, 1973).
Selected Poetry of Andrea Zanzotto (a bilingual anthology), ed. and trans. R. Feldman and
    B. Swann (Surrey: Princeton University Press, 1975).

Critical Writings by Zanzotto

'I "Novissimi"', *Comunità*, no. 99 (May 1962), 89–91.
'Éluard dopo dieci anni', *Questo e altro*, no. 3 (March 1963), 69–71.
'Ricordo di Paul Éluard', *Terzo Programma*, no. 1 (1963), 233–49.
Poesia italiana contemporanea (1909–1959), ed. G. Spagnoletti (Parma: Guanda, 1964),
    713–17.
'Noventa tra i "moderni"', *Comunità*, no. 130 (June–July 1965), 74–9. Republished as

'Il putèl nel poeta Noventa', in *I metodi attuali della critica in Italia*, ed. M. Corti and C. Segre (Turin: Einaudi, 1970), 153–8.

'Sviluppo di una situazione montaliana (Escatologia-Scatologia)', in *Omaggio a Montale*, ed. S. Ramat (Milan: Mondadori, 1966), 157–64.

'Ungaretti: la presenza delle varianti, il mito dell'autobiografia', *Paragone*, no. 254 (April 1971), 29–34.

'In margine a *Satura*', *Nuovi argomenti*, no. 23–4 (July–December 1971), 215–20.

'Infanzie, poesie, scuoletta (appunti)', *Strumenti critici*, no. 20 (February 1973), 52–77.

'Petrarca e i poeti d'oggi. Problemi e illuminazioni', *L'Approdo letterario*, no. 66 (June 1974), 93–100.

'Un letto pieno di libri' (on F. Petrarca), *Il Giorno* (14 July 1974). Republished as 'Una stanza piena di libri', in *Francesco Petrarca: nel VI centenario della morte* (Bologna: Boni, 1976), 81–5.

'Parole, comportamenti, gruppi (appunti)', *Studi novecenteschi*, vol. 4, no. 8–9 (July–November 1974), 349–55.

'Per una pedagogia', *Nuovi argomenti*, no. 49 (1976), 47–51.

'Poesia?', *Il Verri*, no. 1 (September 1976), 110–13.

'Petrarca fra il palazzo e la cameretta', in *Petrarca, Rime* by F. Petrarca (Milan: Rizzoli, 1976), 5–16.

'Nei paraggi di Lacan', in *Effetto Lacan* (Cosenza: Lerici, 1979).

'Pedagogy', *Stanford Italian Review*, no. 2 (Fall 1982), 30–41 (translated from the Italian by B. Allen).

'(Ontology?) (Reference?)', in *The Favourite Malice*, ed. and trans. T. L. Harrison (New York: Out of London Press, 1983), 133–6.

'Verso un "idioma", e poetiche-lampo', *Alfabeta*, no. 84 (May 1986), 15.

INTERVIEWS AND DISCUSSIONS GIVEN BY ZANZOTTO

Interview in F. Camon, *Il mestiere di poeta* (Milan: Lerici, 1965), 149–61.

'Andrea Zanzotto: riflessioni sulla poesia', *Uomini e libri*, no. 23 (May 1969), 46–50.

P. F. Listri, 'Uno sguardo dalla periferia. Intervista con Andrea Zanzotto', *L'Approdo letterario*, vol. 18, no. 59–60 (1972), 185–92.

'Autoritratto', *L'Approdo letterario*, no. 77–80 (June 1977), 272–6.

W. P. Sillanpoa 'An interview with Andrea Zanzotto', *Yale Italian Studies*, vol. 2, no. 4 (Autumn 1978), 297–307.

'Intervista', in G. Nuvoli *Andrea Zanzotto* (Florence: La Nuova Italia, 1979), 3–14.

Interview in S. Battistini and M. Bettarini, *Chi è il poeta?* (Milan: Gammalibri, 1980), 45–50.

Interview in *Sulla poesia: conversazioni nelle scuole* (Parma: Pratiche editrice, 1981), 65–107.

'Autoritratto', *Ateneo veneto*, vol. 18, no. 1–2 (1982), 170–5.

B. Allen 'Interview with Andrea Zanzotto (Pieve di Soligo: July 25 1978)', *Stanford Italian Review*, no. 4 (Fall 1984), 253–65.

WORKS ON ZANZOTTO

AGOSTI, S., 'Zanzotto o la conquista del dire', *Sigma* (March 1969). Republished in *Il testo poetico. Teoria e pratiche d'analisi* (Milan: Rizzoli, 1972), 211–18.

AGOSTI, S., 'Introduzione alla poesia di Zanzotto', in *A. Zanzotto, Poesie 1938–1972*, ed. S. Agosti (Milan: Mondadori, 1973), 7–25.

ALLEN, B., 'Zanzotto's "Grammaticalismo": Positions and Performance', *Stanford Italian Review*, no. 4 (Fall 1984), 209–44.

ALLEN, B., *Andrea Zanzotto. The Language of Beauty's Apprentice* (Berkeley, Los Angeles, London: University of California Press, 1988).

ALMANSI, G., 'Verbal Folly. Andrea Zanzotto: *Filò*', *Times Literary Supplement*, no. 3 (18 August 1978), 985.

ANTONIELLI, S., 'Andrea Zanzotto, *La Beltà*', *Belfagor*, no. 24 (30 September 1969), 627–30.

BALDUINO, A., 'Zanzotto o l'ottica della contraddizione (impressioni e divagazioni su *Pasque*)', *Studi novecenteschi*, vol. 4, no. 8–9 (July–November, 1974), 281–313.

BALDUINO, A., 'Scheda bibliografica per Zanzotto critico', *Studi novecenteschi*, vol. 4, no. 8–9 (July–November 1974), 341–8.

BANDINI, F., 'Zanzotto tra norma e disordine', *Comunità*, no. 23 (1969), 78–83. Republished in *Letteratura italiana 900*, vol. 10 (Milan: Marzorati, 1982), 9756–65.

BANDINI, F., 'Scheda per *Sull'altopiano*', *Studi novecenteschi*, vol. 4, no. 8–9 (1974), 175–83.

BARBERI-SQUAROTTI, G., in *La cultura e la poesia italiana del dopoguerra* (Bologna: Cappelli, 1966), 127–33.

BARBERI-SQUAROTTI, G., 'Zanzotto o gli schemi dell'astrazione', in *Poesia e narrativa del secondo novecento* (Milan: Mursia, 1961 (1), 1978 (2)), 149–56 (1), 206–12 (2).

BO, C., '*Dietro il paesaggio* di Andrea Zanzotto', *La Fiera letteraria* (30 September 1951), 1–2.

CAMBON, G., 'Foreword' in *Selected Poetry of Andrea Zanzotto*, ed. and trans. R. Feldman and B. Swann (Surrey: Princeton University Press, 1975), xiii–xxii.

CONTESSI, P., 'Andrea Zanzotto. *Dietro il paesaggio*', *Il Mulino*, no. 1 (1952), 26–7.

CONTI-BERTINI, L., 'Andrea Zanzotto', in *Dieci poeti contemporanei*, ed. M. Martelli (Florence: Istituto Gramsci, CLUSF, 1980), 199–225.

CONTI-BERTINI, L., *Andrea Zanzotto o la sacra menzogna* (Venice: Marsilio, 1984).

CONTINI, G., 'Prefazione', in *Il Galateo in bosco* by A. Zanzotto (Milan: Mondadori, 1978), 5–7.

CORTI, M., 'Andrea Zanzotto, *La Beltà*', *Strumenti critici*, no. 2 (October 1968), 427–30.

COZZOLI, V., 'Appunti su Zanzotto', *Otto / Novecento*, no. 5, (1981), 327–35.

CRISTINI, G., '*Pasque* di Andrea Zanzotto', *Il Ragguaglio Librario*, no. 6 (June 1974), 213.

CUCCHI, M., 'La Beltà presa a coltellate?', *Studi novecenteschi*, vol. 4, no. 8–9 (July–November 1974), 251–71.

CUCCHI, M., '*Pasque*', *Paragone*, no. 26 (February 1975), 113–17.

DAMIANI, R., 'Un cadavre cher (su *La Beltà* di Andrea Zanzotto)', *Forum Italicum*, vol. 6, no. 3 (September 1972), 317–32.

DAVID, M., in *La psicoanalisi nella cultura italiana* (Turin: Boringhieri, 1966).

DELLA CORTE, C., '"Il latino" di Zanzotto', *Quartiere*, 12 (1962), trans. V. Bradshaw in *From Pure Silence to Impure Dialogue*, (New York: Las Americas, 1971), ed. V. Bradshaw, 335–6.

FALCHETTA, P., *Oculus Pudens. Venti anni di poesia di Andrea Zanzotto (1957–1978)* (Abano Terme, Padua: Francisci, 1983).

FORTI, M., 'Zanzotto o dell'informale', in *Le proposte della poesia* (Milan: Mursia, 1963), 210–18.

FORTI, M., 'La Beltà, l'Oltraggio', in *Le proposte della poesia e nuove proposte* (Milan: Mursia, 1971), 360–7.

FORTINI, F., 'The wind of revival', *Times Literary Supplement* (31 October 1975), 1308–9.

FRATTINI, A., 'Andrea Zanzotto', in *La giovane poesia italiana* (Pisa: Nistri-Lischi, 1964) 273–8.

GARDAIR, J. M., 'L'impossibilité de s'ennuyer', *Critique*, vol. 27, no. 290 (1971), 665–6.

GARDAIR, J. M., 'Andrea Zanzotto. Pâques', *Critique*, vol. 30, no. 335 (April 1975), 361–2.

GIACHERI, R., '*Dietro il paesaggio*', *Momenti*, no. 4 (1951), 40–1.

GIACOMINI, A., 'Da *Dietro il paesaggio* alle *IX Ecloghe*: L'io grammaticale nella poesia di Andrea Zanzotto', *Studi novecenteschi*, vol. 4, no. 8–9 (July–November 1974), 185–205.

GRAMIGNA, G., 'Introduzione a Andrea Zanzotto', in *Elegia e altri versi* by A. Zanzotto (Milan: La Meridiana, 1954).

GUGLIELMINETTI, M., 'La ricostruzione della sintassi poetica', *Studi novecenteschi*, vol. 4, no. 8–9 (July–November 1974), 167–73.

HAINSWORTH, P., 'The poetry of Andrea Zanzotto', *Italian Studies*, vol. 37 (1982), 101–21.

HAINSWORTH, P., 'Andrea Zanzotto', in *Writers and Society in Contemporary Italy*, ed. M. Caesar and P. Hainsworth (Leamington Spa: Berg, 1984), 117–42.

HAINSWORTH, P., 'A Dying Race. Andrea Zanzotto. *Idioma*', *Times Literary Supplement*, no. 2–8 (October 1987), 1083.

HAINSWORTH, P., 'Grasses and Shades, Winters' (translation of a hitherto unpublished poem by Zanzotto, with a review by G. L. Beccaria), *Times Literary Supplement*, no. 1 (February 1990), 15.

HAND, V., 'God and I: "Microfilm" in Zanzotto's *Pasque*', *Romance Studies*, no. 16 (summer 1990), 74–89.

HAND, V., 'Undermining logocentric thought in Andrea Zanzotto's *La Beltà*', *Italian Studies*, vol. 46 (1991), 82–101.

HARRISON, R. P., 'The Italian Silence', *Critical Inquiry*, vol. 13, no. 1 (Autumn 1986), 95–9.

HARRISON, T., 'Introduction: Nietzsche, Heidegger and the language of contemporary Italian poetry', in *The Favourite Malice*, ed. T. Harrison (New York: Out of London Press, 1983), 17–55.

HARRISON, T., 'Andrea Zanzotto: From the Language of the World to the World of Language', in *The Empty Set. Five Essays on Twentieth Century Italian Poetry*, ed. M. Godorecci (New York: Queens College Press, 1985), 66–78.

LUPERINI, R., 'Gel', *Alfabeta*, no. 52 (September 1983), 7–9.

MANACORDA, G., in *Storia della letteratura italiana contemporanea 1940–1965* (Rome: Editori Riuniti, 1967), 398–400.

MENGALDO, P. V., 'Andrea Zanzotto', in *Poeti italiani del novecento* (Milan: Mondadori, 1978), 869–77.

MILONE, L., 'Per una storia del linguaggio poetico di Andrea Zanzotto', *Studi novecenteschi*, vol. 4, no. 8–9 (July–November 1974), 207–35.

MONTALE, E., in *Corriere della Sera* (1 June 1968). Republished as 'La poesia di Zanzotto', in *Sulla poesia* by E. Montale (Milan: Mondadori, 1976) 337–41.

NUVOLI, G., 'Una dialettica della disperazione in prestito', *Studi novecenteschi*, vol. 4, no. 8–9 (July–November 1974), 237–50.

NUVOLI, G., *Andrea Zanzotto* (Florence: 148 Il Castoro, La Nuova Italia, 1979).

PALTRINIERI, M., 'L'affabilità di Zanzotto', *Il Verri*, no. 1–2 (March–June 1987), 19–38.

PANDINI, G., 'Il difficile dire di Zanzotto', in *L'oscura devozione* (Milan: Marzorati, 1977), 119–31.

PANDINI, G., 'Andrea Zanzotto: *Fosfeni*', *Forum Italicum*, vol. 118, no. 1 (1984), 188–90.

PASOLINI, P. P., in *Il Punto* (21 December 1957). Republished as 'Principio di un engagement', in *Passione e ideologia* by P. P. Pasolini (Milan: Garzanti, 1960), 464–6.

PASOLINI, P. P., 'Zanzotto stringe alla gola l'elegia e vince', in *La letteratura del benessere* by W. Pedullà. Ed. M. Bulzoni (Naples: Libreria Scientifica, 1968), 573–6.

PASOLINI, P. P., '*La Beltà* (Appunti)', *Nuovi argomenti*, no. 21 (January–March 1971), 23–6.

PEDULLÀ, W., in *La letteratura del benessere* (Naples: Libreria Scientifica, 1968).

PEDULLÀ, W., in *L'estrema funzione* (Venice: Marsilio, 1975) 314–34.

PENTO, B., in *La Fiera letteraria* (30 September 1962). Republished as 'Andrea Zanzotto. Una poesia difficile' in *Letture di poesia contemporanea* (Milan: Marzorati, 1964), 135–8.

PICCIONI, L., in *Tradizione letteraria e idee correnti* (Milan: Fratelli Fabbri, 1955).

RABONI, G., 'Notizie clandestine sul terrore', *Paragone*, no. 21 (February 1970), 126–8. Republished in *Poesia degli anni sessanta* (Rome: Editori Riuniti, 1976a), 187–9.

RABONI, G., 'La difficile attualità di Zanzotto', in *Poesia degli anni sessanta* (Rome: Editori Riuniti, 1976b), 76–8.

RABONI, G., 'Zanzotto: l'oltraggio, la salvezza', in *Poesia degli anni sessanta* (Rome: Editori Riuniti, 1976c), 169–72.

RAMAT, S., 'Andrea Zanzotto', in *Letteratura italiana 900*, ed. G. Grana, vol. 22 (Milan: Marzorati, 1982), 9730–54.

RAMAT, S., 'Zanzotto nel "ricchissimo nihil"', in *Storia della poesia italiana del novecento* (Milan: Mursia, 1976), 606–12.

RISSET, J., '"Sovraesistenze"', *Studi novecenteschi*, vol. 4 no. 8–9 (July–November 1974), 329–31.

RIZZO, G., 'Zanzotto, "fabbro del parlar materno"', in *Selected poetry of Andrea Zanzotto*, ed. and trans. R. Feldman and B. Swann (Surrey: Princeton University Press, 1975) 307–23.

ROSSI, A., 'La stremata beltà di Zanzotto', *L'Approdo letterario*, no. 42 (April–June 1968), 121–2.

ROSSI, A., 'Articolazione dialettica dei testi di Zanzotto', *L'Approdo letterario*, no. 62 (June 1973), 114–16.

SITI, W., 'Per Zanzotto: Possibili prefazi', *Nuovi argomenti*, no. 32 (1973), 127–42. Republished in *Il realismo dell'avanguardia* by W. Siti (Turin: Einaudi, 1975).

SITI, W., 'Le *Pasque* di Zanzotto', *Rinascita* (12 April 1974), 26.

SMITH, L. R., in *The New Italian Poetry. A Bilingual Anthology*, ed. and trans. L. R. Smith (Berkeley, Los Angeles: University of California Press, 1981).

SPAGNOLETTI, G., in *Poesia italiana contemporanea 1909–1959* (Parma: Guanda, 1959).

SPAGNOLETTI, G., in *Poeti del Novecento* (Milan: Edizioni Scolastiche, Mondadori, 1960).

SPAGNOLETTI, G., in *Profilo della letteratura italiana del novecento* (Rome: Gremese, 1975), 302–5.

TELLINI, G., 'La "subnarcosi" di Zanzotto', *Studi novecenteschi*, vol. 4, no. 8–9 (July–November 1974), 315–28.

TESTA, E., in *Il libro di poesia* (Genoa: Il Melangolo / Università, 8, 1982).

TITTA ROSA, G., '*La Beltà* di Zanzotto', *L'osservatore politico letterario*, no. 9 (September 1968), 107–9.

TROISIO, L., 'La Luna e i Senhals', *Studi novecenteschi*, vol. 4, no. 8–9 (July–November 1974), 273–80.

UNGARETTI, G., 'Piccolo discorso al Convegno di San Pellegrino sopra *Dietro il paesaggio* di Andrea Zanzotto', *L'Approdo letterario*, vol. 3 (September 1954), 59–62.

VARESE, C., '"Solo gli isolati comunicano"', *Studi novecenteschi*, vol. 4, no. 8–9 (July–November 1974), 333–9.

WELLE, J. P., *The Poetry of Andrea Zanzotto. A Critical Study of Il Galateo in bosco* (Rome: Bulzoni, 1987).

WELLE, J. P., 'Dante and Poetic *Communio* in Zanzotto's Pseudo-Trilogy', *Lectura Dantis*, no. 10 (Spring 1992), 34–58.

ZAGARRIO, G., 'Poesia e trasgressione dei significanti', *Il Ponte*, no. 30 (July–August 1974), 801–13.

OTHER WORKS CITED

ARIOSTO, L., *Orlando Furioso*, ed. L. Caretti (Turin: Loescher, Classici italiani, 1982).

BAUDELAIRE, C., *Les fleurs du mal* (Paris: Garnier-Flammarion, 1964).

D´ANNUNZIO, G., *Le laudi*, ed. E. Palmieri (Bologna, 1964).

DANTE ALIGHIERI, *La divina commedia* (London, Oxford, New York: Oxford University Press, 1971). (Italian text with translation and comment by J. D. Sinclair, 3 volumes).

DE´ MEDICI, L., *Scritti scelti*, ed. E. Bigi (Turin: Classici Utet, 1971).

DE SAUSSURE, F., *Cours de linguistique générale* (Paris: 1916).

DELLA CASA, G., *Galateo*, ed. S. Orlando (Milan: Garzanti, 1990).

DERRIDA, J., *De la grammatologie* (Paris: Minuit, 1967). Trans. by G. Chakravorty Spivak as *Of Grammatology* (Baltimore and London: John Hopkins University Press, 1967).

DERRIDA, J., *La Voix et le Phénomène* (Paris: Presses Universitaires de France, 1967). Trans. by D. B. Allison as *Speech and Phenomena* (Evanston: Northwestern University Press, 1973).

DERRIDA, J., *L'Écriture et la Différence* (Paris: Seuil, 1967). Trans. by A. Bass as *Writing and Difference* (Chicago: University of Chicago Press, 1978).

ÉLUARD, P., *Donner à voir* (Paris: Gallimard, 1939).

ÉLUARD, P., *Oeuvres Complètes*, vols I, II (Paris: La Pléiade, Gallimard, 1968).

FLORA, F., *La poesia ermetica* (Bari: Laterza and Figli, 1936).

GIULIANI, A., *I novissimi: poesie per gli anni '60* (Milan: Rusconi-Paolazzi, 1961).

HEGEL, G., *The logic of Hegel*, trans. from the *Encyclopaedia of the Philosophical Sciences* by W. Wallace (Oxford: Clarendon Press, 1874).

HEIDEGGER, M., *Poetry, Language, Thought*, trans. A. Hofstadter (New York: Harper and Row, 1971).

HEIDEGGER, M., *Basic Writings*, trans. D. F. Krell (London: Routledge and Kegan Paul, 1978).

HÖLDERLIN, F., *Sämtliche Werke*, vol. 6, 1 (Briefe Text, 1800–1804) (Stuttgart: Sechsterband, 1954).

HÖLDERLIN, F., *Selected Verse*, ed. M. Hamburger (Harmondsworth: Penguin, 1961).

HOMER, *Odyssey*, trans. E. V. Rieu (London: Penguin, 1991).

HORACE, *The Odes and Epodes*, with an English translation by C. E. Bennett (London: Heinemann and Harvard University Press, 1952).

KAFKA, F., *Metamorphosis*, trans. W. and E. Muir (Harmondsworth: Penguin Modern Classics, 1961).

LACAN, J., *Écrits* (Paris: Seuil, 1966). Trans. by A. Sheridan as *Écrits: A Selection* (London: Tavistock, 1977).

LACAN, J., 'L'instance de la lettre dans l'inconscient ou la raison depuis Freud', in *Écrits* (Paris: Seuil, 1966).

LEOPARDI, G., *Canti*, ed. D. de Robertis (Milan: Il Polifilo, 1984).

LORCA, G., *Bodas de sangre*, in *Obras Completas* (Madrid: Aguilar, 1954).

MIGLIORINI, B. and PELLEGRINI, G. B., *Dizionario del Feltrino Rustico* (Padua: Liviana, 1971).

MONTALE, E., *Ossi di seppia, Le occasioni, La bufera e altro*, in *Tutte le poesie* (Milan: Mondadori, 1984).

OVID, *Metamorphoses*, trans. A. D. Melvill (Oxford: Oxford University Press, 1986).

PAVESE, C., *Il mestiere di vivere (Diario 1935–1950)* (Turin: Einaudi, 1990).

PETRARCH, F., *Canzoniere* (Turin: Einaudi, 1964).

PICCIONI, L., (ed.) *Ungaretti. Vita d'un uomo* (Milan: Mondadori, 1969).

POE, E. A., 'The Masque of Red Death,' in *The Complete Tales and Poems of E. A. Poe* (New York: The Modern Library, 1965), 269–74.

QUASIMODO, S., *Ed è subito sera*, in *Poesie e discorsi sulla poesia* (Milan: Mondadori, 1971).

RIMBAUD, A., *Les Illuminations, Une saison en enfer* in *Oeuvres Complètes* (Paris: La Pléiade, Gallimard, 1946).

ROBBE-GRILLET, A., *Pour un nouveau roman* (Paris: Minuit, 1963).

SAVANIO, P., (ed.) *Ungaretti* (Paris: Éditions de l'Herne, 1970).

SHAW, G. B., *Pygmalion* (Harmondsworth: Penguin, 1941).

STEINER, G., *Heidegger* (London: Fontana Modern Masters, 1978).

TASSO, T., *Gerusalemme liberata* ed. B. Maier (Milan: Rizzoli, 1982).

UNGARETTI, G., *Sentimento del tempo* (Milan: Lo Specchio, Mondadori, 1974).

VIRGIL, *Eclogues, Georgics, Aeneid 1–6*, trans. H. R. Fairclough (Cambridge: Harvard University Press, 1974).

Index